ALSO BY OLIVIA DRAKE

When a Duke
Loves a Governess

OLIVIA DRAKE

St. Martin's Paperbacks

This is a work of fiction. All of the characters, organizations, and events portrayed in this novel are either products of the author's imagination or are used fictitiously.

First published in the United States by St. Martin's Paperbacks, an imprint of St. Martin's Publishing Group

WHEN A DUKE LOVES A GOVERNESS

For information, address St. Martin's Publishing Group, 120 Broadway, New York, NY 10271.

www.stmartins.com

ISBN: 978-1-250-17449-9

Our books may be purchased in bulk for promotional, educational, or business use. Please contact your local bookseller or the Macmillan Corporate and Premium Sales Department at 1-800-221-7945, ext. 5442, or by email at MacmillanSpecialMarkets@macmillan.com.

Printed in the United States of America

St. Martin's Paperbacks edition 2021

10 9 8 7 6 5 4 3 2 1

Chapter 1

"Wait until you hear the news," Lady Farnsworth said to a friend who had just entered the millinery shop. "The Duke of Carlin has lost yet another governess."

Mrs. Ludington gasped. "Why, this one cannot have been in his employ beyond a week."

"Four days. My cousin lives near His Grace in Grosvenor Square, you know. This very morning, her maid spied the woman departing Carlin House with portmanteau in hand."

Tessa James shamelessly eavesdropped from behind the counter. A threaded needle gripped between her forefinger and thumb, she craned her neck to peer past an arrangement of hats. Both ladies were regular patrons of the shop. As they chatted, Lady Farnsworth preened at her aging reflection in the mirror, while Mrs. Ludington tried on a rust-colored toque over her salt-and-pepper curls.

Tessa knew the women only by sight since Madame Blanchet trusted no one but herself to wait on the aristocratic customers. The shopkeeper hovered near the ladies, making suggestions and offering oily praise. Amid the colorful bonnets on display, Madame Blanchet in her severe black gown resembled a raven skulking in a garden of spring flowers.

"Zis *chapeau* is *très magnifique*," she said, encouraging Lady Farnsworth to try on another bonnet.

Tessa curbed the urge to step out from behind the counter and direct the woman to a more flattering style, since the mass of yellow-dyed ostrich feathers made her pudgy features appear sallow. If it were her shop, she would use tact and diplomacy to ensure that every lady walked out looking her very best.

But she was not the proprietor. She lacked the means to set up an establishment of her own. At least as of yet.

A few minutes ago, she'd been called out here to do a minor alteration. It was a welcome escape from the cramped workroom where she and two other employees labored from dawn until dusk. Each hat required hours of toil from start to finish: the shaping of the buckram base, the assembling with wire and crinoline tape, the attachment of the lining, and the addition of trims.

Over the past eight years, Tessa had mastered all the skills of the trade. She had filled a notebook with her own sketches, too, although being allowed to actually make those hats was another matter. Madame preferred ornate monstrosities festooned with ribbons and lace, feathers and birds, silk flowers and papier-mâché fruit. Consequently, the shop was frequented by elderly ladies who had grown up in an era of elaborate powdered wigs.

But times had changed. The current fashion trended toward the elegance of simplicity—a taste shared by Tessa. A few days ago, she finally had been allowed to create one bonnet of her design. How proud she'd been to put it on display yesterday. And how dismayed to learn that—

A prickling sense of being observed alerted her to Madame Blanchet's sharp black eyes glaring from across the shop. Her toadying way with the patrons didn't extend to the staff. Tessa felt sure that Wellington himself could be no stricter a general than Madame.

Hastening to appear industrious, she poked the needle into the stiff interfacing of the bonnet. As much as she'd love to give the woman a piece of her mind, Tessa could ill afford to lose her position. It paid little enough as it was. Every farthing she could scrimp went into the tin box kept hidden beneath a loose floorboard in her tiny flat. Every penny put her one step closer to achieving the dream of one day being a shop owner herself.

For now, she must grit her teeth and oblige her employer by altering this bonnet, the very one Tessa herself had designed. It had a wide chip-straw brim with a gentle pouf of sky-blue satin at the crown. The matching ribbon that crisscrossed the straw was anchored in place by a delicate satin rosette. She had intended the stylish confection to frame the features of some lovely young lady.

Instead, Lady Farnsworth with her multiple chins had cooed over the hat. The woman then had insisted on ruining its elegance with the addition of three huge bunches of pink rosebuds, and Madame had fawningly acquiesced. In one fell swoop, the bonnet had gone from being a work of art to just another overdone atrocity. Tessa's only consolation was being able to listen to the conversation as she halfheartedly stitched the silk flowers into place.

"Carlin must be frightening away his governesses," Mrs. Ludington was saying. "Surely a man cannot spend so many years sailing around the world to remote lands without forgetting the finer points of proper behavior. Heaven only knows what peculiar customs he might have acquired."

"Nonsense, the duke was raised a gentleman even if he never expected to assume the title." Lady Farnsworth tried on another hat, this one of burgundy velvet adorned with a stuffed quail and faux autumn leaves. "As a widower, he is London's most eligible bachelor. And you cannot deny he cut quite a dash at the Sedgwicks' ball the other night by dancing with several of the young ladies."

"But there has to be a reason for all the departures." Mrs. Ludington lowered her voice to a scandalized whisper. "Do you suppose he is making improper advances toward the governesses?"

"When all of them have been bran-faced spinsters? Nay, I daresay it has to do with his daughter running untamed during Carlin's absence. Rumor has it that Lady Sophy terrorizes the ducal household. Her maternal grandparents raised her, and everyone knows what rattlepates the Norwoods are."

"Well, the girl ought to have learned suitable behavior by now. If she is still spoiled at four years, it must be nipped in the bud at once."

"Carlin is in need of a wife to take matters in hand," Lady Farnsworth said in agreement. "My granddaughter will be making her bows in the spring, and it would be quite a plum for her to acquire a duchess's tiara."

"Let us hope that Lady Sophy's manners improve in the interim." Mrs. Ludington examined a gold-fringed purple turban in the sunlight from the window. "The naughty child wants discipline, and swiftly. His Grace must seek a sterner character when he engages another governess."

Tessa's fingers stilled in the act of tying off a thread. The sudden jolt of her heart caught her by surprise. The idea that leaped into her mind was utterly daft. She would have to be mad even to consider such a notion. Yet the words sizzled through her like a bolt of lightning.

Another governess.

The Duke of Carlin had been left in the lurch. He needed

someone on short notice who could handle his disobedient daughter. Perhaps that someone could be Tessa herself.

Living in a ducal household would place her at the center of the aristocratic world. She'd be on a swifter path to acquiring the funds she needed to open her own shop. Partly due to the increase in salary, but also because she finally might find her father.

The man whose name had always been a mystery to her.

She touched the dainty oval shape beneath her bodice. The high-necked gown of gray kerseymere hid the gold pendant that was her most precious possession. In the sixteen years since her dying mama had placed it around Tessa's neck, never once had she removed it. Her fingers traced the small image engraved on the piece. The coat of arms belonged to a noble family—her father's family.

But who was he? Since most of her waking hours were spent here at work, she'd had little opportunity to discover the answer. Tessa didn't dare ask anyone, either. If she were to show it to any of the Quality who patronized the shop, she might be accused of stealing the pendant.

As a governess, though, she could keep her eyes peeled for the coat of arms. Somewhere she might glimpse it on a carriage door or carved into the lintel stone of a house. Once she matched it to a name, she could confront her sire and convince him to advance her a loan.

Yet common sense offered a swift rebuttal. What did she know of being a governess? Next to nothing! Unlike her, they were ladies who had been raised in genteel families. While window-shopping on her half day off, she'd sometimes glimpsed such plain-garbed women shepherding their charges in the posh district of Mayfair.

She could not seriously be thinking about joining their ranks, though.

Governesses had the task of educating upper-class children,

and Tessa's schooling had been sketchy at best. She had taught herself to read by poring over fashion periodicals. From there, she'd graduated to newspapers, playbills, and penny novels rescued from the rubbish bin behind the secondhand shop. She went to church on Sundays partly for the pleasure of reading the hymnal.

However, she knew little of literature or geography or history. Foreign tongues like French and Italian sounded like gibberish to her. And didn't all young ladies require music lessons? Having no such skills herself, Tessa would be exposed as a fraud.

But at four years, Lady Sophy surely wouldn't be expected to know more than a few simple nursery songs. The girl must be just learning her letters and numbers. Tessa's job had made her adept at basic arithmetic like counting and measuring. Even Lady Sophy's difficult behavior should pose no problem since Tessa knew something of bullies from having grown up in a foundling home, where she'd been tasked with caring for the younger girls.

And there was no denying the governess post could put her on the path to fulfilling her dearest dream. By this time next year, she might be proprietress of her own millinery shop.

Tessa succumbed to her favorite flight of fancy. She would lease a storefront on Bond Street, one with a bow window that would be perfect for showcasing her creations. The fashionable set would clamor for her designs, ladies more stylish than the two aging matrons who were presently rummaging through the bonnets here. What should she call her shop? Perhaps Millinery by Miss James. Something as simple and elegant as the merchandise—

"Stop gawping at yer betters."

The hissing voice startled Tessa into pricking her finger

with the needle. Wincing, she saw that her employer stood glaring from the other side of the counter. The French accent slipped into Cockney whenever Madame Blanchet was out of earshot of the customers. They didn't know she'd been born plain Polly Brewster within the shadow of St. Mary-le-Bow church.

"I don't pay ye to stand idle," Madame continued in a harsh whisper. "Ain't them rosebuds attached yet?"

Tessa hastened to tie off the threads and snip the ends with the scissors that dangled from the waistband of her apron. "Aye, Madame."

The shopkeeper snatched up the bonnet and critically examined the work. Her nostrils flared against the stark angles of her face. "Clumsy chit. There be blood on the brim."

Tessa leaned closer, dismayed to see a dot of red on the straw. It must have happened just now when she'd poked her finger with the needle. "I daresay a quick sponging with soap and water—"

"Never mind, 'tis ruined. I should've never let ye wheedle me into makin' such a drab piece, anyhow. Ye with yer fine airs." Sneering, Madame Blanchet dropped the bonnet onto the counter. "Since it ain't me what done the damage, the cost'll come out of yer wages."

"But . . . that will mean months without pay!"

"'Twill teach ye a lesson. Now, back to the workroom."

Tessa stood paralyzed as her employer turned away. How was she to cover the rent that was due at the end of the week, not to mention buy food and a host of other expenses? She was down to a stub of tallow candle and a sliver of soap. In her neighborhood, merchants seldom extended credit to low-wage earners like herself. She'd have to dip into her treasured savings . . .

"No. I won't."

Tessa didn't realize she'd spoken aloud until Madame whipped back around, a thunderous frown on her bony features. Her burning-coal eyes held incredulity, for the employees were usually too wary of her temper to disobey her orders. "Eh?"

Her heart drumming, Tessa felt the fear and exhilaration of stepping off a cliff. All the years of biting her tongue suddenly became intolerable. She was done with being silent. "You heard me," she said firmly. "I quit."

A rapping on the door reverberated through the flat.

The small room might more aptly be described a cubbyhole, but it was home to Tessa. Having grown up in a crowded dormitory, she treasured having space all to herself. It was just large enough to hold a single iron bedstead, a rickety table and chair, and a battered chest of drawers on which sat a spirit lamp where she could make a cup of tea. The single window had a view of a brick wall. She'd spruced up the dreary surroundings with a colorful rag rug on the floor and pages of hats tacked to the peeling wallpaper.

As the knock came again, she paused in the act of unpinning those inspirational drawings. It was rare for her to be at home in the middle of the afternoon. For that reason alone, she should be cautious of opening the door. Although most of the residents in the boardinghouse were hardworking folk like herself, the neighborhood had its share of vagrants and ne'er-do-wells.

But she recognized the summons. Two sharp taps, a pause, then another knock. Tessa hardly knew whether to be pleased or peeved at the interruption in her packing.

Clutching the sheaf of papers to her bosom, she hastened to open the door. "Orrin! Why aren't you at work?

A wiry young man in a brown corduroy suit stepped into the room. Orrin Nesbitt removed his flat-brimmed cap to reveal a thatch of rusty-red hair. Although slightly older than herself, in his mid-twenties, he had a round freckled face that gave him a boyish mien. They'd become friends the previous year when he'd moved into one of the downstairs flats. Since he worked as a typesetter for a tabloid, he'd made a habit of bringing her the daily newspaper.

He held one tucked under his arm but made no move to hand it to her. "Put today's rag t' bed early, so I went t' the shop. Sukie said you pelted off in a rush, leavin' ole Blanchet with her britches in a twist."

Tessa regretted having to abandon her co-workers. "Poor Sukie and Nell. I hope Madame didn't take out her wrath on them."

"Dunno. I hightailed it out o' there and came straight here." Orrin's hazel eyes studied her with stunned curiosity. "Gorblimey, Tess. Wot happened? Tell me you didn't just up an' quit!"

Her stomach clenched. For the hundredth time since marching out of the millinery shop, she questioned her impulsiveness. What had she done? What if she failed to win the governess post? What if the Duke of Carlin saw through her deception? Worse, what if she was never even interviewed? The duke lived in a grand Mayfair mansion undoubtedly guarded by a staff of snooty servants. If she were refused entry, how would she support herself? Steady work was hard to come by, and it might be weeks before she secured another position.

A craven part of her was tempted to slink back and beg Madame's pardon. The woman might be a tyrant, but at least she'd hired Tessa as a fourteen-year-old runaway and had taught her the art of hatmaking.

No. She mustn't regret her decision. She couldn't stay in a position that stifled her creativity and offered little chance of advancement. Her dreams for the future were at stake.

She met Orrin's gaze. "Yes, it's true. I've resigned and I'm not going back."

"What'd the ole battle-ax do t' you?" He shook his brown felt cap in the air. "I oughta go tell that harpy wot for!"

"You mustn't. It wasn't Madame's fault, at least not entirely."

"So you been plannin' t' leave?" He glanced past Tessa at the signs of her packing, the small trunk containing her few possessions. "Without sayin' naught t' me about it?"

His crestfallen face and puppy-dog eyes filled her with chagrin. In her haste to collect her things before proceeding to Grosvenor Square, she hadn't spared a thought for Orrin. He deserved an explanation.

"I only just decided today," she said. "Though I'd have left you a note, of course. You see, this morning I overheard two ladies discussing a lord who needs a governess for his little daughter. I mean to apply for the post."

Orrin let out a hoot of laughter. "Wot, you, a governess? Are you mad?"

"At the foundling home, I watched over the little ones. So I've plenty of practice in dealing with children."

He hastily sobered. "Didn't mean you'd make a shabby one. You're sharp as a tack an' you talk much finer than the likes o' me."

"I've always listened closely to Madame's customers as preparation for opening my own shop. And don't forget, my mother worked for a time as a maidservant. She learned to mimic her employer, and then she taught me."

At least until Tessa was six. Snippets of memory were all she had left. Mama's clear voice singing to her at bedtime. Being cuddled to soft maternal warmth on a cold night. Playing with spools of thread as Mama sewed from dawn till dusk in order to provide for their food and lodging.

The most vivid memory of all was the last one. They'd

been crossing the street to deliver a parcel of finished shirts when Tessa heard the clatter of hoofbeats and the rattle of wheels. In a flash, a carriage careened toward them at breakneck speed. Mama had given Tessa a push that sent her tumbling into the gutter. Her teeth rattled from the hard fall, but that wasn't the worst part. It was seeing Mama lying on the cobblestones, utterly still, her face bloodied. As Tessa scrambled to her with a cry, Mama's eyes had fluttered open. Her hand fumbled for her pendant, sliding the filigreed gold chain over Tessa's head. *"Hide this . . . find him . . . father . . . pain . . ."*

Those halting words had been Mama's final utterance. *Pain*, in particular, was the one that wrenched Tessa's heart. But she hadn't realized the true significance of the rest until much later when, as an employee at the millinery, she'd noticed that ladies often arrived in fine carriages with a lozenge on the door of a type similar to the engraving on the pendant. It had occurred to her then that what she'd viewed as merely a pretty design might actually serve to identify the man who had sired her.

"'Tis him, isn't it?"

Orrin's sharp tone startled her, as did the inquisitiveness in his eyes. "Who?" she asked.

"This lord you're goin' t' see, is he your pa? The one what used your mam an' then tossed her out? Did you find him?"

She'd told Orrin the story about her parentage, although she hadn't shown him the pendant. Keeping it concealed beneath her gown was a habit that had begun as a child at the orphanage, where even a crust of bread must be guarded against theft. "No, I did not. It's the Duke of Carlin who needs a governess."

"A duke, eh? The loftiest o' the toffs." Orrin's upper lip curled. Being something of a revolutionary, he had a low estimation of the aristocracy. "Gorblimey, Tess, you don't do things by halves."

"It's an excellent prospect. With the increase in salary, I'll be able to open my shop all the sooner."

"That's *if* you can bamboozle this duke. He'll be expectin' a blueblood lady. And he'll be askin' for your family connections. You can't be tellin' him you're a hatmaker from the East End."

Tessa had been mulling over that very issue. What little she knew about aristocrats had been gleaned from observation, both at work and while window-shopping along Bond Street on her half day off. But if she let Orrin talk her out of this, she most certainly would never succeed. "I'll think of something. Now I must be on my way lest the duke hire someone else."

That he might already be conducting interviews was a worry that lent speed to her packing. She added a stack of hat sketches to the clothing in the open trunk, then pried up a loose floorboard and extracted the tin box containing her savings. The coins made a satisfactory weight in her palm, though their value fell far short of the vast sum she needed.

After tucking a few pennies in her reticule and concealing the remainder in the trunk, she straightened up to find Orrin eyeing her, his brows knit. "A pity you don't know your pa's name," he said, continuing in his earlier vein. "He must be loaded with blunt. The bleater owes you."

Orrin had skirted close to guessing her true purpose. Too close. Should she apprise him of her secret plan to find the man? Yet a hard-learned caution made her hesitate to reveal the pendant.

"But I *don't* know his identity," she said. "So that's that."

She turned away to don the chip-straw bonnet that Madame had rejected. Tessa had felt justified in taking it in lieu of her monthly pay. The tiny spot on the brim had been eradicated with a bit of careful rubbing. Tying the sky-blue ribbons beneath her chin, she glanced into the little square mirror above the bureau. How pretty the hat looked now that she'd removed the gaudy clusters of rosebuds, how elegant and self-assured it made her feel.

Was it too fine, though?

Lady Farnsworth had described the other governesses as bran-faced spinsters. Such women tended to wear ugly round bonnets that offended Tessa's sense of fashion. Everything in her craved to wear the stylish hat, so she rationalized that the rest of her appearance wasn't memorable in the least. Small in stature, she had blue eyes set in ordinary features, with a hint of fair hair visible beneath the brim. She had changed into her second-best gown, a high-necked one of dark cerulean muslin that made her appear sober and bookish as befitting a governess.

"What was your mam's name?" Orrin asked suddenly.

"Florence." She tugged on her only pair of gloves, the pads of the fingers worn to threads. "Why do you wish to know?"

"I don't like you workin' for this duke, that's why. These noble swells, they're lechers. If one preyed on your mam, it could happen t' you, too."

Disquiet niggled at her. But Lady Farnsworth had pooh-poohed the notion of the Duke of Carlin abusing his governesses. She'd said only that little Lady Sophy had been indulged by her grandparents while the duke had been out of England. What was it that Mrs. Ludington had added?

A man cannot spend so many years sailing around the world to remote lands without forgetting the finer points of proper behavior. Heaven only knows what peculiar customs he might have acquired.

Tessa felt a tingle of curiosity as her natural optimism rose to the fore. "You needn't fret. Sukie showed me how to use my knee to hit a man where it hurts him the most."

Orrin winced slightly. "I still don't like it. If 'tis funds you need, I can track down your pa an' then threaten t' write an article exposing his sins unless he pays you a goodly sum."

"Lud, Orrin, that's blackmail! I won't see you locked in Newgate on my behalf." Tessa didn't intend to use criminal methods to bring her sire up to snuff. If, that is, she managed to identify him. Out of curiosity, she added, "How would you go about looking for him, anyway?"

"By askin' at all the big houses. One of the staff might recollect a maid named Florence James."

"That would have been over twenty years ago. More likely than not, you'd be tossed out on your ear."

"Bah, I've a nose for digging up the truth." Orrin tapped his freckled beak. "Only look how quick I found out who nicked Mrs. Beasley's mutt."

"It was very enterprising of you to uncover that dognapping ring."

"What's more, the story got printed. I brung you a copy." Beaming, he took the newspaper from under his arm, flipped to the last page, and poked an ink-stained finger at a small article near the bottom. "See there? My first published piece."

Tessa scanned the few lines, noticing that the lurid headline lacked an attribution. "Orrin, that's wonderful. Congratulations!"

"No byline as yet, but I'm hopin' t' have one soon. All's I need is a big story. Mayhap you'll keep your eyes open for me, eh? There must be lots o' lords like your pa who are up t' their ears in scandals." He slid her a moony, tail-wagging look. "I won't always be a lowly typesetter, you know. Once I make staff reporter, I'll be able t' support a wife an' children."

Tessa suffered a momentary pang for a family of her own.

Ever since losing Mama, she'd felt the occasional stab of loneliness, a yearning to have someone to love. Yet she had no compelling desire to marry Orrin—or any other man, for that matter. Being beholden to a husband would thwart her dream of opening a millinery shop. Perhaps that was why she felt so reluctant to enlist his aid. She didn't wish to feel obliged to accept his offer.

"That's a fine ambition," she said, smiling to soften her rejection. "But you mustn't expect me to pass along gossip about my employer. Now I really must be on my way."

Orrin agreed to keep Tessa's trunk until she could send for it. As they moved it downstairs to his flat, she ignored his frowning look. She couldn't bear another word of his nay-saying.

Especially when she was already a quivering mass of nerves.

Chapter 2

Guy Whitby, the seventh Duke of Carlin, sat at his desk and tried to concentrate on the packet of papers forwarded by his steward. It didn't help his restless state of mind that he felt like an interloper in the study that had once been his grandfather's domain.

The cavernous room featured gilded moldings and green silk damask hangings, with busts of poets and philosophers on the floor-to-ceiling bookshelves. He'd hung a number of framed botanical paintings from his travels, but the place still didn't quite feel like his own. Every piece of furniture was oversized and uniquely designed to flaunt the eminence of the master. Even the massive desk rested on the outstretched wings of a carved eagle, a tribute to the Carlin family crest.

On the polished mahogany surface before him lay proposals for improving drainage in the west pasture, purchasing a new bull for the herd of milchers, rethatching the roofs of the tenant cottages, and a host of other issues relating to his ducal seat in Derbyshire.

Guy grimaced. How naïve of him to imagine he could devote the afternoon to working on the book he hoped to publish about his four-year voyage around the world. Since his return, there had been an endless stream of legal documents, investment summaries, and detailed reports on the several estates he had inherited—all of them involving problems that required informed decisions. To make matters worse, heavy taxes due to the recent war had eaten into his assets, his stock holdings had been neglected, and he would soon be expected to take his seat in the House of Lords when he didn't give a bloody damn about politics.

It was enough to drive a man mad.

He glanced at his secretary, who was taking notes on a sheet of cream paper. "Snodgrass is even wanting permission to dip the demmed sheep. I don't see why the devil I pay him if he must seek my approval for everything."

"The ducal properties have been without a master since the passing of the sixth duke a year ago," Banfield replied. "Naturally, there is a backlog of issues. Your grandfather believed it to be his obligation to approve any and all expenditures."

Guy detected a faint note of censure in that respectful tone, though no hint of it showed in the secretary's unruffled manner. Banfield was a trim man in his fifties with coffee-brown hair gone silver at the temples, and the sort of nondescript face that blended into the background. He'd served the family for over a decade. On holidays from Oxford, Guy often would see the fellow in this study, taking dictation from his grandsire. He could still hear the old duke's gruff voice snapping orders that echoed down the marble corridor.

A deep ache gripped Guy. It was hard to believe that a man as strong and robust as his grandfather was gone. He'd suffered a heart seizure one night, and Guy hadn't learned of the death until seven months later. While he'd been sailing around the world, collecting botanical samples and sketching plants, his future had been irrevocably altered.

And not in a way that he had ever anticipated.

Growing up, he'd never spared a thought for the dukedom, since he was fourth in line of succession. But through a series of mishaps during his absence from England, the other heirs had died. Uncle Sebastian, the eldest of Grandfather's three sons, had been sailing off the Isle of Wight when his yacht had capsized in rough seas, drowning him and Charles, his only son and heir. Then Guy's father, the second brother, had succumbed to a deadly stomach ailment. The strain of these calamities must have been what had sent the sixth duke to his grave.

It was his grandfather that Guy mourned the most. Despite their differences, the old duke had had a forceful impact on his life, much more so than Guy's father. He and his grandfather often had been at loggerheads, with Carlin urging him toward the life of a noble landowner and Guy determined to follow an academic path. They'd had a flaming row over Guy's decision to outfit a private ship in order to further his interest in the study of plants. Carlin had denounced the round-the-world trip as a fool's errand, and they'd parted ways with harsh words that Guy regretted.

Now *he* was Carlin. He, who had never wanted the title.

Guy had discovered the sequence of tragic events upon picking up several years' worth of mail held for him at a British consul's office halfway around the world. In a state of shock and sorrow, he'd spent hours reading and rereading the letters in chronological order, gossip from various relatives, stern missives from the old duke, and finally the news of Carlin's death from Aunt Delia, along with a host of dispatches from the family solicitors urging Guy to come home at once.

That night, he had stayed awake, drinking and reminiscing until dawn. The unwelcome prospect of having to fill his grandfather's shoes had sorely tempted him to delay his return. But in the end he'd faced his duty, sailed back to England, and taken up the mantle of his inheritance.

London was noisy and crowded after years on the high seas. Society was even worse. His elevation in rank had brought hordes of fawning well-wishers and toadying curiosity-seekers to his doorstep. Only the nagging of Aunt Delia, Lady Victor, had kept him from barring the door and becoming a hermit. Still, a shark attack was preferable to facing a ballroom of young ladies vying for the attention of a bachelor duke.

Little did they know, he was done with marriage.

Banfield's voice intruded. "Perhaps Your Grace would prefer that I make a recommendation on each matter for your approval?"

"An excellent notion." Shoving the mountain of papers toward the secretary, Guy jested, "A pity you couldn't have inherited in my place. You know the role far better than I do."

Banfield flicked him a glance before lowering his gaze to the desk. Guy ignored that startled look. He knew the man found him lacking in proper ducal decorum, but devil take it, Guy had never planned on this life. Maybe in time he'd accept that becoming one of the richest men in England was a blessing, not a curse.

Maybe.

In short order, the secretary began sorting through the proposals, offering advice for Guy's approval. They spent the next few hours wading through the stack and discussing solutions. As they neared completion, a footman entered the study and stood at attention just inside the door. He waited to be acknowledged, his young features immobile beneath a white wig, his posture rigid in blue livery adorned with tiers of gold lace.

Many of the servants had that stiff-rumped manner, Guy had noted, and he wondered if they expected him to be a tyrant like his grandfather. He could only hope that time would ease the misapprehension. "Yes, Francis?"

"Beg pardon, Your Grace. There's a governess come from the agency."

"The appointment is scheduled for eleven tomorrow morning," Banfield interjected. "Kindly ask her to return at the appropriate hour. The duke is far too busy to be disturbed just now."

Guy had found the secretary's diligence in acting as a buffer against unwanted visitors to be useful, especially when ambitious mamas invented an excuse to bring their marriageable daughters to call. However, since this situation involved Sophy, he felt the weight of urgency.

"On the contrary, we've done enough for one afternoon," he said. "Send her in at once."

As the footman departed, Guy pushed back his chair and stood up, his legs cramped from hours of sitting. Pray God this new governess would be more adept at managing his daughter than the others. It perplexed him how one tiny girl could rule the nursery with an iron fist. He knew Sophy needed discipline but couldn't bear to be the one administering it when he already felt culpable for abandoning her.

The trouble was, he couldn't bear for anyone else to punish her, either. It wasn't her fault that her manners been neglected.

As he donned the coat that he'd slung over a chair, Guy feared that he'd failed Sophy. He'd departed England shortly after the death of his wife, Annabelle, believing his infant daughter would be better off raised by her maternal grandparents. After all, how could he succeed at fatherhood when he'd failed so miserably at marriage?

But Lord and Lady Norwood had disregarded his order to dismiss Annabelle's testy old nursemaid, Mooney, and to hire someone more competent. Under Mooney's slipshod

care, Sophy had become a terror. Now half a dozen governesses had come and gone in the past month. The last one he'd
dismissed this very morning when he'd caught her thrashing
his daughter with a switch.

Sophy's bloodcurdling screams had sent him flying up to
the nursery, envisioning her mangled from some horrible accident. As it turned out, she had bitten the governess in a
fit of pique when asked to leave her toys and practice her
alphabet. Her small teeth had left an angry red crescent on
the woman's hand.

Nevertheless, the sight of his tiny daughter lying over the
governess's knee had infuriated Guy. It brought back painful
memories of his grandfather wielding the cane. Sophy had
run to cower in the corner, and even now, the memory of her
woebegone face made his chest clench. By damn, there had
to be a better way to make a four-year-old girl behave!

What that method was, though, eluded him.

He strode to the gilt-framed mirror behind the door to ad-
just his coat. This morning, he had dictated a stern letter
to the agency, requesting they send their most experienced
governess, someone with the skill and competence to handle
a contrary little girl. He grimly resolved to subject this new
applicant to a more thorough scrutiny than the others. She
must be made to understand that he would accept nothing less
than absolute success in taming Sophy's unruly behavior.

Clasping the tidy pile of papers, Banfield bowed respectfully. "I presume you wish for me to finish these in my office?"

Guy gave an impatient wave. "Yes, yes. Go on."

As the secretary started toward the door, the footman
returned. "Miss James, Your Grace."

A petite woman appeared in the corridor. Guy's view was
partially blocked by the door, but he had the impression of
her gawking like a tourist at the opulent surroundings. Her

features half hidden by the wide brim of a chip-straw bonnet, she stepped into the study and halted before Banfield.

Darting a glance up at the secretary, she grasped the skirt
of her dark blue gown and dipped an elaborate curtsy worthy of the queen's drawing room. "I'm ever so pleased to
meet you, Your Grace."

Her voice was soft and melodious yet careful, as if she was
concentrating on the proper enunciation. Before Guy could
step forward and correct her misapprehension, Banfield
spoke. "The agency sent word to expect a Miss Williston.
Nothing was said of a Miss James."

"I'm afraid Miss Williston had to cry off. She . . . was
called away to tend a sick relation. I'm sorry for the confusion."

"You were also to present yourself tomorrow."

"Oh? No one told me so, only that your need for a new
governess is very urgent. I thought it best to come at once,
Your Grace."

Giving her a quelling glance, he gestured toward Guy.
"You may make your excuses to the duke, Miss James. I am
Banfield, His Grace's secretary."

Her swift intake of breath stopped just short of a gasp. In a
rustle of skirts, she swung toward Guy. At once he understood
that Banfield's pursed lips had little to do with scheduling
errors or mistaken identities. She had the smooth features of a
young lady in her early twenties rather than the stern visage
of the middle-aged spinster they both had been expecting.

Miss James studied him with such arrested interest that
he wondered if his cravat was askew. Her cheeks bore a
blush of embarrassment, and the bewitching blue of her eyes
matched the ribbons that were jauntily tied beneath her chin.
A dainty dab of a woman, she radiated a subtle allure despite
the concealment of that modest, high-necked gown.

Guy yanked his mind back to the purpose of the meeting.

Her feminine charms were irrelevant. This was an employment interview, not a ballroom flirtation. Miss James was utterly unlike the string of previous governesses—and that was not a point in her favor. She was far too green for the position.

Frustration filled him. So much for hoping this applicant would be an improvement on all the others. Being not long out of the schoolroom herself, she couldn't possibly have the expertise necessary to handle Sophy.

"Forgive me, Your Grace." She sank into another floor-dusting curtsy, this one to Guy before she arose and glanced at the secretary. "I beg your pardon, too, Mr. Banfield."

He flicked Guy a commiserating look that spoke volumes. It was clear that he, too, assessed her to be all wrong for the post.

As the secretary departed the study, Guy wondered at her use of the term *mister*. Surely she knew that servants were not addressed in so formal a manner. Had she never worked in a large household? The likelihood of that fact further annoyed him.

Blast it, he'd had enough of these mediocre candidates. This was the third employment agency he'd tried, and he was done with all of them. Henceforth, he'd advertise in the journals himself and let Banfield screen the applicants. As for Miss James, she could find work elsewhere.

"I'm afraid you were sent here in error," Guy said bluntly. "I requested someone older, someone with decades of experience as a governess."

She took a step closer. "Oh, but I do have the proper qualifications, sir. I've looked after young children for much of my life, and I've a particular knack for handling difficult cases. Please, won't you at least hear me out?"

Much of my life couldn't mean more than half a dozen years, if that. Yet it was clear from her tense pose that she had a keen interest in this post. She stood before him with her slim shoulders squared and her gloved fingers clutched tightly around her reticule. Guy knew what it was like to face opposition, and he grudgingly conceded that it would be cruel to dash her hopes without even conducting an interview.

"All right, then. I'll grant you five minutes to make your case."

He strode behind the desk and waved Miss James toward the seat opposite him. As she sank onto it, the massive, carved chair served to emphasize the delicacy of her figure. Odd that her bonnet was much more stylish than one would expect from a governess. Its wide brim made a perfect frame for her creamy blond hair and youthful radiance.

"I presume the agency described the situation to you, Miss James."

She nodded. "While you were traveling the world, your four-year-old daughter was spoiled by her grandparents. Since your return, no one has been able to curb Lady Sophy's naughty behavior."

The frank description put Guy on the defensive. "Sophy is a spirited girl. What makes you think you'll succeed where others have not?"

"I've dealt with all sorts of unruly children. There's always a way to bring them around. May I ask, exactly how did Lady Sophy drive away the other governesses?"

Expecting the list of disgraceful incidents would put a dent into Miss James's confidence, he ticked them off on his fingers. "The first governess objected to being scratched and kicked, the second suffered the shame of having her unmentionables tossed out the window onto the street, and the third had a hank of her hair sheared off while she slept. I dismissed the fourth when she allowed Sophy to run away during an outing to the park, and the fifth for administering laudanum to calm my daughter. Then this morning, Sophy bit the sixth."

"I see." Rather than recoil in alarm, Miss James regarded him with a thoughtful frown. After a moment, she went on, "I suppose it must be very upsetting to a motherless little girl to have so many people come and go in her life. Especially when she's so recently been separated from her grandparents. Was she very fond of them?"

Guy clenched his teeth, remembering the disastrous scene when he'd gone to collect Sophy. She had stomped her feet and refused to leave with him. While Lord and Lady Norwood made excuses for her tantrum, Mooney had stood right there muttering darkly about fathers who abandoned their children. He'd been incensed to learn that his instructions to replace the surly old nursemaid had been disregarded. The Norwoods seemed oblivious to her incompetence and had peeled off Sophy's clinging fingers in their haste to be gone to Brighton to attend a party at the Royal Pavilion.

Instead of the happy reunion he'd envisioned, he'd been forced to subject his daughter to a stern lecture. The memory of her tearstained face stung like an unhealed blister. Worse was the loathing of him she'd exhibited, shrinking away when he'd only wanted to hold her hand to take her to his carriage.

He said tersely, "Any child would be fond of those who allowed her to do as she pleased. That is why I need someone with many years of experience to teach her suitable behavior."

Miss James appeared unfazed by his reference to her youth. "It's also important that she have a governess who'll remain in your employ longer than a few days. Pray consider, she was taken from the only family she's ever known, from a home where there were no rules, and thrust into one that is more regimented. A strong-willed child is bound to lash out. This new situation must seem very strange and frightening to her."

"Rather, it is the governesses who are frightened."

"But *I* shan't be. There's nothing your daughter can do to scare me away. I would very much like the chance to prove that to you, Your Grace."

Guy cocked a dark brow. He couldn't decide if her aplomb arose out of naïveté or true skill. One thing was certain, this interview wasn't proceeding the way he'd anticipated. The other governesses had been deferential, proper, *old*. They had not offered their opinions so freely or regarded him with such bold resolve.

Of course, they hadn't shown any inclination to understand Sophy's perspective. He was chagrined to admit he hadn't, either. *Was* there just a frightened little girl hidden behind her malicious outbursts?

He was intrigued enough to lean forward, folding his forearms on the desk. "Tell me about your background, Miss James. What exactly are your credentials?"

The thick fringe of her lashes did several slow blinks. "I grew up in . . . a big family with lots of children. From an early age, I had the task of managing the younger ones, making sure they were tidy and well behaved. A few were wayward, inclined toward mischief like Lady Sophy, but I devised ways to steer them toward good conduct."

"Ways?"

"Every child is unique, so the methods vary. Before deciding on a plan, I would first have to meet your daughter and assess her character."

He couldn't shake a sense of skepticism. "That sounds all fine and good, Miss James, but to be frank I still find your age to be an impediment. You can't possibly know how to handle Sophy better than someone who is older and wiser."

"Oh, but youth can be an advantage. I understand little girls far better than an ancient spinster who's set in her ways. Many a time, I've dealt with willful children who needed a firm hand."

He narrowed his gaze. "So you intend to thrash Sophy into obedience."

The ribbons on her hat swayed as Miss James shook her head. "Oh, no, that isn't at all what I meant. It's far better to treat a child with kindness than with cruelty. I do hope you don't *expect* me to thrash her."

Judging her distaste to be authentic, Guy relaxed. "Certainly not. I'll tolerate no violence against my daughter. But how, then, would you make her behave?"

"It's a matter of inspiring her to conduct herself properly. So that she will take pride in doing what is right. It will require patience and hard work, but you'll soon see excellent results."

If Miss James could really achieve such a lofty goal, he'd hire her in a heartbeat. Yet all she'd offered thus far were glib promises. "So you came from a large family," he reiterated. "What then? You must have left home to become a governess."

"Of course," she said on a modest little laugh. "For the past several years, I've taught two girls in a genteel family, the Blanchets, in Northumberland. Sukie and Nell were quite a handful, but I soon had them on the straight and narrow. When they reached an age to attend a ladies' academy and no longer needed my services, I traveled to London. I much prefer the city, you see."

"Blanchet is a French name. Were they *émigrés*?"

"What? No! Mr. Blanchet is . . . is a country squire. Why, I never even thought of him as being French. He's as English as codfish."

"You needn't look alarmed, Miss James, I'm not accusing you of consorting with spies or traitors. The war is over,

Napoleon's been defeated. Now, I presume Mr. Blanchet has written a letter of recommendation for you."

She blinked twice at him before casting her gaze downward to search through her reticule. After a moment, she uttered a breathy gasp and lifted a gloved hand to her cheek. "Oh! How foolish of me, I must have left it at the agency. Allow me to assure you, milord, everything is in perfect order."

Resisting the allure of those big blue eyes, Guy had an inkling that she was embellishing her qualifications. Perhaps the recommendation offered a less stellar picture of her than she'd painted for herself. Northumberland was distant enough to make checking her story difficult. The last thing Sophy needed was yet another inept governess.

He rose to his feet. "This is most unfortunate. I'm afraid it's impossible for me to hire you without references."

"Wait, please! I'll send a note to the agency. The letter will be in their files, I'm sure. It's too late in the day, but first thing tomorrow morning, I can contact them . . . Oh! What is that?"

Having glanced away during her monologue, Miss James arose from the chair and glided across the study. She stopped before a framed watercolor on the wall. It depicted a tribal headdress consisting of a beaded circlet topped by tall parrot feathers in rainbow hues.

She cast a glance over her shoulder. "Pardon me, Your Grace, but this hat caught my eye. May I ask, is it something you saw on your travels?"

Guy saw no reason not to join her. Though suspiciously timed, the bright-eyed interest on her face appeared genuine. "It's a headdress worn by the people of Brazil."

"The feathers are very striking," she marveled. "I've never seen anything quite like them. Are such hats common among the women there?"

"Actually, this would be worn by a man. It's part of a chieftain's ceremonial garb for special celebrations."

"I see. Did you attend such ceremonies, then?"

"No, the purpose of my expedition was to study botany in the coastal regions of the world. Which is why most of the drawings here are of plants."

He swept his hand toward several other framed paintings on the wall, and she moved closer to examine them. "Lud, they're beautiful. These are all your work?"

"Yes. Sketching helped to pass the time on the long sea voyage."

"Well, they are fine enough to be put in an exhibition. Perhaps they could be displayed at Somerset House. Isn't that where the toffs go to view famous paintings?"

The sparkle of admiration in her gaze gratified him. Despite noticing a trace of common dialect in her speech, he found one corner of his mouth curling up in a smile. "I hardly think my paltry efforts belong with such masters as Turner and Lawrence."

"Then perhaps you should give a lecture here at your house. If you haven't already, I mean. You could talk about your travels. Surely the swells would find your adventures abroad to be fascinating. I know I would."

Guy had been inundated with invitations by scholars and academics to speak to their various organizations. He welcomed the chance to share his knowledge with those who truly appreciated it. Society was another matter. He was viewed as a curiosity, the duke who had spurned polite company in order to travel around the globe.

Yet maybe Miss James was right, and he ought to reconsider.

She went back to gaze again at the painting of the headdress. "The colors of the feathers are so brilliant," she murmured, "especially the blues and yellows. Do you know what sort of dye was used on them?"

"None at all. They're parrot feathers. In the tropics, parrots are as common as wrens and crows are here in England. In fact, I brought a few birds back with me. They make their home in the conservatory."

"Conservatory?"

"It's a large, glass-enclosed room with an indoor garden."

Guy firmed his lips to stop an enthusiastic narrative about the orchids, bananas, and other tropical plants he'd imported to see if they could be coaxed to grow in England's chillier climate. What had gotten into him that he would ramble on about his interests to a prospective employee? Especially a woman he scarcely knew and who might very well be inflating her employment experience. The fact that she'd never heard of a conservatory only confirmed her unfamiliarity with aristocratic households.

"Enough of these distractions," he said, cooling his tone. "We were speaking of your lack of credentials."

"Please, Your Grace, what harm can there be in allowing me a trial period?" Stepping closer, Miss James tilted up her chin to gaze earnestly into his face. "If Lady Sophy doesn't show an improvement, then you'll be justified in dismissing me. Won't you at least give me a chance?"

Guy knew better than to trust a dewy-eyed look designed to charm. Yet Miss James wasn't a flirtatious deb hoping to win the coronet of a duchess. Despite her woeful lack of references and the occasional trace of the common vernacular, she was just a woman who needed a job.

And he was a man caught in the thorns of desperation.

Whenever he visited Sophy in the nursery, her sulky petulance formed a wall between them. How had he ever thought his daughter would welcome him home with hugs and kisses after he'd abandoned her? She regarded him as a stranger because he *was* a stranger. And he hadn't the slightest notion how to fix matters. Perhaps a fresh approach might work where other governesses had failed. If there was even a chance that Miss James could help, he'd be a fool to turn her away.

"All right, then, provided you can show me that letter, I'll grant you one week." Guy paused before adding grimly, "If you can last that long."

Chapter 3

Giddy with success, Tessa followed the Duke of Carlin up the broad steps of the grand staircase. She had done it. She had convinced him to hire her. A jubilant smile tugged at her lips. With seven days in which to prove her worth, she fully intended to succeed where others had failed.

Their footsteps echoed in the vastness of the entrance hall. It was lucky the duke didn't seem inclined toward conversation since she was busy gawking at her new home. Carlin House resembled her vision of a royal palace with its creamy marble pillars, life-sized portraits of his ancestors, and a massive crystal chandelier that sparkled like diamonds in the slanting rays of the late-afternoon sun. The footmen on duty were outfitted in the same elegant gold and blue as the decor. Even the balustrade and woodwork were lavishly encrusted in gilt.

Did her father own such a magnificent home, too?

The question was a sobering reminder of her reason for seeking the position of governess. Her maidservant mother had borne a child by a lord, the man whose crest was engraved on her pendant. He surely lived here in Mayfair with all the other swells. For all Tessa knew, he could be just around the corner.

Or he could be long dead.

The only way to find out was to proceed with her plan to look for his coat of arms while she took Lady Sophy on strolls around the neighborhood. Meanwhile, it was vital that no one guess her secret—especially the Duke of Carlin.

As he led her along an ornate corridor and up another staircase, she studied him from behind. Carlin had a commanding presence, to be sure, but not quite in the way she'd expected. Although smartly garbed in a rifle-green coat and buff breeches, he had longish black hair that needed barbering, skin that was tanned by the sun, and a muscular build more suited to a laborer.

The older gent, Mr. Banfield, had more closely matched her notion of a snobbish, aristocratic duke, which had led to that mortifying mistake. Tessa thanked heaven she hadn't been tossed out right then and there.

While embroidering her past, she'd deemed it wise to stick as close to the truth as possible, inventing a childhood with lots of brothers and sisters since the other orphans had been like her family. One of her assigned tasks at the foundling home really *had* been to oversee the younger ones at their work so they wouldn't be whipped as she herself had once been.

She'd blundered, though, in not having a letter of recommendation.

Tonight, when everyone was asleep, she'd have to nick a piece of paper and a pen in order to forge the letter. Had she known the importance of it, she'd have written one and brought it to the interview. But she knew so little about the ways of the nobs that it was like walking blindfolded through the crooked alleys of Seven Dials.

An even more worrisome problem awaited her on the

morrow when the true applicant for governess was due to arrive. Tessa wondered if she dared to approach Mr. Banfield on some pretext to discover the name of the employment agency, so that she might secretly send word canceling the appointment. Failing that, perhaps the footman stationed at the front door could somehow be persuaded to turn the woman away . . .

Debating possible scenarios, she nearly bumped into the duke, who had stopped at the head of the stairs. She caught hold of the carved newel post to steady herself. This upper floor looked nearly as fancy as the lower ones, with large landscape paintings on the walls and a plush carpet runner on the floor.

"I should warn you . . ." Carlin broke off to scrutinize Tessa. "You're scowling, Miss James. Having second thoughts?"

A window at the end of the corridor cast a halo of light around his powerful form. But the duke looked nothing like the serene angels that adorned the hymnals at church. His roughly handsome features were hewn from granite and honed by the elements. With his brawny build, he resembled a bare-knuckle bruiser. And his dangerously penetrating gaze made Tessa's heart thump against her ribs. It was as if he could peer into her mind and see all her secrets.

Bah! The Duke of Carlin had no divine powers. Despite his rank, he was just a man like any other.

She lifted her chin. "No second thoughts, sir. I was merely trying to memorize the layout of the house. It's larger than the last one where I worked."

"Ah, yes, the Blanchets. I've friends in Northumberland. Perhaps they know your previous employer. You never did mention the name of their town."

"They don't live in a town, but out in the country." Another glib lie rolled off her tongue, inspired by the woodland scene on the wall behind him. "Near a tiny village called Oakville. Now, was there something I needed to know?"

Rather than press further, Carlin merely cocked an eyebrow. "Yes. I expect harmony in my house. No screaming, no mischief, and no tantrums. You're to keep Sophy in the nursery and not let her wander at will."

Tessa stared at him, aghast that he'd confine the girl to her rooms. His order would also put a crimp in Tessa's plan to look around the neighborhood. "Surely you can't mean to treat your daughter like a prisoner. Children need fresh air and outdoor play."

"Then take her down to the garden. It's walled so she can't run away."

"What if her behavior improves? Will you reconsider, then?"

"Perhaps." His tone bristled with doubt that such a miraculous transformation could be achieved. "And let me give you fair warning. Sophy doesn't always misbehave at first, especially when I am present. She seems to have a fear of me, though I've never given her any cause for it."

His mouth was set in a line of pained frustration. The sight made something melt inside Tessa as it dawned on her that perhaps he wasn't merely a tyrant demanding obedience. Perhaps he loved his daughter very much. Yet he'd been absent for most of Lady Sophy's life, and now he must be at his wit's end as to how to repair the rift between them.

"I expect she finds you to be rather large and fierce looking," Tessa ventured. "It's natural for a child to be wary until she comes to trust you. In the meantime, it's a good sign that she respects your authority."

"Well, she won't respect yours," he growled. "So don't be duped into lowering your guard."

He turned on his heel and headed down the passageway.

Tessa had to scamper to keep up with his long strides. She hoped his abruptness was based in concern for his daughter. It couldn't be easy to have half a dozen governesses come and go in the space of a few weeks. He likely expected her to be the seventh failure.

Little did he realize, she understood exactly what it was like to lose the only family one had ever known. To be a motherless little girl thrust into the care of strangers. She, too, had rebelled at first, lashing out in bewildered grief because all that was familiar to her had vanished forever.

And yet, pondering his ominous words, Tessa wondered if she was wrong to think her case was identical to Lady Sophy's. She herself had never been allowed to run wild. Mama had taught her to be respectful, to say please and thank you, and to share what little they had with others less fortunate.

Lady Sophy lacked that firm foundation. She had a history of being naughty and wicked, quite possibly as a means to draw attention. It would be Tessa's job to root out the bad habits and instill the rules of proper behavior in a spoiled girl who was accustomed to having her own way.

You have one week—if you can last that long.

As Carlin waited ahead by an open doorway, his ultimatum echoed in her mind. Those second thoughts he'd suspected her of having now struck with a vengeance. Who was she, a hatmaker from the East End, to think she could train the pampered daughter of a duke? Why had she ever boasted to Carlin of having a knack for handling difficult children?

Oh, why had she even come here at all?

To coax a loan from her father to open her shop, Tessa reminded herself. She envisioned a parade of fine ladies stopping to admire the elegant bonnets on display in the bow window, then coming inside to pay exorbitant prices for a Miss James original. How foolish it would be to give up that dream when she'd already overcome the first hurdle.

Mustering a smile, she joined the duke, whose tense expression seemed locked in place. He was the first and only nobleman Tessa had ever met. Rather than feel awed by his superior status, however, she found much about him to pique her curiosity. For one, she sensed a true concern for his daughter beneath his curt manner. For another, she knew that his mouth was not always set in that firm line. When he'd spoken of his travels, his face had lightened with zeal, and she longed to hear more about his adventures on the high seas. She herself had never once set foot outside of London.

He motioned for her to precede him through the doorway. Upon entering, she paused to take stock of the nursery. Located on the top floor, the long, airy room had lemon-yellow walls and a steeply slanted ceiling. The last rays of sunlight glinted through the windows, and a cheery fire on the hearth warded off the nip of autumn. Beside the carved mantelpiece, a middle-aged woman in mobcap and apron snoozed in a rocking chair.

Nearby sat a little girl at a miniature table. This must be Lady Sophy. She had a tail of dark, untidy hair that was haphazardly tied back with a drooping blue ribbon.

Intent on her task, she didn't look up. Her profile appeared sweet and angelic until Tessa noticed what she was doing. Using a pair of sewing shears, the girl was busily snipping pictures out of a book.

The sight of such vandalism galvanized Tessa. Without thinking, she hastened across the nursery and snatched away the slim volume. Half the pages had already been mangled and ruined. Colorful illustrations of animals lay scattered over the table.

"You mustn't do such a thing, Lady Sophy. Books should be treated with care, not cut into bits."

The girl stared up in startlement. She had the delicate features of a fairy with rosebud lips, a button nose, and golden-hazel eyes fringed by long lashes. Purple jam smudged one cheek, while another blob stained her white pinafore.

The hiss of the fire filled the silence. Then pandemonium erupted.

The servant woke with a snort and hefted herself out of the rocking chair. "Wot's this? Who're ye, miss?"

At the same time, Lady Sophy dropped the scissors with a clatter and jumped up, knocking over her chair. "That's mine! You can't take it!"

She grabbed for the book, but Tessa clutched it to her bosom. "No. Books are meant to be read and cherished, not destroyed on a whim."

The duke strode forward with sharp footsteps. "Miss James! We agreed on harmony, not mayhem."

His daughter turned to him, her lower lip thrust out in a pout. "Papa, she stole my book. Make her give it back to me!"

"That wouldn't be wise, Your Grace," Tessa murmured. Creating a scene hadn't been the ideal way to meet his daughter, but instinct warned her that backing down would only undermine her position.

Gazing at his daughter, Carlin appeared torn by indecision. "The book has already been destroyed. I can buy her another."

"It would be a poor lesson, though. Rewarding bad behavior only encourages more of it."

His troubled eyes searched hers for a moment before he gave a stiff nod. "Sophy, this is Miss James, your new governess. You are to do as she says. Miss James, you'll also wish to meet Lolly, the head nursemaid."

Lolly bobbed a curtsy in the general direction of Tessa, though her wary gaze was on the duke. "Yer Grace, so sorry fer milady's untidiness. The wee mite must've got in the jam pot afore Winnie took the tea tray below stairs."

With the hem of her apron, the servant attempted to scrub at the spot on Sophy's cheek, but the girl twisted free with the slippery agility of an eel.

She stamped her little foot. "Don't want no stinky governess. 'Specially if she takes my book away!"

"Sophy . . ." he began in a warning tone.

"I was only cutting out animal pictures to make a circus. 'Cause nobody ever takes me to a real one."

Sinking down onto the floor, she began to weep loudly, rubbing her eyes in a show of tragic wretchedness. Tessa suspected it to be an act designed to get her way, though Carlin looked stricken. He took a step forward, and before he could take another, Tessa caught hold of his arm to stop him.

Despite the layers of sleeve and shirt, she felt his muscles tense beneath her gloved fingers. He shot her a scowl that made him look remarkably like his angry daughter. Realizing she'd erred in touching his ducal person, Tessa dropped her hand at once. But she was beginning to wonder if he was part of the problem, allowing himself to be manipulated by humbug tears.

"It's a pity you're crying," she told the girl with a sympathetic *tsk*. "You'll only make your papa think you're too babyish to visit the circus."

Sophy miraculously recovered from the bout of tears and scrambled to her feet. "I'm not a baby! I'm almost *five*."

"Five is a very fine age. You're becoming a big girl and must learn how to behave before you can go to the circus. Now, your papa has work to do. Will you come and give him a kiss goodbye?"

Lowering her chin, Sophy eyed him with sulky mistrust. "No."

It was clear the girl wouldn't budge and compelling her to obey would only make matters worse. The duke, on the other hand, regarded his daughter with an expression of strained worry that hinted he was weakening. Tessa couldn't let that happen.

"All right then, perhaps another time. Shall I walk you to the door, Your Grace?" In full sight of the girl, Tessa handed him the butchered book. "I'm sure you'll want to take this away with you."

Carlin reluctantly accepted it. She couldn't decide if he was more irked at being dismissed by an underling, or if he disliked being compelled to deprive his daughter of her heart's desire. Whichever the case, she needed him gone before he caved to Sophy's demands.

Lolly hastened forward to make a fuss over the girl and tidy her hair. Her clucking and Sophy's protests gave cover to Tessa's muted conversation with Carlin as they walked to the door.

He aimed a glare at Tessa. "In the future," he muttered, "I prefer not to be drawn into these nursery battles. Sophy already resents me enough."

"It's important that we show a unified front," Tessa whispered back. "Otherwise she'll play the two of us off each other."

"She isn't so devious!"

"Oh? You're the one who warned me never to underestimate her."

He had no ready answer to that impertinent truth, merely giving Tessa one last frown before disappearing out into the corridor. Once he was gone, she blew out a sigh of relief that he hadn't sacked her on the spot. How strange that she'd never dared to speak to Madame Blanchet in such a cheeky manner but felt at ease to do so with the duke. It made no sense at all.

Before Tessa could ponder the mystery further, a yelp rent the air. Sophy was wiggling in her chair while the maid attempted to comb the girl's tangled tresses. "Ow, ow! That hurts!"

"'Tis a knot, milady," Lolly said placatingly. "If ye'll sit still—"

"No!" Grabbing the comb, Sophy pitched it across the room. "Use the scissors to cut it out."

Tessa knew it was time to start setting rules. Walking briskly across the nursery, she plucked the scissors from the floor before the maid could do the girl's bidding. "That's quite enough," she told Sophy. "There'll be no more snipping of hair or destruction of books."

"Lolly lets me do whatever I want with the scissors."

"Is that true?" Tessa asked the servant.

The maid shuffled her feet, glancing from Tessa to the girl as if trying to decide which of them to offend. "Only when I'm watchin'. Never thought she'd snitch me shears whilst I nodded off fer a minute."

The overturned sewing basket lay behind the rocking chair, the spools spilled in colorful disarray. Tessa hid her exasperation. How could anybody be so careless around a mischief-maker, especially when one of the prior govern-esses had had her hair hacked off during the night? If Tessa couldn't depend on her fellow employees, it would make her job all the more difficult.

"Henceforth, the scissors will be held by me," she said, tucking them in her pocket. "Let me know when you need them, Lolly."

The stout woman nodded, though not without a fearful glance at milady. It was clear the girl reigned as queen bee in the nursery—and she wouldn't give up her throne very easily.

"What if *I* want them?" Sophy demanded, her small hands on her hips.

"You're forbidden for the next week. I'll decide then if you're to be trusted with them. It will depend on you being on your best behavior."

Tessa kept her tone gentle but firm to keep from lighting the fuse of Sophy's temper. Shouting would only make matters worse. If ever she hoped to win the girl's cooperation, it would be necessary to calmly stand her ground.

Sophy instantly put that resolve to the test. "I want 'em *now*. I has to finish my circus!"

"I'm sorry you're angry. But you'll have to manage without them."

The girl screwed up her face into the spiteful mug of an imp. Tessa braced herself for an attack of kicking and biting, but Sophy merely threw herself onto the rug and began to batter the floor with her fists and feet. "I hate you! I hate you! You're *mean*!"

Tessa had dealt with weepy little girls in the past, though never with the overindulged daughter of a duke. At the foundling home, children had never dared to throw tantrums lest the matron apply a cane switch to their tender bottoms. It had taken only once for Tessa to learn to save her tears for the dark of night, muffled by the old flour sack that had served as her pillow.

Afraid the noise would carry downstairs, she went to close the door just as a younger maid with curly auburn hair scurried into the nursery. She bobbed a curtsy to Tessa while her dismayed brown eyes fixed on Lady Sophy.

"See if ye can soothe her, Winnie," Lolly advised.

Winnie crouched beside the girl, rubbing and patting her back, but it only seemed to make Lady Sophy angrier. No amount of petting mollified her. She only squirmed away and increased the volume of her caterwauling.

Just then, Tessa noticed the girl take a peek toward her

and Lolly. The scamp was gauging their reaction to her performance. She wanted people to make a fuss, so perhaps
that was the key. If everyone ignored her, eventually the girl
would realize the futility of her actions.

"Leave her be," Tessa said. "She'll stop eventually if no
one pays her any mind."

Winnie sat back on her heels. "But miss! We daren't let
'er scream."

"The duke'll dismiss us all!" Lolly fretted. "Why just this
mornin', 'e sacked Miss Drysdale fer paddlin' milady an'
makin' her cry."

"If there's trouble, I shall explain matters to His Grace,"
Tessa said in an elevated tone meant to be heard by little listening ears. "Meanwhile, if Lady Sophy wishes to scream
herself hoarse, she'll only lose her voice. It will be her own
fault that she can no longer speak."

It took only a moment for the tactic to show some degree
of success, much to Tessa's relief. The howling died down to
loud snuffling and choked sobs. Sophy scrambled into a sitting position to scrub her eyes with the hem of her pinafore,
pausing now and then to sneak a look up at her elders.

Tessa pretended not to notice as she untied the ribbons beneath her chin. "Lolly, will you please show me to my bedchamber? I'd like to put away my bonnet."

While Winnie kept an eye on the girl, Tessa followed the
older woman down a short passage and found herself in
a cozy room tucked under the eaves. It was beautifully
furnished with a single bed, a washstand, and a small desk
made of polished oak. As she set the chip-straw atop a chest
of drawers, her gaze was drawn to the window, where blue
damask draperies framed a lovely view of the plane trees outside on the square. The leaves had begun to turn yellow and
orange with the onset of autumn.

"'Tis a mighty fine bonnet, miss."

"Thank you, I made it myself." Noticing the maid's puzzlement, Tessa quickly glossed over the unwitting remark. "Trimming hats is a little hobby of mine. My, this is a pretty room. The other governesses must have been reluctant to leave it."

"All they done was grumble," Lolly said, shaking her head. "Threadbare rug, a lumpy mattress, no bolt on the door."

Tessa thought the lock would be useful to prevent nighttime mischief perpetrated by Lady Sophy but had no other objection once she'd sat on the bed to test it. The room even had a small fireplace, a luxury compared with her tiny, unheated flat. "I think it's all perfectly comfortable. Do you suppose anyone will object if I leave for a short while to collect my trunk?"

"One o' the grooms will fetch it if ye write out the directions. The duke would insist on it. 'Tis only right, ye bein' one o' the upper staff."

"Upper? Do you mean upstairs?"

Lolly stared blankly. "Why, 'tis yer rank, Miss. Ye're higher even than Jiggs and Roebuck. Them's the duke's valet and butler. I daresay ye be as high as Miss Knightley, Lady Victor's companion."

"Who is Lady Victor?"

"The duke's aunt. But no mind, ye'll learn soon enough who's who."

"My previous household was smaller," Tessa said glibly. "I hope you'll set me straight if I do anything wrong."

"Aye, miss. If that's all, I'll see to milady now."

Lolly dipped a respectful bob and departed, leaving Tessa alone in the bedchamber and feeling like a fish out of water. How peculiar to have someone curtsy to her—as if she were a born lady. Evidently, the post of governess put her in charge of the nursery servants. There were so many new things to learn about a ducal household that she'd best pay close attention.

But first, she must devise a plan to tame one sassy little girl.

Later that evening, Tessa stood listening outside Lady Sophy's closed door. The angry wails of half an hour ago had gradually died away to stillness. The only sounds came from down the corridor, where the maids were finishing the task of tidying the nursery. To assure herself the girl was truly asleep, Tessa opened the door and peeked into the bedchamber.

A candle in a glass chimney cast pale light over a room decorated in rose and yellow, the colors muted by shadow. She blinked in surprise to see that the bedlinens were no longer heaped on the rug where Sophy had flung them in a fit of pique at bedtime. Tessa hadn't allowed Lolly or Winnie to restore order here. Sophy had made the mess, so she could very well sleep on the floor.

But now alarm struck. Where *was* the girl? Tessa had once read in a tattered gothic novel about a castle with secret passageways. Had she inadvertently let the duke's daughter escape?

She stepped inside to look around and was relieved to discover a small shape curled asleep in the gloom of the four-poster bed. Sophy had dragged the sheets back onto the mattress and wrapped herself in a cocoon of coverings. Her dark hair was spilled in disarray over the pillow, and her hand rested beside her mouth as if she'd been sucking her thumb for comfort.

How odd to see her so peaceful when supper in the schoolroom had been a near-disaster. The girl had bounced up and down in her chair, spilled milk over the table, and kept the maids scurrying. Tessa had diligently corrected each lapse. The last straw had been when Sophy used her fingers to snatch morsels of tender beef off Tessa's plate. Though the meal was only half eaten, the roast and carrots delicious compared with Tessa's usual fare of bread and cheese, she'd ordered both their trays removed to the kitchen.

Bath time had been equally hectic. Sophy had made a game of running naked around the tub while Lolly chased in pursuit. Tessa had stepped in to catch the girl and deposit her into the copper tub. She'd felt not a jot of sympathy when Sophy wiggled and yelped. If not for the consternation of the maids, who believed bathing a child to be beneath the dignity of a governess, Tessa would have done the washing just to show the girl who was in charge.

It irked her that Sophy didn't appreciate the tub of steaming water, for Tessa was used to cold sponge baths from a bucket filled at the street well. The girl had no gratitude for her lavish life here, with toys and books galore, warm clothing and ample food, and servants to see to her every need. Meanwhile, not much more than a mile away in the stews of London, ragged children were forced to labor in workhouses. Or they huddled in doorways, begging for a crust of bread to ease the hollow cramp of hunger. Reflecting on that injustice, Tessa had been sorely tempted to resign her post in disgust.

But now the girl's deviltry had gone dormant, leaving a tiny angel in bed.

Beset by a sudden tenderness, Tessa leaned down to stroke a lock of silky hair from that small cheek. Sophy stirred against the pillow. Without opening her eyes, she gave a whimpering sigh. "Moo-moo. Want moo-moo."

That sad little voice broke Tessa's heart. *Moo-moo?* Did it mean something significant, or was it merely the nonsensical product of a dream?

Whatever the case, she felt certain that what she'd told the duke was true, that Lady Sophy was an unhappy girl lashing out at the world. Tessa knew she couldn't use the position of governess simply as a means to achieve her own ends. She also wanted to help the girl.

Lud, she must not fail Sophy as others had done.

Quietly closing the door, Tessa returned to her own chamber. A candle on a table illuminated the battered old trunk situated against a wall. Since there had been no sly look from the duke's groom when her possessions had been delivered, Orrin must have heeded her note asking him not to drop any hint about her past.

As she sank onto the bed, exhaustion pervaded every bit of her body. She had arisen before dawn to go to the millinery shop, had made a sudden stressful change in her life, then had spent hours caring for a wayward child.

And the day was far from over. Although a yawn stretched her lungs, she still needed to forge that letter of recommendation from the fictitious Mr. Blanchet. An earlier search of the desk in her room had turned up nothing more than scraps of cheap notepaper. Likewise, the schoolroom had yielded only ruled pages in copybooks. A request to Lolly had sent the maidservant trotting below stairs to return with a sheet of elegant stationery. Alas, Tessa could hardly give Carlin a letter that was embossed with his own gold crest.

Somewhere in this vast mansion there had to be a plain piece of paper. She would conduct a search once everyone was asleep—especially the duke.

Longing for the comfort of her old flannel nightdress, Tessa lay down fully clothed on the bed and drew up the covers against the chill in the air. It seemed foolishly extravagant to leave the candle burning, but she would need the light in a little while. To pass the time, she gazed out the open draperies at the crescent moon floating in an inky sea of stars. Her old room had looked out on a brick wall. Such a rare treat it was to have a view of the night sky!

Yet the sight also had the tranquilizing effect of a sleeping draught. Perhaps if she planned activities to pique Sophy's interest, it would help her to stay awake. As disjointed possibilities swirled in Tessa's mind, her eyelids began to feel impossibly heavy. She would close them for a few moments of rest. Just a few moments and no longer . . .

The next thing she knew, morning sunlight was flooding her bedchamber. In horror, Tessa realized she had never written that letter.

Chapter 4

"Ho there, Guy! Come, be a good fellow and talk some sense into Mama."

Guy had been heading down the corridor to his study but felt obliged to detour into the breakfast parlor to greet his cousin and aunt. Though it was past eleven, Edgar Whitby sat at the linen-draped table with Aunt Delia and her companion, Miss Knightley, a quiet, thirtyish spinster.

Guy had returned from abroad to find his relatives ensconced in the east wing of Carlin House. They'd moved in here at his grandfather's decree upon the death of Guy's uncle, Lord Victor. Edgar had been only fifteen at the time and under the duke's guardianship. Guy had had no objection to continuing the arrangement. At least their presence kept him from rattling around this great pile with only servants for company.

Discounting Sophy, of course.

Thinking of his daughter, Guy felt his chest tighten. Would he ever see her settled and happy as a normal child? In light of what he'd just found out, that hope seemed more elusive than ever.

A moment ago, he'd dispatched a servant to fetch the new governess to his study. Miss James would be in a dither, wondering if he'd discovered her secret. Let her wait. She deserved to suffer for her lies.

Having already breakfasted at eight thirty, he ignored the salvers of eggs, kippers, and toast on the sideboard and walked toward the coffeepot. A footman sprang ahead to fill a porcelain cup from the silver urn. "Your Grace."

Guy gave a nod of thanks as he accepted the cup. Perhaps in a year or two or ten, he'd become accustomed to the high degree of service Grandfather had demanded of the staff. It was a far cry from boiling his own tea over a camp stove with water from a crocodile-infested river.

As he walked to the table, he eyed his cousin and heir. Edgar lounged with his legs crossed, bootheels propped on the seat of the neighboring chair. At twenty, Edgar had the air of a Corinthian with a steel-blue coat tailored to fit broad shoulders, buckskins and polished top boots, and a patterned Belcher kerchief tied at his throat. By contrast, Aunt Delia wore the black of mourning into her fifth year of widowhood. She had sad eyes and a droopy mouth, and as usual, her manner exuded all the joy of a funeral.

Guy leaned down to plant a peck on her papery cheek. "I trust you're well this morning, Aunt."

She cast a long-suffering glance at her son. "If only that were so. But I'm afraid my digestion is sorely overwrought today."

"No need to be in a pelter, Mama," Edgar said, cutting a slice of sausage on his plate. "I'm old enough to be at liberty to do as I please."

"Except to put your boots on the dining chairs," Guy said.

His cousin grumbled but lowered his feet and straightened his posture.

"See how he heeds you, Guy, but not me," Aunt Delia

lamented. "Why, I'd told him that very thing only a minute ago and he wouldn't listen. Now, I do hope you can dissuade Eddie from this dreadful course of action!"

"Edgar, if you please," her son corrected. "And it ain't dreadful in the least. Just a few days' jaunt out of town."

Guy sat down to drink his coffee. Edgar was a keen sportsman who relished a challenge and excelled at athletics. "So what is it this time? A boxing match? Fox hunt? Carriage race?"

"Newmarket," Edgar said with great enthusiasm. "Chesterton invited me and a couple of mates to stay with him. His papa keeps a stable near the track where we can watch the horses train. One of his prime nags will be running later this week."

Aunt Delia clutched a black-edged handkerchief to her shriveled bosom. "Only think of all those sharp hooves! Not to mention the drunkards and the gamesters. Why, the very thought of you among them makes me shudder."

"Bother it, Mama, I'm no longer in short pants," Edgar griped. "I've nearly reached my majority."

"Not for another six months. If your grandfather were still alive, he would forbid you from associating with such unsavory characters."

"Fustian! Lord Chesterton is top of the trees, Sedgwick and Hopkins, too. They'd stare to hear themselves described as bounders."

"Be that as it may, Newmarket is teeming with ne'er-do-wells. And you, just out of university! Guy, surely you'll agree that it's far too dangerous."

"A fellow oughtn't be kept on leading strings," Edgar countered. "Tell her, Carlin."

Both mother and son looked to Guy for a verdict. He studied them over the rim of his cup. Damnation, it was a chore to be head of the family. He was forever being drawn into their squabbles. But in his view, any activities that kept a young gentleman out of gaming dens was to be encouraged. Though he didn't wish to upset his aunt, he thought it high time that Edgar be allowed to spread his wings.

"His friends sound unexceptional, Aunt. He has my permission to go for a few days so long as he promises to abstain from deep play. A small wager or two will not be amiss, but nothing more whilst I hold the purse strings."

A grin spread across Edwin's face. He jumped up from his chair so fast he nearly knocked it over. "You're a champ, Carlin. A true blood."

Aunt Delia uttered a strangled cry. "But you've a duty to protect him, Guy. He's heir to the dukedom. Oh, if anything were to happen to my darling Eddie, I would never recover!"

As she fanned herself with the handkerchief, Miss Knightley came to sit beside her, patting the woman's arm. "There, there, Lady Victor. Everything will be fine, you'll see."

"No, a terrible misfortune will befall him, I can feel it in my bones. My only child is fated to die like all the other heirs. It's the Carlin Curse!"

Guy frowned. She was referring, of course, to the passing of his two uncles, his father, and his other cousin, by accidents or ailments. All had happened within a span of five years, and he hadn't realized until now how hard those deaths must have weighed on his aunt, who was gloomy even under the best of circumstances.

"The Carlin Curse," he repeated. "Where did you hear such a slur? I trust the tabloids aren't spreading gossip about our family."

"Mama coined it herself," Edgar said, in an expansive humor now that his wish had been granted. "Quite clever of her, eh? The Carlin Curse."

"You're not to repeat that," Guy commanded. "It's fodder

for rumormongers and exactly the sort of rubbish loved by the news rags."

Just then, a movement across the breakfast parlor caught his attention. One glance in that direction erased all other thought from his mind. Miss James had stepped into the doorway.

Despite the long-sleeved gray gown and the linen cap perched on her blond curls, she looked remarkably alluring. Guy firmed his lips. What the devil was she doing in here? Worse, he had the vexing suspicion she'd eavesdropped on the tail end of the conversation.

Miss James took a few cautious steps forward. Her gaze flitted around the room, scanning the classical statues in niches, the heavy sideboard laden with food, the silver saltcellars and pepper pots on the table, before returning to him. "I hope I'm not intruding, Your Grace. As I was entering your study, I heard your voice from down the corridor and thought to join you here."

Arising, Guy noted that his aunt and his cousin were staring at her with keen interest. He made the obligatory introductions. He'd intended to send Miss James packing before his family even became aware of her presence. The fact that she was employed here at all was a testament to his poor judgment.

Miss James dipped a curtsy to his aunt. "I'd heard mention of you, Lady Victor. And you, too, Miss Knightley."

She smiled at his aunt's companion, who returned the greeting with the same friendly warmth. "Welcome to Carlin House, Miss James."

"I daresay this one won't last long," Aunt Delia murmured to Guy with a mournful shake of her head. "Such a racket I heard coming from the nursery yesterday evening. Poor Sophy's wailing carried all the way down to my bedchamber. It caused a terrible strain on my nerves."

Guy had gone out to dinner with friends at his club, and the house had been quiet upon his post-midnight return. Though he usually took whatever his aunt said with a grain of salt, this particular report added fuel to the fire of his displeasure with Miss James.

"I'm sorry Lady Sophy disturbed you, milady," Miss James said. "I promise you'll see an improvement in her very soon."

"I very much doubt that." Gloom shrouded his aunt's voice. "Alas, I fear the girl is too young for a governess and still needs the care of a nanny. I warned you, Guy. You oughtn't have dismissed Mooney."

Miss James cast an inquiring glance at her. "Mooney, milady?"

Guy noticed that was the second time she'd uttered *milady* in the manner of a lower servant instead of *my lady* as a well-bred woman would say. It only raised more questions about her clouded past. Before his naysayer aunt could continue, he said in a clipped tone, "We'll speak of this later, Aunt Delia. Come, Miss James."

As he started toward the arched doorway, he saw Miss James sink her teeth into her lower lip. The aura of warm interest faded from her face, and her wary eyes darted to him for an instant before she lowered her gaze.

So, she wasn't as oblivious as he'd thought. She knew precisely why he'd called her onto the carpet. Her stiff posture brought to mind a condemned prisoner wearing a brave façade on her way to the gallows. Not that there was any reason in the world why he should feel even a twinge of sympathy for her.

Deceit was the one thing he could never forgive.

Beset by anxiety, Tessa followed the duke out into the corridor. His swift pace and stern expression caused a quake inside her. There could be no doubt he'd discovered the truth—or at least a part of it. Her error in interrupting a family meal had only made matters worse. Oh, why had she gone in search of him? Partly out of the cowardly hope that the presence of others might blunt his anger. But equally awful had been the prospect of waiting in his study for the ax to fall.

All of her plans had gone awry, from falling asleep without having forged that letter of reference, to failing to notify the employment agency that the position of governess had been filled. Her subtle questioning of the nursery staff as to the name of the agency had yielded nothing. As a last resort, she'd meant to tell the footman at the front door to send the applicant away upon her arrival. But Lady Sophy had been too demanding of Tessa's time this morning to allow her even a moment to dash downstairs.

Somehow, she had to extract herself from this tangled web of her own making. Her throat tightened. She couldn't lose this post. Not when it was her best hope of opening a millinery shop. And not when she'd just begun to form a fragile bond with the little girl.

Carlin waved her into the study ahead of him. Walking past his formidable figure, she strove for calm, though his stare chilled her to the marrow. The duke had every right to be furious, Tessa reminded herself. She would think less of him if he didn't look out for the well-being of his daughter. Yet it was crucial to convince him that Lady Sophy needed her and that no other governess would do.

He walked to the desk, perched on the edge, and crossed his arms. Unlike the previous day, she received no invitation to sit. Those unnerving dark eyes studied her. Without preamble, he stated, "You lied to me, Miss James. Imagine my surprise a short while ago when the real governess arrived for her interview."

"I-I feared that might happen, and I'm very sorry for the ruse, Your Grace. If I may explain why—"

"Save your excuses. Since you weren't sent by any employment agency, tell me how you learned of this position."

"I overheard two ladies talking in a shop." He needn't know she'd been an employee, not another customer. "They mentioned that you'd lost half a dozen governesses in the past month or so, and that your daughter was in need of someone with the skill to handle her. It seemed ideally suited to me, so I came at once to apply."

"It never occurred to you to first seek the sanction of an agency?"

"There wasn't time. Had I done so, someone else might have been hired in my place."

"Or perhaps you wished to avoid scrutiny altogether. Due to your lack of any recommendation from a prior employer."

The sarcasm in his voice daunted Tessa. She greatly disliked the need to compound her lies when the duke was only a father looking out for his daughter's welfare. Yet what other choice did she have?

She gazed up at him through the fringe of her lashes. "I confess, no such letter exists. You see, I was dismissed from my last position without reference. Mrs. Blanchet accused me of . . . of making eyes at her husband. But I assure you, sir, it was not true! I would never behave in such a manner."

It took every particle of her willpower to meet his gaze without flinching. Though guilt over the deception gnawed at her, Carlin mustn't guess she was a lowly hatmaker who had grown up in an orphanage, or that she had taken this position in the hope of discovering the identity of her noble father.

Those secrets surely could cause no harm, Tessa rationalized. To make amends, she would do her very best for his daughter—if only the duke would allow her to stay.

"So you expect me to accept your word on this," he said

coolly. "The problem, Miss James, is that you are a proven liar."

She laced her fingers together at her waist. "Only by necessity, Your Grace. No one would hire me without reference, and I could not lower myself to . . . to those vocations to which desperate ladies turn."

"You could have thrown yourself on the mercy of one of your many siblings."

Oh, dear. She had fibbed about that, too, since the other orphans had been like a family to her. "I come from an impoverished background," she hedged, sticking close to the truth. "Perhaps it's difficult for a man of your rank to understand, but . . . my salary is greatly needed."

With the lazy grace of a cat, the duke prowled toward Tessa and stopped in front of her. His nearness increased the trembling disturbance in her depths. With his coal-black hair and intense brown eyes, he commanded her full attention. He was tall and muscled, the epitome of a gentleman in his tailored blue coat and buff breeches. Yet he had an untamed quality that must draw ladies to him in flocks.

"Or perhaps that's another of your havey-cavey tales," he said. "My daughter's governess must be of sterling character. I won't have a con artist teaching her."

Tessa elevated her chin. "I may have embroidered the truth a bit, but I am not a criminal. I'll take excellent care of Lady Sophy. In fact, I daresay I'll be a good deal better than those agency-approved governesses who darted off at the first sign of trouble."

"Oh? Then why was Sophy screaming last evening—so loudly that my aunt could hear her on the floor below?"

"You should know by now that your daughter kicks up a fuss over practically everything. It will take time to break her of that bad habit. But I'm already making some progress.

Just this morning, we had a pleasant episode creating a circus with her toy animals."

At least it had been pleasant until Sophy had lost her temper.

Tessa had had trouble in coaxing the girl to sit still and
learn her alphabet. To make matters worse, she'd been frazzled with worry over the arrival of the real governess. When
Sophy's naughtiness had nearly driven her to the brink, in desperation Tessa had abandoned the lessons and knelt down by
the bins that overflowed with playthings. On the rug, she began to arrange the toy animals into a circus. Sophy had stared
suspiciously at first but quickly took charge of the show that
included an elephant, several horses, a lion, a monkey, and
a spotted long-necked creature that the girl called a *graffe*.
They'd enjoyed a delightful half hour making the beasts
perform tricks—until Tessa had rummaged in the toy chest
and discovered a stuffed cow.

All she'd done was ask if the cow was named Moo-Moo.

The simple question had ruined Sophy's good humor. At
once, the girl had attacked the circus, flinging animals everywhere and making a shambles of the nursery. Not even
Lolly or Winnie had been able to soothe her anger.

"You were supposed to be teaching my daughter her numbers and letters, not playing games."

Carlin's voice snapped Tessa back to the present. Returning her attention to him, she said, "About this nanny that your
aunt mentioned—Mooney. Did Lady Sophy by chance call
her Moo-Moo?"

"Yes. Why do you ask?"

"Last night, when I went to check on your daughter, she
murmured the name in her sleep. She sounded so very sad that
it broke my heart."

Tessa made no attempt to disguise the ache of that distressing incident. It clarified so much about the girl that Carlin

needed to grasp. And she was relieved to see the frown on his face ease into something approaching concern.

"Mooney was a longtime retainer of Lord and Lady Norwood, Sophy's grandparents," he said. "She retired to live with a niece in Essex when I brought Sophy here. She was old, ornery, and negligent."

The Norwoods were the parents of Carlin's late wife, Tessa recalled. She found herself intensely curious about his marriage. "Was Mooney nanny to the duchess when she was a little girl?"

The brief softening of his expression evaporated. She glimpsed a hint of pain before his features became inscrutable. "Yes, though I gained the title only last year, so my wife was never duchess. But enough of these questions. It is you, Miss James, who is under review, not me."

Tessa realized she'd committed a grave impertinence. She oughtn't be probing into his personal life, especially if he was still grieving the loss of his beloved. "Pardon me, Your Grace," she murmured. "I'm merely trying to understand the situation for Lady Sophy's sake. If the Norwoods knew Mooney had grown too old, why didn't they replace her?"

"I instructed them to do so, but they never did. They were too busy with their social life to pay much heed to Sophy's upbringing. While abroad, I was concerned by the infrequency of their letters, but I attributed it to the inefficiency of the overseas mail. I never realized the full extent of the problem until my return."

Veering away, Carlin stalked to the window to stare out into the sunshine. Tessa's heart twisted in response to his bitter admission. Evidently, the duke blamed himself for the state of affairs as much as the grandparents. He was determined to mend his daughter's conduct but kept being thwarted in his search for the right governess.

Tessa had only added to his burden.

Pricked by shame, she yearned to absolve herself by re-forming Lady Sophy. Yet Tessa knew she needed to tread carefully. Never had she been more aware of her ignorance of aristocratic life. There was so much she didn't know, in-cluding the proper age at which a child graduated from a nanny to a governess.

Tessa ventured a few steps closer. Somehow she must convince him that her skills were unique. "Your Grace, I believe there may be some truth to what Lady Victor said. Given Sophy's unruly behavior, perhaps she *does* still need a nanny."

The duke pivoted toward her. "Nonsense, she'll turn five in a few weeks. That's old enough to begin her schooling. En-couraging babyish conduct will only compound the prob-lem."

"Yet your daughter was very attached to Mooney. Lady Sophy must be sad to have lost the one person who was like a mother to her. And that may very well be affecting her be-havior."

"I won't have that woman in my house, if that's what you're suggesting."

"No, of course not," Tessa said hastily. "Only that your daughter needs love more than schoolwork right now. And pray don't give me that mocking stare, please. Sophy's world has been turned upside down. Until I gain her trust, it will be difficult to teach her letters and sums. What I'm trying to say is that she needs someone who can be a blend of both nanny and governess."

He had been listening intently, but now one corner of his mouth took on an ironic twist. "Let me guess. You see your-self in that role, Miss James."

Like Sophy's, his brown eyes had a golden tint in the sun-light, and his jaw was set at the same stubborn angle. For all his size and rank, the duke could be just as combative as his daughter. With both of them, it was important to stand her ground.

"Yes, I do," she said firmly. "If you sack me, you will continue to lose governesses and Sophy's poor behavior will become all the more entrenched. I very much doubt you'll find any agency governess willing to demean herself by taking on the additional job of nanny. Nor will any of them get down on the floor and play circus with milady."

He frowned slightly at that last bit. Had she said something wrong?

Perhaps he found her entire proposition to be absurd. From what Tessa had gathered, nannies and governesses came from different worlds, one from the servant class and the other from the gentry. Melding their roles simply wasn't done. But she had to try. It was the only way to accomplish what was paramount, and that was to keep her post in this house.

The duke startled her by chuckling. "A pity women can't stand for Parliament, Miss James. You're as persuasive as any seasoned politician."

"I trust that means you'll vote for me to stay."

"Under one condition." His intent stare quickened her heartbeat. "Should I discover you've told me any other lies, it shall be grounds for immediate dismissal."

Chapter 5

Several afternoons later, a footman delivered a note to the schoolroom along with the tea tray. Tessa waited until he was gone before she broke the wax seal. To her surprise, it was from Sukie at the millinery shop. Before she could do more than frown at the brief message, the tapping of footsteps distracted her.

Miss Knightley stepped through the doorway. Tall and slender, she wore a modest gray gown with a starched spinster's cap on her chestnut curls. Her mouth was curved in a smile that lent a quiet beauty to her classic features.

"May I come in, Miss James?"

Tessa stuffed the note into her pocket where she kept the scissors. "Of course. Was there something you needed?"

"Only a bit of company if you're not too busy. Lady Victor is napping, and I'd hoped to discover how you've been getting on here." Walking closer, Miss Knightley glanced around the nursery with its little tables and the tidied stacks of books and toys. "Where is Lady Sophy, by the by?"

"Napping as well. I've found that an afternoon rest makes

for a happier child. The only problem is convincing her to remain in bed for an hour."

"I've often faced a similar situation with Lady Victor. Tell me, what is your trick?"

"A promised treat if she's good. I'll read her a book, we'll play hopscotch in the garden, or her favorite, create a circus with her toy animals."

Miss Knightley laughed, a sparkle in her green eyes. "Alas, none of those things will work with my mistress. But often Lady Victor takes a draught of laudanum to help her sleep soundly, and I am free to do as I please."

Delighted by the prospect of having a friend in the house, Tessa waved at the tray. "I was about to have tea. Will you join me, Miss Knightley?"

"Why, I'd love to. But only if you'll call me Avis. It seems forever since anyone has addressed me by my given name."

"I'm Tessa. And I do understand how one can feel alone even when surrounded by a company of people." She wistfully recalled chatting with Sukie and Nell as the three of them stitched in the back room of the millinery shop. Conversing with a child and the nursery staff just wasn't the same.

Tessa fetched another chair and they sat down at the sturdy oak table that served as a desk for the governess. She poured tea into a porcelain cup for Avis, using for herself an extra mug stored on a nearby shelf.

She offered her guest a dish containing a lavish array of pastries. "I must thank you for saving me from stuffing myself. The kitchen always sends far too much for one person. It's so delicious, I'm tempted to eat every bite."

Sampling a piece of gingerbread, Avis gave her a curious glance. "Did you not have a decent cook at your previous post, then?"

"It was a smaller place, so I'm not accustomed to luxury,"

Tessa said with careful vagueness. "I'd never have stood a chance of working in a ducal household had not Lady Sophy driven off the more qualified governesses."

"Why, you must be perfectly qualified! His Grace would never have employed you otherwise."

Avis didn't know she was drinking tea with a fraud, Tessa thought guiltily. She had the precarious sense of living on borrowed time, especially in light of the disturbing note she'd just received from Sukie. It seemed Madame Blanchet had been spreading the word among the other milliners in London that Tessa had stolen a hat.

Her stomach churned. She'd only taken the chip-straw bonnet as compensation for the month's salary she was owed, and after Madame had scorned her design. But now she had been branded a thief.

Lud, how could she clear her name? Would it affect her ability to open her shop? Worse, what if she lost her post here as governess before finding her father? How would she earn a living if no hatmaker would hire her?

The duke's sharp words needled her memory. *Should I discover you've told me any other lies, it shall be grounds for immediate dismissal.*

That mustn't happen. Carlin must never, ever learn the truth about her past. Now, more than ever, it was vital for her to guard that secret.

"You're frowning," Avis said in concern. "Are things so difficult here in the nursery? I was hoping you might be the one governess who will stay."

Picking up a cream bun, Tessa managed a smile. "I'm hoping that, too. I've made some progress with Sophy. Although she still fusses if she doesn't get her way, it helps to remain calm and give her a reason to behave."

"The treats you mentioned."

"That and teaching her that she cannot always have whatever she wishes. I want her to realize she'll appreciate something more if she earns it."

"Alas, that can be a hard notion for children of the nobility to grasp. If their sense of privilege isn't nipped in the bud, they will grow up to believe themselves entitled to whatever they please."

Tessa detected a note of bitter experience underlying those words. Was it in the distant past or in Avis's present situation? "Lady Victor seems a fretful employer," she ventured. "Though perhaps I oughtn't make assumptions based on one brief meeting."

"She *can* be a trial," Avis admitted with a wry twist of her lips. "Only because her glum nature has a tendency to wear one down after a time. It's a relief to have a few moments to myself."

Tessa had the sense that wasn't quite the issue weighing on Avis, but felt their friendship was too new to allow for prying. "Have you been here long at Carlin House?"

"Nearly five years, ever since her ladyship was widowed. I was glad for the position since my own papa had died and left me quite penniless. And really, you mustn't think badly of Lady Victor. Her air of melancholy is largely due to all the deaths in the family."

"Is that what she meant by the Carlin Curse?" Tessa had been curious but hadn't known who to ask. "I overheard part of the conversation the other morning. The duke seemed annoyed by the term."

"His Grace doesn't wish to put ideas in the minds of gossips. But I don't suppose the family's string of misfortunes is any secret." A somber look on her face, Avis took a sip of tea. "You see, the previous Duke of Carlin had three sons. The eldest, Lord Fenwick, drowned in a yachting accident three years ago, along with his heir. The following year, the second son, Lord Nigel, the present duke's father, contracted a deadly digestive ailment. The third son, Lord Victor, had already been slain by highwaymen."

Her stomach curdling, Tessa lost interest in the unfinished cream bun. Poor Lady Victor. That explained why the woman had looked so mournful. Her thoughts strayed to the duke, who had left England after suffering the death of his wife. He surely had been grief-stricken to lose so many other close relatives, too.

"Am I correct to assume that all this happened while the present duke was away on his around-the-world tour?"

"Yes, including the passing of the old duke, his grandfather, last year. It was a heart seizure that took him in his sleep." Avis released a long sigh. "I *am* sorry to have spoiled our tea with such sad tidings. But it will help you understand why Lady Victor has become very protective of her son."

"Surely she can't believe he would suffer such a fate, too."

"My mistress has a proclivity always to fear the worst, especially now that he's the duke's heir. The matter has caused considerable strife between her and Mr. Edgar, who only wishes to go about as all young gentlemen do. But at least he has an ally in His Grace."

Tessa was about to ask Avis to elaborate when the sudden noise of an argument emanated from the passageway. She recognized that childish whine and the scolding of an elderly dame.

When it didn't subside, she pushed back her chair. "Speaking of strife, please excuse me for a moment."

Tessa followed the sound of the quarreling voices. Sophy's door stood ajar, but surprisingly, the altercation came from Tessa's bedchamber. As she stepped inside, her eyes widened to see the girl across the room, kneeling beside the open trunk.

Lolly stood with her plump form bent down toward Sophy.

The two were engaged in a tug-of-war over a small tin box gripped in Sophy's hands.

A strangled breath rendered Tessa speechless. That box contained her life's savings. All the earnings she'd scrimped from years of labor, all the money she'd hoarded toward her dream of opening a millinery shop.

"'Ere, now, milady, ye mustn't take that. It ain't yers."

"Is, too. I found it, so it's mine!"

Sophy gave a mighty yank. She gained her prize, but the force caused her to tumble backward onto her bottom. The tin box slipped from her fingers and sprang open to spill its contents.

Coins rained all over the rug. They rolled into corners and vanished under the furniture. One penny twirled past Tessa and out into the passageway.

A keening cry burst from her throat. She sank down onto the floor, unable to think of anything but recovering her precious coins. Her trembling fingers raked the nearest ones into a pile. Spying a glint of silver in the shadows under the desk, she scooted to fetch the sixpence, and then snagged another from beneath a chair.

As she turned to add them to the pile, the nursery maid was on her knees attempting to peer under the bed. The older woman was clearly too stout to reach very far.

"Stop that at once, Lolly," Tessa ordered. "It is Lady Sophy who should be helping, not you."

Shock had given way to anger, and she aimed a glare at the little girl. Sophy watched from a short distance away, her pinafore wrinkled, her dark hair mussed. Her lower lip was thrust out in a sullen pout, but the wary glint in her eyes made it clear she was well aware of her wrongdoing.

"Well?" Tessa demanded. "What have you to say for yourself?"

The girl pondered a moment, then rubbed her backside in a bid for sympathy. "I hurt my bum."

"Bad things often happen when children are disobedient. You were strictly forbidden to enter this room, Sophy, and you disobeyed."

"You has to call me lady."

"I shall call you lady when you behave like one. Now, enough of your sass. That was my treasure you tried to steal. So crawl under the bed and gather what you spilled."

Perhaps it was the prospect of a treasure hunt that appealed to her, but the girl abandoned resistance and shinnied her small form into the gloom beneath the bed. She emerged a minute later with a string of dust decorating her hair and three coins clutched in her palm. While Lolly put them back into the tin box, Sophy helped Tessa gather the balance of the stash.

"Can we make hats now?" the girl asked when all the money was safely collected.

Tessa had promised the activity for later in the afternoon, but decided a harsher punishment was in order, given the gravity of the crime. It shook her to think of losing even a single penny of her cherished savings.

"I'm afraid not. You were wrong to rummage through my trunk. Those things belong to me and you must learn to respect the property of others. Now it is time for you to finish your nap."

The lower lip stuck out again. "Don't wanna sleep."

"Then you may sit in your bed and look at a book."

"You're mean!"

"Yes, I *am* mean when you're naughty. And you must obey the rules if you wish to enjoy fun projects. We'll make hats tomorrow—provided that you behave yourself for the rest of today."

For a moment, Sophy looked surly enough to kick someone. She was even wiggling the stocking toes of one little foot. Then she cast a sidelong glance up at Tessa's unyielding expression and must have thought better of the action. Grumbling, she marched out the doorway, followed by Lolly.

Tessa spied Avis Knightley waiting in the corridor. "Oh, I'm sorry. I forgot you were still here."

Avis smiled sympathetically as she handed over a penny. "I found this out here but didn't wish to interrupt." Then she lowered her voice slightly. "That was most impressive. How do you stay so calm?"

"With great effort," Tessa murmured, sliding the coin into her pocket as they walked back into the schoolroom. "The girl is a mischievous imp who requires constant watching. I do hope it isn't just wishful thinking for me to detect a slight improvement in her."

"Well, I certainly can see progress. For one, the shrieking that used to carry downstairs has diminished considerably. For another, she actually did as you told her just now. What does His Grace have to say?"

"I don't know. I haven't seen him since earlier in the week."

"Hm, Lady Victor said he's been gone from the house quite a lot lately. No doubt he'll summon the two of you to him soon. Now, I really must go. Her ladyship will be distraught if I'm not there when she wakes."

As Avis took her leave, Tessa stood frowning at the empty doorway. She had been on pins and needles these past few days, expecting Carlin to pop in at any time. He'd brought her here that first day, yet he hadn't returned. Was it unusual for a noble father to visit the nursery? Despite his bluster about wanting the best for his daughter, he'd shown no interest in Sophy since agreeing to let Tessa stay on as governess.

She found herself troubled by his absence. Leaving children to the care of servants might be the way of the aristocracy, but that didn't make it right. Sophy needed his love and attention. And if the opportunity arose, Tessa fully intended to drop the duke a hint.

The following morning, Tessa took Lady Sophy outside to forage for hat trimmings. They both wore shawls to ward off the coolness of the early-October air. Although the duke had barred them from walks around the neighborhood, it was still nice to escape the nursery.

The large garden at the rear of the house reminded Tessa of a park with gravel pathways that wove between beds of late-blooming roses and other plants. A few well-placed trees offered shade from the sun, and the ivy that climbed the stone fence bore the red and orange tints of autumn. She breathed deeply, enjoying the rich scents of earth and humus. To have all the beauty of nature right at one's back door seemed a luxury beyond compare.

She was pleased to see that Sophy appreciated it, too. The girl had already discarded her shawl and was crouched down, poking in one of the flower beds. Her yellow hair ribbon had come half untied, causing a partial spill of dark hair down one small shoulder.

Even though she had not been the precise model of ladylike conduct the previous evening, fussing over her supper and balking at bedtime, at least there had been no screaming fits and she'd heeded all reminders, albeit grudgingly. Tessa thought it best to overlook the minor infractions for now. Being overly harsh would only encourage rebellion in a child who was too stubborn for her own good.

Besides, she wanted Sophy to view her as a friend, not an enemy. That required walking a fine line between ally and autocrat.

Hopefully, a bond of affection eventually would grow between them. As yet, the girl was still too guarded to display fondness toward anyone. But there had been hints of unbending. The previous night, when Tessa had read a bedtime story, Sophy had scooted close, not quite cuddling but almost.

There were also times like now when the girl's eyes shone with delight. She held up a twig. "Look, Miss James! Is this a good decoration for a hat?"

Tessa went over to inspect the broken stick lying in the girl's grubby palm. A squashed red berry dangled from one end. Hiding her amusement, she took a pair of scissors out of her pocket. "Yes, indeed. Holly will look very festive on your bonnet. Shall I clip a few more sprigs from the bush?"

"I wanna do it! Gimme the scissors."

Sophy made a grab, but Tessa held the shears out of reach. "You're not allowed, remember? It hasn't been a full week yet since you cut those pictures out of the book without permission." Seeing a pout darken the girl's face, she added quickly, "Why don't you show me which of these berries you like the best. That's the more important job, anyway."

Thankfully, the girl let herself be distracted. Tessa snipped the chosen stalks and arranged them in the wooden basket that she'd borrowed from one of the gardeners. Then she sent Sophy on a hunt for colorful fallen leaves. The girl hummed to herself while rummaging beneath the trees. It was a joy to see her play for once like any happy child.

Wanting to savor the sunlight, Tessa pushed off her bonnet and let it dangle by its blue ribbons at the nape of her neck. She took the opportunity to study the rear of the mansion. The impressive stone façade had tall windows and a long, covered porch that the servants called the loggia. Her favorite part of the house was at the end closest to her and Sophy, a large circular glass room that extended out into the garden.

Nothing fascinated her more than the conservatory. A week ago, she'd have thought it a hoax if someone had told her the nobs had indoor gardens. Now she felt a burning curiosity. If only she could peek inside! From her present spot, she could see just a tantalizing glimpse of foliage brushing the many windows.

Suddenly, amid the jungle of greenery, a flash of brilliant red and yellow appeared behind one of the glass panes.

Tessa caught her breath. "Quick, Sophy, look! Can you see the pretty bird inside the conservatory? It must be one of the parrots that your papa brought back from his travels."

Sophy scrambled up to stare in the direction Tessa was pointing. An unexpected scowl descended over the girl's face and she let her armful of leaves flutter to the ground. "Papa won't let me go in the 'servatory."

Tessa's heart wrenched. Had she known, she wouldn't have called attention to the parrot. "I see. Well, perhaps he's just afraid you might accidentally let one of the birds out."

"No! It's 'cause he hates me. He never wanted a daughter."

Appalled, she sank down to put an arm around the girl. "Oh, I'm sure that isn't true. He loves you very much."

"Does *not*!"

Sophy squirmed free and darted away. She scooped up a stone from the gravel path and pitched it at the conservatory.

The tiny missile struck one of the windows with disastrous accuracy. The glass made a sharp, sickening noise as it splintered, leaving a hole edged by jagged pieces.

Shock rooted Tessa in place. It had happened so fast she'd had no time to react. To make matters worse, a man's face appeared at the broken window. The duke glared out at them before vanishing from sight.

Sophy stood stock-still, her eyes like saucers and her face ashen. She appeared terrified by her own reckless act. With a choked cry, she made a mad dash for the back door, no doubt to find someplace to hide.

"Sophy!" Tessa called, starting after her.

As the girl reached the broad steps to the loggia, her father came outside. He'd discarded his coat and his shirtsleeves were rolled to his elbows. His irate look could have curdled cream.

Sophy halted in her tracks. She stood there looking wildly around. Then she scurried back to Tessa and took refuge behind her skirts. "I-I didn't mean to do it. Please, Miss James, tell him I didn't!"

Tessa felt the trembling of that small body against her, the hands that clutched the fabric at the back of her waist. Without turning, she reached back to give a soothing rub to Sophy's arm. For the moment, the girl's fear outweighed any well-deserved reprimand.

Carlin stalked down the steps and approached the two of them, where they stood beneath the orange and gold leaves of a beech tree. "What's going on here, Miss James? Is stone throwing one of the skills you're teaching my daughter?"

Tessa stiffened as his sarcasm cured her of any inclination to wilt. "Of course not, Your Grace. It was an accident."

"Stones don't strike windows by mistake."

"You're right, of course. But young children sometimes act without thinking—especially when they're angry at their father."

Tessa's heart lurched. The tart words had emerged of their own volition. She'd meant to drop a hint about his neglect, not a bombshell.

His dark brows clashed in a startled frown. He glanced down at Sophy, then back at Tessa. He had to be irked to be addressed so impudently by a servant, especially one who was charged with keeping his daughter out of trouble—and who had failed miserably at that duty. Yet she couldn't regret having spoken out in the girl's defense.

She bent down to pry Sophy's fingers loose from their death grip on her skirt. "I need a word with your papa, dearie.

Go gather the leaves you dropped and put them in the basket. Then wait for me on the steps."

Sophy kept a wary eye on her father as she sidled down the path. Tessa noticed Carlin observing the girl, too. In those few moments, his ire seemed to subside as his expression took on a hint of worried uncertainty. She hoped that meant he would listen to her.

She clasped her hands tightly at her waist. "I'm very sorry for what happened, Your Grace. It was my fault for not keeping a closer eye on Sophy. You may deduct the cost of the repair from my wages." Lud, it would make a crippling dent in her savings, but that would be better than being dismissed.

"Devil take the expense. What do you mean, she's angry at me?"

"I pointed at a parrot in the window, thinking she'd be delighted at the sight. Instead she became very upset, saying you wouldn't allow her in the conservatory."

"Only because she might leave the door open and let the birds escape. They'd never survive in this cold climate."

"Did you explain that to her? For that matter, have you ever taken her into the conservatory to show her the birds?"

Carlin shook his head. "In case you haven't noticed, Sophy doesn't care much for my company."

"She scarcely knows you. And how will that ever change if you don't spend any time with her?"

"That's why I hired you, Miss James. To correct her wild behavior, train her properly, and transform her into a normal child who will regard me more favorably."

His deep voice held a note of frustration as he again looked at the girl, who was stuffing leaves into the basket. He ran his fingers through his hair, mussing the dark strands. As he did so, the flex of muscles in his bare forearm drew Tessa's interest. His lack of coat and cravat suggested he'd been doing some sort of work inside the conservatory.

The open collar of his linen shirt offered a glimpse of his broad chest, revealing skin tanned from his voyage around the world. A ripple of awareness heated her insides. She'd once read a penny novel about pirates on the high seas. Now her wayward imagination conjured the beguiling vision of him as a buccaneer standing at the prow of a ship, the wind whipping his hair and the salty spray dampening his shirt so that it clung to his sculpted torso.

"What, no cheeky retort?"

His question startled her. She lifted her gaze to see the duke regarding her with a slight, knowing smile. The heat of a blush crept up her neck. Lud, he had caught her ogling him like a common tart when she ought to be using this opportunity to repair his relationship with Sophy.

Wrapping the shawl tightly around her shoulders, Tessa refocused her mind. The duke needed to realize that he was going about matters all wrong. "There's something you should know, Your Grace. May I speak plainly, without mincing words?"

He stepped closer and braced his hand on the smooth tree trunk, crowding her almost like an embrace. "Please do."

The warm intensity of his stare rattled her as did his nearness. Being a nobleman, he'd read a sordid meaning into her question. She hastened to correct his mistaken notion. "It's about Lady Sophy. After she told me that you had refused to allow her in the conservatory, her exact words were, *He hates me. He never wanted a daughter.*"

The duke jerked as if she'd slapped him. All levity vanishing from his hard features, he dropped his arm. "What? Are you certain of that?"

"Perfectly. And I would venture to say, it doesn't sound like something a child would make up on her own. Could she have heard it from someone else?"

Carlin stared into the distance. "It must have been Mooney.

Blast that bitter old woman for planting such a false notion in Sophy's head."

The glimpse of pain in him softened Tessa, and she wanted to help him. "All lords wish to have an heir, don't they? Perhaps that's what your daughter overheard and misinterpreted."

"Don't make excuses. By God, I should have hired a new nursemaid myself before I left England." He struck his fist into his palm. "It was damn foolish of me to leave the matter to the Norwoods."

Tessa hastened to place her hand over his to forestall another outburst. "Please, you mustn't do that." The warmth of his flesh seared her, and she drew back at once. "Sophy will think you're still angry with her."

The little girl was indeed watching them. Hugging her knees, she sat huddled on the steps, the basket beside her. Even from a distance, she looked subdued and scared. Breaking a window was likely the worst offense she'd ever committed.

"I ought to be angry," Carlin growled, though without the earlier fire. "She threw that stone on purpose."

"Only because she feels unwanted by her own father. I'm not denying that she deserves punishment, or that she must learn to control her impulses. However, remember that she doesn't know you. You've been gone for most of her life. To her, you're a tall, fierce stranger who resents her very existence."

Worriedly watching his daughter, the duke released a long breath. He returned his gaze to Tessa, his eyes candid and full of remorse. "I admit to being at my wit's end, Miss James. I don't know how to remedy the situation. I can only hope you've a plan tucked up your sleeve."

"I do, but please don't expect too much at first. It will take time and patience for her to warm up to you. Think of her as a feral kitten, hissing and spitting until she learns to trust you."

"A kitten."

"Yes," Tessa said firmly, praying he'd heed her. "As a first step, now would be an excellent time to give Sophy a tour of the conservatory."

Chapter 6

As Guy followed Miss James toward the house, he had his doubts about the advisability of her method. It seemed too much like a reward to Sophy for lobbing a stone at that window. Whenever he'd committed mischief as a boy, he'd earned the sting of his grandfather's cane. Though that was far too harsh a penalty for a four-year-old girl, Guy wasn't entirely convinced that showing her the conservatory was the proper course of action, either.

Ahead, Sophy sat stiffly on the steps, her dark hair messy, the ribbon dangling loose. Feral kitten, indeed. That description was more apt than he wanted to admit. He suffered a spasm of anguish that his daughter thought he despised her, and that she would express her anger at him in such a manner. It was his own fault for abandoning her as a newborn, for convincing himself she'd be better off raised by her maternal grandparents.

Instead, the Norwoods had allowed Mooney to stuff Sophy's head full of lies. He could hardly blame his daughter for believing what her primary caretaker had said. And it had taken Miss James to figure it all out. To think just a few days ago he'd been ready to banish her from his house.

His gaze lingered on the new governess. In the sunlight her upswept hair was an unusual shade of blond that reminded him of golden buttercream. That high-necked, long-sleeved dark gown couldn't quite hide a feminine figure that was every man's dream. The sight aroused a rush of heat in his core, a sensation that he quickly rejected.

It was dishonorable for a man of his rank to lust for a woman in his employ. Guy had no wish to subject her to unwelcome advances, nor did he want to put her in a situation where she felt compelled to resign. Any temptation that stirred in him must be kept under lock and key.

Reaching the steps, Miss James crouched down to address his daughter. "Thank you for waiting here. Nevertheless, throwing a stone at a window was a very naughty act. As punishment, you will not be allowed to play in the garden tomorrow. Now, what have you to say for yourself?"

The way Sophy sat with her arms tightly curled around her knees suggested distress. Yet her small face wore its usual rebellious scowl. She mumbled, "Sorry, Miss James."

"It is your papa who deserves the apology. That was his window, not mine."

The girl slid a glance upward though she didn't quite meet his eyes. "Sorry, Papa."

The words sounded forced, with an underlying note of mistrust. His chest taut, Guy wanted to grab her up into his arms and declare that he did indeed love her, and she was never to believe otherwise. But Miss James was right, a feral kitten would only scratch and hiss.

Taking his cue from the governess, he hunkered down to his daughter's level so that she had to look at him. The glower on her face was far from encouraging. "I accept your apology." Guy searched for the right words to reach her. "Yet . . . it seems I owe you one, too, for never showing you the conservatory. I'll take you on a tour right now if you like."

Sophy stared suspiciously at him. It was as if she was weighing his sincerity and seeking evidence of some trick in the scheme. Then she shifted her wary gaze to the governess. "Will you go, too, Miss James?"

"Certainly! I wouldn't miss it for all the cream buns in the kitchen."

The girl considered that for a moment. "*I* wouldn't miss it for all the circuses in the world."

"There, you see? Parrots are better than all of our favorite things."

Miss James sprang lightly to her feet just as Guy reached out to offer his assistance. A pity that, for he'd have liked the chance to touch her. In the next instant he scolded himself. Damn, he had to put a halt to such thoughts.

Sophy, too, rejected his proffered hand and stayed close to Miss James, who picked up the basket and tucked the handle in the crook of her arm. The girl gave wide berth to Guy. He had to settle for leading the way into the house, where he ushered them almost immediately through another doorway.

Entering the conservatory was like stepping into another world.

As he closed the door behind them, Guy relished the illusion of being transported to the moist heat of a rain forest. Palm fronds brushed the glass roof amid a tangle of vines and other lush shrubs. Sunlight dappled the flagstone path that meandered through the greenery, and stone benches were scattered here and there to provide spots to enjoy the view.

"Did you bring all these plants back from your travels?"

Miss James asked in wonderment, her neck craned as she scanned the foliage.

"A good number of them. My grandmother had the palms installed many years ago, along with the orange trees and camellias. She liked to hold garden parties out here in the autumn and early spring."

"But how did she keep the place warm? Surely it would take half a dozen fireplaces, and I don't see even one."

"She commissioned an architect to design a network of steam pipes under the floor, as the Romans of old used to do. There's a furnace to stoke the fire in the cellar. Between that and the smudge pots, the air remains quite tropical even in winter."

Her face glowed as she looked around the conservatory. "Lud, I never dreamed such a thing was even possible."

Lud. Odd that an East End dialect would creep into her refined speech from time to time. He sensed there was much more to Miss James than met the eye. Yet perhaps her past was best left a mystery. His primary concern must be her ability to help him to ease Sophy's mistrust.

Miss James returned her gaze to him. She truly had the bluest eyes he'd ever seen. Fringed by long lashes, they reminded him of the deep cerulean depths of the ocean. "Am I correct, then," she said, "to think that it was your grandmother who inspired your love for plants?"

The observation startled Guy. He hadn't ever considered it, but she was right. "Yes, I suppose so. As a boy, I'd often sneak in here and play explorer among the undergrowth."

Much to his grandfather's displeasure. By contrast, the duchess had applauded Guy's antics and had encouraged him to use his imagination. His grandmother had died when he was ten, and now he felt a twinge of wistful regret at the loss of her vibrant charm and unreserved love. She had been a mother to him since his own had passed away when he'd been too young to remember.

Sophy tugged on Miss James's skirt. "Where are the parrots?"

"Perhaps they're hiding among the leaves." Her eyes flashed an appeal to Guy. "Your papa can tell you."

"They're often hard to spot, especially the ones with green feathers," he told Sophy. "You have to look very hard, for they often roost up in the trees."

Even as he scanned the foliage, a sudden hammering broke the aura of peace. The loud banging emanated from across the conservatory and stopped almost immediately. But not before a flurry of wings erupted into the air.

Disturbed by the noise, a dozen birds flew hither and yon in the sunshine. Their raucous cries filled the warm air. Guy enjoyed the delight on the governess's face as well as Sophy's.

His daughter watched with eyes like saucers. "Look, Miss James! They're such pretty colors!"

"How different they are from our dull little wrens and pigeons," she marveled. "Why, they look as if they're all dressed up for a fancy ball."

"Or maybe a circus."

"A bird circus! Now, that would be a sight to see."

Amused by their nonsense, Guy pointed at one that had alighted on a nearby branch. "See that big one with the red head and the blue-and-yellow wings? It's called a macaw. They're larger than the other parrots."

Miss James studied it. "They also appear to have longer tail feathers."

"An excellent observation." He was impressed that she took such an interest when the young ladies he'd known in society would be squealing and clinging to him for protection from the gliding birds.

"What do they eat?" she asked.

"Seeds and fruit, as they do in the wild. I've made their new home here resemble their natural habitat as closely as possible."

"Where are they from?"

"Guiana in South America, the last stop on my voyage before I returned to England." He'd arranged for several mail drops at various places around the globe. At the British consul's office in Georgetown, he'd picked up the packet of letters containing the news of his grandfather's death.

Just then, Sophy began to creep toward a smaller orange bird with a crest on its head that had perched on a rhododendron bush. Miss James took a step as if to stop the girl, but Guy caught her arm and shook his head. "Leave her be," he murmured. "She won't catch him."

"Him? Surely such pretty feathers belong to a female parrot."

"Actually, that one isn't a parrot at all. The locals call it a cock-of-the-rock. The males have fancy plumage in order to attract the females, whose feathers are a brownish gray. Ah, there's his mate now, on that branch above."

"Why, they're just like strutting roosters and drab hens."

"Exactly." He glanced at her simple blue gown with its clinging hint of curves. "We males know how to spot beauty beneath plain feathers."

Miss James had been eyeing the birds when her gaze flashed to his. A blush tinted her cheeks and added charm to the delicate oval of her face. It wasn't like him to play the flirt, Guy thought. He had put those youthful days behind him. Still, as they stared at each other, he experienced a powerful tug of fascination. Did she feel it, too?

A loud flapping of wings broke the spell. The cock-of-the-rock flew up to roost on a high branch near its mate. Sophy had managed to sneak to within a few feet of her quarry.

Now the girl glowered up at the birds and stamped her little shoe. "Hmph!"

"They're very fast," Guy said, chuckling. "That's why we must always keep the doors tightly closed so none of the birds escape."

She stuck out her lower lip. "I only wanted to pet him."

"Perhaps you could look for any feathers lying on the ground," Miss James suggested, glancing at Guy. "So long as your papa doesn't mind."

"Go ahead." Guy remembered himself at that age, hunting for treasure among the vegetation. He wanted Sophy to have similar happy memories. Even more, he wanted her to love him as her father.

As Sophy wandered off, the hammering came again from the other side of the conservatory, accompanied by another flight of squawking parrots. Miss James frowned. "Is that the window being fixed?"

"Jiggs is boarding it up until the glaziers can come to replace the pane."

"Lolly mentioned that name, Jiggs." Miss James looked puzzled. "Isn't he your valet?"

"He's a jack-of-all-trades. Come, I'll introduce you."

As Guy escorted her down the path and through a jungle of plants, Sophy scampered after them. She seemed loath to let Miss James out of her sight. He didn't fool himself for a moment that his daughter was following due to any change of heart toward him. Her wariness was evident in her watchful glances and in her avoidance of venturing within a yard of him.

But at least she wasn't running away.

They emerged into a small clearing across the conservatory, where a leprechaun had just finished pounding a board over the hole in the window. Spotting them, the small man laid down his hammer as a snaggle-toothed grin broke across his leathery face. The black patch over one eye completed his disreputable picture. "Well, well," Jiggs cackled. "If it ain't the two little ladies His Grace's been spyin' on."

"Spying?" Miss James asked.

As she cast an inquiring look his way, Guy felt heat creep up his neck. He shouldn't feel embarrassed to be caught observing his own child. Devil take it, he could hardly avoid seeing the governess, too. But at least now Miss James would realize she'd been wrong earlier to accuse him of taking no interest in Sophy. He'd needed to assure himself that he'd been right to keep Miss James in his employ.

"What he means is that I often work here in the morning, so naturally I noticed the two of you out in the garden. Might I add, you play a lively game of hopscotch." Guy succeeded in making her blush again, thus taking the attention off himself. "Miss James, may I present Jiggs, an old relic who joined me in my travels after my proper valet quit."

"The popinjay was too seasick to make it past Gibraltar," Jiggs scoffed. "He scuttled straight back to England on the next packet."

She sketched a curtsy. "I'm happy to meet you, Mr. Jiggs."

"Now, don't you go mistering me. 'Tis plain ole Jiggs. And this littl'un must be the princess."

"I'm not a princess, I'm a lady," Sophy said as she looked him up and down. "Why do you have that bit of cloth stuck on your face?"

"Pray don't ask rude questions," Miss James chided.

"Ain't no harm done," Jiggs said. "I poked out me eye whilst playing with a stick when I was a naughty little tyke like milady."

Guy knew that was a bag of moonshine. Jiggs had lost the eye in a tavern brawl in Gibraltar and had been left behind when his ship had sailed. Rather than cringe, Sophy merely said to the man, "Do you have any parrot feathers, sir? I want to use them to decorate my bonnet."

"Well now, I jest might know where to find some."

Guy watched his daughter scurry after the short man. It was daunting to see her take to a stranger before her own father. He turned to Miss James. "What's this about decorating bonnets?"

She blinked, then glanced down at the basket that was stuffed full of autumn leaves and red berries. "Oh . . . I thought it would be a fun activity to gather a few things from nature and use them as trimmings for her hat. She needn't wear it out in public, of course."

She seemed nervous about the project, and he could only surmise that she expected him to object to it since he'd been so adamant about Sophy learning her sums and letters. "I daresay this is part of your effort to win her trust."

"Indeed, Your Grace. May I ask, is Jiggs as interested in botany as you are?"

Guy noted how she'd turned the subject but decided to let the matter drop. "Hardly," he said with a laugh. "Jiggs thinks that flowers are too womanish. He spent the voyage grumbling about all the specimens I collected."

"Specimens?"

"Allow me to show you."

He led her to a work area with a table that was littered with utensils, jars of seeds, and glazed pots. A pile of rich black loam provided soil for his experiments. Sophy sat on her heels a short distance away. As Jiggs handed her feathers from a basket, she lined them up in a row on the ground.

While the two were busy, Guy pointed out his current projects to Miss James: banana seedlings that were sprouting tall green shoots, bromeliads that collected water inside the cup of a spiky flower, and the orchids he'd placed in the crooks of tree branches to encourage them to grow as they did in the tropics. Her questions inspired him to describe the varied places where he'd gathered botanical samples, from the dense mangrove swamps along the coast of Mexico to the arid shores of Persia.

"How did you care for the plants aboard a ship?" Miss James asked.

"The roots were packed in damp burlap, and I chose only those types that could survive a period of semi-hibernation. But mostly I brought back seeds, cataloged with notes as to their origin and natural habitat. The bulk of those seeds have been sent on to Greyfriars, to be sprouted in greenhouses come spring."

He felt an intense longing to be at his estate, working the fertile earth, instead of being stuck in London dealing with the myriad duties of the dukedom. Sophy would enjoy roaming the grounds as he'd done at her age. Miss James would relish it, too. He imagined her on horseback cantering over the hills, her face radiant in the sunshine.

"Do you ride?" he asked.

"I-I haven't had much opportunity. Why do you ask?"

"Next month, we'll be heading to the country. My grandfather kept a fine stable, and you must feel free to avail yourself of it."

"Oh! You hadn't mentioned leaving London."

The flicker of dismay in her eyes perplexed him. "You'll much prefer it to the city, I assure you. The nursery is spacious, the gardens are extensive, and the views are breathtaking. Greyfriars is a veritable heaven on earth."

"I shall look forward to it, then," she said with a cool smile. "May I ask, did you bring back anything from your voyage other than seeds and parrots? It seems that a world traveler would have mementos from foreign lands, too. Perhaps gold, frankincense, and myrrh."

"Since my primary purpose was scientific, I resolved not to be distracted by souvenirs. Nevertheless, I can oblige with myrrh in the form of seeds."

She blinked. "But . . . isn't myrrh a perfume?"

"Myrrh is an ingredient of perfumes and incense. It's an aromatic resin derived from a small thorny tree found in the deserts of Arabia. Hopefully, I can coax it to grow in a hot-house."

"I see. Well, I was hoping there might be something from your journey to catch Lady Sophy's interest. Other than parrots, of course."

Guy considered for a moment. "How about a pirate's treasure map?"

"Truly? Oh, you're teasing me, sir."

He enjoyed the thrilled fascination evident in her wide blue eyes and parted lips. "Actually not. The map was indeed sketched by an old pirate who'd been shipwrecked on a desert island for many years. How I came to meet him makes for an interesting story—"

"Miss James, come and see!" Sophy exclaimed.

The governess afforded him one last keen look, then she excused herself to go and admire the two dozen colorful feathers arranged on the ground. Guy followed close behind, sorry their conversation had ended and wondering if his daughter would ever call out to him. He ached to be the one with whom she wanted to share her joys and sorrows. If only he knew how to go about it.

"Why, there's enough feathers to make a chieftain's head-dress," Miss James said. "Wouldn't you agree, Your Grace?"

"A pint-sized one," he allowed.

"I'm making a hat," Sophy insisted. "Don't want a chief's dress."

"A headdress *is* a type of hat. Your papa saw one on his travels and painted a picture of it. Perhaps sometime he would show us how to make one for you." Adding the feathers to her basket, she slipped Guy a cautious glance. "If he has the time to spare, that is. He's a very busy man."

"I'd be happy to lend a hand," he said promptly. "When would be convenient?"

She thought for a moment. "Perhaps later this afternoon after Sophy's nap."

"Don't need help," Sophy protested, kicking a pebble with the toe of her shoe.

"Proper grammar, please," Miss James chided. "And mind, it is always best to seek the advice of experts in order to avoid making mistakes. Now please thank your papa and Jiggs for their kindness."

After Sophy reluctantly did so, Guy watched as the governess ushered the grumbling girl out of the conservatory. He wondered if he'd made any progress at all in winning over his daughter. Trust took time to build, he reminded himself. It would never have occurred to him to show Sophy the birds without Miss James suggesting it. He was too used to the aristocracy's tradition of keeping children out of sight in the nursery.

No, the deeper truth was, he felt unnerved by his own daughter. His ineptness with Sophy had frustrated him these past few weeks. It helped now to think of her as a feral kitten, hissing and spitting because she believed herself to be unwanted by her own father. Learning the source of the girl's anger was one more debt he owed to Miss James.

Guy's chest expanded in a deep breath. Gratitude alone couldn't explain the warmth inside him. It was Miss James herself who'd twisted him into knots with those big blue eyes, soft kissable lips, and irresistible feminine charm. He knew full well that such an infatuation was wrong. She would resign his employ should he be so unwise as to attempt a flirtation. He couldn't risk losing the one person who had a knack for handling Sophy. More important, he had too much respect for Miss James to dishonor her.

What made her so much more effective than the other half dozen governesses? It wasn't just youth and vitality, it was her heart and her fire. Despite having an appearance of delicate porcelain, she had a backbone of steel. She'd stood up to him and fought for Sophy. Her vibrant spirit reminded Guy of his grandmother, who'd never hesitated to get down on her hands and knees to play with him, or to defend him to his grandfather.

There was also that tantalizing whiff of mystery about Miss James. He sensed there was more to her than met the eye. Much, much more.

Chapter 7

That afternoon, guided by Lolly's directions, Tessa walked down a carpeted corridor lined by bedchambers. She stopped in front of a closed door, hesitated, and then knocked. There was no reason to falter. She needed advice and didn't know who else to ask.

Avis Knightley swung open the gilt-trimmed panel. A spinster's cap topped her chestnut curls and she appeared somewhat frazzled, though her green eyes widened with pleasure. "Tessa, what a pleasant surprise."

Tessa returned her smile. "Sophy is napping and I was hoping you might have a free moment."

Avis glanced over her shoulder. "Lady Victor just took a draught of laudanum," she whispered. "I'll need to sit with her until she falls asleep."

"Shall I return in a few minutes?"

Just then, a querulous voice came from inside the chamber. "Who's there?"

"Miss James, my lady."

"The governess? Well, bring her here at once."

With a worried look, Avis ushered Tessa inside, murmuring, "She's especially petulant today, I'm sorry to say."

Tessa gave a nod of understanding. They passed through an elegant sitting room and into a bedchamber with dainty furniture and rose-pink hangings. The closed draperies dimmed the room, while a blazing fire on the grate made the air stuffy.

Lying beneath the covers on the four-poster bed, Lady Victor pushed up on one elbow and blinked anxiously. "Why are you here? Is it my son? Has something happened to Edgar?"

Tessa hastened to the bed and bobbed a curtsy. "Nay, milady. I-I merely wished to inquire how you are faring."

"Oh . . ." Her face settling into long-suffering lines, Lady Victor sank back down on the pillow and plucked at the bedclothes. "How should I be faring with Eddie still gone at Newmarket? Mingling with gamblers and drunkards and other ne'er-do-wells."

"Now, I'm certain Mr. Edgar is just fine," Avis said. She sat down in a chair beside the bed and patted the woman's hand. "Pray recall you had a note from him yesterday saying he'll be returning soon."

"Only if he can elude the danger of highwaymen on the journey home." Shuddering, Lady Victor directed a heavy-lidded look at Tessa. "They killed my husband, you know, those highwaymen. He was the first victim of the Carlin Curse."

A chill tiptoed down Tessa's spine. Though not a superstitious person, she felt a deep-seated unease at the conviction in Lady Victor's voice. The woman truly believed there was a curse on the family. In her defense, there had been a number of deaths over the past few years. Maybe it was only natural that she should worry.

Lady Victor closed her eyes and stirred restlessly on the

bed. "The curse should have claimed Guy, too," she muttered. "He shouldn't have come home. Had he not returned, my dearest Eddie would have been duke . . ."

As the woman drifted into slumber, the dark fog of her words lingered. Guy must be Carlin's first name, Tessa realized. She'd always heard that aristocrats valued position above all else, yet it was hard to believe that Lady Victor regretted her nephew's return from his journey. Would she really rather he had died in order to benefit her son?

The notion repulsed Tessa. Her mind summoned an image of the duke's intense eyes, his strength and vigor, his magnetic presence. Despite the harsh masculine angles of his face, he had a smile that had the power to wreak havoc on her insides. His awkward attempts to befriend his daughter had tugged at her heart, as did his passion for plants. It had been a revelation to discover that despite his high rank, he had hopes and dreams like anyone else. Surely no one could wish death on such an intriguing man.

Perhaps she'd misunderstood the laudanum-induced ramblings of a woman who only wanted the best for her son. A woman who was so mired in the past that she'd forgotten how to be happy.

Avis arose from the chair and motioned to Tessa. Together they tiptoed out to the sitting room. "We can talk here," Avis murmured, seating herself on a rose-and-white-striped chaise and patting the cushion beside her. "Her ladyship shouldn't wake for a time. And pray don't heed her gloomy words. She does go on at times."

Feeling out of her league in such fancy surroundings, Tessa settled onto the edge of the chaise. "Perhaps a rest will lift her spirits."

"One can always hope. Mr. Edgar is her only child after a number of miscarriages, you see, which is why she frets so much about him. But enough of this melancholy. I've been on thorns to know, is there any truth to the rumor that Lady Sophy broke a window this morning?"

It must be all the talk belowstairs, Tessa realized. "Yes, she tossed a stone at the conservatory while we were in the garden. The duke came rushing outside, and the sight of his displeasure isn't something I'll soon forget."

Avis pressed a hand to her cheek. "The marvel is that he didn't dismiss you on the spot. What did you say to him?"

"I convinced him that she'd acted in a fit of pique and it wouldn't happen again." It wasn't Sophy's fault that she'd been duped into believing her father hated her. Only time and patience would heal the rift between them. Unwilling to reveal his private troubles with his daughter, Tessa glossed over the incident. "Once she made her apologies, he took her inside and showed us the parrots that he brought back from his travels."

Avis stared. "Why, His Grace never permits anyone in the conservatory except for Jiggs. You must be very persuasive."

"Rather, I believe the duke viewed it as a chance to spend time with his daughter after being gone for so many years." The visit had been moderately successful, too. Despite Sophy's wariness, the girl had been somewhat calmer during the noon meal and at naptime.

A pity Tessa couldn't say the same for her own peace of mind. The duke had startled her with the news that they'd be departing next month for his estate. Never had she imagined she'd be leaving London. If there was any hope of succeeding in her quest, she must act quickly.

She fingered the delicate gold chain that disappeared beneath her bodice. *Hide this . . . find him . . . father . . . pain . . .* Those had been the last words her mother had spoken after being struck down by that runaway carriage. She'd placed this pendant around Tessa's neck, and Tessa had never

taken it off since that moment. But she was no closer to learning the name of her noble sire than when she'd worked as a
hatmaker.

She turned the conversation to her purpose. "Now that I've
satisfied your curiosity, I wonder if I might ask *you* a question."

"Of course," Avis said, her eyes alive with friendly curiosity.

Tessa slowly drew the pendant from inside her high-necked
bodice and cradled it in her palm. She'd never showed the
piece to anyone for fear of being accused of stealing it. But
she was no longer an orphaned child or a shopgirl. Here, as
governess, she was presumed to be a lady of genteel blood.
No one would blink an eye if she owned a modest article of
jewelry.

She held out the gold pendant. "I inherited this from my
mama. There's a design engraved on it. Do you by chance
recognize it?"

Avis leaned forward. "Your mother didn't tell you anything about it?"

"No, she died when I was very young, and there was no
one else to ask."

"May I have a closer look?"

At Tessa's nod, Avis picked up the pendant and turned it
toward the sunlight coming through a crack in the draperies.
"Why, it appears to be a noble coat of arms."

Tessa was relieved to have that suspicion confirmed at
least. "Yes, though I haven't any notion which family it
might belong to."

"Hm. There are two crossed swords topped by a coronet.
And the winged beasts on either side appear to be griffins."

"Griffins?"

"Fierce creatures from mythology." Avis continued to

scrutinize the piece. "Oh, look. It's hard to see, but there's a Latin word inscribed on the crest . . . VIRTUS . . . yes, that's it."

"Do you know what it means?"

"Indeed, I do. My father was a vicar and since he had no sons, he made me learn Latin. *Virtus* means 'virtue' and likely refers to the family having valor, courage, honor."

Virtue, Tessa thought scornfully, was hardly the proper description for a man who had tossed her mother out on the street upon learning she had conceived his child. "Am I to understand, then, that you've never seen this coat of arms before?"

"No, I'm sorry," Avis said with a shake of her head. "My own family was merely gentry, so I'm no authority on matters of the nobility."

Tessa swallowed her disappointment. "Well, thank you, anyway. Perhaps in time, I'll spot it on a carriage door or affixed to a house."

"Wait, I just had a thought. Why not ask the duke? He must own a book on English heraldry. It surely would have illustrations."

"Oh? I didn't know such a book existed." Fearing her friend might find it odd for a governess to be so ignorant of such matters, Tessa added, "I've never before worked in a lord's house, you see."

"And if Lady Victor read something other than novels, *I* might be of greater assistance," Avis said wryly. "Yet there ought to be such a volume here. Perhaps His Grace will lend it to you."

As the conversation turned to other matters, Tessa vacillated between elation and anxiety. She itched to get her hands on that reference. At the same time, she hesitated to approach the Duke of Carlin. It was one thing to show her pendant to a fellow employee and quite another to do so to the master of the house. He was too clever a man not to ask uncomfortable questions that might unmask her true purpose.

No, there must be another way to acquire that heraldry book. She would just have to formulate a plan.

Later that afternoon, seated at a table by one of the windows in the schoolroom, Lady Sophy howled in anger when Tessa held the needle and thread out of reach. "I wanna do it!"

"You'll prick your finger if you grab like that. First, you need a lesson in how to sew on a bead."

"Don't like lessons."

Tessa curbed a smile at milady's folded arms, tucked chin, and pouty mouth. It wouldn't do to laugh when Sophy was in such a contrary mood. Yet she made such an adorable tyrant that Tessa ached to cuddle her close.

She knew better, though. Not only was Sophy in no humor for affection but Tessa wasn't certain if it were permissible conduct for a governess, anyway. Since the duke had promised to make an appearance here in the nursery, her behavior must be strictly proper.

"Come, dearie, you do need instruction in sewing this headband. Stand in front of me and I'll show you."

Sophy sulked for another moment before thankfully sliding off her chair. Tessa turned the girl and put her arms around her to demonstrate the technique. "Grasp the needle between your forefinger and thumb just so. I'll hold the bead while you stick the needle through it. Careful now."

Though she guided the girl's hand, Sophy was inclined to jab haphazardly, and Tessa was glad she'd had the foresight to wear a thimble. "Aim for the hole. That's better. Now poke the needle through the cloth and pull the thread tight."

Sophy concentrated on the task and her face brightened. "I did it, Miss James! I sewed all by myself."

Though the yellow bead was cockeyed compared with the neat row Tessa had done, she praised the effort nonetheless. "Very good! Would you like to do another?"

Even as Sophy nodded vigorously, a male voice intruded from the doorway. "Good afternoon, ladies. I apologize for being late."

Tessa's heart took a wild leap and she turned to see the duke advancing toward them. She only vaguely noted he was carrying a picture frame at his side. Lud, he looked taller than ever in a formfitting chestnut-brown coat and tawny breeches that accentuated the muscled length of his legs. While window-shopping in the fashion district, she'd glimpsed many an elegant gent out on the strut. But none of those fancy lords could hold a candle to the Duke of Carlin. He had an indefinable quality that rattled her calm and made her feel alive to the core.

Recalling her duty, she arose and dipped a curtsy. "Welcome, Your Grace. I was just now teaching Lady Sophy how to make the beaded band that will hold the feathers."

Carlin scanned the small wooden box of colorful beads and threads, leftover odds and ends that Tessa had collected over the years. Then he eyed the headband. "Very clever, Miss James. You've recalled the headdress perfectly from the picture in my study. Nevertheless, I brought this as a guide." He lifted the frame at his side to display the watercolor painting of the rainbow-hued parrot feathers affixed to a beaded circlet.

"Look, Sophy. Won't you like wearing such a pretty hat?" At the girl's nod, Tessa added, "Your papa saw it during his voyage around the world. He can advise us if we do anything wrong."

"I can certainly try," he said.

Carlin propped the painting on the fireplace mantel for their viewing. He glanced at the miniature chairs, then opted to sit on the nearby window seat, where he folded his arms and watched as Tessa guided his daughter in sewing on several more beads. His imposing presence seemed to fill the schoolroom. Yet there was also a little constraint in his manner, as if he was ill at ease.

Had she been wrong to invite him here? Had she overstepped her bounds? No, it wouldn't do to fret over that. He needed to spend time with Sophy so the girl would come to trust him.

"Perhaps your papa will tell us about the people who made the headdress," she said leadingly.

"They live in South America, which is quite a long way across the ocean from England." The duke went on to describe how he'd been seeking botanical samples in the rain forest just outside the port of Rio de Janeiro when he'd spotted a clan of locals, one of whom had been wearing such a headpiece. They'd kept a wary distance, and having no wish to invade their boundaries, Carlin had remained still while doing a quick sketch of the group before they'd melted back into the trees.

"I daresay they collected feathers from the ground just as you did," he finished. "In the jungle, parrots are as plentiful as pigeons are here."

Sophy's gravely cautious gaze lifted to him. Then she rummaged through the box for another bead. "Look, Miss James. A red one. I like red."

"We'll give it a special place right here in the center, how's that?"

Supervising as the girl attached the bead, Tessa glanced up to see the duke regarding his daughter with a faint frown that seemed to convey a frustrated need. Her insides curled softly. Carlin wanted to be a good father, she felt certain, yet he wasn't quite sure how to go about it.

"I brought you a gift, Sophy," he said. "A memento from my travels."

The word *gift* worked wonders. As he delved into an inner pocket of his coat, the girl abandoned all pretense of ignoring him. She stared wide-eyed as he produced a set of small wooden animals, beautifully carved from pale polished wood, which he arranged on the table.

"Jiggs whittled these aboard my ship after we'd made a stop in Africa. There's a lion, an elephant, a gazelle, and a giraffe."

Longing illuminated Sophy's face, though she made no move accept the offering. Her gaze flicked from the carvings to him and then to Tessa. "Are they truly mine, Miss James?"

A lump rose to Tessa's throat. How sad that the child feared there might be some trick to Carlin's present. She herself would have given much to have had a father who wanted to win her affections.

She smoothed Sophy's tangled hair. "Yes, dearie, and isn't it lovely that your papa remembered how much you like animals? Perhaps you've something to say to him."

"Thank you, Papa," the girl mumbled in a rush. Then she seized the pieces and scurried away to play with them on the hearth rug.

Carlin pensively watched his daughter. "I daresay I should have waited to give them to her. Now she won't help with the headdress."

"It's quite all right, this project is rather difficult for a four-year-old, anyway." While attaching another bead, Tessa murmured from the depths of her heart, "Oh, Your Grace, the animals were a wonderful notion. Now she'll know you were thinking of her during the years you were gone."

"You deserve all the thanks for your talk of souvenirs today. And let's hope those figurines will deter her from snipping any more animal pictures out of books."

The twinkle in his dark eyes flustered Tessa, as did the

sight of him sitting so close, the sunlight haloing his magnificently masculine form. "Never fear, I always keep the scissors in my pocket when they're not in use."

He leaned forward to watch as she deftly tied off a thread and used the shears to snip off the ends. "That ribbon of beads looks wide enough, but isn't it rather flimsy? How will it stay in place?"

"I'll attach it to this strip of buckram, which I've shaped to fit Sophy's head." She picked up the circlet of linen from a nearby chair and frowned. "I've coated it with paste to stiffen it, but alas, the cloth still feels too damp. The fabric must be completely dry before the beads and feathers are attached."

"You're very knowledgeable about fashioning headgear."

She cast her gaze downward on the pretext of hunting for a bead in the box. "Many women have a knack for sewing. I've found it more economical to make my own hats than to purchase them."

"Yet I can't think of a single lady of my acquaintance with the skills to make such a headdress. Have you any other hidden talents, Miss James?"

The teasing note in his voice brought her chin up. A half smile tilted one corner of his mouth, and his dark eyes held a gleam of playfulness. Lud, was he flirting with her? No, surely not. He was merely making conversation. Yet the hint of humor on his granite façade had a curious melting effect on her. It made her breathless, alive with fevered longings that must never be indulged with a man of his rank.

Blessedly, she was saved from replying as Winnie entered the schoolroom with the tea tray. Carlin's face settled back into its usual cool look, as if he, too, had remembered his position and regretted that moment of levity.

He rose to his feet. "I'll take that as my cue to depart."

Tessa watched as he said goodbye to Sophy, and then strode out of the schoolroom. Deep inside her, a quiver lingered that was part attraction and part unease. He was a man who could throw her off balance. A man with eyes sharp enough to penetrate her soul.

One thing was certain. Her search for the heraldry book would have to be done while he was out of the house. And the sooner the better.

As the schoolroom clock chimed midnight, Tessa headed down the servants' staircase. Her candle cast a circle of light on a series of plain wooden steps more suited to a boarding-house than a fine mansion. This utilitarian shaft was designed to keep the staff out of sight as much as possible.

She was grateful that it hid her illicit purpose, too.

Unlike her first night here when she'd intended to hunt for a proper piece of paper in order to forge that letter of rec-ommendation, Tessa had made sure this time not to fall asleep. She had spent the past few hours sketching hats, the one activity guaranteed to keep her mind alert. Her fingers ached from gripping the pencil for so long, but she was quite pleased with several of her new designs, including one of lemon-yellow fluted silk that was adorned with a tasteful cluster of parrot feathers.

Upon reaching the ground floor, she stepped into a wide marble corridor. The flickering light from a wall sconce il-luminated the portraits of ducal ancestors in old-fashioned costume. Tessa spared only a glance for those long-dead fore-bears; her sole concern was to avoid a living, breathing duke.

Discreet questioning of Lolly had yielded the news that His Grace had gone out this evening to a fancy ball. Gossip ran rampant below stairs that he would soon take a bride, and that it was a blessing he'd finally recovered from the terrible blow of his wife's death in childbirth. Tessa knew it was unwise to wonder about his private life. Nevertheless, her wayward mind produced an image of Carlin surrounded by a gaggle of beautiful ladies. At this very moment, he might be flirting with the lucky one he'd chosen to court and wed.

A wistful yearning assailed her, but she stifled it. How absurd to long for a fashionable silk gown made by a seamstress instead of cheap cotton sewn by her own hands—or to imagine herself as Cinderella being whirled around the dance floor by a handsome duke. Having not been raised a lady, she didn't know the proper steps and would only make a laughingstock of herself.

Real life was no fairy tale. She must focus her mind on identifying her noble father in order to procure a loan to open her shop.

Tessa glanced up and down the corridor. The servants were gone to bed except for a footman stationed out of sight by the front door to await the duke's return. Fortunately, her destination lay here at the back of the mansion.

Turning a corner, she tiptoed through a doorway and into the duke's study. This seemed the most logical place to look for a heraldry book. There must be hundreds of volumes on the floor-to-ceiling shelves.

As she glanced around, the feeble light of her candle barely pierced the vast darkness. The black lumps of furniture resembled crouching beasts. Prickles skittered down her spine as the eerie stillness frayed her nerves.

Tessa shook off her foolishness. There was nothing to fear. She would locate the book swiftly and sneak it back to her bedchamber before Carlin could discover her invasion of his private sanctum. With luck, she would return the tome in a few days before he even realized it was gone.

As she began a methodical search, the rows of leather-bound volumes behind the desk turned out to be not books at all but ledgers. The pages were filled with numbers and

notations that gave evidence to the extent of the ducal properties. A gold inscription on each spine listed the years
chronologically, going back well over a century.

A peculiar ache twisted in her as she returned one of the
volumes to its proper place. How lucky Carlin was to possess
such records of his heritage, along with the portraits of his
ancestors. Tessa had no knowledge whatsoever of her blood
connections. Even if she succeeded in finding her father,
he would never publicly recognize a long-lost bastard. He'd
likely grant her the loan just to get rid of her. She very much
doubted he'd know anything of her mother's people, either.
Mama had been a mere servant, after all.

She combed the rest of the study, finding books on a smat-
tering of topics from agriculture to economics. But there
was nothing on heraldry or the aristocracy or even English
history. In truth, it seemed a paltry collection for such a
wealthy duke. There wasn't a single novel to be had, nor even
a ragged volume of Shakespeare's plays. It was odd to think
that Carlin must have little interest in reading when he'd
struck her as a well-educated man.

Thwarted, she decided to abandon her quest for the night.
Perhaps sometime she could inquire at a bookshop.

On her way out of the study, Tessa spotted an object half
hidden in the shadows behind the door. She stopped and
stared. It was a large trunk, and its battered appearance
seemed out of place in this gilded room.

Stooping down, she ran her fingertips over the leather
bindings. The broad oblong top was scuffed and gouged by
long use. Engraved on the front were the gold initials GLW.
Guy L. Whitby? Her interest perked. Was this the trunk that
the duke had taken on his voyage around the world? Why had
it not been put up in the attic for storage?

Perhaps it contained odds and ends like those carved animals. Though he'd claimed not to have collected any sou-

venirs, Carlin might have some strange and unusual items, things that a duke wouldn't deem worthy of mention yet would be of great interest to someone who'd never ventured outside London.

Curiosity nudged at Tessa. She fairly itched to see the contents of the trunk. No one need ever know if she took one little peek.

She was reaching for the metal clasp when a faint noise from out in the corridor broke the silence. Footsteps.

Her heartbeat sprang into a mad tempo. There was an almost stealthy quality to the soft padding of those steps. They sounded nothing like the sharp, measured stride of a footman.

There was no time to run. She pinched out the candle between her forefinger and thumb, then slipped behind the door.

Just in time.

A man strode through the doorway and halted just inside. In one hand, he held a glass-enclosed lamp. Its pale light cast his face into sharp relief, revealing a rugged jaw, granite features, and longish black hair.

The Duke of Carlin.

Barely breathing, Tessa stood perfectly still. Alarm thrummed in her blood. Oh, no! Lolly had vowed that fashionable parties went on into the wee hours of the morning. Why had His Grace come home early?

His elegant garb gave credence to his attendance at the ball. She'd never seen him arrayed in quite so breathtaking a manner. Although he'd shed his cravat, he looked superb in a well-tailored black coat, a watered gray silk waistcoat, and black pantaloons. His stocking feet explained why his steps had sounded muted.

The duke loomed a scant yard from her. Lud, what was she to do now? Her mind was in a whirl.

His gaze scanned the shadows, and she had the horrid feeling that he sensed her presence. He mustn't spot her, Tessa thought feverishly. How would she explain her presence here in the middle of the night?

The moment stretched out in agonizing silence. She willed him to fetch whatever it was he'd come here for, and then go away so that she might dart upstairs to the safety of the nursery.

That hope shriveled as swiftly as it had arisen. He turned abruptly and stared straight at her.

His eyes widened slightly before narrowing again. Those dark orbs glittered like burning coals as he looked her up and down. "Miss James. What the devil are you doing in my study?"

Chapter 8

Pinned by his watchful gaze, Tessa forced herself to relax. It wouldn't do to stir his suspicions. "Forgive me, Your Grace," she said, dropping a curtsy. "You startled me."

"Not as much as you startled me."

"I-I couldn't sleep. I was looking for a book to read."

He glanced at her empty hands. "You don't appear to have met with any success."

"No, and it was presumptuous of me to have come here without your permission. If you'll excuse me, I'll bid you good night."

The duke remained standing in place, blocking her path to the doorway. He towered at least six inches over her, all the better to peer down at her. "Why did you snuff your candle just now?" he inquired. "You were hiding behind the door."

She lifted her chin. "When I heard muffled footsteps coming down the corridor, it didn't sound like a servant. I was afraid it might be a robber. One hears so many hair-raising tales of footpads and thieves roaming the city."

"There's no danger of burglars here. My butler checks

the locks each evening, and a night watchman patrols the grounds."

"Oh . . . well, that *is* reassuring."

"I'm glad. I wouldn't want you to feel unsafe in my home." A slight softening at one corner of his mouth indicated that he'd accepted her explanation, much to her relief. It also lent him an attractive allure that was sure to entice women—as proven by its warming effect on Tessa. "Were you looking for anything in particular, by the by?"

She blinked. "Pardon?"

"The book that you wanted. You can't have thought to find any ladies' novels in my study."

There was no need to mention the pendant and invite pointed questions, she reasoned. A version of the truth would do. "I was seeking something on heraldry, Your Grace. As I'm living in a noble household, it would be helpful to learn the coats of arms belonging to the various aristocratic families."

He raised an eyebrow, studied her for another unnerving moment, then gave a crisp nod. "You would do better to look in the library. I'll take you there if you'll wait a moment."

As he stepped past her, Tessa caught a whiff of spice that smelled rich and alluring. She felt a bit foolish for not realizing that Carlin had a private library somewhere in this enormous mansion. He was an educated man, after all, and wealthy enough to purchase all the books he wished. She herself had yearned to patronize one of the public lending libraries, though the one-guinea subscription fee had exceeded her means.

The duke hunkered down, opened the trunk, and rummaged inside. Her curiosity piqued, she tried to look past him, but his broad shoulders blocked any view of the trunk's contents. Closing the lid, he returned to her side with a thick notebook tucked beneath his arm.

"Come, I'll show you the way."

He courteously took hold of her elbow and guided her out of the study. The duke believed her to be gently bred, Tessa knew. He was treating her with the deference due a fine lady, unaware that she'd concealed her baseborn past.

As their footsteps echoed in the marble corridor, remorse over the deception weighed on her, and she longed to correct his misapprehension. Yet if she confessed the truth, that she'd lied to obtain the governess post, he would sack her at once. Not only would she lose the chance to identify her father, she'd be out of work. No millinery shop would hire her since Madame Blanchet had branded her a thief over that chip-straw bonnet.

What would happen then? How would she earn a living?

Those troubled reflections came to an abrupt halt as Carlin asked, "Did you and Sophy ever finish the headdress?"

"Yes, we did. She liked it so much I had a time convincing her to remove it at bedtime. I told her that the feathers would be sadly crushed by morning."

"A pity I couldn't have stayed, but I had a prior engagement for the evening. I don't suppose she wanted to show it to me?"

Tessa's heart squeezed at his hopeful look, and she felt loath to disappoint him. "I'm sure she'll be happy to model it for you, Your Grace. In fact, I've been thinking we should arrange for you to visit with her on a regular basis, so that she might learn to trust you."

"What would you suggest?"

Tessa thought for a moment. The custom in aristocratic households, she'd gathered, was for children to be brought down from the nursery several times a week for inspection by the parents. But in Carlin's case, the situation called for something less intimidating to his daughter than standing in front of him and being drilled on her activities.

"I don't believe a regimented meeting would be wise. If Lady Sophy is ever to overcome her wariness, you'll need to befriend her—perhaps by engaging in activities together like watching the parrots. You might take her to the park to feed the ducks or to toss a ball back and forth."

Carlin mulled that over for a moment before nodding. "Yes, that's sound advice. But you'll come with us."

The trace of anxiety beneath his command filled her with the desire to help him. It touched her to see such a formidable man, a man who had braved the perils of a round-the-world voyage, hesitate to be left alone with his four-year-old daughter. "Of course, Your Grace."

His eyes warmed as he studied her. "You've done well, Miss James. You've survived your one-week trial and have proven me wrong."

His praise made her glow and she smiled. "I won't deny that Lady Sophy is adept at testing one's patience, but she can be a delightful child, too. You'll soon see for yourself."

"For the first time, I can actually believe that."

He ushered her through a doorway and into a high-ceilinged chamber. Numerous rows of shelves along the walls housed more volumes than she'd imagined existed in the world. Yet for all its vast size, the room had a cozy ambience with a fire burning on the marble hearth and several candelabra to lend a soft gleam of light to the scene. Gold-cushioned chairs provided places where one could curl up and enjoy a good story. Even the air held the pleasant perfume of leather bindings and old paper.

Her hands clasped to her bosom, she spun toward Carlin. "Why, there must be hundreds upon hundreds of books here."

"Some four thousand, I believe. There's another twenty or so thousand at Greyfriars. The library runs the entire length of the house. You'll see it soon when we go there."

The prospect of visiting his ducal estate appealed strongly to Tessa. Yet what if she'd located her father by then? What if she'd left the duke's employ?

She buried an odd pang of regret. "I can't begin to imagine such a treasure trove. What you have right here is quite staggering enough. Have you read all these books?"

"Hardly. Several of my predecessors were bibliophiles. It took over a century for them to assemble this collection."

Her gaze swept the shelves again. Deep in her soul, she hungered to absorb all the knowledge in these works, for they were a stark reminder of her woeful lack of an education. "If it were me, I would devote my life to reading every one of them. Don't you want to do so?"

He chuckled, a rich, velvety sound that wrapped around her senses. "Have patience, I've only just inherited them. Although you'll be happy to know that when I spent my holidays here as a boy, I could often be found reading *Robinson Crusoe* or *Gulliver's Travels*."

When he regarded her like that, his strong features relaxed in a smile, it caused a lurch in her heartbeat. He seemed to relish her delight in the library, yet she sensed something quizzical, too, as if he found her reaction unusual. Perhaps a proper governess would have recognized those titles.

"Well, I confess to be overwhelmed by the sheer number of selections here, Your Grace. I only hope you can direct me to where I might find a book on heraldry."

"*Debrett's Peerage* may include coats of arms. There ought to be a copy around here somewhere." As they strolled over the fine carpet, he tossed the notebook onto a table. Then he took her candlestick and set it down as well. "By the way, there's no need to *Your Grace* me so much. It makes me feel like a doddering old man."

"How else am I to address you?"

"My friends and family call me Guy." He aimed one of

those darkly intense looks at her. "Though I suppose Carlin will do."

Her heart fluttered a warning. She might not be versed in all the rules of society but being on first-name terms with her employer implied intimacy. She could only imagine how aghast Lady Victor would be. Not to mention the other servants.

"Thank you, Carlin." That name at least didn't seem so peculiar since she'd already been thinking of him as such in her mind.

They reached the far end of the library, where the duke held up his lamp to dispel the shadows. His attention half on the books, he cast a droll glance her way. "Now you have the better of me, Miss James. You know my first name, but I don't know yours."

"Tessa. Tessa James."

"Tessa . . . a very pretty name. It suits you." His deep voice was like a caress drifting over her skin. "Is it short for Teresa?"

Swallowing, she shook her head. "Not to my knowledge." Unwilling to admit to an ignorance of what was written on her baptismal record, she said rather quickly, "What makes you think the book is right here?"

"The library is organized into sections. This is where the dictionaries and references are kept, and *Debrett's* is a sort of encyclopedia of the nobility. But I don't see it, so perhaps we should try British history."

Tessa followed him to the opposite corner of the library, where he scanned the books on several shelves. She peered past his broad shoulder, spotting titles like *A Biography of Illustrious British Statesmen* and *Smollett's History of England*. Even such weighty tomes called to her like a new world waiting to be explored. She glided a fingertip down one spine, relishing the smoothness of tooled leather.

She caught Carlin watching her with that slight quirk of

a smile. "If you see something of interest, feel free to borrow it. In fact, here's one." He walked a short distance away, hunted on a shelf, then returned to hand her a book.

She scanned the lettering imprinted on the calfskin cover and reverently touched the gold-edged pages. "*Robinson Crusoe*," she murmured. "This edition looks expensive. What if I were to drop it on the floor or rip a page?"

"Better that books be read and ruined than gather dust on a shelf." The duke gave the section one more inspection before turning toward her. "Alas, I don't see anything on heraldry, and I can't imagine where else to look. I'll ask Banfield tomorrow. Since he was my grandfather's secretary for many years, he knows this library down to the last pamphlet and treatise."

"That's very kind of you." Recalling the interview when she'd first met Banfield, she added in jest, "I certainly wouldn't wish to ask him myself after the embarrassment of having mistaken him for you."

Carlin laughed. "To be honest, I'd as soon he *was* the duke. Then I'd have more time to work on my book. In fact, I was just now going through my diaries and deciding what information to use."

Tessa stared at him, then glanced at the many notebooks that lay scattered on the table by the fire, including the one he'd fetched from the trunk in his study. The long white strip of his cravat had been tossed over the back of a nearby chair, and his shoes had been left near the hearth.

Was that why he'd come home early from the ball? To go over his journals? And why should her heart leap at the notion that there hadn't been a lady there beautiful enough to hold his attention?

The fleeting thought vanished beneath the rise of one equally startling. "You're truly writing a book, Carlin? One that will be published and put into libraries?"

He nodded. "It will be a scientific study of flora in the coastal areas of the world. Not comprehensive, of course, since I haven't been everywhere. Nevertheless, I've an overabundance of material that must be organized and condensed."

She studied the duke with new eyes, seeing him as more than just a privileged nobleman sailing around the globe on a whim. "Lud, I've never before met an author. I'm most impressed."

His teeth flashed in a grin. "Whether the book will make for dull or lively reading remains to be seen. Perhaps you'd care to judge my paltry illustrations for yourself."

The temptation of spending time with him was so potent that she found herself seated beside him on a chaise before her natural sense of caution could warn of any impropriety. The flicker of firelight, the radiance of candles, the stillness of the night all conspired to create an aura of warm intimacy. As she held *Robinson Crusoe* in her lap, Tessa felt a tingling in her veins. Perhaps it was his easy manner or the lack of a cravat that made the duke seem so approachable tonight. He was treating her not as an employee but as a friend, and she didn't know quite what to make of it.

Well, she would only stay for a little while. She dearly wanted to see his work, after all. What harm could there be in glancing at a few sketches?

As he reached for the notebook, she was intensely aware of his masculine presence, the long fingers with their blunt nails and the stark white of his linen cuff against his sunburnished skin. Everything about him called to her senses and hastened her heartbeat. With effort, she doused the dangerous fire of attraction and concentrated on the superb drawings of flowers and plants that he began to show her. There were pictures of birds and animals, as well. Under each one, he had penned a detailed description.

When he turned another page, her eyes widened on the

depiction of a peculiar, doglike creature with a bushy tail, clawed feet, and a pointed head that narrowed to a long tube. She swallowed a gurgle of mirth. "Oh, my. What in the world is that?"

"Whenever the ship put ashore, I sometimes caught sight of unusual animals as I was gathering my botanical samples. This one is an anteater. The snout is designed to poke into ant hills and termite mounds."

Tessa wrinkled her own nose. "Are they dangerous?"

"They're actually shy, solitary beasts who pose no threat to people. Unlike crocodiles that would as soon make you their next meal."

"Crocodiles?"

He leafed through several more pages to the sketch of a lengthy, lizard-like reptile with scaly skin and a set of wickedly sharp teeth. "They thrive in tropical areas all around the world. One must always take care on riverbanks, lest a crocodile snap you up in its jaws. They hide just beneath the surface of the water, and it's easy to mistake them for a floating log. In Australia, one lunged at me as I was crouching down to fill my canteen."

The duke had a gleam in his eyes as if he expected a squeal of terror from her. But it wasn't that faraway incident that caused a shudder in the pit of her stomach. It was the thought that if there really was a Carlin Curse, as Lady Victor believed, he would have died on that riverbank. "It's remarkable you returned alive, then."

"There were as many delights as there were dangers." Carlin related an amusing anecdote about a monkey that had snatched off his hat and then described seeing hundreds of tiny, newly hatched sea turtles scrambling across a sandy beach to the water. His experiences fascinated Tessa, who had never ventured outside the city, let alone crossed oceans to distant lands.

Several pages later, she leaned closer to stare at an amazing sketch. It was a trio of sleek fish leaping out of the sea in formation. Their wild grace captivated Tessa. "Why, I never knew there were fish so large—except for whales, of course."

"It's a school of dolphins. They would sometimes swim alongside the ship for hours, as if they were as fascinated by us as we were by them."

She cast an admiring glance at him. "You've a gift for capturing motion and light . . . the sun glinting on the water, the smooth glide of their bodies, the flow of the waves. And by framing the scene with the rigging of the ship, it makes me feel as if I were right there aboard with you watching the dolphins."

Her words appeared to please him. "You seem knowledgeable about art. Do you draw?"

"A little, although my skills are limited to more common objects." She turned her gaze down to the book. "Nothing so exciting as your voyage around the world. I'm anxious to hear more about it."

His fingers caught her chin and tilted her face back toward him. "Now, don't play coy, Tessa. Tell me what it is you like to sketch."

The interest in his eyes mesmerized her, as did the husky vibration of her name on his lips. She decided it would do no harm to make light of the matter. "If you must know, my attempts are mere doodling compared to your subject matter. You see, I enjoy drawing . . . bonnets."

He raised an eyebrow. "Bonnets. I might have guessed. On the day you first walked into my study you wore a particularly pretty one."

"Thank you," she said, surprised that he'd remembered. "I just had a thought, Carlin. Lady Sophy would enjoy seeing these drawings and hearing your stories. You know how much she adores animals."

"An excellent notion. Yes, I can certainly do that."

He gave Tessa an enigmatic look as if wondering at her reluctance to talk about herself. The firelight added a golden tint to his features, and she curled her fingers around the book in her lap to stop the mad impulse to brush back a lock of black hair that had tumbled onto his brow. The air between them seemed to sizzle as the power of his presence engaged all her senses. Did he feel the attraction, too? The dark depths of his eyes seemed to confirm that suspicion, especially when he glanced at her lips.

Lud, what was wrong with her? One look from him could melt her insides into a pool of longing. Never before had she felt so drawn to any man, especially one who was so wrong for her. It would be fatal to her position as governess to fall in love with the Duke of Carlin. Nothing could ever come of it but heartache.

And yet she found it dangerously easy to forget he was a duke.

She blurted out the first neutral topic that came to mind. "May I ask, how many countries did you visit while sailing around the world?"

"I lost count. Come, it would be simpler to show you."

He set aside his notebook and arose, helping Tessa to her feet. That brief touch of his fingers played havoc with her equilibrium, but she busied herself with bending down to leave the copy of *Robinson Crusoe* on the chaise. Carlin picked up a branch of candles and led her to a window, where gold draperies formed a backdrop for a large sphere that rested atop a carved oak stand.

A globe of the world! Tessa had heard of such an object but had never actually seen one. Unable to resist, she brushed her fingertips over the rounded surface. "I never realized how vast the oceans are."

"Indeed, one can spend months at sea without ever spotting land. Which is why much of my journey followed the continental coastlines." He traced the route with his forefinger. "After setting sail from England, we went south to the Straits of Gibraltar and into the Mediterranean, skirting the shores of Spain, Italy, and Greece before proceeding to the Ottoman Empire and Egypt and then on to Morocco. At many points along the way, we dropped anchor so that I could go ashore to study the local flora."

He launched into a description of the various landscapes and the many botanical specimens he'd collected. Tessa knew only enough about flowers to distinguish a rose from a daisy, and certainly nothing of the unfamiliar Latin names he used for them, and so she was content to let his words wash over her. She loved the sound of his deep voice, the fire of zeal that animated his features. His enthusiasm for botany was akin to her own passion for hats, and it made her feel curiously at one with him to know that they each had a consuming interest in their lives.

It struck her that in a way they were both outsiders to their respective classes. She had the ambition to be more than just a shopworker in a back room, while he had sailed around the world in disregard for what society expected of a fine gentleman. One thing was certain, Carlin wasn't at all what she'd initially anticipated. He was far more personable than the snobbish ladies who had frequented Madame's shop and more industrious than the idle aristocrats she'd observed on the streets.

Tonight, he looked very much the fashionable nobleman in his black coat and gray silk waistcoat. Yet with his longish hair, suntanned skin, and solid build, he didn't fit the mold of a duke. She could more easily picture him standing at the prow of a ship, a dagger gripped in his teeth, like the dashing pirate on the cover of that penny novel she'd once read.

Reminded of something, she touched Carlin's sleeve. He broke off his description of the habitat of the papaya tree and gave a rather sheepish smile. "Forgive me, Tessa. Your eyes must be glazing over from my monologue."

"Oh, no, I merely have a question. When we were in the conservatory, you mentioned meeting an old pirate who'd been shipwrecked on an island. Where did this happen?"

He twirled the globe and then pointed at an expanse of water off the northern coast of South America. "Here in the Caribbean Sea, on a sandy sprit of land containing little more than a patch of jungle. It was off the usual shipping routes, and we'd have never found it, but a hurricane had blown us off course."

"You said the pirate gave you a treasure map." She imagined a wooden chest overflowing with Spanish doubloons. "Did you ever find the buried gold?"

Amusement tipped up the corners of his mouth. "I see you're intrigued. Well, if you wish to learn the rest of the tale, you'll have to attend my lecture here on Thursday evening."

"Lecture?"

"Yes. On the day we met, you advised me to enlighten the swells about my voyage. Since it was your idea, it's only fitting that you should join us."

The opportunity to hear Carlin address a glittering throng appealed to her. But although gratified to know he'd heeded her suggestion, she hesitated to accept the invitation. "What, the governess, mingling with the cream of society in their jewels and silks? Only imagine what people would say."

A look of intense fervor came over his face. Reaching for her hand, he brought it to his mouth and brushed a stirring kiss over the back. "They'll find you beautiful, Tessa, as beautiful as I do."

His sudden declaration robbed the breath from her lungs. The warm feel of his fingers quickened her pulsebeat and triggered a pleasurable throb in the depths of her body. Did he truly find her beautiful? Oh, how she wanted to believe it. Yet surely nothing could be more perilous.

She lowered her eyes, but that was a mistake, for her gaze landed on the strong column of his throat. The absence of a cravat gave a tantalizing glimpse of his chest revealed by the open collar of his shirt. How she longed to touch him, to caress his bare skin. Beset by wayward desire, she looked up again to find him watching her, the ghost of a smile on his face.

Nothing could have been better designed to melt her than that tender look. She leaned infinitesimally closer, and his arms came around her, clasping her to his firm chest. His gaze scorched hers as a visceral heat flashed between them. He brought his head down, his mouth hovering just above hers, his breath warm and inviting. Succumbing to temptation, Tessa arose on tiptoe to meet him halfway.

At the first touch of their lips, fire seared her veins. On some hazy level, she knew she oughtn't allow him such liberties. Yet need outweighed wisdom, and she looped her arms around his neck. How tall and muscled he was, how dizzy and excited he made her feel. It was an enthralling experience to be held by Carlin and kissed with such ardor. The world faded away until there existed only the two of them, taking pleasure in each other.

It seemed utterly natural when his tongue slipped inside her mouth to play with hers. Desire flourished, spreading its honeyed heat throughout her insides. She moaned in her throat. Never had she known that a kiss could be so intimate—or that her body could respond with such passionate eagerness.

One of his hands was flattened to the back of her waist,

holding her close against him, while the other played with the sensitive skin at her nape. All the while she returned his kiss with vibrant delight. Just then, she felt his fingers surrounding her breast. When his thumb stroked across the tip, the thrill generated by his touch made her shiver with the intense desire for something more, a longing to feel his caress beneath her gown, moving over her bare skin. She craved a surrender so forbidden that it snapped her back to her senses.

Shaken to the core, Tessa arched back and thrust at his chest. Even then it took a moment before he lifted his head to regard her in a daze. His passion-glazed eyes cleared, and at once he loosened his hold on her.

She retreated a few steps, her arms wrapped around her midsection. Her mind was in such a tumult that she felt on the verge of a swoon. Shock at her own foolishness made her voice tremble. "Lud! I won't . . . you mustn't . . ."

Carlin reached out as if to touch her again, then raked his fingers through his hair instead. "Tessa." His gaze focused on her, he took a deep breath. "I ought not to have done that. Pray forgive me."

She believed him to be sincere. Neither of them had planned that kiss. Yet it had happened nonetheless and the power of her craving for him made it all the more disturbing.

"I wanted it, too, Your Grace, so you needn't apologize." She used the formal address purposefully to remind herself of his high rank. "But it must never happen again."

He nodded curtly. "Never."

They stared at each other, and her heart thrummed at the fire still smoldering in his eyes. She felt that same fire, too, much to her chagrin. In defiance of good sense, she ached to be in his arms again and to let him do with her as he willed.

She swallowed. "It's best that I return to the nursery."

Carlin made no reply as she pivoted on her heel and fled

the library. Her last view of him from the doorway was of his brooding figure standing in the shadows. His aura of solitude struck a pang in her heart. He had lost his wife and numerous close relatives, cut himself off from society for years, and returned home only to find that his young daughter despised him.

But none of that should matter. It was perilous to view the duke as an ordinary man in need of love. He was her employer, not her suitor.

In near-darkness, Tessa hastened up the servants' staircase. She had forgotten her candle and *Robinson Crusoe*, much to her dismay. Reading would have provided a distraction from her churning emotions.

She undressed by moonlight and climbed into bed, though the folly of their embrace kept her tossing and turning. Her own mother's experience should be a lesson that while a nobleman might woo a servant, he never had marriage on his mind. It would be madness to imagine Carlin's intentions were honorable, or to think she could ever fit into his highbrow world. She had a more sensible dream for her future, a shop to open, a pinnacle to achieve as London's top milliner.

It was best to relegate that kiss to the dustbin of memory.

Chapter 9

On the night of the lecture, Guy stood in the arched doorway of the Blue Drawing Room and greeted his guests as
they entered. The long, cavernous chamber was done in
royal blue with enough gold trim to blind the eye, a ceiling
decorated with cherubs and nymphs, and Rembrandt paintings over both marble fireplaces. Much of the furniture had
been removed to allow space for some two hundred gilded
chairs.

This was a room he remembered from childhood visits
when he'd been called down from the nursery to bid good
night to his grandparents. The duchess had been warm and
loving, but he'd always disliked facing the duke's cutting
criticisms, for try as he might, Guy had never succeeded in
winning the approval of his stern grandfather. Even now, he
felt like an interloper, as if he didn't quite belong at Carlin
House. A ludicrous notion, and one he meant to dispel by putting his own stamp on the place.

Tonight was one way to do so.

Although Aunt Delia had urged him to use the larger
ballroom in order to invite the cream of the ton, Guy had

overruled her. He'd limited the guest list to old friends and their wives, political bigwigs, and scholarly gentlemen. As much as he'd like to enlighten all of society, he was loath to turn the serious address into a frivolous event. The last thing he wanted was a swarm of ambitious mamas pushing their daughters into his path.

That sort of matchmaking nonsense was precisely why he'd returned home early from the Farnsworths' ball three nights ago. The same night that he'd come upon Tessa in his study.

Guy covertly looked for her now as he proceeded to the front of the assemblage. The air hummed with conversations. His cousin and heir, Edgar, was seated at the edge of the throng, drumming his fingers on his knee and likely wishing himself out on the town with his friends. Aunt Delia, draped in funereal black, sat in the last row with her companion, Miss Knightley.

Guy didn't spot Tessa anywhere. Disappointment gnawed at him, for she was a refreshing change from the toadying ladies of the ton. He could have sworn that her keen interest in his voyage would have tempted her downstairs tonight. Her absence, he presumed, must be due to that fiery kiss. No sooner had she leaned toward him with desire in her eyes than his resolve to keep his distance had shattered. At one taste of her soft lips, he'd been consumed by passion, and Guy couldn't honestly say that he was sorry.

He'd seen her only once since then, when she'd brought Sophy downstairs the previous day to look at his animal sketches. Tessa had been cool and deferential as if that ardent embrace had never happened.

He released a long breath. Dammit, he yearned for his warm, alluring companion of that night. He wanted the chance to coax her into telling him all her secrets. For one, he suspected she'd never before seen a private library. For another, there was her occasional lapse into the common vernacular. She was especially adept at changing the subject whenever it centered on herself.

But her past would have to remain a mystery. Miss Tessa James was off limits. Any further dalliance would only invite trouble. He had no desire to marry ever again—let alone engage in an affair with his daughter's governess.

Guy took up a stance in between the two fireplaces. His audience instantly quieted with only a few coughs and murmurs to disturb the silence. "Good evening, gentlemen and ladies. Four years ago I embarked upon a scientific voyage that would take me around the globe in search of strange and unusual plants. Along the way I expanded not merely my knowledge of flora, but also my appreciation for the diversity of the world."

Recognizing that botany alone wouldn't engage their interest, he started by relating a number of vivid anecdotes: outrunning a privateer off the coast of Tripoli, riding out a typhoon in the South China Sea with waves taller than St. Paul's Cathedral, and nearly being trapped in the ice when venturing too close to the South Pole.

Watching their attentive faces was more enjoyable than he'd anticipated. Tessa had been right about widening the horizons of the ton. And they did seem to be hanging on his every word, even when he began to describe the botanical specimens he'd collected during his forays ashore. Guy strolled back and forth, pointing to his framed paintings that had been propped on easels for easy viewing, and focusing on those plants that would draw the attention of an amateur, such as the carnivorous pitcher plant of Southeast Asia that consumed insects caught in the sticky secretions of its flowers.

"One of the most spectacular flowers in the world can be found on the island of Sumatra in the Indian Ocean. The

Amorphophallus titanum has a gigantic burgundy-red bloom with a central green spike that measures several feet taller than I am. The locals refer to it as the corpse plant due to its odor of decomposing flesh—"

"My dear Carlin!" Lady Victor cried out, clutching a black-trimmed handkerchief to her bosom. "Must you include such horrid details?"

Guy made a conciliatory bow. "Pray accept my apology, Aunt. Perhaps you'll find the *Lithops viridis* of southern Africa more to your liking. Because its thick leaves resemble stones, it's commonly called the rock-plant and has a yellow bloom similar to a daisy."

As he directed the audience's attention to another framed watercolor, a movement in the arched doorway caught his eye.

Tessa.

His heart actually skipped a beat. He dismissed the reaction as a temporary madness that would soon pass, as infatuations were wont to do. After all, there was nothing in her appearance that was designed to attract male attention. She wore her usual plain gown, this one of charcoal gray with a high neckline and long sleeves. A lace cap covered much of her upswept buttercream hair. Beneath that spinsterish attire, however, she had womanly curves that were etched into his memory.

His gaze tracked her as she found a seat in the back row near his aunt. He willed her to look at him, but she angled her face toward Miss Knightley. The women whispered to each other and shared a smile. Only then did Tessa turn her attention to the front of the room.

As her gaze locked with Guy's, a bolt of awareness shot through him. The blue of her eyes dazzled him even from a distance. He felt as spellbound as a buck staring at a brilliant flame . . .

"All this talk of plants has been informative, Your Grace,

but do tell us what else you brought back from your travels."
The pompous voice belonged to Lord Churchford, a middle-
aged baron with a well-fed frame and a beaklike nose. An
old crony of Guy's grandfather, he was seated in the second
row. "Surely you have a trove of gold and jewels."

Guy cudgeled his mind back to the lecture. "Actually not.
Pray recall, my purpose was to enrich our scientific understanding of the coastal regions of the world. Although I visited marketplaces in various ports, I never ventured inland
to engage in trade."

"You've no artifacts at all, then?" asked the Honorable
John Symonton. The bespectacled young man was employed
at Bullock's Museum, and he was the only one present with
a notebook into which he had been scribbling from time to
time. "I'm developing an exhibit about South America, you
see, and wondered if you might loan us some items for display."

"I'm sorry to disappoint you." Seeing Tessa lean forward
slightly, listening to the exchange, Guy deemed it time for the
story that he'd promised her. "But perhaps I can make up for
it by telling all of you about an old pirate I met who'd been
shipwrecked in the Caribbean Sea."

Murmurs of interest swept through the audience. Tessa's
face glowed with curiosity, and he was hard-pressed not to
gape at her like a moonling. "The tale began when my ship
was blown off course during a tempest. The storm damaged
the mast, and we were forced to put ashore on an island so
insignificant it didn't even appear on the captain's charts."

Guy had rowed ashore as the crew performed the necessary repairs. While exploring a small patch of jungle, he'd
spied human footprints in the mud beside a freshwater pool.
"My first thought was that natives inhabited the island. I was
about to retreat when a clump of ferns parted and a wrinkled,
bearded face peered out at me. A decidedly English face."

The audience listened raptly as he described how the scruffy man had vanished into the shrubbery and was nowhere to be found. Over the next few days, Guy had left offerings of eggs from the hens aboard the ship, a loaf of bread, a rough linen shirt and breeches. Each morning the gifts would be gone until finally, he'd coaxed the skittish fellow out of hiding.

"It turned out, Nate had been a cabin boy when a great hurricane sank the pirate ship and drowned the rest of the crew. Ever since, he'd been living off figs, plantains, and various roots, along with fish and birds. His age must have been about seventy since he recalled seeing King George the Third's coronation parade when he was a lad. I offered Nate passage on my ship, but having lived so long on the island, he balked at leaving. When I gave him provisions from our stores, he declared his intent to repay me. So he took a page from my sketchbook and scribbled a map that showed where the pirate captain had buried several treasure chests on another island."

A clamor of excited voices broke out. His cousin spoke the loudest. "Thunder and turf," Edgar exclaimed, "d'you mean you've a real treasure map? Why, you might've told your family."

Lord Churchford slapped his knee. "You're a sly one, Carlin. So you did find gold, after all."

"No," Guy corrected, "we sailed from there to Guiana, where I picked up a packet of letters at the consul in Georgetown and learned of my grandfather's death. Naturally, I returned to England at once."

Further questions bombarded him, but Guy held up his hand to quiet the audience. "I shall be writing a book about my travels, so everyone will have the opportunity to read all the details. That concludes my presentation. Please feel free to come and take a closer look at my paintings."

As the guests arose amid an excited chattering and the scrape of chairs, several footmen circulated with trays of champagne. His aunt had arranged for a lavish buffet in the adjoining room, and a number of people wandered in that direction. John Symonton, however, came forward to buttonhole Guy.

"Perhaps you'll allow me a peek at that map, Your Grace," he said, peering owlishly through his round spectacles. "The museum may fund an expedition since the cache could include artifacts of scientific value."

Lord Churchford appeared behind him. "Bah, 'tis likely Spanish doubloons. Gold belongs in a bank, not put on display. I'd pay you well for that map, Carlin."

Guy was half sorry he'd ever mentioned it, though he'd done so to please Tessa. "I'd be a poor friend if I betrayed Nate's trust in me. Who knows if he correctly remembered the location, anyway, after more than fifty years? I'm inclined to think it would be a wild goose chase."

"What, you'd leave those treasure chests buried?" Churchford said in astonishment. "That's as outrageous as placing gold in a museum."

"Well," Mr. Symonton huffed. "At least I am not driven by greed. My sole interest is in the historical nature of the contents."

"The answer is still no. If you'll excuse me, gentlemen."

Leaving them squabbling, Guy made good his escape, thankful to forget about that map. As he wended his way through the crowd, people stopped to butter him up with flattery about the lecture. He accepted their accolades while covertly scanning the throng for Tessa. It wouldn't be wise to pay her special notice, yet surely exchanging a few words with her would not be amiss.

Banfield stood by the arched doorway and directed a guest to the refreshments room. With his trim gray suit and nondescript features, the touch of silver at his temples, he might have been any one of a thousand middle-aged English gentlemen forced by circumstance to work for their bread.

The secretary bowed. "My compliments, Your Grace."

"Thank you. Have you by chance seen Miss James?"

A slight narrowing of the eyes was the only indication that Banfield still disapproved of the governess. "I believe she went down the passage toward the rear of the house."

Guy strode in that direction. Really, the man was as much a stickler as the old duke. His grandfather had hired the secretary more than a decade ago, and it occurred to Guy that he knew as little about Banfield's background as he did Tessa's. But aside from a tendency to be judgmental, Banfield had been a godsend in helping Guy navigate the myriad duties of the dukedom, training that he'd never received in his youth. No one—least of all himself—had ever expected he'd one day succeed to the title.

He was striding past an alcove when a man hailed him. Recognizing those lean features and the rakishly tousled blond hair, he broke into a smile. William Nye, now the Earl of Haviland, had been a close friend during their school years at Eton. Although they'd parted ways at Oxford, with Guy pursuing his studies and Will pursuing his vices, they'd kept in occasional contact over the years.

"By God, it's good to see you, Will," he said as they shook hands with a tight grip. "When I sent the invitation, I never really expected you to attend."

"How could I miss the chance to congratulate the new Duke of Carlin? Well done, old boy, you've come up in the world."

"As have you, inheriting the earldom. My condolences on your father's passing last year."

Haviland grimaced. "It's required me to spend quite a lot

of time at Ainsley Hall, tending to estate matters. You'd have chortled to see me with my nose glued to the account books. You know how I scorn work."

Guy wondered if he was still drowning in River Tick due to his incessant gambling. Although rumors swirled about Will's vast debts, Guy had never broached the topic. As adults, they'd always kept certain aspects of their lives private.

"With privilege comes duty," Guy said wryly. "Though frankly, I could do without all the headaches of the rank."

"I know what you mean. My father left the estate in shambles." Haviland glanced around as if to ensure no eavesdroppers lurked nearby. "Nor was he as virtuous as the world believed. You see, on his deathbed, he admitted to siring a daughter with my younger sister's governess."

The old earl had been as much a despot as Guy's grandfather. It was one of the things that had forged Guy's unlikely friendship with Will. "That must have come as a shock."

"Yes, well, it happened over twenty years ago while we were away at school. The callous old devil cast the poor woman out." Haviland's mouth twisted. "It was only when he was about to meet his Maker that he suffered an attack of conscience and made me swear to find her."

"Did you have any success?"

"My father gave me an address, but the woman died years ago, and her daughter—my half sister—disappeared, never to be seen again. I managed to track down a few leads, but they ultimately led nowhere." He shrugged as if it mattered little; then his mouth tilted in the engaging grin that had made him a favorite with the ladies. "Of course, my adventures have been tame compared with yours. Damme, wouldn't we have loved to have had a treasure map back when we used to play pirates?"

Guy chuckled. "We'd have sneaked down to the docks and

tried to board a ship to the Caribbean, only to be dispatched home in disgrace."

Just then, two women emerged from the throng and strolled in his direction. It was Tessa, deep in conversation with Miss Knightley.

Tessa's eyes widened on him. Guests milled in the corridor, talking and laughing, but Guy noticed only her. He could swear that a current of energy leaped between them. She must have felt it, too, because her aloof expression softened in the instant before she curtsied.

"Good evening, Your Grace."

He bowed in return, disliking the custom that required her to show obeisance to him. Afraid she might continue on by, he drew her closer. "Lord Haviland, if I may introduce these ladies—"

"Miss Knightley," Will broke in.

Guy paused, intrigued to note that Will's face lacked its usual charming smile. A glance from him to Miss Knightley revealed that Will was staring at her as if transfixed and she was scowling back. A flush of color in her cheeks lent a prettiness to her mature features.

Her movements stiff, she curtsied. "If you'll excuse me, Your Grace, I must return to Lady Victor. She will be wondering where I am."

Her head held high, Miss Knightley sailed away and vanished into the crowd. "Later, old chap," Will muttered in Guy's direction before he strolled off in pursuit.

Guy stared after them, then glanced at Tessa. "That was . . . abrupt. I had no idea they even knew each other."

One eyebrow arched, she appeared just as puzzled. "I've never heard Avis mention Lord Haviland. But I've only made her acquaintance recently."

"Hm, you might warn her that he's a gambler and a rake. If in fact she doesn't already know that."

"I'll be sure to mention it." Her expression polite, Tessa stood with her fingers clutched at the sides of her skirt. "The lecture appears to have been a great success, Your Grace. I enjoyed it very much."

"You missed three-quarters of it."

"Lady Sophy dawdled at bedtime. I thought it best not to leave until she was fast asleep. You wouldn't have appreciated her sneaking downstairs to make a surprise appearance."

"Point taken."

Now that he had Tessa in his company, Guy felt as awkward as a callow boy trying to impress his first girl. They stood in an alcove slightly apart from the other guests, and he longed for them to be somewhere private. Someplace where they could talk and trade wits as they'd done in the library. Perhaps then she would cease looking so cool and unapproachable.

"Tessa, I—"

"I've been wanting to—"

They both stopped in chagrin. "Ladies first," he said.

She smiled slightly. "I've been meaning to thank you for asking Mr. Banfield about the book. *A Display of Heraldry* by John Guillim, you said in your note."

"I'm only sorry there isn't a copy here. But Banfield assures me it's in the library at Greyfriars, and he's already written to my butler there. You should receive the book within the week."

"Thank you as well for sending *Robinson Crusoe* up to the nursery. I'm halfway through, and it's been a pleasure to read." Her voice warmed. "Fancy, Robinson Crusoe was captured by pirates! And now you've met a real pirate."

The sparkle that lit those blue eyes had an invigorating effect on him. For a moment, Tessa radiated a vitality that enhanced her lovely features. Her skin glowed like alabaster, and her lips wore a sweet smile that encouraged Guy to take a step closer. "I'll be happy to tell you more," he murmured. "We can sit down together sometime and discuss it."

Her expression changed subtly, the openness shuttering to the blank mask of a servant. "I'm quite busy these days, Your Grace. Lady Sophy is learning her letters and numbers, so of course that must be my primary focus."

Frustrated, he reached for her hand, taking care that none of the guests noticed. She seemed to need the connection as much as he did, for she didn't pull away. Dainty yet capable, her fingers rested in his, and he had a vivid memory of them curling around his neck. "Tessa," he said in a low, rough tone. "Don't turn stiff on me, please. You have my promise that nothing improper will happen between us. Surely we can be friends."

She slowly shook her head. "No. You ask the impossible."

"Nonsense. If you're worried about someone seeing us together, then we'll rendezvous in the library late at night when everyone is asleep."

"Secret meetings would be wrong. You are a duke, and I am a governess. And it is no use pretending otherwise."

Her throat taut, Tessa gazed up at his ruggedly chiseled features and felt such a wrench of yearning that it stole her breath away. For once, she wished to be a fine lady who could be courted by a man of his rank. The warmth of his fingers around hers only heightened her longing for him. She'd never before felt like this about any man, and she feared that if they were alone together, temptation would prove impossible to resist.

His stare burned deep into her soul. Yet she could tell that Carlin didn't truly fathom her dilemma. A man in his exalted position couldn't comprehend the problems faced by a woman of the lower orders. Even if their attraction were innocent, she dared not sit with him as if they were equals.

It would only lead to trouble. For her, not him.

Drawing her hand free, Tessa turned away to walk swiftly down the corridor to the rear of the house. Her steps checked momentarily when she saw Mr. Banfield watching from a nearby doorway. His stern look stirred the disquieting suspicion that he'd seen the duke holding her hand. Lifting her chin, she gave him a cool nod in passing.

Let him think what he wished. His censure was no worse than that of the noble guests. Earlier, some of them had gazed askance at her drab gown. A few of the gentlemen had leered at her as if a governess were fair game for their predatory impulses. With Avis Knightley as company, it had been easier to ignore the swells, to laugh it off and hold her head high.

The stark truth, however, was that she belonged in the nursery, not here among the Quality.

The nobs could stuff it, Tessa decided as she climbed the servants' staircase. They took pride in the money and titles that had been granted to them by birth, while she preferred to take pride in what she earned through her own hard work. Someday, she would have her revenge by charging them exorbitant prices for her bonnets.

On that cheering thought, she entered the nursery. Lolly sat by the fire, mending one of Sophy's pinafores. Seeing Tessa, the woman set aside her sewing and eased her stout frame out of the rocking chair.

"Lady Sophy is still fast asleep?" Tessa asked.

"Snug as a bug in a rug," Lolly said, coming closer to hand over a note. "Winnie brung this up a while ago, miss. A young feller came to the kitchen door to deliver it to ye. I sat up to make sure ye got it."

Mystified, Tessa took the paper. It was folded over several times and sealed with a blob of yellowish candle wax. "Thank you, Lolly. That's very kind of you. Well, good night, then."

The nursemaid peered expectantly as if hoping to discover the contents of the note, but Tessa desired privacy, for it could only have come from someone in her old life. She took a candle and made haste to her bedchamber. There, she carefully peeled off the hardened wax, unfolded the single sheet, and read the few scribbled lines. A frown instantly furrowed her brow.

Clutching the paper, she walked to the window and stared out into the darkness. Pinpricks of light gleamed in the neighboring town houses, and far below, the shadowy shapes of carriages waited around the square for the guests to depart Carlin House.

Tessa scarcely noticed the nighttime scene. Caught in a dilemma, she pondered the message from Orrin. His request would require her to break the rule forbidding servants to have visitors on the ducal property.

Lud, what was she to do?

Chapter 10

In the chill of the predawn darkness, Tessa picked her way through the shadowy garden. An autumnal mist draped the bushes and made it difficult for her to see the path. Shivering, she huddled into her old woolen shawl.

Despite the early hour, the servants were busy baking bread in the kitchen and laying fires to be lit when the family woke in a few hours. But out here, the world was dark and hushed. There was only the sleepy twitter of a bird high in the trees and the scrape of her shoes on the gravel.

Ahead of her loomed the ghostly rectangle of a door in the garden wall. She glanced back to make certain no one was watching from a window. She'd have some explaining to do if anyone—especially Carlin—saw her stealing into the mews like a thief in the night. Thankfully, the house was dark, including the conservatory, where the parrots would be tucked in their nests.

As she reached the gate, the black shape of a man materialized out of the shadows. Tessa yelped in surprise. An instant later, she blew out a sigh of relief. Although the gloom obscured his freckled features and rusty-red hair, she knew that compact figure.

"Orrin Nesbitt, you frightened me half to death." She lowered her tone to a whisper. "You said you'd be waiting in the mews."

He respectfully snatched off his flat cap. "A groom came out o' the stables. So I hopped the fence t' stay out o' sight here."

Yet they were *in* sight of the house, and that made her uneasy. "There's a night watchman on the grounds, so we'd best be quick. Why did you wish to see me? Is it about my mother? Have you learned where she used to work?"

His note had merely asked Tessa to meet him at half past six. He'd offered no explanation. She'd almost declined to come until remembering that Orrin had offered to do some sleuthing on her behalf.

"I've been on your mam's trail this past week," Orrin confided. "I quizzed the kitchen staff at some two dozen fancy houses. Pretended t' be the long-lost son of Florence James. But nobody recalled her from twenty-two years ago. At least so far, anyhow."

His attempt touched Tessa's heart. "Thank you. I do hope you realize, though, I never truly expected you to look for her."

He waved away her gentle admonition. "I'd've found her already if it weren't for me typesetter job at the paper. There's hundreds more houses in Mayfair, but never fear, I mean t' go t' all of 'em even if it takes me a year."

Tessa couldn't let Orrin waste his time trying to find a needle in a haystack. Not when she already had another plan in motion.

"You mustn't put yourself to so much trouble." Clutching the fringed edge of her shawl, she paused, then plunged on, "You see, I've discovered another way to find out where

Mama was employed. I've a gold pendant that belonged to her. For a long time, I didn't realize the design engraved on it was anything important but now I think it's a coat of arms for a noble family."

The darkness was beginning to lighten a bit, enough for her to detect his frown. "You never told me so," he said, sounding injured. "Where is it? Lemme have a look."

She obligingly drew out the pendant from beneath her gown and allowed him to examine it. He squinted down at the engraving and turned it this way and that in his ink-stained fingers. "'Tis too dark t' see much," he grumbled. "Do you mean t' say 'tis from your pa's family?"

"Yes, it must be. Where else would a maid get such a fine piece? He must have given it to her."

"As payment for warmin' his bed, no doubt." Orrin shook his head in disgust. "Hand it over, I'll find the bleedin' toff."

He made a grab to remove the filigreed chain from around her neck, but Tessa stepped back and tucked the pendant back into her bodice. "Thank you, but I'll soon be able to identify the coat of arms myself. I asked Carlin if he has a book on heraldry and he's sent for one from his library at Greyfriars—that's his estate."

"Carlin, is it? Blimey, you sound on cozy terms with His High-and-Mighty Dukeship."

Hostility vibrated in Orrin's voice and she realized to her surprise that he was jealous. With all that had happened, she had forgotten about his hopes for their future together. He mustn't guess about that passionate kiss or her reckless attraction to Carlin.

"Don't be silly," she said breezily. "The duke is a kind, considerate man, that's all. You mustn't think ill of him simply because of his title."

Instead of reassuring Orrin, her speech only seemed to make matters worse. He stood there scowling, his fingers gripped into fists, his manner radiating harsh emotion into the cool morning air. "Tell me the truth, Tessa. The blighter's been tryin' t' charm you into his bed, hasn't he?"

"No! Certainly not."

"Well, if he hasn't, he'll try. It's what them nobs do. Look at your mam, used an' then tossed away like rubbish. We Brits need a revolution like in France t' overthrow the aristos, who think they're better'n the rest o' us."

Picturing Carlin with his neck in a guillotine sent a cold shudder through Tessa. "Hush, that's dangerous talk. You've never even met His Grace. I can assure you he's a person with hopes and dreams, no different from you or me. In fact, he wouldn't even be a duke if not for the Carlin Curse."

"The—what?"

She blinked at him through the misty shadows. "It's nothing, really. Several ducal heirs died within the space of a few years. That is how the present duke came into the title."

"The Carlin Curse, eh? What are their names?"

"Whose names?"

"These heirs what died. 'Tis just the sort of juicy scoop that folks like t' read about in the papers."

Belatedly, Tessa realized that she'd piqued his journalistic interest. He'd asked her once before to keep her ears open for salacious gossip that she could feed to him. Now she'd handed him a story on a silver platter. Lud, she could only imagine what Carlin would have to say about such a scandalous news article. He'd sounded very strict while ordering his aunt never to speak of the Carlin Curse lest anyone repeat it.

She folded her arms beneath the shawl. "Never you mind that. I'll have your promise that you won't write any such article."

"How'll I ever be promoted t' staff reporter without comin' up with good stories? 'Tis the only way I'll earn enough t' marry an' have a family. I thought you wanted that, too."

"Just promise me," she repeated sternly. "I won't have my employer's family name dragged through the dirt."

His puppy-dog expression lapsed back into that jealous pout. "You've changed, Tess. You didn't use t' like the nobs. That's wot comes from livin' in such a posh house."

She bit her lip. Had she changed? Certainly, her horizons had grown with many new experiences, becoming a governess, inventing ways to coax Lady Sophy into good behavior, learning about other lands. And by kissing Carlin. That had opened up a whole new world in and of itself. A world of desire and decadence the likes of which she'd never known.

All of a sudden, Orrin sprang forward to pull her against him. She snapped out of her reverie to realize that his face loomed mere inches from hers. "I want you t' come home with me," he declared. "You should be my wife, not a slave for some toplofty duke. He'll never love you the way I do."

Orrin lowered his head and mashed his lips against hers. Tessa was so shocked by his uncharacteristic behavior that she stood as stiff as a marble pillar. How different his wiry form felt in comparison with Carlin's solid, muscled build. With Carlin, she had been swept away into a sea of excitement, the outside world fading until there was only the two of them. But Orrin inspired none of those soaring sensations. Nor did she lose herself in his arms. She felt the chilly air at her back and heard the clatter of a cart out in the mews. There was no rise of passion, no sense of being one body and soul.

Perhaps if she'd never known that thrilling ardor with Carlin, she might have been gratified by Orrin's declaration of love and more amenable to his kiss. Instead, his embrace reminded her of being licked by an over-eager puppy. And it wasn't a pleasant experience in the least.

She turned her head to the side so that his lips slid wetly over her cheek. "Don't, Orrin. That's enough!"

"Aw, lemme kiss you. We're soon t' be wed, after all."

"I've agreed to no such thing. Now let me go."

When she squirmed, he loosened his hold and leaned back, though his hands still gripped her upper arms. He wasn't much taller than her, so she didn't need to tilt her head back as she did with Carlin.

In the half-light, he wore an injured frown. "You never used t' put on airs with me. Is it your half-noble blood? P'raps I'm not good enough for you anymore."

"Don't be ridiculous. How can you even think such a thing?"

"You're all I think about, Tess, you an' me, together as man an' wife."

The yearning in his voice stirred guilt in her, and she remembered what a good friend he'd been, fetching medicine when she was sick, telling her all the neighborhood gossip on nights when she worked late, bringing her newspapers hot off the press. She'd sensed that he wanted more from her, though, and now it seemed he'd developed even stronger feelings than she'd anticipated.

She lightly placed her hands on the shoulders of his fustian jacket. "Please try to understand, Orrin. I don't mean to hurt you, but it's best that you put me out of your mind. I'm in no position right now to think about marriage—nor are you."

"Hmph. So you *are* dallyin' with the duke. Mayhap you're hopin' t' be showered with jewels and gold as his mistress."

His incessant jealousy frustrated her, especially since his suspicions held a grain of truth. She had indeed dallied with Carlin, just not to the extent that Orrin had suggested. Yet it was insulting to be thought of as the grasping sort who would sell her favors to the highest bidder. If Orrin meant to persist in such mistaken beliefs, well, she was tired of arguing with him.

"There's no reasoning with you," she said, too exasperated to defend herself anymore. "I think you had better leave—"

The slam of a door interrupted her. She turned her head toward the house. Her heart jumped as a dark figure emerged onto the loggia.

Having tied his cravat, Guy turned away from the long pier glass and sat down on a leather-padded bench. The large dressing room resembled a men's club with chestnut-paneled walls, paintings of horses and hunting scenes, and an abundance of cabinets, the majority of which were empty since he possessed only the essentials in clothing. Luckily, he had a valet who cared as little about fashion as he did.

Jiggs handed him one boot, and then the other, while Guy tugged them on. The valet squinted with his one good eye while using a rag to rub at a spot on the glossy black leather. "Sure ye don't want breakfast, Yer Grace?"

"Later." Guy surged to his feet. "Dawn is the best time to ride. The park is empty, and I can go for a gallop."

A cackle escaped Jiggs. "Too much time at yer desk, I s'pose. Sets a man t' itchin' fer action."

"Precisely."

Being in no humor for chatter this morning, Guy donned a forest-green riding coat and went into the darkened bedchamber that had once belonged to his grandfather. Gloom cloaked the heavy furnishings and the four-poster bed on its dais against the wall. Since he'd arisen early, no servant had yet come in to light the coals in the marble fireplace. He'd slept fitfully due to that encounter with Tessa after the lecture.

You are a duke, and I am a governess. And it is no use pretending otherwise.

Her parting words had needled him. She was right, of course, they oughtn't be meeting late at night, no matter how much they relished each other's company. The danger wasn't so much the risk of being seen together. Rather, it was the heat smoldering between them that eventually would burst into flames. They would end up in his bed—and then what?

Marriage was out of the question. She knew as well as he that they were not social equals. Such a match would be regarded with horror by the ton, not to mention his aunt and various other family members. Besides, he had sworn to avoid the institution. Once was enough to sour him.

In his youth he'd been dazzled by Annabelle's beauty and eager to speak his vows to her. By the time the fire of infatuation had burned away, and he'd discovered the shallowness beneath her charms, it was too late. Their marriage had grown increasingly contentious. Annabelle had craved balls and frivolities, the constant fawning of others, and she'd sulked whenever he'd devoted any time to scientific study. The endless pouting, the tearful quarrels, had stirred contempt in him until they'd spent more time apart than together.

The memory left a bad taste in his mouth. Over the years, he'd made his peace with the past, though wedlock still wasn't for him. But he'd always be grateful to Annabelle for one reason. She'd given him Sophy.

Guy's chest tightened. He would never forget the joy of cuddling her tiny form for the first time. Yet he'd felt frightened, too, that he'd fail her as he'd failed at marriage. If he wasn't fit to be a husband, he surely wasn't fit to be a father, either. Hounded by that fear, he'd sailed away from England, believing his daughter to be better off in the care of her grandparents.

Yet that, too, had been a terrible mistake. Sophy now believed her father hated her. And he needed Tessa's help to convince her otherwise.

For that reason alone, Guy knew he must resist his bodily desires. After having neglected his daughter for years, he couldn't rob her of the one person she was beginning to trust. He could not set up Tessa in a discreet house for his pleasure, as was common among gentlemen of his class. She'd never agree to such a demeaning arrangement, anyway. Nor did he wish to dishonor Tessa, no matter how much he ached for her.

You are a duke, and I am a governess. And it is no use pretending otherwise.

Those words were a grim reminder that his life was no longer his own. Along with the title came the duties of running several estates, overseeing myriad holdings and investments, and directing enough employees to populate an entire town. Any spare time he could eke out of his busy schedule must be devoted to the book he was writing, to his research in the conservatory, and to redeeming himself in the eyes of his daughter. Nothing else mattered.

He couldn't keep losing sleep over his obsession with a woman.

That was the real reason why he'd decided to go for a ride, to clear his mind and regain his focus. He was looking forward to an hour of freedom. During the years of sailing around the globe, he'd missed the invigorating briskness of an English autumn.

It had been pitch dark when he'd woken but now the sky had grown lighter. He walked to a window to assess the weather. A lustrous pink glow on the horizon tinted the neighboring houses and heralded the dawn. It looked to be a cool, fair morning, just the sort of fresh air he needed to sweep away the cobwebs. As he was turning to head down to the stables, however, a movement below in the garden made him pause.

Near the stone wall, two people stood close together in conversation. A man and a woman. There seemed to be something furtive about their meeting. Then his gaze sharpened. Tessa? Yes, that had to be her. No other woman on his staff had that creamy blond hair or that dainty figure wrapped in a shawl.

But who the devil was her companion? A footman? A groom?

Abruptly, the man pulled her into his arms and kissed her. Tessa made no attempt to push him away. In fact, she appeared to have no objection at all to the close embrace.

In an instant, Guy's blood went from a simmer to a full boil. He strode across the bedroom, threw open the door with a bang, and plunged down the darkened staircase. His brain was so agitated that he couldn't form a coherent thought.

His bootheels echoed sharply in the marble corridor. Here, several sconces had been lit, and a maidservant toting a brush and bucket backed against the wall as he went rushing past her. At the rear of the house, he wrenched open the door and went out onto the loggia.

The chilly air did little to mitigate his overheated senses. Tessa's lover turned to peer at Guy as he stalked down the steps. The dim light revealed him to be a stranger in workman's garb with a round, youthful face. Abruptly the fellow made a mad dash for the garden gate.

Guy hastened his pace, his footsteps crunching on the graveled path. "You there, stop!"

But the coward scuttled out into the mews and vanished. When Guy sprang after him, Tessa moved in front of the gate. "Please, Carlin, let him go. He means no harm."

Far from mollified, he swung toward her. "Who was that mawworm? Why did he come here?"

"Orrin? He's merely a friend. He . . . wanted to see if I was settled into my new post."

She had to be lying. There was tension in the fingers that gripped her shawl. The pearly light barely illuminated the pale oval of her face, but it was enough for him to see that her lips looked reddened and slightly swollen.

"How do you know him? You told me you were new to London."

"I've made some acquaintances," she said, lifting her chin. "While I was seeking employment, I lived in a boarding-house. Orrin Nesbitt was a resident there and we became friends."

"Friends—or lovers?" Realizing he was on the verge of shouting, Guy bit off his words. Just yesterday evening she'd rejected his offer of friendship and not ten hours later, she'd slipped downstairs at dawn to meet another man. It was like getting a kick in the shins. "You were kissing him, Tessa. I saw you from my bedroom window."

She recoiled, glaring at him. "Orrin is not my lover. And I don't appreciate you spying on me."

"Well, I don't appreciate my daughter's governess creep-ing out of the house to rendezvous with strange men in my garden."

"I already explained, Orrin isn't a stranger. And . . . oh, never mind. Pray forgive me if I caused any trouble. If you'll excuse me."

Guy remained planted as solid as an oak. Something wasn't right, and he intended to get answers. "Your duty is to stay in the nursery with Sophy. I hope you realize that what you've done is grounds for dismissal."

She drew in a sharp breath. "Lady Sophy is asleep at this hour. I would never neglect her. You know that I wouldn't."

The devil of it was, he believed her in that. No other gov-erness had ever displayed such devotion to his daughter. As perturbed as he was, Guy didn't truly want to dismiss her. "If you wish to keep your post, there will be no more secret trysts with Orrin Nesbitt—or any other man. Is that clear?"

Tessa visibly stiffened. "Perfectly, Your Grace. And let me reassure you, I don't have a harem of men at my beck and call."

With that, she stepped into the flower bed to get past him before returning to the path and marching toward the house. Guy found himself in the unaccustomed position of taking up the rear instead of leading the way. Eyeing the sway of her hips, he didn't know whether to snap at her or to admire her gall.

Upon reaching the loggia, he automatically reached for her upper arm and felt stung by a spark of heat. There it was again, that sizzling contact he experienced only with Tessa. As she glanced up at him, her eyes aglow in the shadows, he detected a quiver of awareness in her, as well. He had to restrain the powerful impulse to kiss her, to brand her as his and make her forget all other men. Especially one in particular.

"What does he do for a living?"

She blinked. "Who?"

"This Nesbitt fellow."

"He's a typesetter. Though I don't see why it should matter to you."

Guy opened the door to let Tessa precede him into the house. It was a leveling notion to discover that she preferred a common workman to him. Yet it was odd, too. No genteel lady would kiss a man of the lower orders—especially not with such passionate gusto.

"Of course it matters," he said tersely. "You're my daughter's governess. If this man is your beau, I should know something of his character. It also makes me wonder, did you enter my employ under false pretenses?"

She stopped dead in the corridor. In the flickering light of a sconce, her fine features wore a startled, almost guilty expression. "Why do you ask?"

"Don't dissemble, Tessa. Are you or are you not planning to marry him?"

"Oh!" she said on breathy note. "You mean Orrin."

"Who else would I have meant?" He shook his head, irked that they seemed to be talking in circles. "If you were already affianced when you accepted a position in my house, then you've done a grave disservice to Sophy. She's grown fond of you and she'll be distraught when you leave here."

"I wasn't. Engaged, I mean."

"And what about now? That kiss appeared entirely too fervent for mere friends. I deserve to be told if you're intending to turn in your notice soon."

Tessa parted her lips and stared at him, her fingers twisting the fringe of her shawl. The blue of her eyes held a peculiar haunted quality. "I . . ."

Her gaze shifted to peer past him. Only then did he hear the hurried approach of footsteps along the corridor. Guy turned to see Banfield striding toward them. The secretary exuded an unusually agitated air as he made a quick bow.

His gray eyes flicked to Tessa, in particular to Guy's hand on her arm. "Your Grace, if I might have a word in private."

It was unlike Banfield to neglect to say good morning. Something was clearly disturbing the man. But Guy had no intention of letting Tessa off the hook until he had satisfactory answers to her puzzling behavior.

"Wait for me in my study," he told the secretary. "I'll be there shortly."

"I'm afraid this is too urgent a matter for any delay," Banfield said grimly. "You see, a thief broke in during the night and ransacked your study."

Chapter 11

Heading down the marble corridor, Tessa half ran to keep up with the long strides of the men. Carlin's already taut features had turned even harsher at the news. A thief! She would have been hot on his heels even without his hand on her arm, towing her along at his side. What could have been stolen?

The only bright spot, she reflected guiltily, was that the robbery had distracted him from that disaster in the garden. She ought never to have gone out to meet Orrin. It had been a mistake from start to finish. And now the duke rightfully suspected that she was up to something.

Lud, what would he say if he learned that she'd come to Carlin House under false pretenses? That she had planned all along to leave his employ once she'd identified her father? Her mind had gone blank at his accusation of duplicity, and she hadn't been able to come up with a ready excuse. She felt miserable even to imagine how he'd despise her if he knew the truth. It was becoming harder and harder to continue the deception. And to complicate matters, he'd forced her to face another uncomfortable fact.

You've done a grave disservice to Sophy. She's grown fond of you and she'll be distraught when you leave here.

In the beginning, Tessa hadn't imagined her departure would be any different from that of all the other governesses who had come and gone. Yet now that she knew Sophy better, had learned the cause of her bad behavior, and had seen a steady improvement in her, the situation had been radically altered. She had come to care for the motherless girl who had been raised to believe her father hated her.

Tessa's heart felt steeped in a brew of worry and regret. What would happen if—when—she left Carlin House? Would the next governess even attempt to repair the broken relationship between the duke and his daughter? There was no guarantee, and that made it more difficult for Tessa to envisage herself leaving. Yet if she stayed, it would mean postponing her millinery shop, possibly for years.

She bolstered her spirits with the reminder that nothing was settled. Everything depended on how quickly she could identify the coat of arms, if her truant father would grant her a loan, and if he were even still alive. He could be dead and buried for all she knew. There were enough variables for her to postpone fretting about the matter for now.

If only she could hold her warm feelings for Carlin at bay as well.

His face grim, the duke ushered her into the shadowed study. A single candle on a table provided the only illumination, but it was enough to reveal a shocking sight. A blizzard of papers covered the carpet. Every drawer in the desk hung open. Books had been tossed down from the shelves, Carlin's framed paintings scattered. The place looked like the nursery after the time when Sophy had gone on a rampage and emptied out all the toy cabinets.

Looking around, Carlin plunged his fingers through his

hair, rumpling the black strands. "Good God! Who could have done this? And when?"

Mr. Banfield shook his head, then picked up the candle to light the tapers in a candelabrum. "I arose early to write out some letters that needed your signature," he said somberly. "Otherwise, the burglary might have gone unnoticed for another hour or two."

"Have you determined what's missing?"

"No, Your Grace. The moment I saw this, I could think only of catching you in the stables before you departed on your ride."

For the first time, Tessa noticed that Carlin was handsomely attired in a dark green coat, tan breeches, and shiny black boots. So that was why he'd been up at the crack of dawn. But he hadn't been in the stables, and the disapproving glance that Mr. Banfield aimed her way made Tessa feel uncomfortable. Really, he ought to be happy that she'd delayed the duke.

"There's no telling if anything has been stolen until this mess can be tidied," Carlin said curtly.

"At least the safe doesn't appear to have been tampered with," the secretary noted as he moved a landscape painting aside to reveal a hidden steel door in the wall. "That means no cash or jewels were taken."

"Well, that's something."

While the men talked, Tessa stepped to the windows and opened the draperies, fastening the gold tasseled cord to the wall hooks. Although it was still dark outside, the sun was coming up and daylight would soon make the candles unnecessary. When she returned, the duke was barking out orders.

"Send Roebuck in here at once. And Peabody, as well. Then interview the staff. Find out if anyone noticed anything unusual."

"As you wish." Banfield cast a sidelong glance at Tessa. "But if you'll first allow me a word, Your Grace."

Frowning, Carlin accompanied the secretary out into the corridor. Tessa suspected the starchy fellow wanted privacy to urge the duke to banish her to the nursery, but when Carlin returned alone a minute or two later, he did no such thing.

Since he seemed willing to tolerate her presence, she picked up some books and replaced them on the shelves. The duke began to collect the papers that were scattered near the open trunk. How odd that this had happened on the very night after he'd given his lecture, she mused. But she didn't want to interrupt him with chatter when he appeared engrossed in the task of putting his research documents back in order.

They worked in silence, though once she intercepted a cool stare from him before he turned away again without a word. That look was a stark reminder that he had not forgotten their quarrel.

She ought to be thinking up a way to placate him, but her mind kept dwelling on the robber. Why would someone break into a duke's house yet make no effort to crack the safe? Had he been interrupted while committing the crime? Or had he been seeking something other than jewels? That would suggest he was no ordinary picklock from the stews of Seven Dials.

Just then, Roebuck entered the study. The butler had a mane of silver hair and a stately aura that put Tessa in awe of him. This morning, however, his normally impassive face held dismay as he assured the duke that all the doors and windows had been locked as usual. He'd seen to the matter himself once the guests had departed after the lecture.

A similar assurance came from Peabody, the burly ex-soldier who patrolled the grounds at night. The only thing of interest Tessa discovered was that Peabody always went down to the kitchen for breakfast at six, which explained how Orrin had evaded the man's meaty clutches.

The butler took an order for coffee from the duke and departed along with the guard. Left alone with Carlin, Tessa ventured to comment, "I don't wish to gainsay Roebuck, but what he told you isn't entirely true. When I went out to the garden this morning, the back door was unlocked."

The duke's eyes narrowed on her. He made no reply, nor did he return to sorting his papers. Bathed in the first rays of dawn, with his hands on his hips, Carlin resembled an avenging angel. Her heart began to pound. She had never witnessed such a look of cold contempt directed at her.

Lud, she must have underestimated the depths of his displeasure. Or perhaps his frustration over the burglary had amplified it.

Retreat seeming the wisest action, she curtsied. "Lady Sophy will be waking up soon, Your Grace. I had best return to the nursery."

"No." The word was punctuated by the click of the latch as he turned to close the study door. "Sit down, Miss James."

That formal address increased her uneasiness. Her nerves frayed, she sank into the massive carved chair that she'd used during her first interview, the one that made her feel like a doll sitting on a throne. She was forced to tilt her head back to regard Carlin, who remained on his feet.

"I've already explained about Orrin," she said in a conciliatory tone. "I am not engaged to marry him. I'm very sorry for disobeying the rules and it won't happen again. There is really nothing more I can say."

"I have quite a lot to say. In particular about the burglary."

"Oh." She let herself relax a little. So this wasn't about her taking the governess post under false pretenses, after all.

Maybe he just wanted to discuss what had happened. "Have you determined yet if anything is missing?"

"All of my diaries," he said in a clipped tone. "I placed them in the trunk yesterday evening. But now they're gone."

Aghast, she stared up at him. "That's dreadful! Your lovely drawings and your notes . . . they must be irreplaceable. But why would someone take them?"

"I believe the thief was seeking that pirate's map. It could be worth a small fortune in gold."

"Oh. Then perhaps the culprit was someone who heard about it at your lecture."

"Or someone who'd already known of its existence." Still wearing that strange accusatory expression, Carlin prowled back and forth in front of her. "I first mentioned the map to you on the day that you and Sophy were in the conservatory. The same night I came upon you hiding here in the darkness. Right over there by my trunk."

Icy fingers crept over her skin. Was he suggesting that she was behind this robbery? Surely not. "I was looking for a book on heraldry."

"In my study? I found that odd at the time and even more so now." He slowly shook his head. "I suspect you were hunting for the treasure map. When I took you to the library, you asked about it again. Tell me, was that kiss designed to put me off my guard?"

She bristled at his wrongful interpretation of events, even as a part of her cringed that he could think her so devious. "Certainly not. Carlin, you must believe me."

He stalked closer, planted his hands on the arms of her chair, and stared straight into her face. In the early sunlight, the gold flecks in his brown eyes flashed like sparks of fire. "Stop lying to me, Tessa. You've been lying all along. And I presume you have a partner in this scheme."

"A-a partner?"

"Orrin Nesbitt. Did you pass those notebooks to him just now in the garden?"

"No! I swear I did not."

His lips compressed. "I've sensed from the start that you were not who you claimed to be. I should have heeded my instincts, Banfield's too. He also saw you with Nesbitt in the garden."

So that was why the secretary had looked so suspiciously at her and had requested a private word with the duke. Her spirits sank even lower. "I already explained to you, Orrin is merely a friend."

"Enough of these Banbury tales. A constable will be summoned to take you to Bow Street. The Runners will uncover the truth. If necessary, you'll be arraigned before a judge and charged with theft."

Tessa gazed at him in horror. It would be her word against the testimony of a duke. She could well imagine how that would turn out. She'd be confined for the rest of her life in prison. Orrin, too. When the diaries weren't found, Carlin would accuse him of having already sold them to the highest bidder.

A knock broke the tense silence. As if from a distance, she saw Carlin go to open the door. A footman entered, bearing a silver tray, and the duke directed him to place it on a table by the hearth. Her mind felt so mired in panic that she couldn't think. It might have been a moment later or ten minutes that the duke took her arm and drew her up out of the chair.

She stiffened at his touch. Visions of iron-barred cells swam in her head. "Where are you taking me?"

"Over here. Now sit, you look pale enough to swoon."

Tessa collapsed onto a chaise near the hearth. She scarcely

felt the softness of the cushions. A fire burned on the grate, though she could not recall seeing anyone light it. The radiating heat caused her to shiver, making her realize she felt frozen to the core.

Carlin pressed a cup into her hand. "Take this."

She obediently wrapped her fingers around the hot porcelain, took a sip of dark scalding liquid, and grimaced. "Ugh, coffee. And it's far too sweet."

"You've had a shock, and this will restore you. Drink it."

Tessa lacked the strength to defy that brusque command. She choked down the coffee, wishing it were tea. But at least it helped to thaw her body from that terrible chill.

Carlin sat down opposite her and drank his own coffee. He took a jam tart, then offered the plate of pastries to her. She shook her head. Her stomach felt so cramped that not even a cream bun could tempt her.

Within a few moments, though, she rallied enough to say, "You should be happy for me to swoon. Then you needn't bother with chains when you haul me off to prison."

"I wouldn't need chains for a dab of a woman like you."

The remark did nothing to bolster her confidence. She was well aware that a man of his tall, muscled build could easily overcome any resistance from her. It was hard to fathom that this hard-eyed stranger was the same warm man who had kissed her with such passion, who had shown her his parrots and his plants, who had sought her advice about his daughter's conduct.

But perhaps that was a big part of this, Tessa thought wretchedly. The duke had confided in her and now he felt betrayed. As much as it pained her to admit it, the circumstances were damning. By her own foolish lies, she had landed herself in hot water. And she couldn't fault him for thinking the worst of her.

He leaned forward, his elbows on his knees. "You should know that you didn't succeed in stealing the treasure map. It wasn't in my notebooks."

She blinked. "Oh?"

"Do you understand what I'm saying, Tessa? It means you've failed, and those diaries are useless to you. If you'll return them at once, I might be persuaded to drop all charges."

A flicker of hope in her wanted to believe he still harbored a modicum of faith in her. But he didn't, and the only way to restore that faith was to admit everything. Not just to save her own skin but to offer restitution in the form of honesty. Even if he dismissed her, even if she ended up on the street with nowhere to go, she must do what was right.

Collecting her courage, she set aside her cup and folded her hands in her lap. "I will confess, Your Grace. But only to the charge of coming here to Carlin House under false pretenses. The truth is . . . I've never before worked as a governess. In my previous position, I was a milliner's assistant."

"A hatmaker!" His startled gaze burned into her. "You swore that you were experienced with children."

"I am. I grew up in a foundling home, where it was my job to watch over the younger girls. If you doubt me, you may check the records at St. George's on Mercer Street, where I lived for eight years. When I was fourteen, I found work at a millinery shop." She lifted her chin. "And you cannot deny that Lady Sophy's behavior is much improved. I've succeeded where your more proper governesses failed."

"Of course I can't deny that." Carlin eyed her skeptically while refilling his cup from the silver pot. "Yet your speech is too refined for someone who grew up in the East End."

At the orphanage, Tessa had been taunted by the matron for her fancy airs and had learned to pepper her words with local color. "I paid close heed to the ladies who frequented the shop. But more important, I was taught proper speech by my mother. Mama picked it up while working as a maid in a lord's house, until he got her with child and turned her out onto the street."

That drew a sharp frown from Carlin. She expected him to recoil at her base birth, but he merely said, "Which lord?"

"I don't know. That is the crux of the matter, and the reason why I came here to Carlin House. I was hoping to discover his identity."

Carlin set down his cup with a clatter. "Good God. If you're implying he was someone in my family—"

"No, I'm not. Let me explain." Tessa drew out the delicate gold pendant and let it rest in her palm. "My mother was struck down by a carriage as we were crossing the street. As she lay dying, she gave me this necklace. She said it would help me to find my father. But being only six years of age, I had no notion of-of what she meant."

As her voice choked, the duke's expression seemed to soften. But in the next instant he flicked a doubtful glance at the pendant. "You expect me to believe that no one at this foundling home noticed that you were wearing a gold chain around your neck, let alone ever tried to steal it?"

"I made sure always to wear a high-necked gown or a shawl at my throat. Mama had warned me to guard it, you see. It wasn't until recently that I realized the design on it is more than just a pretty decoration, it's the key to identifying my father. You'll understand if you take a closer look."

Carlin left his chair and sat beside her. He picked up the pendant and leaned closer to give it a cursory inspection in the sunlight. The mere brush of his fingers disturbed her heartbeat, as did his scent of dark spice. It brought the haunting reminder of how low she'd fallen in his esteem.

"It's a coat of arms," he said flatly.

She nodded. "My father's coat of arms. I've tried for the past year to look for this crest on carriage doors or on a house here in Mayfair. But while working at the millinery I had only one afternoon free a week. That's why I took the position here, in the hope of having more opportunities to walk around the neighborhood. Alas, you forbade me to take Lady Sophy off the premises."

"An elaborate ruse when you needed only to consult a book on heraldry."

"Perhaps you'll think me stupid, but I didn't realize that such a book even existed until Miss Knightley told me. That was on the very afternoon before you found me here in your study."

Carlin dropped the dainty pendant back into Tessa's palm. "For all I know you could have picked up that necklace in a pawnshop."

Bitter frustration clogged her throat. "Then ask Miss Knightley. She can confirm my story. Or would you rather believe that I bought an article of jewelry on the off chance that I might need to con my new employer with it? As if I could even afford such an expensive piece on the pittance I was earning!"

His dark brows snapped together in a frown. He seemed to consider her words a moment before gruffly saying, "All right, then. Presuming you're telling the truth, what do you mean to do once you've learned this man's name? Blackmail him?"

"Certainly not," she said through clenched teeth. It wouldn't do to antagonize the duke when her life hung in the balance. "All I have ever wanted in life was to open my own millinery shop. So when I find my father, I intend to ask the callous lecher to advance me a loan. It's the least he can do to make up for his years of neglect."

Angling away from Carlin, Tessa turned her head lest he spy the hot moisture welling in her eyes. Her fingers trembled from the force of her emotions as she tucked the pendant back inside the bodice of her gown. It was clear that the duke still mistrusted her. Was that any surprise after she'd confessed to being a liar?

All of her hopes and dreams had come crashing down around her. She had not identified her father, she would never have her shop, and she'd be lucky to escape this awful quandary with her neck intact. And she had only herself to blame.

She drew a ragged breath and blinked away tears before pivoting back toward Carlin. He hadn't bothered to return to his seat. He was lounging beside her on the chaise, watching her. A certain grimness lingered at the corners of his mouth, yet that harsh severity had eased, and he merely looked like the arrogant duke of their first meeting.

If his mood had mellowed, even a little, then she desperately needed to press her advantage. The alternative was to be imprisoned on false charges. "Please, Carlin, you must believe me," she implored. "I've told you everything. And I beg you not to have Orrin arrested. He came here today only to tell me that he's been making inquiries about where Mama may have been employed. So take out your wrath on me if you like, but not on him."

During her speech, Tessa unthinkingly extended her hand across the cushion to touch Carlin's. How warm and strong his fingers felt, how dearly she wanted him to caress her as he'd done in the library. Then she realized her foolishness. Lud, now he would think she was trying to work her wiles on him.

Yet when she tried to withdraw, he gripped her fingers for a stirring moment and gave her a brusque nod before releasing her. "I won't turn either of you in to the law. But I intend to do a thorough investigation. As to your father, we'll see what can be discovered when the book arrives."

Relief welled up in her and bubbled forth in a tremulous

smile. "I-I don't know what to say except . . . thank you. I vow, I didn't come here to steal any treasure map. I knew nothing about it when I applied for the post." Seeing the value of a little self-enhancement, she added, "I'm truly sorry for lying, but pray consider, if I'd confessed my background from the start, you wouldn't have hired me. And Lady Sophy would still be terrorizing the nursery staff."

An appreciative glint lit his dark eyes, though it didn't quite reach his lips. He stood up. "We'll discuss my daughter later. For now, you're to stay inside this house. Do I make myself clear?"

"Yes, of course." Tessa also arose, feeling as light as air without the weight of her secrets. A way to make restitution occurred to her. "I was thinking . . . even if I were to find my father, I needn't leave your employ at once. Lady Sophy will require a proper governess eventually, but it's too soon yet and you won't want her to lapse back into bad behavior. Of course, that's only if . . . if you wish for me to remain here for a time."

"We shall see. I've other things on my mind at present."

The robbery. In all the turmoil over her own fate, she'd nearly forgotten there was a thief to apprehend. She glanced around at the remaining chaos. "This was no ordinary burglary, Carlin. If it was about the treasure map, surely that confirms the culprit was someone who was here yesterday evening."

He raked his fingers through his hair. "Frankly, I don't know what to think."

Because he'd been certain it was her and he hadn't yet considered anyone else. So Tessa speculated on his behalf. "Well, if *I* were a thief, I'd have hidden myself somewhere in the house after the lecture. There are any number of places on this floor, or perhaps even upstairs in one of the unused bedchambers. Then I'd have waited until everyone was asleep, searched for the diaries, and left by the back door. It was unlocked, you'll recall."

Carlin went to pull the bell rope. "I'll assemble the footmen who were on duty last night. They'll know if any visitor was not observed to have departed."

"Of course there's another possibility," she mused, picking up one of the framed paintings from the floor. "The villain may have left through the front door and then sneaked back inside by way of the garden before Roebuck locked the doors. In which case, it won't do any good to question the footmen."

"Very true. Has anyone ever told you, you have the mind of a criminal?"

"Yes, you have."

Her tart retort wrested a chuckle from Guy. He was relieved to be back on friendly footing with Tessa. If truth be told, he'd never wanted to believe her capable of the crime. But once he'd noticed that his diaries were missing, logic had forced him to assemble her actions into an inescapable conclusion. The inconsistencies in her personal history. His discovery of her in his study that one night. Her rendezvous with Orrin Nesbitt in the garden.

All of it had pointed toward her guilt. However, Guy had been missing half the pieces of the puzzle. He hadn't known the truth about her background or her reason for seeking the position of governess.

When Roebuck entered, Guy tasked him to fetch the footmen. Then he set to work hunting for the guest list among the papers strewn across his desk.

As he did so, Guy surreptitiously watched Tessa, who was absorbed in straightening his books. A hatmaker, by God. One couldn't help but admire her audacity. She was a clever, plucky woman, and as much as he despised her deception, he could understand why she had done it.

Her story was perfectly plausible. Growing up in an orphanage explained her unfamiliarity with aristocratic homes, her unorthodox approach to child rearing, and her occasional lapse into a lower-class dialect. As for the gold pendant, however, he remained dubious. Perhaps the necklace *had* come from a lord—there were plenty of noble by-blows in England. Yet a six-year-old's memory of her dying mother's words seemed a bit unreliable.

Tessa believed it, though, he was sure of that. Her voice had held the passion of conviction. In particular, he winced to recall that glimmer of tears before she'd turned her face away from him. Then as now he felt the powerful urge to protect her.

The early-morning sunlight kissed her buttercream hair and lit the delicacy of her face. The fine manners of the upper class seemed to come naturally to her, yet no society lady he knew would ever have pitched in to clean up this mess. Perhaps that was why he vastly preferred Tessa's company to that of any of the debutantes who were considered suitable for a man of his rank.

The footmen trooped into the study, half a dozen of them, and he painstakingly reviewed the names on the guest list with them. Once he glanced up and spotted Tessa edging toward the door, but he motioned to her to stay. He didn't want her returning to the nursery just yet. Not when she might offer some insight on the attendees. At least that was the excuse he gave himself.

In the end, only one guest had not been observed by anyone to have departed. His identity left Guy numb with surprise. He swore the footmen to secrecy, dismissed them, and stood frowning at the empty doorway.

Tessa appeared at his side. "So the culprit is Lord Haviland. If I may ask, how well do you know him?"

Guy turned a bleak eye on her. "We've been friends since our school days. Blast! It just can't have been Will."

"You did mention that he's a gambler. Perhaps he's in desperate need of funds and hopes to enrich himself with the treasure map."

"Still, I cannot believe it of him. Despite his faults, he's always had a certain sense of honor."

She was silent a moment, then said, "Well, perhaps there were others at the lecture with a reason to steal the map. Remember, the robber may have left by the front door and then reentered at the rear in order to throw you off the scent. There was a middle-aged man with a beaky nose who kept hounding you about the treasure."

"Lord Churchford. He's as rich as Croesus yet he's always greedy for more gold. Yes, I could see him funding an expedition if he had the map."

"Then add him to your list. Is there anyone else?

Mentally reviewing the guests, Guy prowled back and forth on the plush carpet. "Another possibility is the Honorable John Symonton. He's a scholar at Bullock's Museum."

"Was he the young gent wearing spectacles?"

"One and the same. For Symonton, it would be less about the gold and more about the archaeological value of the treasure. Such a find could be the makings of a young man's career."

Tessa's eyes shone. "There you go, Carlin. You have some likely suspects to investigate. One of them had to have stolen your diaries."

For a bare moment, it crossed Guy's mind to wonder if Tessa wanted to make the men look guilty in order to avert suspicion from herself. Then he quashed the notion. Despite her lies, she was no criminal. Nor was she Annabelle, attempting to twist him to do her bidding. If truth be told, Tessa was the opposite in every way of that pampered beauty.

"Well," Guy said crisply, "I had best make haste before the scoundrel realizes the map isn't in the notebooks and destroys them."

He placed his hand at the small of Tessa's back to guide her out of the study. As always, the burn of desire afflicted him, but he firmly doused it. He had to keep his base cravings in check. Any feelings he harbored for her must not be allowed to flourish for more reasons than he could name.

As they went through the doorway and into the passage, an unexpected sight greeted them. Sophy was running toward them, a white flannel nightdress flapping around her small bare feet. Her childish voice echoed in the marble corridor. "Miss James, Miss James!"

Winnie was hot on her heels. Panting, she bobbed a nervous curtsy. "Sorry, Yer Grace, milady escaped."

Sophy hurled herself forward and wrapped her arms around Tessa's waist. A tragic look made her lips wobble. "When I woke up, you were *gone*. I thought you went away like Moo-Moo."

Tessa leaned down to return the hug. "I was merely speaking with your papa for a few minutes. Will you give him a good-morning kiss?"

Sophy aimed a suddenly shy look up at him. "Morning, Papa."

But she didn't venture forward, and Tessa threw a glance over her shoulder at him, her lips curved in an apologetic smile. He knew it was too soon to expect kisses from his daughter, yet his chest felt curiously tight as he stepped forward to stroke her soft cheek. "Good morning, monkey."

Her eyes rounded. "I'm not a monkey!"

"Oh? Scurrying down the passage just now, you looked just like one that I once saw swinging through the jungle."

A burble of mirth escaped her. "Did you hear that, Miss James? I'm a monkey."

"Lady Monkey, we'll call you," Tessa said. "But even monkeys need to eat breakfast. Come along."

A half smile on his face, Guy watched them troop toward the staircase. Sophy was holding Tessa's hand and skipping along like any happy little girl. That was Tessa's doing, and he breathed a prayer of gratitude that she had succeeded where the other governesses had failed. For that reason alone, he must exert control over his passions.

Besides, he didn't need any distractions just now. His plans for the future had been struck a serious blow by the theft of those diaries. He could attempt to reconstruct them, but that would take months and he likely would forget vital details. If ever he hoped to write a book about his voyage, he must track down the villain at once.

Chapter 12

Tessa kept busy for the next few hours helping Sophy practice her alphabet on a slate, teaching her simple sums by moving buttons around on a felt board, and correcting her table manners during the noon meal. Afterward, they had story time, with the little girl reclining on the rug while Tessa read to her from one of the many books on the nursery shelves.

It was their favorite activity, and one that Tessa usually relished, but today she was preoccupied by that encounter with Carlin. She lost her place several times and had to be prompted by an indignant Sophy. At last, though, the girl began to yawn and went willingly with Lolly to lie down for a nap. Determined to put the hour of freedom to good use, Tessa left the nursery on a mission.

She tracked down Avis Knightley, who was working on a basket of sewing in an antechamber on the first floor. Across the corridor, in the Blue Drawing Room, Lady Victor was entertaining a circle of ladies. From afar, their voices sounded like the squawking of crows.

Avis smiled and let the lace chemise she was mending fall to her lap. "Tessa, how lovely to see you. Do keep me company while I wait for her ladyship. There's been a deluge of visitors today who want to hear all about the lecture last evening."

Settling onto a gilt chair, Tessa thought it ill mannered of Lady Victor to exclude her companion from the gathering. But perhaps that was the way of aristocratic households. "I wonder, is it really the lecture that's drawn them here—or the robbery?"

Avis's face sobered. "Word does get around swiftly, doesn't it? Everyone wants to learn the scandalous details, although I believe His Grace has put about that nothing of value was taken aside from some of his papers. And I'm dying to hear if it's true that you were present in his study when the theft was discovered this morning."

Tessa detested being the subject of belowstairs gossip. Lud, did the other servants know that Carlin had charged her with the deed? Surely not, for he had made his accusations in private.

"I happened to wake early and went out to walk in the garden," she hedged. "I was returning inside when Mr. Banfield came running with the news. His Grace had been on his way out to the stables, and he asked me if I would mind helping him straighten up the mess."

The story sounded unconvincing even to her ears, and it elicited a curious look from Avis. She took a few stitches while musing, "I must say, it's shocking to think of a criminal breaking into this house. As you can expect, Lady Victor was in a dither this morning when she heard the news. She's certain we will all be murdered in our sleep."

"It didn't seem to me to be a typical burglary, though. No money or jewels were taken, only some notebooks belonging to the duke. Please don't mention this to anyone, but it's possible the culprit was looking for the treasure map that was mentioned at the lecture."

Avis's green eyes widened. "Ah, that would make sense.

But how horrible! Does His Grace have any notion as to who it might have been?"

"There were some two hundred guests, so it could have been any one of them, I suppose." Trusting that Avis would presume the duke wouldn't confide in a mere governess, Tessa sought a way to casually work the conversation around to her purpose. "I'm afraid I knew no one in attendance but the family. Did you know any of the people who were there?"

"Having been with her ladyship for nearly five years, I recognized a number of them by sight. But I cannot speak for their character since I was never truly a member of the ton."

"I believe you do know one of them, though." Tessa leaned forward to place her hand over Avis's. "I don't mean to pry, but I had the distinct impression that you were closely acquainted with Lord Haviland."

The woman's fingers stilled on her mending. Her cheeks turned pink and distress clouded her eyes. "Oh, my. Was it so obvious?"

"Never fear, I very much doubt that any of the guests noticed." Tessa didn't want to upset her further by mentioning that Carlin had come to the same conclusion, too. "Yet he knew you by name and I couldn't help but notice the way you two looked at each other."

Sighing, Avis glanced out the window. "I daresay it would do no harm to tell you the story. It's quite ancient history, really, having happened some ten years ago in Sussex, where my father was vicar of a small village church. It was just Papa and me, and I served as his housekeeper. One day I went out to the woods to pick blackberries to make jam when a storm blew up suddenly. There was so much thunder and lightning that I was frightened near to death. Then from out of nowhere, the handsomest man I'd ever seen came riding by and rescued me."

A soft smile curved her lips, and she seemed almost to

have forgotten Tessa's presence. "He swooped me up onto his horse and just as the rain came down in a torrent, we took shelter in a gamekeeper's hut. William—Lord Haviland he is now—said he was visiting a friend on a neighboring estate. I'd never in my life met such a charming man. One thing led to another and . . . oh, you must not think matters went *that* far. But we proceeded to kiss each other most thoroughly . . . until I came to my senses and fled."

Having experienced passion in Carlin's embrace, Tessa could fully understand. "He *is* very handsome. One can see why you were bowled over."

"I learned only later of his reputation as a rake. Oh, he apologized most fervently and even called a few times at the vicarage, but I refused to be beguiled by his banter." Her lips firmed. "I think what angered me the most is that Lord Haviland seemed to take for granted that I would succumb to his charm. As if a vicar's daughter ought to be grateful for the attention of an earl's heir. I want nothing to do with such a brash man."

"He followed you last night. Did you ever speak with him?"

Avis bit her lip and nodded. "He enticed me outside into the garden and then tried to cozen me that he'd changed and was no longer a rogue. But we quarreled and he went storming out through the gate."

So, Haviland had not returned to the house. Tessa filed away that bit of information. "He doesn't sound indifferent to you," she said.

"I can't imagine why he would bother with an old maid like me after so much time has passed . . . except perhaps he views me as a challenge. I'm the one woman who has managed to resist him."

Tessa studied her friend's sparkling eyes, the flushed cheeks, and the glossy chestnut curls beneath her ruffled spinster's cap. "It's clear to me why he would bother. Have you looked into a mirror lately?"

Her blush deepening, Avis busied herself with her sewing. "Oh, fiddle. Having achieved the grand old age of thirty, I am quite firmly on the shelf. Besides, Lord Haviland would never marry a penniless lady without any advantages of family connections."

Thirty didn't seem so very old when love was involved. And Tessa had the suspicion that Avis still pined for him despite her protests to the contrary. Yet she was right, Lord Haviland wasn't likely to rescue her from the drudgery of being Lady Victor's paid companion. In that way, she and Avis were alike, for Carlin would also eventually wed a lady of high rank, one who would bring him a large dowry and enhance the family honor. It was a dismal thought.

"I suppose it's just as well," Tessa said. "I can't imagine it would be wise to marry a gambler. Do you know how deeply he is in debt?"

"Lord Haviland claims to have turned over a new leaf since attaining the earldom last year, and that he no longer frequents gaming dens. He also said that he's never forgotten me. But who knows if any of it is really true?" Avis paused, her fingers taut on her sewing and her face stricken. "You don't suppose *he* could have stolen the map, do you? All that gold would be tempting to a man in dire straits. Or am I being too hard on him to suspect him of such a criminal deed?"

Tessa hoped for her friend's sake that he wasn't guilty. "Only time will tell. We must wait for His Grace to uncover the truth."

The following day, Tessa was bringing Sophy back inside after an outing in the garden when the sound of upraised voices carried along the marble corridor from the front of the house. She could not make out any words, but a lady was chastising someone in a haughty tone while a gentleman added his own blustering commentary.

Sophy's face lit up. "Gammy!"

Yanking her hand out of Tessa's, the little girl went racing down the passageway, forcing Tessa into hasty pursuit. Lud, there would be trouble if these were callers for Lady Victor. "Sophy, come back here at once."

Sophy either didn't hear or chose to ignore the order. Tessa arrived at the grand entrance hall in time to see the little girl fling herself at the visitors, who had been railing at a hapless footman. They were an older couple, the well-padded woman clad in a stylish gown of bottle-green muslin and a matching felt hat adorned with a flat ostrich feather. The dapper man at her side had receding gray hair, a hazelnut-brown coat, and a gold-topped cane.

"Gammy, Gammy, I missed you!"

The lady batted Sophy away. "Let me first dispose of my wrap, child, before you smother me." Only when the footman accepted her crimson pelisse did she grant her attention to the girl, holding her back by the shoulders. "Good heavens, your hands are filthy! Who has your papa tasked with taking care of you these days?"

"Miss James," Sophy piped up. "We've been making a house for fairies with twigs and leaves."

Tessa dipped a quick curtsy as she drew out a handkerchief to rub the dirt from Sophy's little fingers. "I am Miss James. I must apologize, for Lady Sophy has just come in from playing in the garden."

The man held up a quizzing glass that magnified one blue eye as he looked Tessa up and down. "Romping in the flower beds, by Jove! I shall have a word with Carlin about this shocking lapse in the girl's hygiene, not to mention the neglect of her education."

Tessa had a strong suspicion about the identity of these

newcomers. It irked her to have to tolerate such criticism when it was their neglect that had turned their granddaughter into a spoiled imp. With cool politeness, she said, "And who may I ask are you, sir?"

"We are Lord and Lady Norwood," he said. "And we have come to see about the safety of our precious granddaughter."

Lady Norwood lifted a gloved hand to her generous bosom. "We returned from Brighton the very instant we read that terrifying account in the papers about what happened here. Oh, our dear baby girl might have been—"

"Lady Sophy is in perfect health, as you can see," Tessa cut in, not caring if she was rude. How could they be so foolish as to refer to the robbery in front of a four-year-old? Sophy was gazing up in curiosity, for the servants had been strictly warned not to frighten her with tales of burglars. "May I suggest that you discuss any matters of concern with His Grace in private."

"Carlin is out," Lord Norwood said, his knob of a nose twitching as if the duke's absence had been planned as a personal affront to his in-laws.

"*So* inconvenient," drawled his wife. "Well, we should like to visit with dear Sophy in the drawing room as we haven't seen her in ages. I shall send for strawberry tarts. Those are your favorite, aren't they, darling?"

Sophy bounced up and down. "Jam tarts, jam tarts!"

Tessa scarcely knew what to do. "But, milady, it will spoil her luncheon."

"Nonsense," Lord Norwood huffed. "A little treat never hurt any child. Now where is that blasted footman?"

The poker-faced servant in blue-and-gold livery came forward to lead the way up the staircase. Upon being shooed away again by her grandmother, Sophy slipped her hand into Tessa's as they mounted the steps and went along a wide corridor to the magnificent gilded drawing room. All the while, the Norwoods kept up a critical commentary about the decor. *Annabelle would have found that rug a bit threadbare.* Or *Annabelle would have changed those draperies to a paler blue to lighten up the room.*

"It is a dreadful misfortune that our daughter never had the chance to become duchess," Lady Norwood said, picking up a china shepherdess from a table and turning it over to check the maker's stamp on the bottom. She eyed the painting over the mantel as if to calculate its value before sinking onto a chaise and arranging her skirts. "Annabelle would have been the perfect mistress of so grand an establishment. She would have spruced up this house and turned it into a showpiece."

Tessa was so flabbergasted that anyone could find fault with the palatial mansion that she couldn't formulate a reply. Not, of course, that the Norwoods would care about the opinion of a governess, anyway.

"Ann-bell was my mama," Sophy said proudly, tugging Tessa over to a chair. "She was the prettiest mama ever."

Sophy had never known the mother who had died shortly after her birth. Touched by the girl's devotion, Tessa smiled. "Very pretty, indeed, I'm sure."

"Pretty?" Lord Norwood scoffed as he used his cane to lever himself into a chair. "Why, she was so beautiful, so charming, so utterly delightful that all the gentlemen called her the Angel."

Tessa's mind instantly produced an image of Carlin kneeling in adoration before his wife, a haloed beauty draped in a gauzy white gown. Annabelle the Angel. An ache assailed Tessa's bosom. How could a man ever recover from losing the love of his life? No wonder he had gone away to wander the world for so many years. He must have needed time to overcome his grief.

Lady Norwood's voice pulled her back to the present.

"Such a pity you don't have your mother's green eyes, So-phy. Like perfect emeralds, they were. But then, you take after your Papa's side."

As the frowning girl stuck out her lower lip, Tessa said quickly, "I think Lady Sophy's eyes are a lovely shade of to-paz."

Lady Norwood's mouth pursed, and she lifted her fin-gers in a dismissing wave. "Pray sit over by the door, Miss James, you oughtn't be here with the family. And do not speak unless you are spoken to first."

Tessa had no choice but to do as she was told.

From her new perch a short distance away, she fumed in silence to see how the Norwoods permitted Sophy to do as she pleased, whether it was knocking over the stack of unlit coals on the grate or grabbing several tarts from the tea tray that had been delivered. They scolded the girl halfheartedly, then immediately undermined the correction by indulging her pleas for more sweets. All the while, they had the nerve to flash accusatory looks at Tessa as if it were all her fault that a four-year-old couldn't restrain her impulses.

A number of hours had elapsed since breakfast, and Tes-sa's stomach rumbled. She was offered nothing, even though there was an extra cup on the tea tray and plenty of pastries left. Despite their fine airs, the Norwoods had manners that struck Tessa as unconscionably rude. She could name a dozen friends and neighbors from the East End who were kinder and more cordial.

Lord and Lady Norwood alternately pampered Sophy and ignored her. As they began gossiping about parties they'd at-tended in Brighton, the girl grew increasingly whiny. She tugged on her grandmother's skirt. "I want to see Moo-Moo. Why didn't you bring her, Gammy?"

"You might ask your papa that question. It was he who sent her away. He didn't want the dear old woman in this house."

Sophy kicked the leg of the table. "Papa's mean, I hate him."

"Here now," Lord Norwood said gruffly. "Stop that racket at once."

"Such a rag-mannered child," his wife added in distaste. "Since your mama was a perfect angel, I daresay the bad temper comes from your papa's side of the family."

That only made the girl angrier. She struck the table so hard that the tea tray might have slid off the polished surface had not Lord Norwood bestirred himself to catch it. Then she threw herself onto the floor and burst into tears.

Tessa had witnessed quite enough. Leaving her chair, she marched toward the group. "I'm afraid Lady Sophy must return to the nursery. She's already missed her luncheon and it is nearly time for her nap."

"Don't want no nap!" the girl wailed, pounding the carpet with her fists.

"Well!" said Lady Norwood as she arose in self-righteous indignation. "I do hope you will teach the child proper grammar along with manners, Miss Johns. This behavior is the outside of enough!"

Tessa didn't bother to correct the mangled name. She unclenched her teeth long enough to say in cold civility, "Good day, milady, milord."

As the pair trotted out of the drawing room, muttering about insolent servants, she turned her attention to Sophy, who was still actively engaged in a tantrum, kicking and sobbing and writhing on the floor.

Her skirts pooling around her, she knelt to gently rub the girl's back. The poor child was trembling and crying, and Tessa couldn't blame her. How could anyone treat their granddaughter with such callous disregard? And to walk out while she was weeping!

At least now Tessa had a better understanding of the

appalling household in which Sophy had grown up. Meeting the Norwoods had left Tessa in a state of simmering anger. It was easy to see how Sophy had been influenced into hating her father. The Norwoods had encouraged just that.

All Sophy wanted was to be loved by her grandparents, but they were too selfish to see beyond their aristocratic noses. They had overindulged her with sweets, compared her unfavorably with their daughter, and thrust her away instead of kissing her.

"There, there, dearie. I'm sorry you're so unhappy. You'll feel better in a few moments. Come, let's go upstairs, and I'll read you a book."

Sophy lifted her head, her face stained with tears. She scrubbed her sleeve across her eyes and gave one last hiccuping sob. "Two-two books?"

"Yes, my clever little monkey," Tessa said with a tender smile. "Two books it is, then. But only if you come straightaway without making a fuss."

The girl clambered to her feet and placed her small hand in Tessa's. Aside from a few sniffles, she was calm enough to let herself be led upstairs to the nursery. The outburst appeared to have sapped her of energy, though, and she submitted to Lolly's fussing over her having missed luncheon and let Winnie change her out of the jam-smeared pinafore. Then, much to Tessa's delight when she sat down in the rocking chair to read to the girl, Sophy climbed into her lap instead of sitting on the floor as she usually did.

With that small body snuggled against her, Tessa felt a sweet rush of love. She knew she shouldn't encourage such closeness. Carlin had not yet said how long she'd be permitted to stay, and if she was forced to leave here soon, she oughtn't be fostering dependency in the girl. Yet it crushed her heart to imagine pushing Sophy away as her grandparents had done.

Sophy must not have the same unhappy childhood Tessa herself had known. All children deserved to be loved unconditionally. Now more than ever, she was determined not to abandon the precious little girl.

Shortly after supper that evening, Tessa received a note from Carlin requesting her presence in his study at her earliest convenience. The brevity of the message gave her no clue as to why. Was this the moment she had feared, then? Now that he'd had time to reflect upon her lies, had he decided to dismiss her from his employ?

She fervently hoped not.

Nonetheless, she welcomed the opportunity to talk. Having not seen the duke since the robbery, she needed to tell him what she'd learned about Lord Haviland. She also wanted to discuss Lord and Lady Norwood and to ask what might be done to protect Lady Sophy from their noxious influence.

Regrettably, Sophy was still exhibiting a degree of fretfulness after the visit of her grandparents. At bedtime, she fussed and clung to Tessa. It was past nine when the girl finally dropped off to sleep and Tessa was free to go to her bedchamber to spruce herself up for the meeting.

She had decided that if Carlin meant to sack her, she would not wear a frumpy high-necked gown that served well enough in the nursery. She would primp a little in case he could be swayed to change his mind. Deep down, Tessa knew it was also her attraction to him that influenced her to want to appear at her best. He was an admirable man whose good opinion had come to matter a great deal to her.

With that in mind, she donned her finest gown, a sky-blue muslin that she'd sewn the previous year to wear to the wedding of a friend. The dress might not have been costly by noble standards, but it was the only one in her sparse wardrobe that had the low-cut neckline and puff sleeves popular with ladies of the ton. And since there was no longer any need for concealment, she would leave off the fichu she usually wore to hide her delicate gold pendant.

You are a duke, and I am a governess. And it is no use pretending otherwise.

Despite her admonition to Carlin, Tessa felt a fizz of excitement while pinning her hair into a sleek chignon. It was nighttime, they would be alone, and perhaps he could be enticed into a little indiscretion. Though it was wrong to encourage a man who would never marry her, she could not repress an errant longing for him, no matter what the cost.

For the first time, Tessa had an inkling as to how a woman could set aside her principles and engage in forbidden acts with a man. She had a burning desire to feel Carlin's hands on her body and his flesh pressed to hers. The dread of being asked to leave his house weighed heavily on her. If she might never see him again after tonight, she mustn't pass up what could be her last chance to be clasped in his arms.

Would she really succumb if Carlin wanted more than just a kiss?

She draped a cream-colored shawl around her shoulders. There was only one way to find out.

Chapter 13

A short while later, Tessa paused in the partially open door-way and peeked into the study. Carlin was seated at his desk and hadn't noticed her arrival. His attention was concentrated downward on a book that lay open on the mahogany surface. As was his habit when he was working, he had removed his coat and cravat. Clad in a white linen shirt, he peered through a magnifying glass at the page before him. The light from a branched candelabrum made his hair gleam as black as a raven's wing.

The house was very quiet. Most of the servants, she knew, would have gone to bed by now. A veil of shadow draped the palatial proportions of the room, creating a cozy aura that was enhanced by the fire burning on the hearth. The scene looked like the perfect place for a romantic tryst.

Tessa drew a deep breath to calm her jittery heartbeat. There was still time for her to turn around and make a silent retreat. It would be wiser to present herself to the duke in the morning sunshine when there were others around to act as a shield against folly.

Her folly, not his.

Just then, Carlin lifted his head. His gaze met hers for a long moment before making a slow downward trek to her hem and back up again, lingering at her bosom and returning to her face. Admiration flashed in his dark eyes.

She was suddenly very glad that she had come.

He set down the magnifying glass and rose to his feet. "You're looking exceptionally fine, Tessa. Is there a ball here tonight that my aunt failed to inform me about?"

"Even if there was a ball, the governess wouldn't have been invited. But thank you, anyway." Feeling a little shy under his scrutiny, she strolled to the desk to give herself something to do. "Am I interrupting? You appeared to be very engrossed in that book."

"It's your book, the one on heraldry. It arrived from Greyfriars this afternoon. I've been looking through it this past hour or so."

Nothing could have been better designed to capture her attention. Tessa craned her neck to peer across the desk, catching a glimpse of mostly printed text along with a few illustrations. Somewhere in there must be the one nugget of information that would grant her the means to achieve her dreams. Yet any sense of excitement about that prospect seemed to have deserted her.

She forced herself to ask, "Have you identified my father's coat of arms, then?"

The duke shook his head. "I'm afraid I couldn't recall all the details. Many of these family arms look remarkably similar. That's why I called you down here, so I could take a closer look at your pendant." He paused, a hint of firmness to his masculine features. "At least that's partly the reason."

Tessa braced herself. Lud, he was going to announce her departure from this house. To forestall him, she said, "I hope you're referring to Lord and Lady Norwood. They came to call today while you were out."

"So I heard." His jaw clenched, though whether at the visit or her mention of it, she didn't know. "None of the servants could tell me what happened, except that a large number of tarts were consumed, Sophy had a fit of sobbing, and my in-laws left in a huff."

Tessa bit her lip. Since it was her duty to watch over his daughter, she hoped he didn't hold her to blame. "That's a fair summary. However, a few key details have been left out."

"Ah, I had suspected as much. Come, you must fill me in on what's missing." Carlin waved her toward the chaise by the fireplace. "Would you care for a glass of wine?"

"Er . . . yes, please."

Seating herself, Tessa hesitated to mention that she'd never tasted wine before. Or any other type of liquor, for that matter. She had never felt inclined to squander her hard-earned coin on ale or gin, as folks in her old neighborhood were wont to do. But apparently ladies often partook of wine, as they'd done at the reception after the lecture. And a part of her did so long to be a lady so that she might win the affections of the duke.

Carlin went to a table that held an array of crystal decanters and filled two glasses, then came to press one into her hand. At the brush of their fingers, a thrill tingled over her skin and she wondered if he felt it, too. But aside from an intense look, the duke gave no indication of it.

As he sat down beside her, she sampled the ruby wine and found it smooth and rich to her tongue. There was so much about his world that remained a tantalizing mystery to her. How lovely it would be to experience it all, to partake in every aspect of his life, to be allowed to enjoy his kisses as she had that one night in the library.

"Now," he said, "tell me what happened."

She blinked to chase away the lovely fantasy of him drawing her into his arms again. "Lord and Lady Norwood read about the burglary in the Brighton newspapers, so they returned to London. They said they were afraid that Lady Sophy might have come to harm."

Carlin swore under his breath. "They spoke of this in front of my daughter?"

"Just a little. I interrupted before Lady Norwood could finish. I knew you wouldn't want Sophy to be frightened of robbers roaming the house."

Tessa took another drink of wine to steady her nerves. She must keep in mind that the Norwoods were the parents of Annabelle the Angel, and Carlin might not appreciate hearing too forceful a criticism of them. At the same time, he must be made to recognize how harmful they were to his daughter.

Choosing her words carefully, she reported what had been said during the visit, leaving out certain parts pertaining to Annabelle, except those times when Sophy had been compared unfavorably to her mother. "I don't mean to be a tattle-tale, Carlin, but I saw how Sophy was hurt by their careless talk. Yet she also seemed to crave their love and attention."

"Yes, I noticed her strong attachment to them when I returned from my voyage and went to bring her home." He stared into the fire a moment as if looking into the past. "Needless to say, she did not wish to leave and fought me every inch of the way."

It was clear that the memory pained him, and Tessa longed to give him comfort. "In Sophy's view, she was being wrenched from the only home she'd ever known and sent off with a stranger. It would have been far less alarming to her had she trusted in your love for her. But she had been led to believe that her papa despised her."

Carlin sprang to his feet and prowled back and forth by the hearth. "Blast Mooney. I told the Norwoods to get rid of that bitter old woman and hire a younger nursemaid."

Tessa collected her courage. He wouldn't like what she had to impart, but it needed to be said. "Are you sure it was really Mooney who filled Sophy's head with lies? After today, I can't help but think there's more to the story."

"What do you mean?"

"I wonder if it's Lord and Lady Norwood themselves who are to blame. If it was they who turned Sophy against you."

He aimed a scowl at her. "They're my daughter's grand-parents. What reason would they have to do so?"

"I can't say, it was just the way they spoke about you, Car-lin." Refusing to be intimidated by that ducal stare, Tessa kept her gaze steady on him. "When Sophy asked about Mooney today, they said it was your fault that she'd been forced into retirement and that you'd refused to have her in your house. Then your daughter cried out that you were mean, and that she hated you. Lady Norwood didn't correct her. Instead she told Sophy that her bad temper had come from your side of the family."

"That can't be true."

He looked genuinely startled and she hastened to add, "It is indeed true. I clearly heard every word. That was when I put a stop to the visit."

Carlin raked his fingers through his hair. "Good God. They always seemed to me to be just silly fribbles. It was Mooney who openly resented me."

"How so?"

"As an old family retainer, she was given more latitude to speak her mind than most servants. She made plain her dis-approval of my courtship. She thought Annabelle deserved a title, and at the time, I was a mere mister."

Tessa was of the opinion that too much emphasis was placed on noble monikers. "Then I daresay Annabelle must have loved you more than a title."

He flicked her a slight frown as he continued to pace.

"Mooney also never missed a chance to complain that I was luring Annabelle from her home at too tender an age. My late wife, you see, made her bows at seventeen. Since I myself was a stripling of two-and-twenty, that didn't seem too young to me. I was drawn to her beauty, and we wed just after her eighteenth birthday."

Yet it was Lord and Lady Norwood who had allowed their daughter to enter society when she was barely out of the schoolroom, Tessa reasoned. Judging by their actions today, they must have been the sort of parents who had given in to Annabelle's every whim and then blamed Carlin for it all. "Well, it seems to me that they might have put a stop to Mooney's criticisms. The fact that they didn't only suggests that they agreed with her."

His brows drew together in a considering look. "Perhaps."

Tessa hoped to hear more, but he didn't offer any further insight. He tossed a few more coals onto the fire and used the iron poker to stir the flames. Then he resumed his seat, swirled the wine in his glass, and stared down into its dark red depths. He looked like a man who was still tormented by his past.

She yearned to put her arms around him. But she didn't have that right and besides, the matter of his in-laws had yet to be resolved in a manner that protected Sophy. "I might add, the visit with her grandparents caused your daughter to slip back into her old habits, at least temporarily. It was a very upsetting experience for her, and there was little I could do since they'd ordered me to be silent."

"Did they, by God? As I've placed Sophy under your care, they should have allowed you to comfort her."

His fiery glare warmed Tessa. "Well, I'm just a servant, after all," she said demurely. "That's why I wanted to suggest that Lady Sophy not be permitted to visit with the Norwoods without you being present."

"You're right, of course. I shall instruct Roebuck to turn them away whenever I am out." Then Carlin's wrathful expression lightened, and he aimed a crooked smile at her. "It seems I am once again in your debt, Tessa. Had I not been out chasing miscreants today, I'd have been home to deal with the ones on my own doorstep."

She sipped her wine to hide the dizzying effect that his smile had on her. It wasn't just that his praise pleased her. It was the fact that unlike other aristocrats, Carlin did not hold himself above the rest of humanity. He was not too proud to admit when he was wrong, or too arrogant to heed the advice of an underling. His fairness was one of the traits that made him so very appealing. She could always count on him to listen, even when he'd suspected her of theft and had learned how she'd lied about her background. In fact, Tessa found him to be far less dangerous a man when he was angry than when he was gazing at her with tender admiration.

At times like this she felt in dire peril of losing her heart.

Flustered, she cast about for another way to make herself so useful to him that he would never let her go. "Speaking of miscreants, I've discovered something of interest about Lord Haviland."

"Oh? Tell me."

"Yesterday, I had a talk with Avis—Miss Knightley. It seems she and Lord Haviland met some ten years ago when she was living in Sussex with her late father, the local vicar. The earl attempted to court her, but she knew he was a rake and would have nothing to do with him."

"Sensible of her. Respectable ladies aren't Will's usual cup of tea."

Tessa made no mention of the passionate kiss in the gamekeeper's hut that had been told to her in confidence. "That isn't all. Apparently, she and Lord Haviland quarreled in the garden after the lecture. Avis said that he stormed out by way of the garden gate."

Carlin gave a low whistle. "So that explains why he was so tight-lipped yesterday. He threw me out of his house when I asked why no one had seen him depart after the lecture. He must have been protecting Avis's reputation."

Tessa found that commendable of Lord Haviland. Perhaps he truly did care for Avis. Yet if Lady Victor were to find out that her companion had been alone with him, there would be an uproar. And the parallel between that situation and Tessa being here with Carlin tonight was uncomfortably obvious.

He was sitting close to her, and more than once she'd caught his gaze dipping to her bosom, as it did now. Being unaccustomed to revealing any flesh, she was surprised by how effective even a modestly cut bodice could be in luring a man's attention. And by how a mere glance from him could quicken her heartbeat.

She took a bracing sip of wine. "Does this exonerate Lord Haviland, then?"

His gaze snapped back to hers. "Not entirely. Don't forget, he might have returned later and slipped inside the house before Roebuck locked up."

"What about the other gentlemen? Have you found out anything yet?"

The duke shrugged. "Little enough. When I tracked down Churchford at his club yesterday, he spent the better part of an hour trying to talk me into letting him finance an expedition to find the pirate's gold in exchange for a cut of the proceeds. That isn't something he'd have done if he had the diaries. There wasn't sufficient time for him to have combed through them and to realize he didn't already have the treasure map."

"Perhaps he was attempting to throw you off the scent."

"Perhaps, although I'm leaning toward a not-guilty verdict for him."

Picking up the decanter, Carlin offered to refill her glass, but Tessa shook her head. She was giddy enough in his presence. When he leaned back and propped his feet on a leather ottoman, she, too, wiggled into a more comfortable position. She batted away the fleeting thought that it wasn't appropriate for a governess to slip off her shoes and tuck her feet beneath her skirts. But Carlin didn't seem to mind, so what did it matter?

"As for John Symonton, I'm less certain," he continued. "I called on him this morning and we had a long conversation about my travels. He attempted to persuade me to give him the map in the hope that the treasure might include artifacts of value to the Bullock Museum. The best I can say is that he's dedicated to his studies to the point of obsession, and that such a passion could lead a man to rationalize a crime as being for the good of science."

Tessa pondered that for a moment. "A reasonable conclusion. Yet there must be other possibilities, too. Have you been investigating anyone else?"

His face sobered. "As a matter of fact, yes."

That grave expression made her uneasy. Perhaps it was a family member like his cousin, Edgar, who also had attended the lecture. As the moment of silence stretched out, she ventured to ask, "Won't you tell me who?"

"Indeed. I was investigating *you*, my dear."

Chapter 14

Guy watched the play of emotions across her lovely features. In the firelight, Tessa looked startled at first, then worried and watchful. She sat very still, her expressive blue eyes vigilant on him. He wanted to take her in his arms and calm her fears, but given the intensity of his desire for her, he knew that would only lead to trouble.

More trouble than he could afford.

From the moment she'd stepped into the study, he had been captivated by her presence. Her insightful conversation and astute observations had further drawn him under her spell. He felt perfectly at ease in her company and knew she felt the same with him, judging by her unconventional way of curling her stocking feet beneath her. Yet now her delightful warmth of manner had gone underground, and it was evident that she believed him to be repelled by what he'd found out.

If only she knew, his visit to St. George's Home for Girls had stirred an entirely different reaction in him.

Upon stepping out of his carriage at the orphanage, Guy had been greeted by the unpleasant sight of a vagrant with an empty gin bottle lying in a stupor on the street. The neighborhood in the slums of Seven Dials had been crammed with pawnshops, secondhand warehouses, and rickety tenements. But at least the dingy brick orphanage had showed some signs of careful upkeep. Though the windowpanes were cracked, the glass sparkled, and the front steps were swept clean of debris.

A girl of perhaps twelve in a starched white apron answered his knock. She stared openmouthed at Guy, and upon learning his identity, left him in a cramped office and scampered off to fetch the matron. Glancing around, he saw that the piles of papers on the desk looked tidy and an attempt had been made to beautify the place with a few scraggly flowers stuck in a chipped blue vase. The air held the acrid scent of a cleaning solution, and he could hear girlish voices reciting their alphabet somewhere down the corridor.

The gaunt, middle-aged dame in black bombazine who hurried into the office introduced herself as Mrs. Plunkett. She dipped a curtsy and afforded him a look of more restrained curiosity than the girl's. "How may I be of assistance, Your Grace?"

"I'm seeking information on a Tessa James who once lived here."

Mrs. Plunkett obligingly removed a battered ledger from a shelf, searched the records, and found confirmation that matched the dates he provided her. "Departed here at age fourteen, eh? Why, we never let 'em go until sixteen, when they're better prepared to deal with the harsh world out there." Her mouth formed a thin line. "But then, 'twas before my time, milord. The last administrator had to be cast out for mistreating the girls."

"What do you mean?"

"She used the orphans to pad her own pockets, that's what."

Mrs. Plunkett revealed a number of disturbing facts, then

took him on a tour of the house, from top to bottom, where he saw for himself that the girls looked happy and industrious at their studies. They were garbed in clean though patched clothing, and it was painfully obvious from the stark surroundings that funding was scarce.

"You mustn't think ill of us, Your Grace. That bad apple is long gone, thank the Almighty. We take good care of our dear orphans now, and their schooling is of the utmost importance. Of course, there are always books and chalk and slates to purchase, but I do my best on what little we have."

Guy hadn't needed that hint to empty his pockets, giving Mrs. Plunkett a handful of gold guineas and promising to dispatch additional moneys in the future. Her effusive thanks had stirred only shame in him for having neglected charitable works until now. Although he'd always been aware of the poor, it had struck him deeply to actually witness children suffer such scarcity when his own daughter lived in the lap of luxury.

Now, seeing Tessa's anxious expression, he felt a powerful wish to erase all her bad memories of growing up in that place. "As you will have guessed," he said, "I visited St. George's, and you'll be happy to hear that it's under new directorship. It is no longer a workhouse where the girls are forced to stitch clothing from dawn until dusk. Now it is a proper school."

Hopeful disbelief lit her face. "Truly?"

"I saw the children in their classrooms myself." Mindful of how she would react to the rest of what must be said, Guy softened his voice. "I also saw the records book. Your name was in there, Tessa, with the notation that you had run away to escape an apprenticeship."

She blinked, then glanced toward the fire. "Yes."

Seeing that she needed a nudge, he went on, "You might also be interested to learn that the previous matron was arrested five years ago. She was convicted of peddling the older girls for nefarious purposes."

Her stark gaze flashed to his. "Good!" she said fiercely. "I sent an anonymous letter of complaint to Bow Street as soon as-as I was able. I hope Mrs. Cobb is rotting in prison. Hanging is too quick for the likes of her."

"I wholeheartedly agree. Will you tell me what happened to you?"

She regarded him with haunted eyes, then lowered her gaze to her lap. "After Mama's death, I was taken there at the age of six. Though St. George's was called a foundling home, it was really a workhouse where we sewed cheap clothing. In time, it became my job to train the younger girls, to make sure they met their daily quotas while I also completed my own. The worst part was trying to keep their spirits up when they were sad or exhausted." She looked at him again. "Even the little ones, girls no older than Sophy, had to sort threads and fold clothes. They should have been in school or playing with friends."

At the anguish in her voice, he reached out to clasp her hand. It felt small and delicate in his, and for the first time, he noticed the slight calluses on her fingers from years of hard work. Now he could understand better why she had succeeded with Sophy where others had failed. Tessa's affinity for children was deeply rooted in the sufferings of her past.

Not wanting to distract her, he reluctantly drew back. "And then?"

"When I was fourteen, Mrs. Cobb informed me that I was to be apprenticed to a modiste, a dressmaker. Though I disliked leaving the other girls, especially the little ones who needed me, I was happy for the chance to escape the drudgery, to work with pretty fabrics instead of coarse fustian, and so I went willingly enough. But she took me to a house on

the pretext of needing to speak to the landlord. And . . ."
Shuddering, Tessa stopped.

A frustrated anger gnawed at him. If only he could have
been there to rescue her! Although Guy burned to know the
full story, he said gruffly, "If it's too painful, you needn't
go on."

"You might as well hear the rest," she said in a subdued
tone. "I-I glanced into the parlor and saw several gents who
were . . . fondling women in scanty garb. Mrs. Cobb was gripping my collar while she haggled with the procuress. That's
when it struck me that . . . I was being sold. This was the
apprenticeship, and I would be forced to behave like those
women. When Mrs. Cobb let go of me to take her cash payment, I seized my chance to run. There was a big bruiser
guarding the door, but I managed to duck past him." Tessa
drew a shaky breath. "Looking back, I can scarcely believe
my luck in getting away. For several days I applied to dress-
makers but could find no work until Madame Blanchet hired
me at the millinery."

For next to nothing, no doubt. Guy clenched his jaw and
imagined her as a frightened young girl wandering London
alone, sleeping in alleys and scrounging for food in rubbish
bins. But even that was not as horrifying as the fate that he'd
feared had befallen her at the brothel.

With the weight of that worry gone, he felt a portion of
his tension dissipate. "It is by the grace of God that you're
here now, and safe."

Despite his fervent words, Tessa stared forlornly into her
empty wineglass. "I felt so . . . so stupid, though. Other girls
had been taken away for apprenticeships, you see, and I had
thought nothing of it. I'd envied them, in fact. I'd never once
realized what had really become of them."

"Of course you didn't," he said, his voice rough with

feeling. "You were a child of fourteen, confined to a work-house. What could you have known of such matters?"

She gave him a sad little smile, then set down her glass. "Well, Carlin. Now you have discovered the full extent of my fraud. I'm a baseborn hatmaker who barely escaped be-ing sold as a lightskirt. Wouldn't it set society on its ears if they knew you'd hired a governess with such a disreputable background and no formal schooling at all?"

He disliked hearing Tessa denigrate herself. "Devil take them. As you delight in pointing out, you've dealt with So-phy far better than anyone else. Whatever knowledge you lack can be studied and acquired. By the way, how *did* you learn to read?"

"Mama had taught me my alphabet and a few simple words. Once I left St. George's, I was determined to educate myself. I read whatever I could find, from fashion journals to hymnals to penny novels."

"Then your abilities are all the more noteworthy. I've met many a lady with every advantage of education who had nary an intelligent thought rattling inside her head."

Tessa raised her chin. There was a desolate quality to her expression that reached into his heart. "Oh, pray don't be so gentlemanly, Carlin. It really isn't necessary. If you intend to dismiss me, I wish you would just do it."

"Dismiss you?" he said blankly.

"Yes, you said yesterday morning that you needed time to consider if I might stay in your employ. After what you've discovered, there surely can be only one course of action. Isn't that why you summoned me here?"

"Frankly, no. It was any number of things. The heraldry book, the Norwoods, and yes, the orphanage, but only to find out what had happened to you there." When she still looked unconvinced, Guy brought the back of her hand to his lips for an ardent kiss. Rashly, he added, "I also simply wanted to see you, Tessa. Two days was too long to be separated from you. I crave your company, more than that of anyone else of my acquaintance."

A glow flickered to life in her eyes and softened her face. All the anxiety melted away as a tremulous smile hovered on her lips. Her bosom rose and fell with several ragged breaths. "Carlin."

She flung her arms around him, burying her face in the crook of his neck. He was instantly bewitched by her lush breasts and hourglass curves. Holding her close, he rubbed his cheek against her hair and savored her spellbinding scent. Everything about her supple form was soft and feminine, yet he very much liked that her inner spirit was strong and resilient, too. An unwavering warmth of sentiment held sway over him. He didn't care to examine the feeling too closely; he knew only that no other woman had ever affected him as profoundly as Tessa. His fingers were actually trembling as he brushed back a lock of silky blond hair and tipped up her chin.

He settled his mouth over hers and kissed her long and deep. The wild beating of his blood banished all wisdom to the farthest reaches of his mind. She tasted of wine and desire, a potent combination made more powerful because she was Tessa. He had been burning for her ever since that scorching encounter in the library. No, long before that. He'd been lost since she had first walked into his study more than a fortnight ago, with a jaunty chip-straw bonnet framing the finely etched cameo of her face, all pert manners and sapphire eyes, charming her way into his heart.

Yet he oughtn't be feverishly wondering how he could smuggle her upstairs to his bed to spend the night in a heaven of heated lovemaking. Now more than ever, Tessa must be forbidden fruit. Intimacy would lead to disastrous consequences for everyone—Tessa, Sophy, his family, himself.

He simply could not indulge in an affair with his daughter's governess.

With the utmost regret, he broke off the kiss and pulled air into his lungs in an effort to clear his passion-fogged mind. Then he disentangled himself from her arms. "Tessa . . . we can't do this."

"Mm." She nuzzled his throat. "But I like kissing you, Carlin. Don't you like kissing me?"

The tickle of her warm breath on his skin sent a bolt of temptation straight down to his loins. "I like it entirely too much. That's why you're returning to the nursery right now."

By a forceful application of willpower, Guy sprang up from the chaise, then offered his hand to assist her to her feet. The moment she stood upright, however, Tessa swayed against him, her fingers clutching at his shirt. An infectious giggle tumbled from her lips as she looked up at him with dancing eyes. "Oh, dear. My foot must have fallen asleep."

At her giddy smile, he fought back a grin. "Tessa, surely you can't be bosky from one glass of wine."

She shook her head in vehement denial. "Oh, no, I feel perfectly fine. Though the wine was delicious, by the way. Might I have more, please? There's really no need for me to go just yet."

Guy wrapped his arms around her slender form to stop her from reaching down to the table for her glass. "Not another drop."

Keeping Tessa glued to his side, he guided her to the partially open door of the study. He must ensure she made her way back upstairs without being seen. It had been unpardonably reckless of him to have engaged in that steamy embrace when anyone might have walked in.

"Oh, no! It seems Cinderella has lost her slippers." Tessa twirled away from him and lifted the hem of her gown to allow a provocative view of slim ankles and toes clad in only white stockings. In the doing, she bumped into the door, shutting it with a click. "Perhaps you'd be so kind as to walk me back over to the chaise. I must don my magic slippers before the clock strikes twelve. Otherwise, you might turn into a frog."

Guy was so much taken with this flirtatious side of her that they were halfway across the study again before he realized he ought to have just fetched the shoes for her. "I believe you're mixing your fairy tales."

She tapped a finger to her cheek. "That may be so since they're all new to me," she said. "I've read any number of wonderful stories to Sophy these past few weeks. Did you know that in *Mother Goose's Tales*, there are children who live in a shoe?"

As Tessa seated herself, he knelt before her and picked up one of her plain leather slippers, so much more practical than a lady's satin heels. "I daresay it was a bigger shoe than this one."

"Perhaps like the ones worn by the giants in *Gulliver's Travels*. Have I thanked you for sending that book up to the nursery?"

"I'm pleased to hear you enjoyed it."

Those inadequate words couldn't begin to describe how much Guy wanted to give her all the books that she hungered to read, all the knowledge that she had been denied, all the experiences that a woman of her keen intellect craved to learn. Though he knew it wasn't his place to provide a governess with an education, his desire to do so persisted nonetheless, especially after what he'd learned about her today.

Then he made the mistake of glancing up at her.

Forgetting about the shoe he was chivalrously restoring to

her foot, he found himself riveted by the way the firelight gilded her smooth skin and buttercream hair. A few curls had sprung loose to give her the enticing look of a woman who had just arisen from bed. Most captivating of all was the soft, sensual smile on her lips.

She leaned closer and glided her fingertips over his cheek, and that gossamer touch sent another dart of heat through him. "Please don't ever turn into a frog, Carlin. I like you much better as a man."

He liked her too damn much as a woman. Therein lay the problem. He needed to view her dispassionately, as just another one of his servants.

But her forward movement had offered him a better view of her bosom, and what red-blooded man could resist such a sight? The delicate filigreed chain of her necklace was like a trail of bread crumbs leading downward into the valley between her breasts. Alas, the small gold pendant enjoyed privileges that he did not have.

Resolutely, he eased the shoe onto her dainty foot. "The slipper fits, which means it's time for Cinderella to retire for the night."

"Bah, that isn't the way the story goes. I seem to recall the prince taking her into his embrace." She shimmied closer and looped her arms around his neck. "It would be most inconsiderate of him to banish her from his sight."

The warmth of her pliant body was almost too tempting to bear. Damn, he was in circumstances more treacherous than a storm at sea. The lust he felt should never be directed at a woman in his employ. Least of all one who had been used and abused for much of her life.

Still kneeling, he placed his hands firmly on her shoulders. "Tessa, I'm very flattered that you enjoy my company. But if you stay, we'll end up removing our clothing and making love."

That blunt assertion didn't deter her as he'd expected. Instead of recoiling, she regarded him with heartfelt sincerity. "I want that, Carlin. I feel such a great need for you, a craving that I've never felt for any other man."

"That's the wine talking," he said hoarsely. "You can't know what you're saying."

"Oh, but I do." With a tender touch, she framed his jaw in her hands. The eyes that gazed into his were perfectly sober and candid. "I fear that I must make a confession. I came here tonight wanting . . . hoping for more than just a kiss. For once, I wish to experience the fullness of pleasure. To bury the past by creating a perfect memory of the here and now—with you."

Those fervent words sealed his fate. And what a dazzling fate it was.

As she touched her lips to his, a white-hot desire seared him, burning his scruples to ashes. He molded her to his chest and returned her kiss with unbridled passion. Her eager response fed his own need to draw her essence into himself, to become one with her. How could he deny her when he, too, felt the fiery urge to merge their bodies?

But kissing her mouth was only a prelude to the feast. Guy wanted to taste all of her, every curve, every dimple, every hidden secret. As he blazed a trail down the uncharted territory of her throat and bosom, she arched her neck and threaded her fingers into his hair. Her quick, shallow breaths scorched him with the desire to press their bodies together, skin-to-skin.

While his tongue traced the whorls of her ear, he loosened the row of buttons down her back, his fingers clumsy with impatience. When at last it was done, and as he tugged at her gown, she assisted him by drawing her arms out of her sleeves so that her bodice slipped down to her lap.

He knelt before her like a supplicant to a goddess on her

throne. Her undergarments had no frills or lace to distract from the smooth beauty of her figure, and he skimmed his hands over the warm contours of her waist and bosom. Only then did he allow himself to untie the strings of her corset and to slide his hands inside to open the stiffened fabric.

Freed from their prison, her breasts were a fête of femininity, with dusky rose nipples and lushly full globes. In the soft luminosity of the fire, they appeared the perfect size to fit his large palms. As he tested that notion and found it to be an excellent guess, the tremor that quivered through Tessa captivated him.

Her eyelids were at half-mast, her lips parted with pleasure as she pushed her breasts deeper into his hands and undulated her body against him. His own body responded with a hot pulse of desire. Bending his head, he took one taut peak into his mouth and laved her with his tongue before affording the same loving treatment to the other until she was gasping, her fingers moving restlessly over his shoulders and back.

She lowered her hands to tug rather impatiently at the hem of his shirt. "Shouldn't you . . . may I see . . . ?"

Guy perfectly understood her disjointed speech. "As my lady wishes."

He paused only to drop another kiss on her soft lips. Then he dragged the linen shirt over his head and tossed it away without a care for where it landed. He was too intent on watching the light of interest on Tessa's face.

She glided her palms over the muscles of his bare chest. As her fingertip traced one flat nipple, he groaned at the inferno she fanned in his loins. She looked at him in naïve confusion. "Did that hurt?"

A hoarse chuckle broke from him. "It felt far too good. I'm aching for you, Tessa. Unbearably so."

Understanding dawned on her face, along with a blush

and then a wise womanly smile. She slid her hands lower and let her fingers lightly play along the waistband of his breeches. He sucked in a ragged breath. Half maiden and half coquette, she possessed a natural sensuality that drove him wild.

He leaped to his feet and drew her up as well. In between deeply arousing kisses, he stripped away her gown and undergarments until only her stockings saved her from full nudity. With a blissful sigh, she slipped her arms around him and rested her cheek against his chest, her breath warm and unsteady against his overheated skin. "Oh, Carlin, how I've longed for you."

"Guy. Say my name."

"Guy," she whispered, and turned a smile up at him.

That winsome air had the power to kindle his passions every bit as much as her naked form. He felt consumed by the desire to please her, to make this an experience she would never forget. His hands trekked along the indention of her waist and the curve of bare bottom, savoring the satiny smoothness of her skin. The pins had come loose from her hair, allowing thick waves to tumble over her shoulders and bosom, and he loved the softness of it to his touch. "What a darling you are, Tessa," he murmured, rubbing his cheek against hers. "Warm, graceful, lovelier than any other woman I've known."

She gave him a dubious look, but it was true. He had met many ladies deemed by society to be diamonds of the first water—indeed he had married one—and yet none of them could hold a candle to Tessa. Hers was a quiet beauty, lit from within by the brilliance of her spirit. In some still-functioning corner of his brain, he damned the strictures of class that separated them. If they had but this one night, this one encounter to savor, he intended to make the most of it.

He kissed her lingeringly, keeping his own fierce urges on

a tight leash. Only when she began to move restively against him did he lower her onto the chaise. He could scarcely contain the mad impulse to join their bodies. Yet he took his time untying her garters and unrolling the plain cotton stockings down her legs, his mouth tasting the bare flesh that he uncovered.

Every part of her held him enthralled, the dainty toes, the shapely legs, the nest of her womanhood. He kissed a slow path upward to suckle her breasts again until she was moaning, clutching at his back. He then glided one hand downward to lightly palm her mound. As he slipped a finger inside to find her slick and hot, she shuddered. With one swirling stroke from him, a sigh of intense yearning eddied from her.

"Ahh . . . that feels so . . ."

Her voice trailed off into mewling sounds of delight as he continued to play with her. She tilted her head back and parted her legs in honeyed invitation. Her hips moved sinuously, arching against his hand, and that untutored action strained the limits of his willpower. It took everything in him to keep from tearing off his breeches and claiming what he craved. But he would have her pleasure first, and it happened in a sudden quivering of her body, the dig of her fingers into his shoulders, and a sobbing cry of exultation.

His own ravenous hunger could wait no longer. He stripped himself naked and then lay down to cover her with his body. She regarded him with dreamy eyes and a contented smile, at least until he positioned himself to enter her. As he pushed past a slight resistance to bury himself inside her, he heard her choked whimper through a haze of exultation.

Panting, Guy reveled in her tight, hot depths even as he lamented having caused her pain. Her eyes were wide open now, and a wince firmed her lips. Devil take it, he hadn't spared a thought for her innocence. What knowledge could she have had of lovemaking with no female relatives to inform her?

Bracing his hands on either side of her tumbled curls, he reined in his urges with great effort while nuzzling her stricken features. "Forgive me, dearest. Are you all right?"

As she cautiously wiggled her hips, the bud of a smile began to bloom on her lips and the ardent fire again lit her eyes. "Yes, perfect." She pressed a lingering kiss to his jaw. "I never imagined anything so wonderful, Guy . . . we are truly one."

Truly one.

Those adoring words wrapped around his heart and intensified the scorching demands of his loins. Abandoning thought and reason to the irresistible allure of passion, he thrust into her slowly at first to ensure her pleasure. Much to his gratification, Tessa displayed an eager readiness, and her enthusiasm made his own excitement build to a fever pitch.

As she lifted her hips to receive him, he drove harder and quicker until she was gasping, begging, moaning as they moved in perfect rhythm. The delicious torture grew for timeless moments until her ecstatic cry of release hurled him to the edge. Only by a thread of awareness did he have the presence of mind to withdraw to spill his seed in hot spurts of rapture against her thigh.

The blissful pulsations waned, leaving him sprawled with Tessa in a haze of idyllic exhaustion. In unison with his, her rapid heartbeat gradually evened out along with her erratic breaths. She snuggled her cheek against his shoulder as her desultory fingers stroked over his back. He could not recall a time when he had ever felt so perfectly replete.

We are truly one.

No, they were not one, Guy knew with a pang. She had said that while in the throes of desire and must soon recall the impossibility of their situation. But he was feeling too good to spoil the moment with thoughts of tomorrow.

He raised his head slightly to give her a lazy grin. "I hope our tryst has met with Cinderella's approval," he said, brushing a spun-gold lock of hair from her cheek. "Though I fear you've fractured the story again."

"How so?"

"I very much doubt," he said, tracing her rosy lips with his finger, "that Cinderella seduced the prince. Not, of course, that I've any objection."

Her eyes sparkled like stars. "It seems to me that we seduced each other. I merely helped by shutting the door."

He chuckled. "Minx. So that artful stumble was done on purpose."

Tessa regarded him with a flirtatious tilt of her head. "Naturally. I knew that *you* wouldn't have closed it."

Guy marveled at how often she managed to surprise him. It was one of the many traits that set her apart from other women. "Allow me to express just how thrilled I am that you did." He lifted her hand to his lips and grazed a kiss across her knuckles. "Now, if you'll wait here a moment."

He disentangled himself and walked across the study to fetch a folded handkerchief from an inner pocket of his coat. On his return, Tessa reclined on her elbow while eyeing his naked form. There was a furtive quality to her scrutiny that stirred tenderness in him. For all her boldness, she could also display a natural shyness that wrapped silken threads around his heart.

Sentiment was a dangerous quagmire, he reminded himself. It was best to view this encounter as a moment out of time. An infatuation and nothing more.

Turning his mind to a more practical matter, Guy sat down beside her and gently wiped away the remnants of their union. "I took care not to spill my seed in you. So there shall be no consequences nine months from now."

Her eyes widened, and she brought her arm across her bare bosom. "I hadn't considered . . ."

"Passion has a way of overriding rational thought. I believe we both can attest to that."

He also knew that was precisely why they could not continue to meet like this. It was unfair of him to take any risks with her future. In fact, by society's standards, he should dismiss her from his employ. Yet he couldn't—wouldn't—do so. Tessa oughtn't suffer for his own breach of conduct. And losing her was not something he wished even to contemplate.

As he leaned forward to lift her arm from her beautiful bosom, Guy's attention was caught by a glint of gold. Her necklace had fallen to one side and hung suspended over the curve of one breast. From his present perspective, the firelight perfectly illuminated the tiny coat of arms.

Suddenly jarred, he picked up the pendant to examine the engraving more closely. "I forgot all about this. But I believe I saw this insignia tonight."

Tessa came alert. "Are you sure?"

"There's one way to find out."

He stepped into his breeches and hastened to the desk, where he sat down and began to page through the thick heraldry book.

Tessa came hurrying to his side. It did not escape his notice that she had drawn on her gown without bothering with undergarments. Nor could he be unaware of her tantalizing scent and tempting closeness. But his keen interest in her must be set aside until he'd untangled this mystery.

He focused his attention on the book. "What is unique about your pendant is the griffins. At first glance the other day, I mistook them for dragons. Because of the wings, you see."

"The wings?"

"In heraldry, the English usually portray the griffin with the wings closed. But on yours, the wings are open." He glanced up at her. "Would you mind very much to remove the pendant so that I might see it better?"

Tessa drew the necklace over her head and placed it on mahogany surface of the desk, where it lay bathed in the glow of the candelabrum.

In short order, he found the proper page and used the magnifying glass to compare the sketch to the pendant. "Yes, by God, these are one and the same. There are the winged griffins on either side, the crossed swords, the coronet at the top, and at the bottom, the motto, VIRTUS."

"Whose is it?" Tessa asked, leaning over in an attempt to view the fine print.

Guy stared down at the family name. He found it highly unlikely that this elderly lord could be Tessa's father. Surely the fellow was too much the stuffy Puritan to have sired a child out of wedlock. Perhaps the pendant had come into her mother's hands by some other means.

He lifted his troubled gaze to Tessa. "The coat of arms belongs to one of my grandfather's old political cronies. The Marquess of Marbury."

"The Marquess of Marbury," she repeated in a reverent tone. A stunned smile on her lips, she fell into the chair on the other side of the desk. "Oh, Guy. I can scarcely believe it. You've found my father."

He hardly knew how to reply. Tessa had looked forward to this discovery for a long time. It was the very reason she'd taken the post of governess in his house. Yet he couldn't bear to think of her being sorely disappointed.

He reached across the desk to enfold her dainty hand, rubbing his thumb across the back. "Tessa, you can count on my help in this matter, but I also must warn you. Marbury is the very definition of a curmudgeon. He's an elderly recluse who may deny ever knowing your mother."

"He can't deny it. Not when I have the pendant as proof."

"Then he may accuse her—or even you—of stealing it. And even if you do convince him, he's tight-fisted. He's not likely to be willing to fork over funds for your millinery shop."

A martial light lit her eyes. "We'll see about that."

Despite her confidence, Guy couldn't shake the worry that Marbury would reject Tessa as his bastard daughter. By God, he must do everything in his power to keep the marquess from breaking her heart.

Chapter 15

The following morning, after placating Sophy with a promise to read her an extra story upon her return, Tessa made her escape from the nursery. Carlin's note had given her little time to prepare. Fearing to be late, she raced down the servants' staircase and arrived at the entrance hall to see him approaching from the opposite corridor with his secretary.

The duke afforded her a distracted nod. "Have those papers ready for my signature upon my return."

"Of course, Your Grace." Mr. Banfield took one glance at Tessa's shawl and bonnet, and his gray eyes sharpened. "Miss James is to go out with you?"

"Yes."

"Might I inquire as to your destination?"

"No, you may not."

As Carlin turned to accept his curled beaver hat and tan gloves from Roebuck, Tessa was thankful that he'd dismissed secretary's intrusive question. She was acutely aware of the butler's slight elevation of one starchy eyebrow, and Mr. Banfield's more obvious disapproval. Clearly, it was unfitting for a duke to set forth with his daughter's governess.

Though neither man could know about that tryst the previous evening, nor about Lord Marbury being her father, the situation still made her quake when she was nervous enough already about meeting the marquess.

As Carlin escorted her down the front steps and handed her into the waiting carriage, she could not even enjoy the rare treat of riding in a fine vehicle with crimson brocaded upholstery, squabs as soft as clouds, and gold-tasseled blinds drawn back from sparkling windows. She gripped her gloved fingers in her lap and drew several deep breaths in an effort to calm her thrumming heartbeat. But it was no use. She still felt anxious and uneasy, her future in a turmoil.

And the duke wasn't helping matters.

He had taken the seat opposite hers when she would have liked to have him beside her, holding her hand to lend her courage. That was an impossible wish, of course. Their romantic liaison could not continue. Though a short drive through Mayfair was hardly the time to discuss it, she suspected that Carlin shared that view, judging by his detached manner today.

This morning, he was once again the granite-faced duke. Elegant in a slate-blue coat and fawn breeches, a snowy white cravat at his throat, he sat frowning out the window at the passing houses. One would never guess that his fine clothing concealed a tender lover who had whispered such marvelous things to her, who had taken her to heights of glory.

The previous evening, they had parted ways after a lingering kiss. She had been in such an agitated state over identifying her sire that it hadn't occurred to her until later, lying in bed and remembering that wonderful joining, that he had never said a word about prolonging their affair.

And why should he? Carlin had striven to avoid the entanglement from the start. She was one who had pursued him. She was the one who had abandoned all restraint. Even now,

Tessa felt a desperate longing to hurl herself across the carriage and into his arms. Only the impossibility of the circumstances kept her anchored in place.

She had entered into the assignation with her eyes wide open, knowing that he could never wed a baseborn commoner who had been raised in a workhouse. A woman who was not even qualified to be governess to his daughter. As for all their whimsical banter about Cinderella, well, that had been merely a product of wine, firelight, desire . . . and Guy.

Never again must she address him so familiarly. In the throes of lovemaking they had been equals, two people drawn together to fulfill a mutual passion. But in the cold light of day she knew it was best to accept reality.

You are a duke, and I am a governess. And it is no use pretending otherwise.

Her soft sigh was lost to the rattle of the carriage wheels. Tessa rallied herself with the reminder that she would soon regain her spirits. Once she persuaded Lord Marbury to give her the funding, she finally would have the means to set up her shop and fulfill her dream of becoming the premier milliner in London. There was no reason at all to feel low.

It was just that things had happened so fast. She hadn't had time to absorb all the changes in her life. And now she was hurtling headlong into another change without having fully settled the last one.

For that reason, it would be best to reestablish her former footing with the duke. "I owe you an apology, Carlin."

His gaze swung to hers. "Why?"

"I'm keeping you from searching for the stolen diaries. Truly, I could have visited my father on my own."

"I've hired a Runner to assist me in the investigation, so there's no time lost. As for this meeting . . ." He shook his head. "I would never leave you to face Marbury alone."

The keenness of his stare, the firmness of his tone, caused

a treacherous warming in her bosom. "Surely you can't think I'll need protection from him."

"My presence will ensure that you're allowed through the front door. Marbury is a crotchety old fellow who doesn't care much for visitors. Luckily, in response to my note, he has agreed to receive me." Carlin smiled slightly. "Of course, I mentioned nothing about bringing his long-lost daughter."

She summoned a small smile of her own. "Thank you for not warning him. If he were prepared, it would have been too easy for him to hide the truth." Tessa paused. "If I may add, I would greatly appreciate you allowing me to do the talking. This is my concern, after all, not yours."

"As you wish." He paused, eyeing her. "Have you considered what you'll do if Marbury doubts your story about the pendant? After all, you were only a little girl when your mother died. He could say that your memory is playing tricks."

That dreadful scene unfolded in Tessa's mind as if it had just happened. The speeding carriage. Mama falling onto the cobblestones. The blood pooling beneath her head. "My memory is clear as crystal. She placed the necklace around my neck and said, *Hide this . . . find him . . . father.* And . . . *pain.* That was the last word she ever uttered."

Tessa swallowed. It was hard to reflect on the agony her mother must have suffered. But she wanted Carlin to understand why this was so very important to her.

"Pain?" he repeated in an odd tone.

"Of course. She was struck down and . . . and she'd hit her head."

His harsh expression eased slightly, though he still gazed intently at her. After a moment's silence, he said, "I don't mean to upset you, Tessa. It's just that I'm acquainted a little with Marbury since he was a friend of my grandfather's. I must warn you, I find it difficult to view him as a man who carries on with chambermaids."

"It would have occurred some twenty-three years ago, when he was younger." Tilting her head, Tessa dared to add, "And I should think any man could be tempted into an indiscretion."

At that, Carlin's veil of reserve vanished. His coal-dark eyes lit with a scorching gleam, a look that turned her insides to molten lava. Though he wasn't touching her, he might as well have been, so swiftly did her blood race.

"A fair point," he said silkily. "We shall have to wait and see, then."

Tessa had the distinct impression Carlin was referring to more than this meeting, that he wished to revisit their intimate relationship. The raw erotic hunger that emanated from him seemed to fill the confines of the carriage. She could feel it in the air, wrapping around her like an embrace. Her breasts tightened, heat suffused her limbs, and passion pulsed in her depths. Since she'd already concluded the affair was at an end, this latest development threw her off kilter.

What did he want out of this? What did *she* want?

Before Tessa could answer those questions, the carriage came to a halt and a footman opened the door, offering his gloved hand to help her alight. In something of a daze, she found herself standing in front of a brick town house in the damp autumn chill. The familiar coat of arms etched into the triangular pediment above the entry brought her crashing back to reality.

She was about to meet her father.

Her skin prickled from a shiver. Carlin appeared at her side and tucked her fingers in the crook of his arm. "Chin up, Cinderella," he murmured. "You have more pluck than any woman I know."

"Then why does my spine have all the substance of a cream bun?"

"Even the brave feel fear. Courage is taking necessary action in spite of that fear."

As he escorted her into the house, she raised her chin and found that it did indeed bolster her confidence. The entrance hall featured a curved staircase that was lit by a domed skylight. Despite the elegant architecture, the decor had a tired look and the pistachio-green wallpaper had seen better days.

A footman accepted Carlin's hat and gloves. Tessa kept her shawl and the chip-straw bonnet with the blue ribbons that went well with her best gown, the same one she'd worn to the rendezvous with Carlin. A stylish hat of her own design was a fitting reminder of her purpose here.

The footman slid a glance at Tessa. "Might I inquire as to the lady's name, Your Grace?"

"No," Carlin said. "Pray inform Lord Marbury that I'm here."

The fellow trotted away and returned a moment later to lead them down a corridor and through a doorway. They entered a library, smaller than the one at Carlin House, but comfortable with stuffed leather chairs and a desk at the far end. Most impressive of all were the many books. They filled every nook and cranny and were crammed on shelves, stacked on tables, and piled here and there on the worn Oriental carpet.

Beside a hissing fire sat a white-haired man who was employing a silver-knobbed cane to lever himself out of his seat. Carlin sprang forward to offer assistance and was soundly rejected.

"I'm no invalid," Lord Marbury grumbled. "It's this demmed rheumatism, always acts up when the weather turns chill."

He achieved his feet and held himself so proudly that Tessa

didn't notice for a moment that he was no more than an inch or two taller than herself. Lines of age carved his face into a majestic visage that brought to mind a sketch she'd once seen of Moses parting the Red Sea.

She felt numb rather than angry or resentful. So this was the Marquess of Marbury. The man who had abandoned Mama. The man who had rejected his bastard daughter and left them to live in poverty.

Carlin's stride having carried him a few steps ahead of her, he bowed to the marquess. "It's an honor to see you again, sir. I hope you are otherwise well."

"Never mind all that nonsense," Lord Marbury snapped as he looked the duke up and down. "Well, well. So you are Carlin now. You're the spit of your grandfather in his younger days. I hope it isn't just skin-deep and you can adequately fill his shoes. You were a great disappointment to him, you know, when you sailed away from England on a whim."

Even with Carlin's back to her, Tessa sensed his stiffness. A tide of antipathy swept away her stupor as she stepped to his side and made an obligatory curtsy to Lord Marbury. "It was no whim, milord. His Grace was conducting important research and making scientific discoveries. And he intends to write a book about his travels, too."

Carlin fixed her with a warning frown. "We'll discuss this later."

"Tell that to Lord Marbury, not me."

Tessa braced herself for a lecture from the old sourpuss and belatedly realized that contentiousness was no way to butter him up for a loan. He'd likely toss her out on her ear as he'd done her mother.

But to her surprise, Lord Marbury didn't appear irked. Rather, his mouth hung open and his wrinkled face had turned as white as bleached linen. He wore a peculiar expression that seemed to be equal parts shock, disbelief, and, strangely, joy.

In a strangled voice, he uttered, "Flossie . . . ? *Flossie?*"

Leaning heavily on his cane, the marquess attempted to step toward her but swayed on his feet. Carlin hastened to guide him back into his chair. Then the duke poured a measure of brandy into a glass and held it to the man's pale lips. It was a testament to Lord Marbury's weakened state that he didn't fuss, but meekly swallowed the liquor.

Tessa ventured closer. He had clearly mistaken her for her mother, she realized, and it had given him a nasty start. Her anger evaporated, leaving remorse in its place, for she could not wish to be the cause of him suffering a heart spasm. "I beg your pardon. Are you all right, milord?"

He looked up at Tessa, then passed a gnarled hand over his face. "You're not Flossie. Don't know what I was thinking. Your hair's too light. Couldn't see it for that demmed bonnet. And she'd be older now, past forty."

"Flossie, was that what you called her?" Tessa asked, hoping to coax the story out of him. "I daresay you thought Florence too grand a name for a maidservant."

"Maidservant? What the deuce are you babbling about?" Recovering a measure of vinegar, he shook his cane at her. "Who are you to malign Lady Florence in so vile a manner and under her own roof?"

She blinked in confusion. "*Lady* Florence? Lady Florence James?"

"Payne," he corrected impatiently. "Lady Florence *Payne*. That is my family name."

"Oh! But-but how can that be? I know her surname to have been James." Utterly confused, she looked at Carlin. "It *is* the same coat of arms."

"Indeed," he said slowly, glancing from her to the marquess. "I believe what Lord Marbury is saying is that Lady Florence was his daughter."

"You!" Lord Marbury turned a bitter scowl on Carlin. "What is your role in this piece of treachery? Did you unearth that ancient scandal and devise a trick to play on an old man by presenting an imposter as my daughter? I would never have thought Carlin's grandson could be so cruel."

"Rather than cruel, sir, I hope you will find this a blessing," he said. "If I may introduce you to your granddaughter, Miss Tessa James."

Tessa had been standing with her feet rooted to the floor as she struggled to absorb this new revelation. But now her legs weakened, and she sank down before Lord Marbury's chair to gaze earnestly at him. He looked as stunned as she felt. Her grandfather! That truth whirled in her mind. She'd been wrong all these years. Mama had been referring to *her* father, not to Tessa's.

"It can't be," he muttered brokenly. "This is some ploy."

"No, it isn't," she said in a strained voice. "Florence was my mother. Lady Florence, it would seem, though she never breathed a word of that. Look, I have her pendant."

Opening her shawl, Tessa lifted the dainty gold necklace and held it out to Lord Marbury. The acrimony faded from his features as he took it into his trembling hands and ran a knobby finger over the engraving. "I gave this to Flossie on her eighteenth birthday. 'Twas shortly before she ran away. I never saw her again. How did you come by this?"

The quaver in his voice touched her heart, and she realized he didn't even know his daughter was long dead. Kneeling before him, she gave an abbreviated account of what little she could recall of her early life, including her mother's death and glossing over her days in the foundling home. "I worked in a millinery shop for a time, then took a post as governess to His Grace's daughter. Carlin is the one who identified the coat of arms on the pendant."

"Then who was your papa?" Lord Marbury asked.

"I-I don't know. I thought you were, milord. You see, when she gave me the pendant, her last words were, *Hide this . . . find him . . . father . . .*"

"And *pain*," the duke added. "She was telling you her family name was P-a-y-n-e, though given the circumstances, it's understandable why you would misinterpret it."

"Lud, Carlin, you're right!" Thunderstruck, she glanced up at him, then returned her gaze to her grandfather. "Then where did James come from?"

"James is my given name," Lord Marbury said, his gaze absorbing her features as if to make up for all the lost years. "Perhaps that is why Flossie chose it. And if she was living under an alias, it explains why I was never able to find her."

"But . . . why did Mama run away? Why would she turn her back on a lady's life to become a maidservant?"

"I fear 'twas entirely my fault," the marquess admitted. He glanced into the fire, the flames lighting his stark features. "As a girl, Flossie always had a wayward streak. Her mama had died young and I left her at my country seat in the care of servants. She grew up charming and lovely, but she was also saucy and strong-willed. Rather than allow her a London season where I feared she might embroil herself in scandal, I deemed it best for her to have a solid, dependable husband in the hope that bearing children might settle her down. But the marriage I arranged to Bucklesby wasn't to her liking."

"The Earl of Bucklesby?" Carlin asked, one eyebrow cocked. "He must have been thirty years her senior—and as dull a dog as they come."

"Forty is a perfectly respectable age for a nobleman to wed, as I myself did." Then Marbury's brusqueness dissolved into a look of wretched remorse. "Ah, but Flossie would have nothing of him. And though she begged and pleaded, I was foolish enough to be adamant. On the morning of her wedding, she went missing. Her bed hadn't been slept in. I searched for years, but she'd vanished from the face of the earth. Had I heeded her wishes, found a man more to her liking, I would never have lost her."

The fire whispered into the silence. Tessa imagined her mother as a spirited young lady, pressured to wed a man old enough to be her father. Poor Mama! She must have been truly horrified by the match to prefer servitude over it. And once she'd borne a child out of wedlock, it would have been impossible for her to return home.

Lord Marbury's bony hand sought Tessa's. "But now you have come to me in my old age. My granddaughter. I never envisioned such a miracle."

The misty look in his eyes touched her deeply. Never had she imagined having a grandfather. "It's truly a marvelous dream," Tessa murmured.

He studied her closely for another moment; then he gained his feet with the help of the cane. "Come, there is something you must see."

He led them slowly up two flights of stairs and into a dim bedchamber. Carlin strode to the window and opened the blinds. Sunlight bathed the room in brightness, and Tessa could see feminine touches in the rose print wallpaper and the daintiness of the furniture that was shrouded in cloth.

"This was Flossie's room," Lord Marbury said, touching a set of mother-of-pearl brushes on a dressing table. "I left everything exactly as it was."

In case she ever returned. Those words hovered unspoken in the stale air of a room kept closed for over two decades. Tessa's breast ached to envisage her mother living here, a girl full of hopes and dreams.

And then suddenly, there she was.

"Mama," Tessa breathed as she made haste to the painting that hung above the marble mantel. It was the portrait of a slender young lady with toffee-brown hair, standing at a window, smiling dreamily out at a green vista. She wore a gauzy white gown with the dainty gold pendant at her throat.

"I can see why you mistook Tessa for her," Carlin told the marquess.

Stepping protectively to her side, Lord Marbury gave him a sharp look. "You address your governess in familiar terms, Duke."

"There *is* something of a question as to how she ought to be addressed," Carlin said adroitly. "Shall I call her Miss James? Or Miss Payne?"

"Miss Payne, of course," Lord Marbury said, easily distracted by such a pertinent issue. "My granddaughter is a rightful member of this family. And as such, she can no longer be employed by you. It would be proper for her to remove from your house and to live here instead."

Startled, Tessa spun around. "I beg your pardon?"

"You heard me. You are Lady Florence's daughter. I have no other living children, so you are all I have left to continue the line."

"But . . . I'm bastard-born. I don't even know the name of my father."

"Bah. We shall concoct a story to explain your absence from England all these years. Perhaps Flossie ran off to Italy, where she wed an Englishman by the last name of James." Devising his plans, he limped around the bedchamber, the tip of his cane thumping on the carpet. "Ah, then you must remain Miss James, after all."

"I don't speak Italian!"

His age-spotted hand waved away the argument. "Then let us say Canada. All that matters is that it be a distant locale, somewhere not easily disproven. People may whisper, but no one will dare to question my word that you are my long-lost granddaughter."

"I should rather you would lend me the funds to open a millenary shop."

"My granddaughter in trade? Never! No, you shall join me in this house and prepare to take your rightful place in society."

His obstinate face made Tessa's heart sink. Lud! Her entire life had been turned topsy-turvy. She had come here with the simple hope of securing the means to design elegant hats for ladies—not to be taken into a noble family and expected to *be* one of those ladies.

"I couldn't possibly live here, milord. We're strangers to each other. And there's Lady Sophy—His Grace's daughter—to consider. I can't simply abandon the child."

Lord Marbury parted his lips to argue, but Carlin spoke first. "This has all been very distressing for Miss James. It would be most kind of you to allow her a few days in which to accustom herself to the news."

The marquess wasn't happy, but in the end he agreed. He needed time, anyway, to prepare the house, to hire additional staff, to write to a spinster cousin and command her to London at once to act as his granddaughter's chaperone. He seemed brighter and livelier, as if he'd gained new life from the news. He was still scheming as they departed his house.

In something of a stupor, Tessa entered the carriage and sat down. So many thoughts were darting around in her head that she hardly knew how to focus on any one of them. She had a blood relative; no longer was she alone in the world. And if her grandfather enjoyed books, as his overstuffed library would indicate, she thought he might be an interesting conversationalist.

Yet to enter the ton, to hobnob with the swells! She, who

had never attended a single society event except Carlin's lecture, would be expected to know how to waltz, to play cards, to ride horses, to chitchat with nobles, and a thousand other highbrow skills. The very notion threw her into a panic.

"Well," the duke said coolly, "I cannot say that I've ever seen Marbury so animated about anything. He was always a dour fellow, and it's good that he took the news of a long-lost granddaughter so well."

"Good?" Tessa burst out. "No, Carlin. I cannot do this. I can't move into his house and pretend I'm one of the Quality. I don't wish it."

He gave an incredulous laugh. "Not wish it? Tessa, you've acquired a very wealthy and powerful family connection. If Marbury wants to acknowledge you publicly, I'd strongly advise you to take his offer."

"But I scarcely know the man. And the life he expects me to lead is not at all what I had planned for myself. You know that."

"Becoming a shop owner can hardly compare to becoming a lady. Of course you must give it all up. It will be an adjustment, but in time you'll see the value in accepting your heritage."

She goggled at Carlin, who seemed utterly oblivious to her concerns. How could she have ever thought him a fair man, one who would listen to her? And why were his eyes narrowed on her, as if he, too, were scheming? His frown suggested that he disliked the situation, yet he was still urging her to accept it.

"How dare you presume to dictate what I must give up," she said heatedly. "I'm accustomed to labor, not luxury. Even my childhood years were spent at hard work. I may have noble blood, but I certainly didn't grow up in a mansion staffed with servants. I know nothing of music and dancing and all the other accomplishments of a lady."

"You can sew, you can draw, and you have a natural grace of manner. Any other skills can be acquired from tutors." Looking every inch the high-and-mighty duke, he sat unsmiling as the carriage transported them over the cobblestoned streets. "It would be wise to put our minds to creating a foolproof background to explain where you've been all these years. Something you could feel comfortable in adopting as your own."

Tessa stiffened. His alignment with Marbury's plan felt like a betrayal. "So after denouncing me for lying about my past, now, when it suits your purposes, you wish me to lie about my past again. Some would call that hypocrisy."

He firmed his lips. "I should rather call it pragmatism."

She fumed in silence for a moment before trusting herself to speak. "What matter is any of this to you, anyway? It is my life, not yours. I don't see why you should have any dealings with it at all." She paused in frustration, wondering at his coolness of manner and comparing it with the lustful heat she'd sensed in him earlier. "Perhaps you wish to remove temptation from your sight because you'd intended to set me up as your mistress—and now you daren't do so. Well, allow me to enlighten you, Your Grace, I would never have agreed to any such arrangement. One night was all I ever wanted."

That was not quite true, she admitted to herself. Even now, she longed to be clasped in his arms with his lips upon hers. But she would never, ever admit that aloud.

To her consternation, Carlin gave an odd laugh and shook his head. He studied her for a moment before uttering in a rough tone quite unlike himself, "Then you will be pleased to know how wrong you are. I trust you will do me the honor of accepting my hand in marriage?"

Tessa felt instantly robbed of her wits. Of all the things he could have said! But he could not mean those words. He must have flung them out in a pique over her rejection of his lovemaking. Dukes didn't marry governesses. They chose well-bred ladies like Annabelle the Angel. As verification of that truth, Tessa could detect no light of affection in his eyes, no tenderness in his hard features, no ardent air of the lover.

Her breast heaving, she leaned forward, her gloved fingers fisted in her lap. "Spare me your mockery, sir. It is beneath you."

One eyebrow lifted. "Mockery? Hardly. We've no choice in the matter." Then, instead of extolling her beauty or declaring his undying love or even kissing her hand, he made an even worse blunder. "You must see that marriage is required after our tryst last night. As Marbury's acknowledged granddaughter, you are a lady now. And having ruined you, I owe you the protection of my name."

His terse explanation only made her spirits sink lower. Well, at least that explained the chill in his manner. This proposal didn't spring from any tender longing of his heart. "So you feel forced into offering for me. Never fear, your sacrifice isn't necessary. I should rather be a shop owner than a duchess."

He stared at her a moment; then his features softened as he leaned forward to grasp her hand. "Forgive me, Tessa. That was poorly done. I meant no offense. It's just that . . . I never thought to marry again. This has come as a shock to me as well as to you."

The remorseful sincerity in his eyes tempted her. She could even understand that his plans for his life had been thrown into disarray as much as hers.

But though her imprudent heart yearned for him, it was bitterly obvious that Carlin was acting out of gentlemanly duty because of her blue blood. If he felt any true fondness, he'd have proposed the previous night when she had been a common nobody. Now everything in her rebelled at entering into a loveless marriage to a man whose affections must still belong to his late wife. A man who felt obliged to offer matrimony. A man whose high rank would prevent her from fulfilling her life's dream.

As the carriage rolled to a halt in front of Carlin House, she pulled her hand from his. "*You* may have no choice, Your Grace, but *I* am a free woman. And my answer is no. I will not marry you. Not now or ever."

Chapter 16

Guy spent the next several days dismally aware of how badly he'd bungled his marriage proposal to Tessa. He had plenty of time to reflect during his fruitless hunt for the stolen diaries. His days were spent checking in at Bow Street, following up on leads, and questioning the highbrow attendees at the lecture who required more delicate handling than could be expected of a rough-mannered Runner. His mind wasn't entirely on that mystery, though, because all too often he would think back on that clumsy offer.

From the moment he'd confirmed her connection to Marbury and had seen that the marquess intended to bring her out in society, Guy had faced the inevitability of the marriage. Admittedly, he had been angry, not at Tessa but rather at the circumstances. He had vowed never to wed again. Like her, he'd had his life arranged, and a wife did not figure into it.

Nevertheless, he oughtn't have blurted out the proposal like that—in a carriage, by God!—when she'd already been in a state of distress over the encounter with her grandfather. He should have had the brains and the courtesy to choose a more appropriate time and setting. Tessa of all women deserved the trappings of romance, the flowers, the diamond ring, and the suitor down on one knee to plead for her hand.

Instead, his wits had deserted him. He had behaved like a clodpate, citing her newfound status as his rationale for the union. He had presented the offer with all the charm of a business deal, and in fact had given her little choice but to agree to it. Worse, he'd been arrogantly certain she'd welcome the solution, as it meant she could share his bed, would become Sophy's mama, and needn't reside with her grandfather except for the short period of the betrothal. Not, of course, that he had even bothered to voice any of those advantages.

No wonder she'd thrown his words back into his face. It had not been an offer, it had been a decree. And her refusal had left him dumbfounded and dissatisfied when he ought to have been celebrating his escape from the shackles of wedlock.

The devil of it was, he had warmed to the notion of having Tessa as his wife. He enjoyed her company, her lively curiosity, her witty conversation. He would relish the pleasure of providing a few siblings for Sophy, too. And given Tessa's disgust of society, she wouldn't force him to squire her to endless balls and parties as a well-born lady would do. In fact, he suspected she'd far prefer to sit in the library of an evening, curled up beside him, absorbed in reading a book, at least until he leaned over and kissed her . . .

Yes, they were compatible in many ways, and he'd been a fool not to have recognized that from the start. He fully intended to revisit that botched proposal, once she'd had a few days in which to cool down.

In the meantime, he had attempted to restore himself to her good graces. He had sent her books from the library, especially chosen to entice her interest. He had ordered cream buns delivered to the nursery each day because he knew she

liked them. He had invited Sophy to the conservatory for another look at the parrots, in the hope that Tessa would come,
too, though it had been the nursemaid, Winnie, who had escorted his daughter.

Today, however, he had decided to take more direct action. By shamelessly exploiting the occasion of Sophy's fifth
birthday, he intended to tempt Tessa out of her self-imposed
exile.

Directly after that botched offer four days ago, he'd had
the foresight to ask Banfield to procure ringside tickets to Astley's Amphitheatre and had shelled out an exorbitant fee for
an entire private box, which normally would have seated a
dozen or so people. Then this morning, he had dispatched a
note to the nursery, asking Miss James to accompany him
and his daughter to the afternoon's performance.

Alas, the passage of time appeared not to have softened
her.

During the carriage ride, Tessa paid him little heed. She
encouraged Sophy to engage him in a game of seeing who
could spot more dogs on the street. Guy enjoyed the interac-
tion with his daughter, although Tessa resisted his every effort
to coax her to participate. All cool courtesy, she was back to
hiding her beauty with high-necked, long-sleeved gowns,
this one a charcoal gray. She also wore a matching gray bonnet with a discreet cream bow that somehow looked stylish
despite her obvious effort to fade into the background.

Guy suspected it was her way of showing disdain for the
rank of duchess that he had so ineptly presented to her. She
took pride in being a member of the working class. And that
put him at a distinct disadvantage. While other ladies viewed
the acquiring of a title as a prized asset, Tessa spurned it as a
hindrance. She scorned the trappings of status, and his misbegotten proposal had failed to take her views into account.

For that, he bore her cold shoulder as his rightful penance.

He hoped this outing would help make amends and restore their camaraderie. Without any rapport between them, his wooing of her was doomed to failure.

As he ushered them into their box on the lowest tier, Tessa placed Sophy in between them. Despite it being October, when London was thinner of company than in the spring season, most of the seats were filled. There were benches for the masses while a finer circle filled the more expensive boxes. He spied a few familiar faces, members of the ton who were here with their families, and he thought it best not to catch their eye. If they were to visit this box, he had no confidence they might not snub Tessa and turn her even more against joining their ranks.

They were situated just above the circular shallow pit and could not have had a more perfect view. Laughter and chatter enlivened the air, along with the scent of sawdust and the discordant sounds of an orchestra tuning its instruments. At one end of the ring stretched a large stage where roustabouts were preparing scenery backdrops for one of the events.

Sophy bounced up from the seat and hung her elbows over the low ledge, her lacy petticoats visible beneath a lemon-yellow gown. "Look, Miss James! That man is throwing three balls in the air all at once."

A juggler and a few other performers were warming up the crowd before the start of the main show. Her eyes alight with interest, Tessa appeared as excited as Sophy, and Guy suspected this was her first time at any such venue.

"I'm sure *I* would drop them," she said. "Oh, my, now he's added two more balls. And do you see those acrobats doing cartwheels?"

"There's a clown, too," Sophy said, "riding in a wagon pulled by a dog."

Listening to his daughter's happy giggles, Guy smiled. As much as he hoped to win Tessa, he also had a strong wish to please Sophy. She had expressed a longing to visit the circus, and although this entertainment would be largely equestrian, it was as close to a circus as anything in London.

The show commenced to great fanfare and the roar of the crowd. They were treated to a series of performances, trick riders doing handstands and other amazing feats on the backs of cantering horses, then a quartet of mares dancing the minuet in perfect time to the music, and next, fencers on horseback, the clash of steel blades ringing out with the trample of hooves.

Sophy cheered and clapped. She and Tessa looked especially awed as the show switched to the stage, where tightrope walkers nimbly performed stunts high above the ground. Women in fancy skirts danced with elegant gents on the high wire, bowing and dipping and twirling.

When one couple teetered, having to catch their balance, Sophy scrambled onto his lap, much to his surprise, and hid her face against his coat. "Ooh, Papa, they're going to *fall!*"

His heart melted as she wrapped her small arms around his waist. In wonder, he held his daughter close, acutely aware that this was the first time she'd ever shown any true sign of trusting him. How he longed for her to turn to him for comfort—always.

"Never fear," he said soothingly, "they've practiced for hours and hours. And I daresay the rope is much sturdier than it appears to us from a distance."

Sophy considered that for a moment and then peeked back at the stage to watch with restored confidence.

Stroking her silken dark hair, already untidy, he glanced over to see Tessa observing them. A soft smile curved her lips. As their eyes met, the smile lessened somewhat, though it didn't quite disappear, either. What did vanish was the crowd, the whistles, the applause, and the show itself until it was just the three of them, joined together as a family.

The allure of her held him spellbound. His brain addled, Guy knew he ought to say something to advance his suit, yet no words rose handily to his tongue. Her gaze sparkled, her cheeks were flushed, and he hoped it was as much for him as the entertainment. No other woman had ever tied him into such knots. He had the unsettling thought that this fascination he had for her might surpass mere infatuation.

The crash of cymbals shattered the moment, and she returned her attention to the stage. As the tightrope walkers shinnied down the ropes to a wild ovation from the crowd, Guy took a deep, restorative breath. Tessa wasn't entirely indifferent to him, that much was certain. No doubt she was still miffed with him, yet there had been a glow in her eyes, too.

"Look, clowns!" Sophy exclaimed.

She slid off his lap and went to the wooden ledge, leaning on it to get a better view of the riders that came trotting into the ring. They were garbed as jesters with masked faces and garishly striped clothing, and the full-grown men looked ridiculous mounted on little ponies.

Taking advantage of their momentary privacy, Guy edged closer to Tessa and murmured for her ears alone, "I've you to thank for taming the feral kitten. How, pray tell, did you achieve this miraculous change?"

"By citing your better qualities these past few days. It *is* what you hired me to do, after all."

A cool veil had come over her face, so he attempted a jest. "In light of that clumsy offer, I'm pleased you could find something good to say about me."

"I would never let our quarrel stand in the way of Sophy's happiness. Like any child, she deserves to know that her papa loves her. Now do let us enjoy the show."

As she returned her gaze to the arena, Guy was stymied by her abrupt end to the conversation. How was he ever to win her if she wouldn't speak to him? Then he reminded himself that now was hardly the time or the place to woo Tessa. He'd already made that mistake with his misbegotten proposal.

Stifling his frustration, he watched the performance and found himself enjoying it. He chuckled along with everyone else as the pony-mounted jesters engaged in a chaotic battle, riding in circles and shooting at each other with toy pistols. To make the spectacle more real, there were occasional flashes of gunpowder that elicited shrieks of thrilled alarm from the audience.

Years ago as a young man, newly wed to a lady who preferred ballrooms to circuses, he would never have attended such a silly display. But seeing it with Tessa and Sophy changed all that. It transported him back to his childhood when he'd come here with his grandmother, who'd had the same fun-loving spirit as Tessa.

Just then, he noticed that Sophy was leaning too far over the ledge for his comfort. He bent forward with the intention of drawing her back to safety. At the very moment he moved, a sharp jolt struck his upper arm.

Knocked off balance, he bumped into Tessa and nearly jarred her from her seat. An instant later, a starburst of hot pain permeated his shoulder.

Glancing down, he saw a neat hole in his blue sleeve that was rapidly turning dark with blood. Good God, he'd been shot!

Tessa gave him a startled look. "What—?"

He seized hold of her and Sophy and thrust them to the floor. Sophy cried out in protest while Tessa protectively put her arms around the little girl.

"Stay down," Guy urged. "Don't move."

Keeping one hand on their crouched forms, he sat up to take a quick glance around the arena. He fought off an en-

croaching wooziness and made himself concentrate. The
show was in full swing with the jesters racing their ponies
hither and yon and pretend-shooting each other. With all the
tumult of the mock battle, the audience continued to cheer
without having noticed that one of the shots had been genuine.

But Guy noticed. His arm stung like the very devil. He
pressed a folded handkerchief to the wound to stanch the
blood saturating his sleeve. All the while, he scanned the pit
and the spectators, seeking the gunman.

The jesters were using fake weapons ingeniously rigged
to appear to fire multiple times. Had one of them picked up
a real gun by mistake? If it had happened once, it could happen again.

He stood up, intending to shout out to stop the show. A
split second later, he saw one pony cut away from the others
and trot toward the exit. The rider seemed hell-bent on escape.

That had to be the culprit. He must have realized what he'd
done. Damn the blighter to hell! He could have killed Sophy
or Tessa.

A rush of rage infused Guy. The intensity of his need to
catch the shooter drowned out all pain. He bounded up onto
the low ledge, gauged the distance down to the sawdust pit,
and braced himself to jump.

Chapter 17

Tessa looked up in bewilderment. She couldn't fathom what could have induced Carlin to thrust them onto the floor, and had been too busy soothing Sophy to ask, but when he leaped onto the ledge and then sprang out of sight, there was no way she was going to obey his order to stay down.

She lifted her head to peer over the wooden barrier. He'd landed in a crouch and now he took off running, keeping to the outer edge of the ring.

What in the world—?

A roustabout dashed forward to intercept the duke. So did one of the riders, who turned his pony into Carlin's path and forced him to dodge. Viewing the chase as part of the spectacle, the throng thundered its approval.

Sophy tugged on Tessa's skirt. "I want to watch! Why can't I see?"

"Shh, dearie. It's only for a moment."

As she glanced down at the girl, Tessa spotted a blood-soaked square of cloth lying on the bench. Her eyes rounded in horror. That was Carlin's handkerchief; she'd seen him draw it out and clap it to his shoulder. Quickly she pushed it out of sight so that Sophy wouldn't notice.

All of a sudden, everything made terrible sense. Carlin had been shot! That must have been when he'd fallen against her. Now she could only guess he'd seen the shooter and had gone after him.

Her heart pounding, she looked out again to see that the duke was arguing with the roustabout, gesturing at his arm, and trying to get past him. Then the big bruiser bobbed his head, and they both took off running toward a small open gate in the ring.

Meanwhile, the performers had gotten wind of the incident and stopped the show, milling around and talking excitedly to one another. Several of them spurred their ponies after Carlin, who had disappeared from the ring.

Awareness rippled among the spectators, followed by cries of shock and fright. It was clear that the news was spreading about someone having been struck by a real bullet, so Tessa decided it would wise to whisk Sophy away at once before panic ensued.

"Come, the show is over. It's time to return to the carriage."

"But where's Papa?" Sophy said with a tragical air. "We can't leave without him!"

"I promise, he'll find us. Here, I'll carry you."

When Tessa picked her up, Sophy didn't object but wrapped her small arms around Tessa's neck. Though Tessa talked cheerily, her worry must have been sensed by the girl because she didn't whine or fuss. She merely clung tightly as Tessa left the box and made her way through the crush of people gathering in the corridor.

Exiting the building, she blinked at the afternoon sunshine, so much brighter than the interior torchlights. An attendant summoned their vehicle, and they were soon nestled inside after having told the coachman what had happened. The footman went dashing off into the throng to help the duke. Meanwhile, she kept Sophy entertained by discussing which performance had been their favorite, all the while keeping a watch out the window for Carlin.

Where was he? How badly had he been hurt? And how had it all come about? She could only think it must have been a terrible accident.

To her great relief he appeared at last, taking his leave of a stout, fawning gent who kept bowing to him. The footman then assisted the duke into the carriage. Carlin sat down opposite them, his neckcloth tied around his upper arm in a makeshift bandage. The fine linen was stained an alarming red. "Ah, I've found you, Lady Monkey. I feared you and Miss James had run away with the circus."

Sophy stared with saucer eyes. "Papa, why are you bleeding?"

"A mere scratch. Once we arrive home, Jiggs will fix it and I'll soon be as right as rain."

The girl seemed satisfied, although Tessa thought he looked entirely too pale beneath his sun-bronzed skin. She could tell that his smile was forced, his manner stiff from pain. He sank against the cushions, using his good arm to support the afflicted one. Although she itched to know if he'd caught the shooter, and how such a mishap could have happened, she thought it best to divert Sophy with reviews of the most amusing acts they'd seen.

It seemed to take forever to reach Grosvenor Square, and from the instant of their arrival, the household was in an uproar. The footman no sooner opened the carriage door and helped them out than he dashed into the house, and a moment later Roebuck came hastening down the front steps to meet the duke halfway.

"Pray lean on me, Your Grace," the butler said, his usually dignified features taut with shock. "You look to be on the verge of collapse."

"I'm perfectly capable of walking."

"Don't argue, Carlin," Tessa said firmly, having noticed his unsteady gait. "You *will* accept his help."

The duke flashed her a grimace; then he grudgingly submitted to the butler's steadying arm as they all proceeded toward the house. Tessa was a little surprised that Carlin would heed her decree. Either he truly was dizzy, or it had done him good to have his coldhearted proposal rejected.

Once inside, Roebuck barked orders that had the other footmen running for bandages and hot water. Another was dispatched to summon the family physician. In the mysterious way of servants, the news spread like wildfire and in the time that it took for the butler to assist Carlin across the expanse of marble to the grand staircase, a number of the staff had found some excuse to scurry out to the entrance hall to gawp at their wounded master.

Winnie came dashing down the corridor, and Tessa bent down to give Sophy a kiss on the cheek before transferring her into the nursemaid's keeping. "Winnie will fetch your tea, dearie, and later I'll read you a book."

"I want jam tarts," Sophy said, ever on the alert for a way around the rules. "A dish big enough for a giant!"

"One tart," Tessa corrected.

"Two," Carlin countered, having brushed away Roebuck to take hold of the staircase railing. "A special treat since a girl only celebrates her fifth birthday once."

"Thank you, Papa, and for taking me to the circus, too." Without prompting, she flung her arms around his waist and tilted an earnest look up at him. "I hope your booboo is better soon."

"It shall be, never you fear."

As he stroked the girl's hair, the softening of his harsh

features brought a lump to Tessa's throat. These past few days she had used every opportunity to erase the damaging hatred instilled in Sophy by Lord and Lady Norwood, and to replace it with gentle reminders of how kind her papa had been in showing her the parrots even though Sophy had broken his window. He had let her collect feathers in the conservatory, and he loved her enough to take her to the circus for her birthday. Having never known her own father, Tessa was determined that Sophy not feel alone and unloved. Today, seeing the little girl climb into his lap during the tightrope act had been a marvel beyond compare. Nothing had ever touched Tessa's heart more than fostering a closeness between Carlin and his daughter.

Yet one searing question remained. Now that she'd accomplished her purpose, what else was there to keep her here?

Only the prospect of never seeing him—or Sophy—ever again.

Nevertheless, Tessa knew she could not remain in his employ much longer. Although she loved Guy, the man who had kissed her with such tender passion, she bitterly resented the stern duke who viewed marriage to her as a duty. Ever since her rejection of his callous offer, he had attempted to charm her with books and cream buns. But it was all pretense designed to cajole her into doing his bidding. She would not be duped into accepting him for anything less than love.

And perhaps not even that was enough.

Even if he pledged his undying devotion to her, wedding Carlin had one insurmountable obstacle. It required her to be a duchess. She would become mistress of this grand house, the recipient of bows and curtsies, the receiver of noble visitors, the hostess of balls and dinner parties and who knew what else? She would be pitchforked from the bottom rung of the social ladder all the way to the pinnacle. The very thought was unnerving.

Besides, his cavalier dismissal of her dreams still smarted. *Becoming a shop owner can hardly compare to becoming a lady. Of course you must give it all up.*

She knew that a career of any sort was forbidden to a duchess. The swells despised even a whiff of trade among its exalted members. Yet all she had ever wanted was to design hats, to own her own millinery, and as the wife of a duke, she would be barred from doing so.

That quandary flew from her mind as she saw Carlin favoring his left arm while carefully mounting the grand staircase. Roebuck shadowed him, and she hastened to follow the two men up the marble steps. For now, nothing else mattered but the need to see to Carlin's health and comfort.

Jiggs met them at the top of the stairs. With his eye patch and leathery skin, his short legs planted wide, he resembled a miniature pirate. "Well, ain't ye a pretty sight, Duke? Sent ye off t' the circus an' ye come back half dead."

"Pray don't hasten my death with any of your blasted remedies."

"Ye were grateful for 'em that time ye got poisonous sap on yer hand. Darn near blistered yer skin right off."

"The manchineel tree in Mexico." Carlin gave a strained chuckle. "And you were grateful when I saved you from being eaten by that shark near Australia. A tough little morsel you'd have been."

They continued to trade outrageous insults as Jiggs badgered him down the corridor. In the midst of her anxiety, Tessa had to bite her lip to stop the unseemly urge to laugh. The situation was far from amusing, but they did look ridiculous, with tall, broad Carlin leaning on the gnome-like Jiggs.

As they disappeared through an open doorway, Roebuck marched close at their heels. He turned to close the door, but Tessa stuck her foot into the opening, earning herself a rare scowl from the usually stoic butler. "Miss James! You cannot enter the master's bedchamber."

She conjured a haughty duchess stare. "I was present when His Grace was shot, and I intend to see to his care. Now step aside."

"Certainly not. That would be beyond the pale."

"Let her in," Carlin called out. "When Miss James gets a bee in her bonnet, there's no sense trying to stop her."

Tessa sailed past the perturbed butler, though an antechamber, and into a splendid room fit for a duke. The furnishings were heavy and masculine with chests and tables and a writing desk. Dominating the chamber was a canopied four-poster bed—on a dais, no less—with royal blue hangings and gold silk fringe. A shield above the headboard displayed the Carlin coat of arms, an eagle with outspread wings, flying ribbons, and a ducal coronet.

Carlin sat on a chaise near the hearth, where a maidservant was pumping a bellows to coax the glowing coals into flames. Jiggs had untied the makeshift bandage and was now tugging off the duke's coat, which Carlin tolerated with a clenched jaw.

A footman delivered a pitcher of hot water, while another brought a quantity of rolled lint along with linen bandages. Both servants found reason to dawdle, no doubt hoping to learn news to relay belowstairs. Mrs. Womble, the stout housekeeper, scurried in with a basket containing a variety of ointments, salves, and other mysterious bottles, and immediately started touting their various restorative properties.

Tessa stood off to the side, wishing there were a service she could contribute to justify her barging in here. Removing her bonnet, she tied knots in the ribbons out of a desire to do something. One thing was certain, she wasn't budging before knowing how badly Carlin was hurt.

Jiggs cast a baleful glare at the hovering servants. "Out, all o' ye. This ain't no Punch-and-Judy show."

The maidservant scurried from the room at once, as did the footmen, though Roebuck firmed his lips as if to argue. But apparently recalling that this chamber was the valet's territory, the butler promised to leave a footman stationed outside the door should His Grace require anything. He himself would wait downstairs and bring up the physician the instant he arrived. Even Mrs. Womble was sent on her way by Jiggs, after being assured that he knew all of her remedies and then some.

Once they were gone, Tessa flung her bonnet onto a chair and went to help Jiggs, who was having trouble tugging the duke's shirt up over his head without hurting his arm. The valet cast her a quick, one-eyed glance, but she was beyond caring what he might think of her presence.

She reached in her pocket for the scissors, then realized she'd left them behind for the excursion to Astley's. "Pray fetch me a pair of shears," she told Jiggs. "The shirt is already ruined, so it would be better to cut it off."

"This'll be quicker," he said, whipping out a dagger.

"Give that to Miss James," Carlin said. "You may be able to spear a grape from a distance of twenty-five yards, but I'd sooner trust her with my neck than you."

Jiggs chortled as he passed the weapon to Tessa. "Mind, 'tis sharp."

The small grip fit her hand perfectly. "Is this the knife you used to carve the wooden animals that His Grace gave to Lady Sophy? She plays with them every day."

"'Tis pleased I am t' hear it. Mayhap I'll whittle her a few more."

As Tessa leaned over Carlin, the blade sliced easily through the front side of the linen garment. Seeing the tightness of pain at the corners of his mouth, she chattered to distract him. "I've often thought it would be helpful for men to have buttons down a shirt. Tell your tailor, and you might start a new style."

"A novel notion if only I cared a fig for fashion. Blast! Are you trying to kill me, Jiggs?"

Now that the shirt was cut, the valet had lost no time in peeling it off. "'Tis stuck t' yer hide, is all. There, that'll do."

With Carlin's broad torso bare, Tessa could see the long, ugly gouge on the outside of his upper arm. Blood oozed sluggishly from the wound, and she unrolled a length of soft lint, using it to apply pressure. Her mind grappled with the horror of how much worse the injury might have been. If the bullet had struck just a few inches over, in the middle of his chest . . . no, that nightmare did not even bear considering.

"Let me see," Carlin said, craning his neck as Tessa obliged him by lifting the absorbent gauze. "What's the verdict?"

Jiggs peered closely. "Bullet plowed a deep furrow, but went straight through, so I won't be needin' t' dig it out. Demmed lucky, I say. Beggin' yer pardon, milady."

"Miss James," she murmured.

"Might as well accept *milady* as your due," Carlin advised. "Or would you prefer *Your Grace*? I can arrange for that if you like."

Her gaze flew to his to see a glint of dark humor in the midst of his pain. She hardly knew whether to laugh or scold. "I'd prefer you keep silent and preserve your strength."

Marching to the bed, Tessa brought several feather pillows and propped them beneath his injured arm. He flinched a little, then blew out a sigh of relief once it was elevated. Yet that telltale twinkle lingered in his eyes. "I'm surprised you aren't trying to coax me into bed."

His gravelly chuckle made her cheeks burn, and Tessa

gave him a quelling frown. "You must be delirious, sir. All the more reason to be quiet."

Luckily, Jiggs wasn't paying attention. He'd gone to a nearby table to pour a glass of brandy, which he delivered to the duke. "Ye'll need this when the sawbones starts pokin' ye."

"Might as well bring the decanter, then."

Carlin was downing his second glass when a footman came in to report that the foremost physician in London, on retainer to the Duke of Carlin, was presently tending the Lord Chancellor's gout but should arrive within the hour. Unless, of course, His Grace wished a different doctor to be summoned.

"I don't need a doctor at all, so send him away when he comes," Carlin growled. "Jiggs will handle this."

Once the startled footman retreated, he told the valet, "Fix me up, will you? You must have some crackpot treatments in your bag of tricks."

"Aye, Duke. I'll fetch me kit."

Jiggs scampered across the bedchamber and through a doorway, leaving Tessa alone with Carlin. While applying gentle pressure to the wound, she took the opportunity to ask, "How did this happen, Guy? Was it one of the performers? I was down on the floor and couldn't see—and then you jumped over the ledge. You might have killed yourself, by the way."

One eyebrow cocked, he regarded her over the rim of the brandy glass. "It's a relief to know that you care whether I live or die."

Her heart squeezed as she found herself the subject of those penetrating brown eyes. He looked far too appealing, sprawled bare-chested on the chaise, with a lock of black hair dipping onto his brow. She wanted nothing more than to hug him close and tuck her face into the crook of his neck. But that would mean abandoning her resolve. "Of course I care," she said briskly. "I would never want Sophy to see her papa leap to his death."

He groped for her hand and stroked his thumb across her palm. "It was no more dangerous than jumping off the stable roof when I was a lad. And of course we won't mention that time I had to swing from a vine over a cliff—"

"To escape a herd o' wild boar," Jiggs said with a cackle as he came trotting back with a leather case. "Thought we was both done fer that time."

As he unbuckled the strap to display a number of tins and bottles inside, along with bundles of dried herbs, Tessa removed her hand from Carlin's tempting clasp. A plethora of aromatic odors tickled her nose. "What is all that?"

"Medicines from around the globe," Carlin said. "While I was cataloging plants, Jiggs was studying their healing properties."

"You said earlier that he could kill you with his remedies," she said in alarm. "Why not just use basilicum powder from Mrs. Womble's basket?"

"Because I've been hoping for an opportunity to do some research on these herbs. What curatives do you have there for bullet wounds, Jiggs?"

"Sweet broom leaves an' pawpaw seeds, I reckon," the valet said, dropping a few dried items into a pestle. "An' a pinch of calabash bark."

As the man began grinding them with a mortar, Tessa prayed he knew what he was about. She sprang to her feet, poured warm water into a bowl from the pitcher, and leaned over the duke to clean the crusted blood around the lesion with a piece of dampened lint.

Although she was careful, Carlin winced. "It's best to leave this to Jiggs. It isn't a matter for a lady. In fact, perhaps you ought to go on up to the nursery. Sophy will be wondering where you are."

Tessa tried out her duchess stare on him. "If you intend to experiment on yourself to the risk of death, the least I can do is to ensure you are clean."

"If you insist, then."

He meekly leaned back to endure her gentle ministrations. Despite his casual manner, his arm had to be causing him considerable discomfort, Tessa knew. He was watching her in a way that made her heart skip a beat, and she hoped he wouldn't take the wrongful notion that the rift between them had been mended. She could tend to him in an emergency without consenting to join his world and give up her dreams.

She patted his arm dry, then tucked a towel beneath it to catch any seepage. "There, you may do your doctoring now, Jiggs."

The valet proceeded to sprinkle a powdery brown concoction into the deep gash. Seeing that he was about to thoughtlessly use a bloodstained strip of linen to bind the wound, she took it from his stubby fingers and set it aside. "I shall do the bandaging, if you please. And it's time His Grace told us exactly what happened today."

Carlin exchanged a droll look with the valet. "Overbearing, isn't she?"

"Best t' just do as yer told," Jiggs advised as he refilled the duke's glass. "So start talkin', Duke."

Carlin took a swallow of brandy. "I was shot during one of the performances. There were some two dozen jesters riding on ponies while using toy pistols that were rigged to fire without ammunition. When I noticed that Sophy was hanging over the ledge too far, I leaned forward to pull her back. That's when the bullet struck me."

Tessa paused in the act of winding a clean strip of linen around his arm. Her throat felt so taut that she could barely speak. "Do you mean to say that if you hadn't moved, you might have been killed?"

He attempted a shrug and grimaced, his mouth white at the edges. "There's no use speculating on what didn't occur. To continue, I thought it was a fluke, an accident. One of the jesters must have picked up a real gun by mistake. Then a rider broke away from the group and made for the exit. I guessed him to be the culprit, so I went after him."

As he paused to drain his glass, Tessa relived that awful moment of seeing him leap from the ledge. Her heart had come near to stopping, and even now, her fingers trembled as she finished securing the binding.

"Go on," Jiggs prodded. "I take it ye didn't catch the blighter?"

"No, several workers tried to stop me from cutting through the arena. It took a minute to explain what had happened, that I wasn't some drunkard trying to disrupt the show, but the delay was enough to enable the fellow to escape. Since he was wearing a mask, I never saw his face."

"If he's employed by Astley's," Tessa said, "then someone will surely be able to identify him."

"Unfortunately, the fellow was a substitute since one of the regulars had taken ill. All I could gather was that he was of medium height and build like half the men in London, and his eyes were either blue or gray or brown depending upon who I asked. In other words, I've no description of any use."

Tessa found the whole thing to be peculiar. As she arose to wash her hands, she wondered why there had been a replacement. With so many other riders, the audience wouldn't have known that one was missing.

"Sounds mighty fishy," Jiggs said with a shake of his grizzled head. "Where'd 'e get a real gun unless 'e brought it with 'im? An' if the shot were only a blunder, why'd he run off?"

"Perhaps he was afraid of bringing the law down on his head." Carlin flinched slightly as he adjusted his injured arm on the pillow. "The manager has promised to get to the bottom of it. He'll notify Bow Street and report here on the morrow. There isn't much more to be done at the moment."

As Tessa dried her hands, uneasiness churned in her belly. What if the shooting hadn't been an accident? What if it had been deliberate? But why would anyone wish to harm Carlin? Even as that gruesome question hovered on her tongue, two upraised voices came from out in the passageway.

One belonged to the butler. She gasped to recognize the other as the Marquess of Marbury's querulous tone. "I'm no stranger to this house, so out of my way, Roebuck. When the sixth duke was alive, I wouldn't have been turned away on some trumpery excuse!"

"The duke is indisposed, milord. He mustn't be disturbed." Roebuck hastened into the bedchamber. "Pray pardon the intrusion, Your Grace, but Lord Marbury was most insistent."

"Never mind," Carlin said. "Let him in."

As the butler retreated, the marquess tottered inside, leaning on his cane. "What's this I hear about a gunshot—?" Then his rheumy eyes focused on Tessa. "Blister it, Carlin! What have you done to my granddaughter? Why is she in your bedchamber?"

Dismay riveted Tessa in place. She could imagine the scene through Lord Marbury's eyes, with Carlin in a state of undress and her hovering at his side. What made it so acutely awful was that she'd reconciled herself to the prospect of moving in with her grandfather—at least for a time—once she left here. She'd decided to use the rare opportunity to further an acquaintance with her only blood kin and to learn about her mother's early years. Moreover, she'd been considering how to convince Lord Marbury not to launch her into society. Then perhaps—just perhaps—she could eventually persuade him to fund her millinery shop.

Now he might very well abandon her altogether.

To her vexation, Carlin looked remarkably calm. "There's no need for alarm. Miss James was kind enough to bandage my wound just now. Jiggs, will you fetch my dressing gown?"

The valet tramped into the next room and returned a moment later with a russet silk garment. By dint of Carlin leaning forward, and Jiggs and Tessa each taking a sleeve, they managed to restore the duke to a semblance of decency. His face looked pale, his jaw tight with pain, but at least he was covered. Since his one arm was useless, Tessa tied the gold tasseled sash for him.

The valet retreated into the dressing room while she straightened up to face Lord Marbury. A thunderous glower on his wrinkled features, Marbury was leaning on his cane like an aging lion about to roar. She drew a gilt chair closer. "Pray, sir, won't you sit down?"

The marquess levered himself onto the seat and glared at Carlin. "This is an outrage. My granddaughter is not your physician."

"No one would dispute that," Carlin said blandly. "She's a lady with an admirable compassion for the injured, for which I am most grateful."

Tessa seated herself on an ottoman and attempted a demure look. "The doctor was delayed, milord. Since I was with His Grace when he was shot, I could scarcely abandon him."

"What's that? You were with him when he was shot?" The marquess fixed Carlin with a gimlet stare. "What sort of havey-cavey household is this, Duke? Roebuck babbled some nonsense about a circus, but I daresay the truth is that you were engaged in a duel. I won't have my granddaughter endangered by rakes and rattles."

"I am neither a rake nor a rattle, and you will be pleased to learn that Roebuck did not lead you astray." Carlin proceeded to explain how he had taken Tessa and Sophy to Astley's Amphitheatre for his daughter's birthday when he'd been struck by a stray bullet during one of the performances.

The marquess harrumphed. "That does not excuse your shabby conduct here. If word gets out that Tessa was in your bedchamber, her reputation will be ruined. Any story we devise to explain her background will be in grave jeopardy."

"Jiggs has been present the entire time," Carlin assured him. "Please know that I have the utmost respect for Miss James. And perhaps it will ease your mind to learn that I intend to pay my addresses to her."

Tessa sucked in a breath. He must not lead her grandfather astray with such talk. "That is a private matter—"

"Forgive me, darling, but your grandfather deserves an explanation," Carlin broke in, the gleam in his eyes urging her to play along. "Although nothing between us is settled as yet, surely he has a right to know that my intentions are honorable." He shifted his gaze back to the marquess. "Lord Marbury, will you be so kind as to allow me to pay court to your granddaughter?"

Lord Marbury's anger vanished in a twinkling. A look of beatific approval came over his wrinkled face. "So a betrothal is in the works, eh? Well, that does shed a different light on matters. Still, you ought not to have Tessa here in your bedchamber."

"It was the pain of my injury that made me overlook the proprieties. But your support will help to quiet any wagging tongues."

"The gossipmongers won't dare to prate in my presence," Lord Marbury stated, thumping his cane on the carpet. "You may be certain I shall put a swift end to any slander."

Tessa had heard enough. "Milord," she said urgently, "you must not mistake the situation. I have not agreed to this courtship."

The marquess leaned over to pat her hand. "My dear, you

will soon come to realize what an honor it is to chosen as bride by the head of such a venerable family. Once Carlin has recovered, he and I shall discuss the marriage settlement. You will not find me a skinflint, I assure you."

"Settlement? I've asked nothing of you beyond a modest loan to open a millinery shop."

"Bah, ladies must never dirty their hands with trade. You may purchase all the bonnets you please with the pin money Carlin will provide you."

Her further protests fell on deaf ears. As Marbury launched into a homily about a grand alliance between two of the oldest houses in England, Tessa stewed over Carlin's maneuvering of the situation. Perhaps he'd taken her solicitousness toward him as a sign that she had softened her opposition to the match. She burned to set him straight, yet the lines of pain around his mouth, the clenching of his teeth whenever he shifted position, stirred a reluctance in her to scold him in his present condition.

She was relieved when Lady Victor swooped like a black cloud into the bedchamber, bringing the sharp scent of the vinaigrette flask clutched in her hand. Sinking beside Carlin on the chaise, she scrutinized him as if he lay at death's door. "My dearest nephew, I just now awakened from my nap to such horrid tidings! How badly were you hurt? Where is the doctor? Oughtn't you be in your bed?"

Carlin gave her a reassuring smile. "There's no need to trouble yourself, Aunt Delia. It was merely a scratch. I'm perfectly comfortable now, thanks to Miss James's superior nursing skills."

Lady Victor gazed askance at Tessa. "This is most improper, Guy. What can a governess know of medicine? She belongs in the nursery!"

"Not if I've any say in the matter," the marquess interjected.

"Why, Lord Marbury! Pray forgive me for failing to greet you. It is this shocking event that has me all aflutter." Her overwrought nature even more pronounced, Lady Victor went on, "You oughtn't be in the duke's bedchamber, either. Roebuck should have bade you await me in the drawing room."

"Fiddle. I didn't call on you, Delia. I came to visit my granddaughter."

"I beg your pardon?"

"Miss James is my granddaughter," he clearly delighted in revealing. "You'll recall that my daughter Lady Florence ran away many years ago? Well, as it turns out she emigrated to Canada and married a fur trader by the last name of James. Upon the deaths of her parents, Tessa traveled to England and took the governess post here while she was trying to find me."

Lady Victor's jaw dropped. Astonishment momentarily banished her doleful expression as she focused her pale blue gaze on Tessa. "I do remember that scandal. But my lord, are you quite *sure* . . . ?"

"Absolutely. She has the pendant I gave to Flossie on her eighteenth birthday. And she is Flossie reborn, except for the lighter hair."

"Well! Aren't you a sly one, Miss James, never breathing a word about your true identity? You simply must tell me all about your past!"

Tessa wanted to sink into the floor. How was she to speak intelligently about Canada and fur trading when she knew nothing of those things? If only she'd had the good sense to leave the moment Carlin had been bandaged, this awkwardness could have been avoided. Luckily, she was saved from any explanations by the arrival of another member of the household.

Mr. Banfield looked agitated, his silvering brown hair

mussed as if he'd just come in from outdoors. He bowed, his gray eyes intent on the duke. "Do pardon my absence at such a critical time, Your Grace. I've just returned from Lincoln's Inn, where I was filing the last of your legal papers. But never mind, what is all this about you being shot? And at Astley's, no less!"

"A bullet winged me. I daresay I'll survive."

Lord Marbury thumped his cane again. "These blasted circuses ought to be regulated. Imagine, using guns around crowds of people! You may be sure I shall take up the matter with the prime minister."

"It was not their usual practice," Carlin pointed out. "The performers were issued toy pistols. The manager has promised to call in Bow Street to do a thorough investigation of the matter."

"Bow Street?" Mr. Banfield questioned, one eyebrow raised. "Surely you don't suspect foul play."

A shiver tiptoed down Tessa's spine. *Foul play.* To hear her own nebulous fears put into words made her skin crawl. It couldn't be true. What possible reason could there be for someone to want Carlin dead?

"At the moment I scarcely know what to think," the duke said testily. "But you may be sure I intend to get to the bottom of this."

"Well, I know precisely what is to blame," Lady Victor lamented. "I warned you once before, Guy. It is the Carlin Curse!"

Chapter 18

Guy was inclined to scoff at his aunt. Being prone to hysteria, she had a tendency to imagine problems where none existed. Only look at the way she always tried to stifle his cousin Edgar with her excessive worrying, conjuring up every possible accident that might befall him.

Yet today's incident cast a different light on matters. Might there be a grain of truth to what she said? Was something sinister going on that he was missing? Even so, it could have nothing to do with hocus-pocus sorcery.

"There is no curse on our family," he said, the dull throbbing of his arm making him irritable. "You must not go on about that, Aunt."

"How am I to remain silent when so many have died?" she said, her downturned mouth quivering with distress. "Six family members in the past five years, including your dear Annabelle. And now *you* have been attacked!"

"It's too soon to label today's incident an attack. It may well have been an accident."

"Perhaps," Tessa interjected. "Yet I believe you should seriously consider the possibility, Carlin. After today, there does seem to be cause for concern. If you hadn't moved, that bullet likely would have killed you."

Guy regarded her, sitting on the ottoman, her hands folded in her lap. Despite her prim posture, her eyes held a keen worry that touched him deeply. She'd been largely silent since he had placated Marbury with that hint of a possible betrothal, and he'd feared he'd gone too far. More than that, though, it disturbed him to hear her say the shooting was no accident. Unlike his aunt, Tessa had too much common sense to engage in flights of fancy.

"I must concur," Marbury said. "Your grandpapa had three sons who all died in their prime. A grandson, too, who was ahead of you in the succession."

Lady Victor ticked them off on her fingers. "The eldest, Lord Fenwick, drowned in a freak accident three years ago, along with his son Charles, when their yacht capsized off the Isle of Wight. Then the second son, Lord Nigel—your papa, Carlin—contracted a deadly digestive illness. It came on him so suddenly there was naught the doctors could do to save him. And the third son, my dear husband, Lord Victor, was slain by highwaymen."

"Don't forget, old Carlin himself was discovered dead of a heart seizure in his bed last year," Marbury added grimly. "He was in vigorous health, too. I was inclined to call it all misfortune, but after today, one must wonder."

To consider the deaths laid out in a pattern greatly troubled Guy. Annabelle he discounted, for she had died of childbed fever, but the others, all his close blood relatives, had succumbed in ways that could have been random fate . . . or murders that had been cleverly planned to arouse no suspicion.

A chill infiltrated him. He felt witless for not having put two and two together before now. But the deaths had been spaced at the rate of one per year, not close enough to raise questions. Besides, he hadn't been present here in England to have noticed any irregularities. He'd been sailing the world with little contact from home.

If his family were being targeted, who could have a reason to do so? Someone with a grudge, someone who'd felt wronged and wanted revenge? His grandfather had been a stern tyrant, especially in the House of Lords. But surely revenge based on a political quarrel would be aimed only at him, not at his entire family.

Frustrated, Guy turned to his secretary, who was standing discreetly by the wall, a slight frown on his brow. "You've worked in this house for over a decade, Banfield. What have you to say on this matter?"

The man slowly shook his head. "This has taken me quite by surprise, Your Grace. I never imagined there was anything nefarious about these unfortunate deaths. However, there is something we have all forgotten. That is the stolen diaries."

"Yes, I heard you'd been burglarized, Carlin," Marbury said with a sharp glance at Guy. "Has the culprit been caught?"

"No," Guy said curtly. "I'm sure it was someone who attended my lecture and wanted the pirate's treasure map. But go on, Banfield."

"My point," the secretary said, "is that I cannot think it a coincidence that the theft and the shooting occurred only a week apart. There must be a connection. I would suggest something else is going on, something unrelated to the deaths of these family members. Perhaps today was meant as a warning, Your Grace, to stop you from asking questions about who stole your notebooks."

Guy welcomed the theory. It was certainly a more palatable explanation than imagining a killer picking off his family members one by one. "The thief must know by now that the map isn't in the notebooks. So what purpose would it serve to kill me?"

Banfield considered for a moment. "The perpetrator may be hoping to procure the remainder of your papers upon your death. After all, what use could such things be to your heir? Mr. Edgar has no real interest in leaving England on a treasure hunt, and he would gladly sell the map to the highest bidder."

John Symonton, Guy recalled, had already petitioned him for the papers to be donated to the Bullock Museum—and Symonton had not been pleased by Guy's refusal. "I take your point. Then the relevant question is, who among the attendees at the lecture would have known that I'd be at Astley's today?"

"Oddly enough, I know of one," Banfield said rather grimly. "On my return from purchasing the tickets four days ago, I chanced to encounter Lord Haviland on the street. We exchanged a few pleasantries, and I mentioned to him the purpose of my errand."

That news gave Guy a nasty jolt. He'd written his friend off as a suspect after learning from Tessa that the earl had departed by way of the garden gate after the lecture. "Would anyone else have heard of my plans?"

"Oh, my dear boy," Lady Victor said in a tragical tone, "I hope I may not be the one who endangered you. The other day when I was entertaining some ladies, they remarked on how lovely it is that you've finally been reunited with Sophy, and I said that you were taking her to the circus for her birthday. But I am *very* certain that none of my friends would shoot you!"

"Of course not," Guy said, hard-pressed not to sound impatient. "But they may have told someone else, so pray give me their names."

"There was Lady Jersey, Mrs. Ludington, Mrs. Young-blood"—she paused to tap her chin—"oh, and Lady Church-ford."

That last name snared Guy's attention. Lord Churchford had expressed a keen interest in funding an expedition to find the gold. Although he was too stout a man to have ridden a pony, he could have hired someone else to do his dirty work.

"That clutch of biddies likely gossiped to others, too," Marbury pointed out. "In the space of twenty-four hours, the entire ton could have learned you were attending the performance today."

There was no topic of greater interest to chattering ladies than the doings of a bachelor duke. Little did they know, however, he had his sights set on one woman. His gaze sought the cameo loveliness of Tessa's face. She looked far too somber, and he longed to see the lively sparkle back in her eyes, the enchanting smile on her lips again. But as attentive as she'd been to him today, he knew she must be seething about that betrothal ruse. And ironically, he found her independent spirit to be a part of her charm.

"Well, I don't believe for an instant that this has anything to do with the stolen diaries," Lady Victor declared. "Let us not call it the Carlin Curse, but the Carlin Killer! And he may well be after all of us." She clutched at his hand. "I implore you, Guy, find out who is behind this. I've a dreadful fear for you . . . and for my dearest Eddie."

He gently extracted himself from her clawlike grip. As much as the soreness in his arm made him want to snap at her, he kept his voice even. "I'll do my best, Aunt. Now perhaps Miss James will be kind enough to escort you back to your chamber."

Tessa frowned slightly, her gaze flashing to his. It was clear that she had a few pithy comments to utter to him in private, but in his current state of strain, he would as soon postpone their inevitable quarrel. Thankfully, she arose without a word and offered Lady Victor her assistance.

As they started toward the door, Marbury reached out to catch Tessa's hand. "I shall return soon, my dear, so that Carlin and I can discuss your nuptials."

"Nuptials?" Lady Victor inquired.

"Indeed, I am most happy to say that Carlin has requested my permission to pay his addresses to Tessa. He and my granddaughter will soon be betrothed."

Lady Victor lifted the small vinaigrette flask to her nose. "Betrothed . . . to my nephew? *Miss James?*"

Banfield, too, gave a start of surprise. More important, though, Tessa had that rebellious glint in her beautiful blue eyes again. Guy groaned inwardly, wishing Marbury had kept his mouth shut.

"Nothing has been settled," Guy stated, his stern gaze sweeping the small gathering. "I trust I can rely upon everyone here to remain silent on the matter."

"A wise notion," Marbury agreed. "And until such time as the announcement is put in the papers, it would be best for Tessa to live in my house, to spruce up her wardrobe and to introduce her to a few select members of society. I hope I may call on you to help with that, Lady Victor."

"I'd be honored, my lord. But oh, this news has my head spinning. Perhaps Miss James will be good enough to explain how it all came about. It seems I have been kept very much in the dark!"

Leaning on Tessa's arm, his aunt went out of the bedchamber. Banfield also departed, as did Marbury, leaving Guy alone to sort through his tangled thoughts.

Rubbing his brow, he knew he'd sunk deeper into the suds with Tessa. Now she would be forced to enlighten Aunt Delia. Tessa would be grilled on her relationship with him and quizzed on her fictitious life in Canada—and she would resent him all the more for landing her in such an awkward spot.

Yet as troubling as that situation might be, it was the least of his worries.

He leaned back on the chaise and strove to ignore his throbbing arm. The shooting today had been no fluke. For whatever reason, someone had deliberately attempted to murder him. It unnerved him to think that Tessa or Sophy might have moved in the way of that bullet.

Finding the gunman had to be his top priority. He must dig deeper, discover the whereabouts of suspects like Churchford and Symonton when the incident had occurred. In addition, he must take a closer look at all who had attended that lecture. And he must not discount the possibility, either, that today's attack was related to the other deaths in his family.

That would certainly broaden the scope of his investigation.

Yet his morbid reflections kept returning to one man in particular. Had it been Haviland, his old friend, behind the jester's mask? Had the earl's addiction to gambling driven him to take such a drastic step to acquire the treasure map? It was time to discover the full extent of Haviland's debts.

The following morning, Tessa headed downstairs in answer to a summons from the duke. She had left Sophy in high spirits, happy to abandon her arithmetic lesson in favor of playing circus with Winnie. Tessa's spirits were high, too, from an eagerness to release her simmering anger at him.

She was still seething at his audacity in duping her grandfather into believing an engagement was imminent. Carlin had placed her in an untenable position, forcing her to fob off Lady Victor yesterday with a promise to confide in her

later. Tessa had been greatly tempted to return to the ducal
suite the previous evening to confront him. Only a thought
for propriety and compassion for his injury had stopped her.

But today he surely would be improved, and she needn't
suffer the slightest reluctance about giving him a piece of her
mind. He had to tell her grandfather the truth—and swiftly.
Today, if possible, before Lord Marbury concocted more
plans to pave her path into society.

Tessa paused outside the library and marshaled her
thoughts. One thing was certain, Carlin must not be permitted to orchestrate her future. Not even if he played the
charmer, buttering her up with compliments and flattery and
melting looks. His purpose was to cajole her into accepting
the marriage offer that he viewed as his gentlemanly duty.

Braced for battle, she stepped into the sunlit library. The
shelves of tooled-leather books looked as appealing as they
had on that glorious night when Carlin had kissed her here
for the first time. As duchess, she could devote her life to the
pleasure of reading all of these works. The thought held her
transfixed, and only with effort did Tessa drag her mind
back to reality.

She wanted to be a hatmaker, not a lady of leisure.

The duke was seated by the window, his frowning attention focused on the newspaper he was perusing. Daylight
gleamed on his raven-dark hair and put his harshly handsome
features into sharp relief. He wore a loose jacket in a dark
bottle green rather than a tight-fitting coat that would have
been difficult to don over a bulky bandage. With his left arm
in a sling, he cut a dashing figure, and her wayward heart
lurched, beset by a rush of longing.

She clamped down a rise of warmth and glided purposefully toward him. "Good morning, Carlin. I hope you're feeling well today. No fever, I trust?"

He looked up to observe her approach. Rather than the

suave smile and alluring eyes that she'd prepared herself to resist, his mouth formed a thin line, and his gaze held a steely glint that nearly made her falter. "I was considerably better," he said coolly, "until I saw this."

Tessa took the newspaper that he thrust at her. With a quiver of shock, she recognized it as the tabloid where Orrin worked as a typesetter. Her gaze widened on the front-page article with the headline emblazoned at the top in large letters: THE CARLIN CURSE.

Drained of stamina, she wilted into a chair. A swift reading of the piece confirmed her worst fears. It related a luridly embellished tale of the Duke of Carlin being shot at Astley's Amphitheatre, then went on to describe in sensationalist detail the deaths of other family members. It concluded with flowery, overwrought speculation that the present duke was the current victim of the curse and might not be long for this world.

The byline identified the reporter as Orrin Nesbitt.

Her stomach knotted, she lifted her stark eyes to Carlin's face and was shaken by the iciness there. "Oh, no."

"Is that all you have to say? I should think you'd be scrambling to convince me of your innocence in the publication of this disgraceful piece."

"My w-what?"

The duke snatched the paper from her and flung it onto a nearby table. "Don't prevaricate, Tessa. You must have run to Nesbitt yesterday after you left my bedchamber. There's no way he could have thought up the name of this ridiculous curse on his own. *You* had to have passed the story on to him."

The unwarranted attack helped to rally her wits. "I most certainly did not. I haven't had any contact with Orrin in a week."

"Then what explanation can you offer for this outrageous article being penned by your friend?"

"I . . . I recall mentioning the curse to him that morning you saw us outside in the garden. It was just a silly, offhand comment, though. I never meant for him to write about it. In fact, since he hoped to become a reporter, I expressly ordered him to forget he ever heard me say it. Believe me, I'd have stopped him had I known."

Sunk in misery, she reflected on the extent to which Orrin had disregarded her request. He must have begun researching the article immediately, for he couldn't have gathered so many facts about the duke's family history since just yesterday. Then he'd added the Astley's event and used the breaking news to convince the publisher to print the story.

How could he have betrayed her like this? Of course, there was his wish to increase his income in order to marry her. Apparently her refusal hadn't deterred him from that course. No matter what their class, she reflected bitterly, men did as they pleased without regard for a woman's wishes.

Carlin sprang to his feet and prowled the library. "It's too late to stop the scandal. No doubt this edition has been distributed all over London. As head of this family, I have a duty to uphold our name. But now we will become a laughingstock, the object of gossip and speculation in every drawing room and club across the city. My aunt won't be able to hold up her head."

Tessa rather thought Lady Victor with her taste for gloom would enjoy the notoriety but refrained from saying so since Carlin looked so grim-faced. "I know how distasteful you find this, and I'm truly sorry. Please believe I would never have encouraged Orrin to write such a story."

The duke's eyes narrowed on her in a speculative stare. "You say Nesbitt aspired to become a journalist. A piece of rubbish like this could launch his career. That makes me wonder if he made his own news."

"Pardon?" She snatched up the paper to scan it again. "The

prose is certainly overblown, but the basic facts appear to be true."

"You mistake my point. I'm suggesting that he may have garbed himself as a jester and taken that shot himself."

His conjecture rocked her to the core. "Carlin, you surely can't think so. Orrin would never harm a flea. And how would he have known where we were going, anyway?"

"He could have discovered it the same way he nosed out all the other family secrets. By chatting up the servants in the stables or in the kitchen. You may be sure I'll instruct Roebuck to have a word with my staff about tattling to strangers." The duke came closer to tower over her. "This proves Nesbitt isn't your friend, Tessa. You don't know him as well as you thought."

Tilting her head back to view Carlin, Tessa detected a hint of heat in his glacial gaze. Despite her distraught state, it thrilled her to think that a man of his rank could be jealous of a common workman. She was tempted to spite him by singing Orrin's praises, but since she was also angry at Orrin, she deemed it wiser to abandon the notion.

"It's absurd to imagine that Orrin shot you," she said. "And besides, I doubt the ton reads this rag, anyway. It's sold to the masses on street corners. There may be little scandal at all."

"My aunt subscribes to this rag. That's why Roebuck delivered it to me at once."

Tessa cringed to think the damage might be more widespread than she'd wanted to believe. Carlin prided himself on duty and honor. She regretted having caused him trouble, however unintentionally, at a time when he'd suffered a gunshot wound and still hadn't recovered his diaries.

Perhaps it was best to distract him with another possible suspect.

"Speaking of your aunt, there's something I must tell you."

At his inquiring frown, Tessa went on, "I was in Lady Victor's bedchamber a few weeks ago when she was about to take her nap. As she was falling asleep, she seemed unhappy that you'd returned from your trip. She said that if you had died on the voyage, then her son would have become duke. Do you suppose she could have been repeating what she'd heard from him?"

Carlin stared as if she'd gone mad. "Good God. I hope you're not suggesting that Edgar is trying to murder me."

"Why not? It's only logical, since he's next in line to inherit your title."

His mouth tight, the duke resumed pacing. "It isn't logical in the least. My cousin is too sports-mad to covet the responsibilities of the dukedom. I can't even coax him to learn the ropes of the estate he inherited. His mind is too preoccupied with boxing and horse racing."

"And hunting? Whoever fired at you yesterday had to have been a very good shot, don't you think?"

"Yes," he said curtly. "But Edgar couldn't have done it. He's gone out of town to a prizefight."

"Perhaps that's just a handy excuse. Can you be certain he didn't sneak back into the city to don a jester costume and a mask?"

Carlin scowled at her. Then a gradual easing of his expression and a slight lift at the corners of his lips gave him a rueful look. "If it will set your mind at ease, I'll look into it. But I suspect Edgar's guilt is about as likely as you meekly agreeing to marry me."

His warmly teasing tone set Tessa all atremble. She ached to be held by him, to feel their hearts beating as one, to forget all the rules and restrictions of his highborn world. But wasn't this exactly what she'd feared would happen, for him to use his considerable charm to coax her into doing his bidding?

Collecting her defenses, she arose from her chair. "There will be no betrothal, Carlin. You should never have raised Lord Marbury's hopes."

"It was necessary since you were discovered in my bed-chamber, with me stripped to the waist. Marbury's anger was justified. Nothing less would have served to pacify him."

"But we weren't alone. Jiggs was present. And you were hardly in any condition to . . . to do anything."

"A valet can be sent out of the room. And there was quite a lot we could have done, then. A bullet wound wouldn't have stopped me."

The glint in his eyes suggested all manner of wicked acts. She remembered in vivid detail the weight of him lying over her, the intense joy of their bodies joined in passion. A keen yearning to experience that again whittled away at her common sense. Of all the men in England, why, oh why, had she fallen in love with a duke? A man who felt compelled to wed her only because he'd discovered her to have noble blood?

Fighting a blush, Tessa lifted her chin. "Well, I won't be a party to any sham courtship. It's cruel to mislead my grandfather. You must write a note to him today saying that I've decided you and I don't suit."

"Not just yet." All playfulness fading, Carlin closed the distance between them and gripped her hand. "Give it a little time. There's too much else going on right now to think about this now. You can always cry off later."

"There's no point in waiting, though. I shan't change my mind." Yet despite her firm speech, Tessa could not bring herself to draw her fingers from his warm clasp. "Please understand, Guy, I was raised to work, not to live in luxury. And anyway, I could never marry a man who derides my dreams."

"I never did!"

"In the carriage on our way back from meeting Lord Marbury, you told me that becoming a shop owner could hardly

compare to becoming a lady. And that I must give it all up."
It was hard to keep bitterness from creeping into her tone.
"As if I had no choice in the matter."

Remorse knit his brow, and he brought her hand to his
lips for a kiss. "Forgive me, Tessa. I oughtn't have been so
blunt. That particular morning was not my most eloquent moment."

"Yes, you were busy wrestling with the unhappy realization that because you had ruined Marbury's granddaughter,
you had no choice but to do your duty and marry her."

"Nonsense. You and I are exceedingly well matched . . .
in more ways that I can name. Surely you can see that."

In a burst of unbridled passion, he drew her close and
crushed his lips to hers. She melted against him, not out of
forgetfulness of their rift, but because she was acutely aware
this might be their last kiss. Wanting to savor every moment
of it, she returned his fervor with his own, gliding her hands
over him, memorizing his face and body and wishing his
arm were not in a sling so that he might hold her even tighter.

"Tessa, Tessa," he murmured against her hair.

She clung to him, breathing in his scent and relishing
the heat of his embrace. Despite his enticing kiss, however,
she knew that only unhappiness could arise from such a dis-
parate marriage. He would eventually come to regret his
choice of a wife, perhaps even be ashamed of her, and that
would break her heart.

Reluctantly she stepped back out of temptation's reach.
"Oh, Guy," she murmured, shaking her head in anguish.
"There has to be more to a marriage than desire. Similar
backgrounds, for one. That is why this will never work."

"We share more than that. We have the ease of friendship,
we both love Sophy, and we enjoy each other's company."

"How long will that last before you grow tired of me?
Will I embarrass you when I address some great lord by the

wrong title or when I let the truth slip out about my past or when I make a thousand other blunders? We're from two different worlds."

"Any skills you lack can be learned."

"So, in addition to educating myself about my fictitious birthplace of Canada, now I shall have to change who I am in order to fit *your* view of a duchess. It's no wonder you resented having to offer for me."

He thrust his fingers through his hair, disheveling the black strands. "Tessa, I never resented you. It's just that . . . I had sworn off marriage. I had no intention of ever taking another wife again. That's the real reason I was troubled that day."

A tiny devil seized hold of her tongue. "Because you could never find any woman to measure up to Annabelle the Angel."

His sharp gaze pinned hers. "Measure up? To Annabelle—?"

The sound of a clearing throat made them both jump. Carlin uttered a harsh curse under his breath as they turned to see Roebuck standing in the doorway of the library.

"Your Grace, there is a Mr. Gumbleton to see you. I informed him that you are not receiving callers, but he was most insistent."

"The manager at Astley's. Yes, yes, send him in at once."

Tessa welcomed the interruption. There was no solution to their quarrel, anyway. Carlin would never see matters from her perspective since he was too fixed on fulfilling his perceived obligation as a gentleman. Besides, it was best not to prolong the conversation when she was referring to his late wife in a manner that sounded uncomfortably close to jealousy.

He caught her arm as she headed to the door. "We'll speak of this later, Tessa. Only promise you won't cry off just yet."

There was a gravelly urgency to his voice that called to her bruised heart. "All right, but in return you must promise to keep me informed as to your search for the killer."

Three evenings later, after settling Sophy in bed, Tessa felt too fidgety to read as she usually did. Wrapped in a shawl, she had been sitting in the lamplit schoolroom for over an hour, unable to keep her mind on the book about Canada. Carlin had sent it to her the previous day along with a brief note saying he'd learned no new information about the gunman.

That had been his only communication with her. He hadn't said a word about who he'd interviewed, what clues he was pursuing, or even what Mr. Gumbleton had had to report. According to kitchen chatter relayed by Winnie, His Grace had departed after luncheon today on some unknown errand. Now darkness had fallen, both nursemaids had retired to their bedchambers down the corridor, and Tessa had no idea if Carlin had ever returned.

Fear and frustration gnawed at her peace of mind. Although he'd taken a coachman and a footman, he could be in danger. It stood to reason that a killer who was bold enough to strike in a crowded amphitheater could devise some clever means to attack again. And Tessa could not rest until she had assured herself of his safe arrival home.

She set the book aside and picked up the pewter candle lamp. Going belowstairs to fetch a cup of tea would provide her with an excuse to make a casual inquiry. She would likely endure a few stares from the kitchen staff. Ever since she'd gone to Carlin's bedchamber on the afternoon of the shooting, the other servants had taken to giving her curious looks, as if they suspected her of casting her lures at His Grace.

She had no intention of enlightening them that it was *he*

who was pursuing *her*. Nothing was settled, anyway. She was still in a limbo of anxiety about her future. If she was so certain about her decision to leave Carlin House, then why did her heart feel ravaged at the prospect?

Because she loved Guy. She loved Sophy, too. Tessa could think of no worse fate than to lose them both. Yet she could see no other solution.

Pondering the dilemma, Tessa left the nursery. Immediately she spied the faint glow of a candle coming from the staircase at the end of the gloomy corridor. The approach of heavy male footsteps on the steps gave her a start. Carlin! Since the hour was past nine o'clock, it surely could be no one else.

Spurred by an unreasoning joy, she made haste down the carpeted passageway. It would be useless to dupe herself into thinking she sought only news from him when it was Carlin's presence that she craved. She ached to put her arms around him, to reassure herself of his strength and vitality.

But the man who came around the bend at the top of the staircase wasn't the duke, after all. It was his secretary.

She checked her pace before continuing toward him, forcing a smile to mask her disappointment. "Mr. Banfield. What brings you up here?"

He didn't return her smile. The light of his candle wavered over his creased brow and the worried expression on his middle-aged face. "Miss James, I'm thankful that I found you so swiftly. You must come with me."

"What's wrong? Is it Carlin?"

"Yes, I fear His Grace has been injured again, this time with a knife. He's waiting outside in his carriage, and he asked me to fetch you at once."

Her heart lurched. It was exactly as she'd feared, the killer had struck again. "We must tell the footmen to bring him inside. And summon a doctor."

As she started toward the stairs, Mr. Banfield motioned to her to follow him. "The servants' staircase will be swifter. And His Grace said I was to bring only you, Miss James, and to not say a word to anyone else. Since he looked to be in a bad condition, I thought it best not to plague him with too many questions. This way."

They went through a nondescript doorway and proceeded down a set of plain wooden steps. The house seemed preternaturally quiet. Lady Victor must have retired early, Avis Knightley would be with her, Mr. Edgar was still out of town, and Guy—oh, Guy was hurt and bleeding again.

As they reached the ground floor, she said, "Wait, we'll need bandages."

"There's a footman already tending to the duke. The one who accompanied him today. Now hurry, there's no time to waste."

Mr. Banfield went out into the darkened garden. He paused only long enough to blow out his candle, leave it on a table, and take her glass-chimneyed lamp. Having expected the carriage to be parked in front of the house, she was a little surprised that it was at the back. But the mews would be more private if Carlin had some dire reason for secrecy.

"Do you know what happened?" she asked.

"Only that he had a fight with the Earl of Haviland."

Lord Haviland! So he was the culprit, after all. Poor Avis, she would be devastated to learn that the charmer who had once swept her off her feet with a passionate kiss had attempted to kill the duke. And poor Guy, he would have been at a disadvantage, having not yet recovered from his bullet wound.

As they made their way along the gravel path, her teeth chattered as much from anxiety as from the damp, autumnal mist. Mr. Banfield cast a swift glance backward before proceeding through the gate. Though she couldn't have said why, she had the fleeting impression he was looking at the house, instead of checking to see if she was still behind him.

The pungent aroma of horse droppings permeated the mews. At the far end nearest to the street stood the boxy black shape of a carriage. The dark form of a coachman sat huddled on his high perch.

Her heart in her throat, she hastened her steps. Mr. Banfield was quicker, opening the carriage door and motioning for her to enter. She started to do so but stopped halfway.

To her bewilderment, the interior was that of a hired hackney cab rather than the plush ducal coach. Even more confusing, it was empty. Where was Guy? Had he changed his mind and gone into the house?

Or was this some sort of trick?

Even as that suspicion entered her mind, a punishing blow struck the back of her head. Pain splintered her skull and she plummeted into darkness.

Chapter 19

The first thing she noticed was the cold. It raised gooseflesh
on her skin and penetrated deep into her bones. The slightest
movement jarred her aching head. She was sitting upright
on a hard floor, and when she attempted to lift her eyelids,
a jabbing needle of light made her shut them again.

One by one, she sorted through a jumble of sensations.

A gritty surface against her back. A sooty odor in the air.
An inability to move her hands and feet. That last one stirred
alarm as she came to an awareness that her limbs were bound.

Memory flooded back. Carlin was hurt. The empty carriage. The blow to her head. Then . . . nothing.

Tessa forced her eyes open. She squinted against the painful
brilliance of a lantern. It hung from a hook on the other side
of a smallish room. As her vision adjusted, she discerned
filthy brick walls, a dirt floor, and at one end, an enormous
black pile of . . . coal.

She was in a coal cellar.

Mr. Banfield had struck her. He must have dumped her
here. But why? And where was he?

Even as those questions plagued her throbbing head, he stepped out of a gloomy corner and strolled closer. With his back to the lantern, his face was in shadow so that she had to strain to make out his features. "Ah, you're awake, Miss James. I was afraid we might not have a chance to chat before I depart."

That cool, unruffled voice sent a centipede of dread crawling down her spine. He spoke as if they were exchanging pleasantries over a tea tray. Lud, Banfield must be the killer. He was the one who had shot the duke. Panic threatened to scramble her brain. The awful fear that Guy might already be dead paralyzed her throat.

Swallowing hard, Tessa lifted her chin and forced her dry tongue to function. "Where-where is Carlin? What have you done with him?"

"Why, nothing. At least as of yet."

Pray God he was telling the truth. Nevertheless, that word *yet* sounded ominous. Somehow she had to warn Guy. Covertly, she twisted her bound wrists behind her back. But the rope was too strong for her to slip her hands free.

The magnitude of her situation horrified Tessa. There was no hope of rescue. Even if her absence was discovered, no one knew where she had gone. She was entirely on her own. Being trussed up as tightly as a Christmas goose, she could do nothing but pretend weakness on the slim chance of coaxing Banfield into releasing her.

Injecting bewilderment into her tone, she said, "I-I don't understand, sir. Why have you brought me here?"

"Family secrets. You're familiar with the concept, I gather."

"Don't speak in riddles. My head is aching too much already."

"Well, then, Miss James, you'll be interested to hear that

you and I have one attribute in common. I, too, am a noble bastard. My father was the sixth Duke of Carlin."

"Pardon?"

"You heard me. I am the eldest son of the previous duke. I would have succeeded him had he had the decency to marry my mother." The topic clearly inflaming him, Banfield began to pace back and forth. "He sired me with a lady who gave birth in secret, and when she died I was placed in a genteel family. They never let me forget I was an unwanted orphan." His mouth tightened. "You may be sure that my adoptive father suffered for his treatment of me. And before he died at my hand, he admitted that it was the Duke of Carlin who had paid for me to be schooled as a gentleman. It was the duke's intention that I never know his identity."

Banfield was Guy's uncle, Tessa realized in shock. In his warped mind, he now sought revenge on the ducal family. Lady Victor had been right to make a fuss over those deaths. They weren't the result of a curse, though. They must have been Banfield's horrific doings.

As he prowled the coal cellar, the lantern cast his elongated black shadow onto the wall. "Never once did he deign to visit me, his firstborn son. Yet that proved to be a boon, for when I applied for the post of his secretary, my own father didn't recognize me."

"Did you . . . did you ever tell him who you were?"

A smile touched his lips without reaching his ice-gray eyes. "Indeed. But only after I'd savored his anguish over the demise of his legitimate sons. Victor was the first to die, a simple matter of slipping a sack of gold into the pocket of a highwayman. For Fenwick and Charles, I hired a man to drill a hole in the hull of their yacht and to plug it loosely so that once out in rough seas, the plug washed out and sank the boat. Then there was Nigel, the present duke's father. He was a drunkard, so I laced his wine with a purgative and slipped additional doses into Mrs. Womble's tonics. Such misery my poor middle brother endured! But it was my father who suffered the most. It was worthwhile to see the old goat's reaction when I told him all this—right after I'd administered digitalis in his nightly brandy. His heart stopped just as he was about to throttle me."

Tessa was hard-pressed not to gulp. Banfield's resentment must have festered for years. He'd gone after the heirs one by one, taking his time to plan each murder in order to make them appear as accidents or illnesses.

And now Guy was his target.

Dear God, she could think of nothing to do but to humor Banfield, to find out his scheme, in case by some miracle she escaped his clutches. "Was that you, then, at Astley's? You must be an excellent shot."

"On occasion my father was magnanimous enough to allow his lowly secretary to join a hunting party. For that, he required me to practice my marksmanship. Many a time I considered shooting him in the back—by accident." Banfield extended his arm and sighted down an imaginary barrel before lowering it again. "But I couldn't risk being caught. That would have been fatal to my mission."

"I daresay you were angry when Guy moved and spoiled your shot."

His lips curled in distaste. "No matter, I've devised another clever ploy that will do quite nicely for my nephew."

"Ploy?"

"This is the Earl of Haviland's cellar. It will appear that he abducted you in order to force Guy to exchange you for the treasure map. I've already hidden the incriminating diaries in his study."

Lord Haviland! It was a crumb of luck to know that Banfield hadn't transported her out of London, that she was still in Mayfair. He'd made up that story about telling Haviland that Guy would be attending the circus. It was all a trick to make the earl look guilty. "So you stole the diaries, too. And you told His Grace that I had done so."

"Guy was sniffing at your skirts. I couldn't take a chance that he might get you with child. I hoped he would take a disgust of you, but he didn't." His calculating stare seemed aimed at her midsection. Did he think she was expecting? That only confirmed he meant to kill her, too.

Before she could vanquish another surge of panic, he went on, "I daresay it was Marbury who forced him to court you. Dukes don't willingly wed bastards. Especially one so different from a lady like Annabelle. Guy was madly in love with her, you know."

Tessa's heart wrenched. She mustn't listen to his poison, she must find a way out of this impossible predicament. "Your plan won't work. Lord Haviland is bound to have an alibi. Someone will surely swear to his whereabouts tonight."

"He returned this evening from his estate in Dorset. After traveling all day, he won't be going out again tonight. He's sent his servants off to bed and is now ensconced upstairs in his library."

The news riveted Tessa. Once Banfield departed, she would scream herself raw in the hope that Haviland would hear her.

"The earl has become something of a recluse this past year," Banfield continued. "His father left him quite destitute, and the authorities will be persuaded he had ample motive to have committed murder for that treasure map." He glanced around. "I daresay these walls are too thick to allow any cries for help to penetrate. But just in case . . ."

He whipped out a strip of linen, stuffed it between her teeth, and tied it behind her head. Tessa recoiled as much from his loathsome touch as from the pain of him brushing

the sore lump he'd inflicted. The whiff of his masculine co-
logne might have been the foul stench of a demon.

Damn him! She was only sorry she hadn't cursed him blue
when she'd had the opportunity. Though her tongue had been
silenced, she let her eyes speak eloquently of her disgust.

Straightening up, he appeared amused by her glower. "I
daresay you're wondering how I can be so certain of Haviland's doings. These past few days, I've been cajoling one of
his maidservants, a spotty-faced goosecap whom I made sure
to visit each morning while she was polishing the brass on
the front door. She was putty in my hands and gladly told me
all the household gossip." He shook his head. "Alas, she isn't
long for this world. She, along with you and Guy, will suffer
tragic deaths at Haviland's hands."

Tessa controlled a shiver. Though Banfield appeared to be
the sober, upright gentleman, he was in truth a raving madman who belonged in Bedlam. He spoke of killing people as
calmly as one might mention going to the market.

Then he withdrew a knife from inside his coat. He turned
it in his fingers so that the steel blade flashed in the lamplight.

Her body went rigid. He meant to kill her this instant! She
would never see Guy again, never know the joy of his embrace. Her desperate cry muffled by the gag, she yanked fu-
tilely at her bound hands.

Banfield crouched in front of her. His lips were curled
into a caricature of a smile as if he savored her terror. She
braced herself as he brought the knife closer. Would he cut
her throat or plunge it into her bosom?

Instead, he uttered a nasty chuckle as he caught a lock of
her hair and sliced it off. "Never fear, you'll live until Guy
is present to witness your death. This is merely bait to lure
him here."

Arising, he sheathed the knife and then examined the

curl of hair in the light of the lantern. "An unusual shade of blond," he mused, "rather like buttercream. Do you know this color is the signature trait of a certain noble family? Once one considers the possibility of a resemblance, it becomes easier to recognize it."

Tessa was too shaken by the close call even to make sense of his words. She could only stare at him, willing her heart to slow its frantic beating.

He tucked the little bundle of hair, along with the knife, into an inner pocket of his coat. Then he surveyed the coal cellar with an air of satisfaction. "I must say, this scenario has a certain poetic flair. It will appear as though Guy was killed by his old friend, and you by a man who might be your half brother. Think about that whilst I'm gone. Do excuse me now."

He took the lantern and ascended a steep flight of wooden stairs. A moment later the room went black and she heard the rattle of a key in the lock.

Tessa huddled cold and alone in a darkness so absolute it might have been the stuff of nightmares. Her situation was utterly hopeless. She couldn't move, she couldn't scream. The very walls seemed to close in, threatening to suffocate her. Disjointed phrases kept running through her brain.

I've devised another clever ploy . . . you and Guy will both suffer tragic deaths at Haviland's hands . . . a man who may well be your half brother . . .

Her panicked brain could not sort out the meaning of those last words. He must mean Haviland. But she could not even recall the earl's hair color. The one time she'd met him, at the lecture, her attention had been on Guy.

What did it matter now, anyway? She mustn't waste time pondering the lunatic ramblings of a madman.

Banfield had gone to lure the duke into his trap. Guy would come here, prepared to confront Haviland and ready to exchange the treasure map for her release. He would have no inkling that death awaited him at the hands of his secretary, for Banfield was extremely clever at tricking people.

Her anguish deepened. She had never told Guy she loved him and now she would never have the chance. They would both die in this cold, dank cellar.

Then another dreadful realization shook her. If Banfield was determined to eradicate everyone with Carlin blood, that meant he would eventually go after Edgar . . . and Sophy, too.

A wild fury arose from the depths of her despair. She could not just sit here and wait to die. If there was the slightest chance she could save Guy and Sophy, then she had to try. She wrenched at her bonds again only to find them maddeningly secure. Even if she wriggled loose, how could she escape with the door locked?

Now that her eyes had adjusted to the darkness, she spied a faint oblong outline near the top of one wall. A window? No, that must be the coal chute, where the coalman would dump his cartload into the cellar. Though she couldn't see it in the gloom, there was an enormous stockpile for the impending winter. If she could climb to the top and squeeze through the narrow chute, perhaps there might be a chance.

With renewed energy, she squirmed and writhed as the twine abraded her wrists. It was impossible! The rope was too tight to work her hands free. She was about to succumb to tears of frustration when, during the course of her struggles, her elbow bumped something hard at one side of her skirt.

Scissors!

Oh, bless Sophy for snipping animal pictures from that book. Ever since, Tessa had made a habit of keeping the shears tucked in the pocket of her gown.

But retrieving them posed another problem. By a series of painstaking wiggling movements of her hips, she managed to twist her skirts around far enough so that her fingers could just reach the scissors. She was panting by the time they dropped out onto the dirt floor. Then it took another few torturous minutes to maneuver one blade in between her wrist and the rope.

At last she began sawing at the strands of hemp. It was a tedious process that forced her to pause now and then to uncramp her fingers from their unnatural position. All the while she was conscious of time ticking, ticking, ticking.

How long had Banfield been gone? The darkness made it impossible to tell. It could have been an hour or only twenty minutes. She prayed the villain would be delayed long enough for her to escape.

And if she did escape—*when* she did—it would take all of her courage and ingenuity to thwart the killer and save the man she loved.

Chapter 20

"You needn't have waited up for me," Guy said as he handed his greatcoat to Roebuck. "The night footman could have opened the door."

"I wouldn't have slept a wink, Your Grace. Not when you are still recovering from that bullet wound. I trust you haven't done yourself a harm by staying out until nearly midnight."

Guy bit back a smile. He couldn't recall a time when the stately butler had fussed over him so much as the last few days. It gave him a curious sense of homecoming, as if this house were truly his own now rather than still his grandfather's sanctum. "I'm perfectly well. But go on to bed, that's an order."

He took a candle from a table, then headed up the grand staircase. Although he hadn't told the butler, his arm was still sore despite the sling. A glass or two of brandy would work wonders before he hit the feather tick.

However, upon nearing the ducal suite, Guy decided those creature comforts paled beside a greater allure. He continued down the corridor and mounted the stairs to the nursery.

He'd been negligent about keeping Tessa informed as promised, and he felt a powerful need to share the details of his long, fruitless day.

The afternoon had begun the same as the past few, with a parade of curiosity seekers arriving on his doorstep. Ever since that blasted article about the Carlin Curse, along with the news of the shooting, a steady stream of the ton had come to gawk at him. Although he had initially forbidden Roebuck to admit any visitors, Aunt Delia had sulked until he'd rescinded the order and allowed a few of her particular friends into the house. That number had grown as Lady Victor reveled in being in the center of such a sensational story.

He himself had escaped the gossips by going out in search of the culprit. Unfortunately, his efforts had yielded no definitive answers. Neither Churchford nor Symonton had an iron-clad alibi for the afternoon of the shooting, which meant they could not be eliminated as suspects. Churchford had gone for a drive in the country, while Symonton had been squirreled away in a deserted room of the museum working on an exhibit. Still, it proved nothing. Either man could have hired a ruffian to take that shot.

Not even a team of Bow Street Runners had succeeded in tracking the gunman. The mask and jester costume had been abandoned in an alley a block away from Astley's Amphitheatre, and the pony had been recovered wandering a nearby street. Beyond that, there had been confused reports of various strangers walking away from the arena, but all had checked out to be innocent of the crime.

As well, Guy had been unable to locate his cousin. One of Edgar's friends said that he'd met a woman at the prize-fight—a lightskirt, no doubt—and had gone off with her to his hunting box. That sounded just like Edgar. Having recently completed his studies at Oxford, he was enjoying having the freedom to kick up a lark.

He was simply too carefree to be a murderer.

Logic told Guy that the culprit was a man with dark secrets. A man with a grudge powerful enough to induce him to kill multiple times. As much as he'd wanted to believe the shooting had been connected only to the treasure map, he could not discount the unusual number of deaths in his family prior to his return from abroad. Consequently, he had spent a considerable amount of time seeking out his grandfather's old political cronies.

Guy was by no means finished with the interviews, yet he had the growing suspicion that he was tilting at windmills. There was something else going on, and today he had hit upon a half-formed notion as to who was targeting his family. He had yet to find proof, though, and hoped that talking it out with Tessa would help him to focus his thoughts.

He entered the nursery to find the schoolroom dark save for the glow of banked coals on the grate. The book about Canada lay open on a table as if Tessa had recently been reading it. That she had to contrive a new history for herself was one more negative mark for him, one more mountain he had to climb in order to win her as his wife.

Out of respect for her wishes, he'd avoided her company these past few days. It frustrated him that he couldn't properly woo her until he solved the mystery. And he couldn't blame her for being wary of the gulf between them. Theirs would be a mésalliance in the eyes of the world. It was unheard-of for a man of his rank to marry a woman with a sketchy past. With Marbury's help, though, he intended to wield his power to silence any critics.

Yet he knew that gossip was not the real issue. It was convincing Tessa that marriage to a duke didn't have to mean changing her true self.

As he headed down a corridor, the first door was his

daughter's. He went inside to see her small form huddled asleep in the canopied bed. Sophy had kicked off her blankets, and as he tucked them back in place, his chest tightened with the fierceness of love. The best decision he'd ever made was to hire Tessa as governess. To think he'd almost turned her out after discovering she'd lied about having a letter of reference.

The intense need to see her burned in him. He wanted them to be a family. Forever and always.

He tiptoed out and proceeded down the passage. Tessa would be asleep at this late hour, and the prospect of waking her appealed immensely to him. How he craved to see her lashes lift, her eyes soft with sleep, her mouth curved into a smile. He would kiss her awake before she had time to remember all the reasons why they didn't suit.

Much to his surprise, though, he found her door open. Even more troubling, the single bedstead had not been slept in. He held up the candle to see that the coverlet was neatly made, the feather pillow still plumped. Even the curtains were open to the night sky as if she hadn't been in here since the afternoon.

Alarm gripped him. Had she left his house for good, then? Perhaps she had walked out in order to avoid another quarrel. Perhaps she'd gone away because her feelings for him weren't strong enough to grant him another chance.

Yet a swift look around revealed that her trunk was still here, her clothing tucked in the drawers, her brush and comb on the dressing table. Even her favorite chip-straw bonnet was hanging from a wall hook.

He steadied his breathing. How foolish of him to think the worst. She might leave *him*, but she would never abandon Sophy without first badgering him to hire a new governess. Knowing Tessa, she would insist on interviewing the candidates herself.

Then where the devil could she be in the middle of the night?

The library. Yes, that was the one room in the house that held enormous appeal to her. At this very moment, she was likely curled up on the chaise reading something more interesting than a dry tome on Canada.

Guy hastened back down the stairs to the ground floor and went along the marble corridor. Much to his consternation, however, the library was dark and deserted, the ashes cold in the hearth. Could she have gone to his study? Or down to the kitchen? He was heading out the doorway again when Banfield came striding from the direction of the entrance hall.

The secretary bowed. "Your Grace, I wondered where you might be. Jiggs hadn't seen you."

"Yes, well, I'm home now. Good night."

The last thing he wanted was fall into a conversation about some urgent estate business that needed tending. He had a number of vital questions to ask Banfield tomorrow, but not right now, not until Guy had had the chance to discuss his theory with Tessa. As he went past the man, however, Banfield did the unusual act of stepping into his path.

"Do pardon me, but this note was slipped under the front door just now. The directive on the outside said to deliver it to you at once."

The oddity of that caught Guy's attention. Letters came by the daily post or by a private courier who would place it directly into the hands of a footman. Perhaps one of the Runners wished to inform him of a development in the case.

He seized the note. Even before opening it, though, he knew it hadn't come from Bow Street. The elegant script bespoke a gentleman's education. When he broke the seal and unfolded the paper, something fell out onto the marble floor.

He reached down to pick it up. It was a curl of hair, soft and silken, buttercream blond. Tessa's hair.

Infused by icy horror, he scanned the brief message. *If you wish to see Miss James again, bring the pirate's map to the coal cellar behind my house. Come at once, unarmed, else she will suffer the consequences. —Haviland*

Guy stared down at the words. Though it had been a long time since they'd passed notes in school, he recognized that penmanship. The waxen seal had been an *H*, as well. If this was a trick, it was cunningly done.

Then again, the culprit was diabolically clever.

His fingers clenched into a fist around the note. Fear spawned a rage so powerful that he felt on the verge of explosion. Giving vent to it, however, could hinder Tessa's rescue.

He forced himself to think. Haviland might be a scoundrel, but he'd never stoop so low as to endanger a woman. Having also uncovered the truth about his friend's finances, Guy found it dubious to think that the earl would commit such a desperate act.

Of course, people often saw only the face that a man chose to show to the world. And the murderer was adept at hiding the dark secrets in his soul.

"Is something amiss, Your Grace?"

Guy looked into Banfield's gray eyes. He'd never before noticed how utterly devoid of emotion they were. "Lord Haviland has abducted Miss James. He wants the map in exchange for her. I'm wondering how he ever got his hands on her."

"Abducted! Perhaps she went out for a walk. Or received a note that lured her away. The bigger question is, what will you do?"

"Go after her, of course."

Turning on his heel, Guy walked rapidly to his study and tossed the note and the lock of hair onto his desk. If Tessa came to harm, he would never forgive himself, for he had no doubt it was his interest in her that had made her a target.

With effort, he kept a tight rein on his seething emotions as he swiftly formulated a plan for her rescue.

He set down the candle, moved aside the painting on one wall, and used his key to open the safe. Reaching past a casket of jewels and several bundles of cash, he picked up the map that had been torn from one of his notebooks. After tucking it into an inner pocket of his coat, he removed a large leather case, which he brought over to the desk to open.

Against the blue satin lining gleamed a pair of perfectly matched dueling pistols with mother-of-pearl inlaid stocks. He took one of the guns, along with a sack of shot, and began to efficiently load it.

As he'd expected, Banfield had followed him into the study and now hovered at his side. "Forgive me, Your Grace, but I glanced at the note. It instructed you not to bring a weapon."

"This villain won't escape justice." Guy aimed a narrow-eyed glance at the secretary. "I'll take great pleasure in putting a period to his existence."

"At least allow me to accompany you, then. You daren't go alone with your arm still in a sling."

"Jiggs will come with me."

Banfield frowned. "Your Grace, you may not know but I am a skilled marksman. Your grandfather insisted upon it, as he sometimes required me to join a hunting party at Grey-friars."

"Now that you mention it, I do seem to recall that. I daresay he was glad of the company since his three sons were indifferent hunters."

There was a certain tightness to Banfield's lips as he nodded. "I pray you will agree to me taking one of the pistols. I shall remain hidden from sight. Haviland need never know I'm there."

Guy considered all the ramifications of his plan. He had

a strong intuition that tonight would finally bring an end to this wretched mystery. Matters would likely turn deadly, though, and with Tessa's life at stake, he didn't wish to appear careless enough to deny the need for backup.

He handed Banfield the pistol. "Call for the carriage, then. Haviland lives only two blocks away, but Miss James may require assistance in returning here. Go on, don't dally."

The moment Banfield scurried out of the study, Guy swiftly loaded the other pistol. He had purposefully not revealed his entire strategy to the secretary. After tucking the weapon in his waistband, he sprinted upstairs to his bedchamber to put the last piece of his hasty plan into place.

A full moon cast an eerie glow over the narrow garden behind the Earl of Haviland's residence. It was sufficient to allow Guy to make his way from the gate without stumbling into the rosebushes on either side of the path. He could hear the pad of Banfield's quiet footsteps behind him.

When Guy had called on Haviland earlier in the day, the butler had reported that the master was expected to return from his country estate by evening. Now the rear of the brick town house was dark except for one window on the first floor, where a sliver of candlelight escaped the closed curtains. The library, Guy recalled.

Haviland was here. The stage was set. The action was imminent.

"Where the devil is the coal cellar?" he muttered.

"Near the service entry to the kitchen, I should guess," Banfield whispered. "There's a path along the left wall. See?"

"No, I don't see. You had better go first."

Guy stepped aside. Banfield hesitated before taking the lead, creeping toward the corner of the house. Their movements disturbed the low mist so that it swirled like frolicking ghosts over the shrubbery. But the chill Guy felt had little to do with the dank night air.

Where was Tessa? Pray God she was tied up in the coal cellar. As uncomfortable and frightened as she must be, that was the safest spot for her. If there was any shooting to be done, he intended for it to happen right out here in the garden.

His thumb on the hammer of the pistol, he followed Banfield around the corner. The residence was located at the end of a row of town houses, which allowed for a side entry for deliveries. The secretary proceeded to the second door nearest the street.

Unerringly, Guy noted.

He needed no further confirmation that his suspicions were correct. Banfield had planned all this. He'd fired that shot at Astley's, and when it had failed, he'd set up this elaborate scheme. No doubt he intended for Haviland to take the blame for murdering the Duke of Carlin and his governess. Guy could even make a fair guess as to the motive behind the killings.

Banfield stepped aside, waving his hand at the door. "There is a key in the lock. Lord Haviland must have left it for you."

"Don't just stand there. Open it."

"As you wish."

The instant the secretary turned toward the door, Guy quietly drew out his pistol. He would come up from behind and take him captive. Then he'd force a confession out of the weasel.

But before he could advance even a step, a black form flew out of the bushes. It landed on the pathway in between them. A long silver claw flashed in the moonlight as the snarling creature pounced on Banfield.

The man spun around, defensively raising his arm. Too

late. The beast struck flesh, wresting an inhuman howl from Banfield. With lightning-quick reflexes, the secretary seized the squirming entity, and the claw clattered onto the ground.

Guy stared. A pair of scissors?

Just then, the struggling figures moved into the moon-light. The ethereal glow revealed a dainty face smudged with black. The sight was a hard punch to his gut.

Tessa!

"Let me go," she cried out, straining against Banfield's grip.

A cauldron of rage erupted in Guy. His fingers clenched around the stock of his pistol. Only a thread of rationality en-abled him to keep a hold on himself. Banfield would stop at nothing, and Guy dared not risk harming Tessa.

Besides, he still had an ace up his sleeve. Two aces, in fact.

"You heard the lady," he snapped. "Release her. This is between you and me."

He brought out his pistol and cocked the hammer.

So did Banfield.

The man jammed the barrel of the matching pistol into the side of her neck. "Lay down your weapon, Carlin," he grated in a voice quite unlike his customary coolness. "Else I'll shoot her dead."

Chapter 21

Tessa ceased struggling at the feel of that cold round circle pressed against her skin. One bump of Banfield's hand could end her life in an explosive flash. Since the mere touch of his body against her back was repulsive, it took all her willpower to hold herself still. For an older man, he possessed a wiry strength, and she hoped Guy would not underestimate him.

But at least she had hurt Banfield. The tip of the scissors had ripped through his sleeve and sunk into his flesh. She could feel the warm blood dripping from his forearm down onto the front of her gown.

The duke stood like a granite statue in the shadows. Though she could not read his expression, the sight of him made her ache with love and despair. She couldn't see any way out of this standoff, at least not for herself.

Yet she had no regrets for having attacked Banfield. She had caught him off balance and upended his diabolical scheme. He would no longer have the advantage over Guy in a physical fight.

"Shoot him, Carlin!"

"And lose you? Don't be absurd, my dear."

To her anguish, he eased back the hammer and leaned down to place the pistol on the ground, shoving it beneath the bushes. Then he straightened again, his hands open, palms up. "There, Banfield. I'm all yours. Now let her go."

"How touching," Banfield mocked. "The Duke of Carlin trading his life for a mongrel."

"The only mongrel I see is you," Guy said coolly. "I'm guessing you're my grandfather's bastard. Quite probably his eldest. Once I hit upon that theory, all the deaths in my family began to make perfect sense. You've been eaten up by envy of us."

"Shut up," Banfield hissed, his breath hot as a demon's against her ear. "I would have made a much more dignified duke than you, your father, or any of your uncles."

"Oh, much better, I'm sure. I never wanted the title, anyway." Guy paused, his pose still one of surrender. "But you won't wish to murder me out here in the garden. The noise of the gunshot would wake all the neighbors. Not to mention it would bring Haviland running."

During this exchange, Tessa could feel tension quivering in Banfield. Now that his scheme had been revealed, he no longer exuded a cold superiority. It was Guy who radiated control despite the dire situation, and she could only pray he had devised some plan of his own. Yet she could not see how it was helping matters to goad a madman. He would get himself shot!

Unless that *was* his plan. To save her by sacrificing himself. Dear God, he must not do it. For Sophy's sake if nothing else.

Banfield jerked his head toward the door. "Enough chatter. Get into the coal cellar, Carlin. If you value the wench's life, don't try anything foolish."

"I'll cooperate. But only so long as you promise not to hurt her."

The secretary uttered a vicious laugh. "You aren't in charge here, Duke. I've had enough of your orders these past few weeks."

Tessa felt herself drawn backward a few steps by Banfield to allow space for Guy to reach the door. The cold steel never wavered from the side of her neck. The thought of him walking into a death trap caused her throat to constrict. "Don't, Guy. Don't go down there. He intends to kill you."

"I know."

As he turned to look at her, his hand on the doorknob, the moonlight revealed a calm passivity on his face, a fatalistic acceptance of his doom. It was an expression she'd once read described in a gothic novel about a nobleman riding in a tumbrel to the guillotine during the French Revolution.

Guy must believe the situation impossible to escape. She had been mistaken to think him confident. Rather, he was resigned to his fate. Their fate because she would not elude death, either. She felt her own courage ebbing, and only with effort did she bolster her spirits. No! If he wouldn't fight back, then she would have to save them both somehow.

Even as she watched for her chance, a flash of movement jarred her. Guy spun around and seized her, yanking her against him. In the same instant, she felt Banfield's finger jerk on the trigger.

A scream of pure terror tore from her lips. She braced herself for a pain that never came. Instead, the world tilted crazily. She was falling . . . falling with Guy's arms wrapped tightly around her.

As they hit the ground, his body shielded her from the impact. She realized in a daze that she hadn't been shot. Guy, however, uttered a strangled groan and fell still.

Had the bullet struck him? Was he dead?

She pushed up on one hand to frantically examine him in the shadows. Running her fingers over him, she found no blood. Only then did it occur to her that she'd never heard an explosion of gunpowder.

A snarl of rage yanked her attention to Banfield. He loomed against the night sky like an avenging devil. She stared in frozen horror as he pointed the pistol at them. There was no time to move, nowhere to escape. Yet as he pulled the trigger again, it clicked ineffectually.

His teeth bared in a curse, he hurled the gun aside and dug in his pocket as if seeking another weapon. Then the oddest thing happened.

He clapped his hand to his neck and staggered sideways. He stood for a moment, swaying like a tree buffeted by a gust of wind. Much to Tessa's astonishment, he crumpled into a motionless heap in a bed of roses. Not even the thorns could rouse him.

A bandy-legged leprechaun stepped out of the gloom by the back gate. As he came scurrying forward, she gave a choked gasp of relief and leaped to her feet. "Jiggs!"

"Is ye hurt, milady?"

"Not at all. But I fear Guy has been shot."

"Nonsense."

The deep, disembodied voice came from near her feet. She caught her breath for a second time to see the duke slowly sitting up. Quickly, she bent down to grasp his good arm and assist him when she would have much rather showered him with kisses. "Guy! Are you all right? Did you jar your wound when you fell?"

He got to his feet and dusted off his clothes. "I merely had the air knocked out of me. Neither of us was in danger of being shot."

"I beg your pardon?"

"Banfield was using one of my dueling pistols. When I received the forged note with a lock of your hair, he insisted on accompanying me as protection against Haviland. Though he was standing right beside me in my study when I primed the gun, he never even noticed that I'd palmed the bullet. His arrogant belief in his own cleverness was his undoing."

"You *knew* it was him?"

"I realized it only today," he said grimly, "after coming up empty with every other suspect. It was then that I started considering who else had been in my family's orbit for the past five or more years. And I took a hard look at Banfield. It was merely a theory, one I'd hoped to discuss it with you, Tessa. But when you weren't in the nursery and I went looking for you, Banfield approached me with the note, insisting that I read it. It was then that I knew for certain."

She shivered. "He must have been reaching for another gun in his pocket when he fell . . ." A thought distracted her. "Why *did* he fall?"

"'Twas me knife," Jiggs said, kneeling beside Banfield's unmoving form to search him. "Blimey, 'e 'as two more pistols."

"Jiggs was the other ace up my sleeve," Guy said. To the valet, he said, "You took your sweet time throwing that blade."

"'Twas milady bein' in the way. Ye scared the bejesus out o' me, missy, when ye bust out of them bushes!"

"I'll second that," Guy said on a rueful laugh. "I thought her a hell-born beast. And just when I was about to nab Banfield and force him to confess at gunpoint."

Tessa was glad the darkness hid her blush. The black dust disguised her better than she'd imagined. Every inch of her must be covered, for she'd had to climb a mountain of coal in order to wriggle through the chute, escape the cellar, and position herself near the door. Just in time, too, for a moment later the gate had creaked open and they'd entered the garden.

Though as it had turned out, Guy hadn't needed her help. He'd already deduced the truth and had a plan of his own.

Just then, the back door opened, and a tall man slipped stealthily out of the house. As he peered in their direction, his fingers were clenched into fists as if he anticipated trouble.

"Come join the party, Will," the duke called out. "Unfortunately, you've missed all the fun."

Haviland vanished inside and emerged a moment later with a glass-chimneyed lamp. As he came down the pathway, it was clear from his dressing gown of mulberry silk that he'd settled in for the night. "I heard a scream. What the deuce is going on here?" He glanced at the three of them, then lifted the lantern to illuminate Banfield's fallen form. "Damme, isn't that your secretary, Guy?"

"Regrettably, he's also the Carlin Killer. For rest of her life, my Aunt Delia will be telling everyone about her role as oracle in the infamous tale."

Haviland regarded him with a trace of ironic amusement. "It seems I did miss all the fun. And in my own backyard, no less."

"Be thankful he didn't succeed in his scheme, or the Runners would be clapping you in irons to hang for murder. It's a long story."

"I'm all ears," said the earl.

Guy gave a concise summary of the events, and Tessa contributed what she'd learned from Banfield's gloating confession while she was tied up in the coal cellar. "He stole Guy's diaries, milord, and hid them in your library in order to incriminate you."

The earl regarded her in slight puzzlement, as if he was trying to figure out how the governess had become involved and why she was on a first-name basis with her employer. But he merely commented, "I wonder how he managed to creep into my house. And to filch the key to my coal cellar, too."

Tessa shrugged, unwilling to betray the fact that one of

his maidservants had fed information to Banfield, as he'd told Tessa in the cellar. She didn't want the hapless girl to be tossed out on the street for the naïve mistake of being conned by a villain.

Haviland glanced again at Banfield's still form, under guard by Jiggs. "Well, Carlin, unless you want more vulgar news articles about your family like the one I was just reading upstairs, I would suggest removing this fellow from my property."

"I'm thinking he was set upon by footpads," Guy said. "But not in Mayfair. Too upsetting to the neighbors."

"And messy," the earl agreed. "But it can't be too far away if he merely went out for a walk. Piccadilly, perhaps? Covent Garden?"

"That's too respectable," Tessa said tersely, the memory of her ordeal in the coal cellar still fresh in her mind. "He can have gone to a bawdy house. I can show you the location of several in Seven Dials."

That earned her another stare from Haviland and a chuckle from Guy.

He took hold of her hand, his gaze scanning her in the lamplight. "Thank you, my dear, but you've had enough adventure for one night. You're going back to Carlin House for a bath. Jiggs will escort you in the carriage."

His dismissal made her more aware than ever that she didn't know how to behave like a proper lady. Here she was, covered in soot like a climbing boy, and babbling about houses of ill repute. Though Guy was polite enough not to show it, he must certainly find her an embarrassment in front of his friend. It was disheartening to realize just how much she craved his love and esteem.

While he went to tell Jiggs, she shivered, chilled by the night air and her dismal thoughts. She turned her attention to Lord Haviland, in particular to his pale blond hair, some-what tousled in the lamplight.

Now was hardly the best time to speak, but with her future so uncertain, this might be her only opportunity. "I must tell you something, milord. But you may think it to be very odd."

He raised a brow in lazy interest. "Nothing could be odder than finding a dead man in my garden. But do go on."

"It's something Banfield said to me while I was bound and gagged in your coal cellar."

"Had I known you were there . . ."

"Never mind that. He said that my unusual shade of blond hair is characteristic of a certain noble family. *Your* family."

Every trace of idle humor vanished from Haviland's face. He stared at her so hard that Tessa felt self-conscious and regretted her loose tongue. "Forgive me, sir, this was ill advised. I know my hair is covered in coal dust . . . and Ban-field was likely just needling me, anyway. You see, he found out somehow that I was looking for my natural father."

Heedless of her disclaimer, Haviland said rather intently, "We met at the lecture, did we not? I'm sorry, I was a trifle distracted at the time. What is your name?"

"Miss James. Tessa James."

"Tessa James." His eyes widened in a startled manner. A slow smile lifted one corner of his mouth, and she feared he must be laughing at her to imagine they could be related by blood. Guy had returned to join them, and Haviland said to him, "Do you recall that deathbed confession of my father's that I mentioned to you?"

"Something about him siring a child with the governess."

"He begged me to look for the girl, my half sister, and to do right by her. But I hit a brick wall on discovering the govern-ess had died in an accident and no one knew what had hap-pened to her daughter. The governess was Florence James. And her daughter's name was Teresa."

Guy looked from her to Haviland and back again. "Tessa, you said your mother was a maidservant, not a governess."

"Yes, that's what I believed." She scoured her memory. "Mama talked about working as a servant in a fine house, and I suppose I just assumed . . ." Her heart pounding, she raised her hands to her cheeks and smiled wonderingly at Haviland, taking in his roguishly handsome features and the dark blue eyes full of deviltry. "Oh, milord. Could it be possible?"

He smiled back, taking her hand and grasping it firmly. "More than possible. It would seem we are brother and sister. Well, half siblings at least. Wait until my younger sister—your sister, too—finds out she has someone else to hector besides me. By the way, her name is Margaret, she's rather tall, and if ever you wish to tease her, just call her Leggy Meggy."

"Oh! I could never—!" Tessa said, shocked at the very thought of uttering something so rude to this unknown lady. *Her sister.*

She had a brother and a sister. It didn't seem quite real.

Nevertheless, jubilation filled her. Though she had once feared to be rejected by her noble relations, Haviland appeared pleased by the discovery. And to think they'd already met on the night of the lecture. He'd been looking at Avis, while Tessa had been too entranced by Guy to take note of anything so absurd as a similarity in her hair color to Haviland's.

They parted with a promise to talk more on the morrow. As she went off with Jiggs to the carriage, she felt enveloped in a wonderful dream. She was accustomed to making her own scrappy way in life without any relatives, though she'd often longed to have loved ones. Now she had a brother, a sister, a grandfather. It was all too bewildering to absorb.

Yet one thought shone as clear as the full moon against

the night sky. How could she truly be happy without Guy and Sophy?

Watching Tessa disappear out the garden gate, Guy had to restrain himself from going after her. He craved to settle matters between them, to ensure that she wouldn't leave him now that she'd acquired a family of her own. But he could hardly abandon Haviland to deal with the body lying in the bushes. They must wait for Jiggs to return with the carriage.

"I daresay you've stolen my scoundrel's crown tonight," Haviland said on a droll note. He'd set down the lantern and leaned a shoulder against the brick wall of the town house. "There I was, sitting in the library like a decrepit old codger, catching up on a week's worth of newspapers, and now thanks to you, I've acquired another sister and there's a dead man in my garden."

Guy chuckled. "You may keep your crown. Though it would seem you're not so much of a scoundrel anymore, either."

A certain stiffness entered Haviland's expression. "You've been investigating me. I should draw your cork for that. There was a time when you trusted my word."

"Forgive me. It was necessary for the protection of my family. But pray know that when Banfield handed me that note summoning me here tonight, I knew him at once to be the culprit. *You* would never have abducted a woman in order to steal a treasure map. Not even if you were still deeply in debt."

"So you've looked into my finances, too?" Frowning, Haviland glanced away. "It was my father leaving Ainsley Hall mortgaged to the hilt and in a state of utter disrepair that shook me awake. After he died, I decided not to spend my life dodging creditors while my estate fell to rack and ruin."

He paused to take a deep breath. "I've even deemed it time to produce an heir."

"You, marry? You swore a blood oath it would never happen."

"Yes, when I was one-and-twenty and had just been spurned by the girl of my dreams for being an incorrigible rake." As if he were looking into the past, a slight smile touched his lips. "Now that I've found her again, I'm determined to convince her that I've turned over a new leaf. And since she has no living relations, I shall ask your permission to pay her my addresses. Miss Avis Knightley is, after all, in your employ."

Guy stared. "My aunt's companion? I'd have sooner pictured you chasing after some sweet young Venus."

"It's been ten years since we first met, and she's still the sweetest young Venus I've ever known." His smile took on an uncharacteristically soppy quality before vanishing into sternness. "Speaking of romance, I demand an explanation for this improper closeness I noticed between you and my newfound sister. What exactly has been going on under your roof?"

It was Guy's turn to stiffen. Not for the world would he mention that passionate interlude in his study. "My intentions are honorable, I assure you. In truth, I've already offered for Tessa, though she hasn't accepted—yet."

"You should be asking permission of her elder brother."

"You'll have to fight Lord Marbury for that right. He's her grandfather on her mother's side. There was a scandal a long time ago. Marbury's daughter disappeared when he tried to marry her off against her will. Apparently she ended up at your father's house as governess under an assumed name."

Haviland whistled. "You don't say! Tessa has acquired a whole host of noble relations, then. What happened to her,

Guy, after her mother died? Where has she been all these years?"

"In a workhouse as a child, then a millinery shop. It's another long story, which I'm sure she'll be happy to tell you. Suffice to say that she's been on her own for most of her life." Wondering if Haviland would fund her shop, Guy firmed his jaw. "So as far as paying my addresses, it isn't your or Marbury's permission that matters. It's Tessa's."

Chapter 22

Still in something of a daze upon her arrival back at Carlin House, Tessa was startled to be escorted by Mrs. Womble to a bedchamber on the floor reserved for the family. Jiggs had sent the night footman to wake the housekeeper, and in turn, she had rousted several maids out of bed. As they carried in cans of hot water to fill a large copper tub by the fire, Mrs. Womble in her nightcap and robe directed them.

Tessa felt compelled to protest to the venerable woman. "A pitcher in my nursery chamber will do. Really, I don't mean for you to go to any trouble on my behalf."

"Mercy sakes, Miss James, you need a more thorough washing than that. I can't imagine how you came to be in such a state unless you was climbing the inside of a chimney in the middle of the night. Though of course it is not my place to inquire, only to obey His Grace's command."

Tessa thought it best to avoid satisfying the housekeeper's curiosity and to let Guy determine what the staff was to be told about the circumstances of Banfield's death. "This is much too fine a room for me."

"It's merely a guest chamber, one of a dozen. Why, you're

saving the maids the trouble of toting them heavy cans all the way up to the nursery and likely disturbing Lady Sophy. I expect that's why His Grace ordered it so. He was always considerate, even as a lad."

Now that was a subject of interest to Tessa, to hear stories about Guy's childhood, about visiting his grandparents in this house. She would have liked to have asked, but Mrs. Womble was busy supervising the maids at various tasks. One ran upstairs to fetch Tessa's nightgown, one kindled a fire on the hearth, and one laid out towels, soap, and a brush. Within minutes, yet another maid delivered a tea tray from the kitchen.

The housekeeper bobbed a respectful curtsy to Tessa. "Ring the bell if you require anything else, miss. Or shall I leave Sally to assist you?"

"Oh, no," Tessa exclaimed. "Pray return to your beds, all of you. I shall be fine and . . . thank you."

Alone at last, she shed her filthy clothes and immersed herself in the steaming water. She didn't know how nobles suffered having so many servants around. Yet the extravagance of a tub filled nearly to the brim made her sigh with pleasure. She'd have to be a saint not to appreciate such luxury.

Studiously, she avoided thinking about all that had happened. Her brain needed a rest from worry and strain. After a few minutes of mindless relaxing, she set to work scrubbing away the coal dust from head to toe. The cake of soap smelled deliciously of lavender, and in guilty delight, she used a liberal quantity of it. Only when the water began to cool did she emerge to dry herself with a towel and to don the soft familiar flannel of her old nightdress.

Armored in comfort, she perched on a fringed ottoman by the warmth of the fire. She took care to avoid the sore spot at the back of her head while running a brush through her damp hair. As it dried, she drank a cup of tea and savored a cream bun from the tray. Two cream buns, for it seemed a shame not to indulge when such a plentiful amount sat on the plate. Then, having nothing else with which to occupy herself, she gazed around the room and marveled to think that her mother had grown up in similarly lavish surroundings.

A branch of candles illuminated a chamber of fairy-tale splendor with a canopied bed and rose silk hangings. Her bare toes curled appreciatively into the plush carpet. Even the brocaded ottoman felt luxurious to her work-worn hands. This could be her life if she accepted Guy's proposal.

But she was no Cinderella destined to marry the prince.

That particular tale had ended with a glorious promise of happily ever after, with no one questioning exactly how Cinderella had adapted to living in a palace after years of sleeping in the ashes. And surely it must have been extremely odd to wear a tiara instead of a servant's mobcap, and to have others bow to her when she had always been the one to do the curtsying.

Of course, any such adjustments were made easier for Cinderella because she basked in the certainty of the prince's love.

Love. That was the key.

Tessa knew that one missing element could greatly mollify her own doubts about marrying into the nobility. But Guy had made his offer out of duty. He'd even admitted that he hadn't intended to wed ever again. His heart, she suspected, would always belong to the ghost of his departed wife.

She rallied her flagging spirits. How could she possibly despair when she had gained a family in Lord Marbury and Lord Haviland? That they would welcome her into their lives was the answer to her dreams.

Removing the gold pendant, she ran her fingertip over the

engraved coat of arms. How pleased Mama would be to know that her daughter had finally found her grandfather. That had been her dying wish, after all. Upon leaving Carlin House, Tessa would go to live with him, and she would make every effort to forge a bond with her brother and sister, too.

And perhaps someday, she would forget that she had once loved a duke.

The quiet ticking of the clock on the mantel drew her attention. It was half past two in the morning. Sophy would be awake by eight, and if Tessa hoped to get any sleep at all, she had best return to the nursery straightaway.

She lay the pendant on the table, intending to braid her nearly dry hair. No sooner had she reached up her hands to do so, though, than a quiet tapping sounded. As she whirled around, the door opened, and Guy peered into the bedchamber.

A spontaneous joy uplifted her soul. All of her lethargy dissipated as she felt buoyed by the anticipation of his embrace. Oh, she'd been mistaken to think him unloving, because surely he'd come to lay his heart at her feet . . .

He entered the room and closed the door behind him. Instead of approaching her, however, he paused. "I thought you'd already be asleep. When I saw a glimmer of light under the door, I decided to check on you."

From across the room he studied her somberly, his hair in attractive disarray, his cravat gone, and his arm still in its sling. There was an indefinable weariness to him that touched her deeply. Yet she found it difficult to read his impenetrable face, and his coolness was far from encouraging. If he loved her, surely he would have rushed forward to seize her in his arms, to cover her with kisses.

Tessa abandoned the braid and let her hair fall loosely around her shoulders. "It's very late. I was about to go upstairs to bed."

He frowned. "I told Jiggs very clearly to convey that you're to stay right here tonight. I won't have Sophy waking you at the crack of dawn. You need a little time to recover from all that's happened."

Her throat taut, she folded her arms and returned his steady stare. "I belong in the nursery. I-I don't feel comfortable here."

"Not comfortable?" He glanced around the well-appointed bedchamber. "Was there something you lack?"

Your love, Tessa thought, though she felt too disheartened again to say that aloud. Guy was fond of her, but merely as a friend, and he would wed her out of nothing more romantic than gentlemanly obligation. She craved wild, reckless ardor, the closeness that had immersed them in the bliss of their one night together. But on that occasion she had been naïve enough to mistake fleshly passion for heartfelt sentiment.

Feeling treacherously close to tears, she turned her head to gaze into the fire. "There's nothing," she murmured. "Your servants were all very kind."

He strode to her side. "Yet you look so desolate. You've told me very little about your ordeal. Come, my dear, sit down for a moment. It will do you good to speak of it."

Sliding his arm around her waist, he guided her to the ottoman, then knelt in front of her and grasped her hands in his. The firelight revealed the anxiety etched in the lines of his face. "I have to know, Tessa. What did that brute do to you? How did he lure you away from here?"

"Banfield told me you'd been injured again, that you needed me to come outside to your carriage. But when we went to the mews, there was only a hansom cab and as I looked inside, he struck me from behind. I daresay it's lucky that I have a hard head."

Guy didn't chuckle at her attempt at a jest. His jaw tight and his face grim, he growled, "He knocked you out?"

"Yes. When I woke, I was tied up in the coal cellar."

He turned her hands over, palms up, and regarded her reddened, abraded wrists. Though his expression was hewn from granite, his touch was soft as he brought them to his lips for a kiss. "You should never have fallen prey to Banfield's clutches. It's a wonder you don't hate me."

"Hate you? No, those scrapes were only caused by me trying to loosen my bonds," she said, trying to keep her voice light. "Luckily, he didn't notice that I had a pair of scissors in my pocket. Once I'd sawed through the rope, I scrambled onto the pile of coal and managed to wriggle through the chute." An involuntary shudder ran through her at the memory of slipping and sliding her way up the coal stack only to be very nearly daunted by her escape hatch. "It was quite narrow, and there was a moment when I feared myself to be stuck."

A muscle clenched in his jaw as he held tightly to her hands. "Damn Banfield to hell! And damn me for never seeing the evil in him. I always sensed a certain coldness in him but put it down to reserve. I never imagined he was my uncle, let alone that he'd been plotting revenge on my family."

"How could you have guessed? He fooled everyone, even your grandfather." That reminded Tessa of another horror, something she felt obliged to tell Guy. "While I was tied up, he confessed all of it to me . . . exactly how he'd murdered your family, one by one. Pray don't ask me the details just now. But . . . I could only think he meant to do the same to you, Guy. And that I had to . . . I had to stop him."

Hot tears began to slide down her cheeks. She couldn't control the flow despite her best efforts. He uttered a gruff exclamation and she found herself folded into his arms, clutched securely to his chest. Tessa tucked her face into the curve of his neck while she sobbed out all the residual fear and terror bottled up from that nightmare. Guy had very nearly died at the hands of a murderer, and she rejoiced to be sheltered in his embrace again, absorbing his heat and vitality, feeling the strong beat of his heart against her bosom.

He nuzzled her hair, while his hand rubbed soothingly over her back. "Ah, my darling. I'd have given my life to have spared you that anguish."

Through hiccupping sniffles, she uttered, "But then you'd be dead, and that would be even *worse*."

A chuckle rumbled deep in his chest. He tilted up her chin and dabbed her wet cheeks with a folded handkerchief. Then he kissed the tip of her nose, though it must surely be red and unsightly from her weeping. Yet he was regarding her with a gaze so adoring that she felt like the most beautiful woman in the world.

"What I find so wonderfully admirable about you, Tessa, is that you grew up an illegitimate child under the worst of conditions. Yet you never harbored bitter resentment over the circumstances of your birth as Banfield did."

She glowed. "In all fairness, I owe the man a debt of gratitude. He's the one who suggested that Lord Haviland is my brother."

Guy idly twisted a curl of her hair around his finger. "My powers of observation must be failing me. I never even noticed that you two have the same unusual shade of hair—and he's my childhood friend. By the way, you'll be pleased to hear that your brother has become remarkably respectable. Not only has he cleared his debts and abandoned his rakish ways, he also told me tonight that he hopes to marry Miss Knightley."

Tessa's eyes widened. "Truly? Oh, how happy Avis will be! She's never forgotten him, you know."

The duke's smile slowly faded into a more serious look. Still holding her close, he said, "You're now a member of two powerful noble families, Tessa. You're sister to an earl and granddaughter of a marquess, both of whom are your staunch supporters. Do you still think you don't belong in society?"

She drew a shaky breath. When Guy gazed at her with such intensity in his dark eyes, it was difficult to remember all the reasons why she had balked at the prospect. "It's a world I've never known. How could I possibly fit in?"

"You're underestimating yourself, darling. You're bright and witty and exceedingly charming. You'll have Marbury and Haviland as your allies, as well as me. It's time you took your rightful place as a member of the nobility—and as my duchess."

Though her heart thumped with longing, this second offer was hardly better than the first. He'd slipped it in almost as an afterthought.

She pulled herself free, sprang up from the ottoman, and turned to face him. "Even if I wanted to be a duchess, which I *don't*, I would never marry a man who's . . . in love with another woman."

He gaped up at her in flagrant surprise. Then his expression cleared, and he leaped to his feet, the hint of a smile curling one corner of his mouth. "Are you referring to Annabelle the Angel?"

Tessa lifted her chin and crossed her arms. "Don't regard me so . . . so mockingly. Lord and Lady Norwood said she was the most perfect lady ever. Even Banfield told me you were madly in love with her."

"My dearest heart, are those really the opinions you wish to trust? The truth is that her *Angel* moniker went only skin deep. She was shallow and self-absorbed, outwardly beautiful but inwardly empty. I was young and infatuated when we spoke our vows, but soon realized that we had very little in common. She had no interest in my scientific work, and I had no interest in attending an endless array of balls and parties. Afterward I swore I'd never again be taken in by a pretty face." His wry smile deepened. "At least until you came into my life."

The revelation was a balm to Tessa's maimed spirits. So was his phrase *my dearest heart*. It made her feel vibrant with hope. "Is that why you were determined never to marry again?"

He nodded ruefully. "In a nutshell. But I'm botching it again, aren't I?"

All trace of humor gave way to an intent earnestness. He closed the short distance between them, fell to one knee, and clasped her hand, gazing up at her with a worshipful warmth in his eyes. "Tessa, my dear, I love you with all my heart and soul. I know with absolute certainty that my life will never be complete without you as my wife. I promise to cherish you always. Will you put me out of my misery at last and do me the great honor of accepting me as your husband?"

An airy lightness swept away most of her misgivings. Her eyes misted, this time with happiness, and she threaded her fingers through his thick dark hair. "Oh, Guy, I love you, too, so very much. But pray don't kneel before me. We must be as equals. Do stand up at once."

"Not until you agree. If I need must remain in this position from now until kingdom come, I shall suffer my fate gladly."

A gurgle of laughter escaped her. "But I can't be a duchess. I truly don't know how."

"Oh? You're acting like one now, issuing orders, telling me what to do." Smiling, he cocked his head to one side. "I envision you as an unconventional duchess, wielding your power for good works. Being provided with generous pin money, you'll have the means to purchase a millinery shop. Then you can design the hats and hire girls from the foundling home as your workers." Temptingly, he added, "Just think of all the orphans you could help."

For a moment, Tessa felt too choked up to speak. It was the answer to all her dreams. To marry Guy yet not be forced to subjugate her interests to his will—or that of society.

Since he refused to stand, she sank to her knees, framing his face in her hands. "But dearest, think of the gossip. Even if I'm discreet, my grandfather will find out I'm a shop owner."

"Marbury will come around eventually. As for my wishes, you may be as eccentric as you please. Given all my wanderings around the globe, I'm something of an eccentric myself, which makes us the perfect couple."

Tessa's heart melted, and her happiness beamed forth in a tender smile. "Then we had best be wed at once. I wish never to be apart from you again."

His harsh features softened with an expression of tender joy that she'd have found mawkish in any other man. "Finally!"

With that, they fell into each other's arms to share a kiss of fiery passion and boundless promise. She felt in perfect harmony with Guy, as if at last she had found her home, the one place where she belonged. She reveled in the taste of his lips, the feel of his body, as her smoldering desire for him was fanned into flames.

When she tugged at his shirt, he sprang up and pulled her over to the bed, where they divested themselves of clothing in a mad rush. Yet concern made her hesitate as he settled back onto the mattress. "Your arm," she said, eyeing the binding. "It isn't yet healed."

A gleam shone in his eyes. "Then minister to me, my love."

He pulled on her hand and brought her tumbling down, draped over his powerful naked form. She was straddling him with her legs parted and her palms braced upon his firm chest. The novelty of the position seared her veins with excitement. Her breathing fast and eager, she lowered herself until he was sheathed to the hilt within the damp heat of her body.

Her long hair formed a curtain that closed out the rest of the world. There was only the two of them awash in lush sensations and an abundance of pleasure. While moving her hips, she uttered soft moans of uninhibited enjoyment, especially when he slipped his hand between them to caress her intimately. Within moments, she felt the rise of rapture enticing her over the edge into blissful madness. Even as the spasms rocked her, he cried out her name, thrusting upward, his body shuddering with his own white-hot release.

As they lay entwined in the aftermath, Tessa knew the joy of perfect contentment. Never had she realized that marrying didn't have to mean bondage; it could actually free the soul. Yet she wanted Guy to have his dreams, too.

She let her fingers skim over the beloved contours of his face. "I love you so much, my dearest duke. But what about the pirate's map? Don't you wish to go back and find the gold doubloons?"

"You're treasure enough for me." Smiling, he brushed a kiss over her lips. "I'd sooner stay in England, where I've far more enjoyable things to do."

"Like helping me invent a new past?" she teased.

He groaned. "About that . . . what do you say we forget Canada entirely and use your true background? That will mean you can openly acknowledge Haviland as your brother."

Taken by the notion, Tessa caught her breath. "Do you

really think I could? But only imagine how people will talk if they learn I'm baseborn and grew up in a workhouse."

"Let the hens cluck," he said, the tender glow in his eyes warming her through and through. "After all, what's one more scandal so long as we have each other?"